Susan Temby wa
sheep farm, and
where she graduated in Arts majoring in English Drama and Theatre Arts. She also has a Masters of Arts in Writing from University of Technology, Sydney. Susan spent some years acting in professional theatre both in Australia and in London. She has directed plays, and taught creative drama to children, writing and producing films with them. She has been a drama coach and dialogue coach for film and television and a university tutor in writing. She lives on the edge of a national park in outer Sydney.

THE BREAD *with* SEVEN CRUSTS

SUSAN TEMBY

THE BREAD *with* SEVEN CRUSTS

The extract from Giacomo Leopardi's poem, 'L'Infinito', appears courtesy of translator John Heath-Stubbs, from his translation *The Infinite*, published by Carcanet.

The extract on p. 1 from 'Edge' by R. D. FitzGerald comes from his *Forty Years' Poems* and is reproduced with the permission of HarperCollins*Publishers*.

Flamingo
An imprint of HarperCollins*Publishers*, Australia

First published in Australia in 2002
Reprinted in 2002
This edition published in 2003
by HarperCollins*Publishers* Pty Limited
ABN 36 009 913 517
A member of HarperCollins*Publishers* (Australia) Pty Limited Group
www.harpercollins.com.au

HarperCollins*Publishers*
25 Ryde Road, Pymble, Sydney, NSW 2073, Australia
31 View Road, Glenfield, Auckland 10, New Zealand
77–85 Fulham Palace Road, London W6 8JB, United Kingdom
Hazelton Lanes, 55 Avenue Road, Suite 2900, Toronto, Ontario M5R 3L2
and 1995 Markham Road, Scarborough, Ontario M1B 5M8, Canada
10 East 53rd Street, New York NY 10022, USA

National Library of Australia Cataloguing-in-Publication data:

Temby, Susan.
The bread with seven crusts.
ISBN 0 7322 7425 7.
1. Prisoners of war – Australia – Fiction. 2. Prisoners of war – Italy – Fiction. 3. World War, 1939–1945 – Social aspects – Fiction. 4. Man–woman relationships – Fiction.
I. Title.
A823.4

Cover photograph © Darrell Lecorre/Masterfile
Cover and internal design by Christa Edmonds, HarperCollins Design Studio
Typeset by HarperCollins Design Studio in 11/15 Minion
Printed and bound in Australia by Griffin Press on 70gsm Bulky Book Ivory

6 5 4 3 2 1 03 04 05 06

Norm and Rene

Author's Note

The historical setting for *The Bread with Seven Crusts* has been carefully researched. Occasional slight adjustments have been made to dates. Some incidents have been taken from life, but all characters are fictitious.

Among the many sources used in research, one of outstanding value warrants a mention: *Italian Farming Soldiers* by Alan Fitzgerald, Clareville Press, 1998.

Acknowledgments

I am greatly indebted to Lazzaro and Myriam Bonazzi who gave me the translations and a delight in and understanding of my subject, and to Ro Johnston and Debbie Campbell who gave me their theses and their valuable research, and to the following people who gave me of their memories and learning: Jim McAllester, Laurel Blythe, Erna Forrester, Jack MacNamara, Emily Roper, Terry Butler, Ric Pisatura, Sebastiano Gatti, Aladino Carboni, Charles Butler, Mary Duffy, Munro Alexander, Margaret Pellow, Tom Bullock, Margaret Billson, Jocelyn Maddock, Jacqueline Templeton, Fiona Powell and Eddie Pollis.

Jenny Anthony and Bill Bunbury put me in touch with people I needed to meet, and Toll and Merrilyn Temby gave technical advice. Paula Hamilton polished up my history, Jan Hutchinson and John Dale kept me on track, as did my readers, Cath McKinnon, Bronwyn Rodden, Kim Morrison, Phil Voysey, Trisha Rothkrans and Jennifer Mellet.

For her encouragement, guidance and kindness I will always be grateful to Glenda Adams. Linda Funnell, Nicola O'Shea and Belinda Lee at HarperCollins have earned my great respect and gratitude. For her representation, excellent advice and sense of humour, thank you, Mary Cunnane.

For their love and support, thank you, Mim, Jack and Rick.

Contents

Part One — Edge

Part Two — L'Infinito

Part Three — Martyr

Part One

Edge

Knife's edge, moon's edge, water's edge,
graze the throat of the formed shape
that sense fills where shape vanishes:
air at the ground limit of steel,
the thin disc in the moon's curve,
land gliding out of no land.
The new image, the freed thought,
are carved from that inert bulk
where the known and the unknown
is cut down before it — at the mind's edge,
the knife-edge at the throat of darkness.

ROBERT D. FITZGERALD

BARBED WIRE DISEASE

It is less than twelve hours since he arrived and already he has a new name. They call him Joe Lazarus. For half a minute he is put out. Then he sees it is a way for them to include him. Giuseppe Lazaro is not a difficult name to pronounce, but how can he judge what is difficult to an Australian tongue? Vincenzo is happy to be Vince instead of Enzo, but Carlo is incensed and will not answer to Charlie. Giuseppe decides that a change of name is no sacrifice if it means that he can be released into the world.

It is dawn. He has left the warmth of his bed to explore his new home. He is leaning against a strainer post in the crisp air looking across the paddock to a stand of shiny trees — slim, straight trees around ten metres high with shiny green trunks that spiral like corkscrews, trees he will learn to call gimlets. He can be happy in a place that can create such an elegant structure to make a tree strong. Because he is an engineer, he knows that people invent very little. They observe and copy. He's had to be a close observer of people in the last two years. Closer than he would have chosen. He needs space and peace now and is willing to work hard to have it. In the wide, beige grassland before him he sees promise. At last he can think about the events that brought him here with a quiet mind.

He remembers the relief and disbelief. It is 5 January, 1941. General Bergonzoli has surrendered. They are captured. Forty-five thousand Italian soldiers and their groaning wounded. Giuseppe is not thinking of right and wrong. He is not even thinking of survival. He is thinking only of an end to the carnage, and of the heart and lungs of his sergeant that he scraped from the shoulder of his greatcoat, and of the lies he will invent for parents of dead sons, erasing terror and shattered flesh and faeces and hours of slow unattended agony. He has lost all but three of the men in his platoon. Before they died, they had their brief and bloody share of killing. For three days no one rested, except the dead. The living slept on their feet.

North Africa is obliteration. First by sandstorms then by war. They scorned the safety of home for this hell. They have come to the moon and been captured in a meteorite storm not by moon men but by Martians who are taking them back to their outer kingdom. Or else it is true that in the first two months of 1941, 130 000 Italian soldiers have been taken prisoner. The North African division, all of it. Giuseppe's battalion was captured by Australians at the Battle of Bardia on the border of Egypt and Libya. Mussolini called the Australians barbarians in a broadcast to the troops from Rome and said that they numbered a quarter of a million. There were no more than eight thousand. Mussolini had become an unreliable source of information. This did not surprise Giuseppe. It did not appear to surprise anyone.

The British will have to remove them from North Africa before Germany invades. Most will go to India, and the rest will make a long and shameful journey to Australia. The men fear imprisonment by a people whose soldiers are fierce and bloodthirsty. Giuseppe tells them that Australians are Europeans like themselves and that the Aborigines are peaceful and few. Families from his mountain have been sacrificing the youth of their sons to Australia for a hundred years. They spend their good years excavating mines or logging forests to send money home. He is not curious about Australia. He knows it is a rough place of rock and ragged bushland, but he will not miss the dust storms of the Libyan desert. He will miss the distant Bedou caravans and the plovers in the sage. There are things that stay in the heart.

The three days of battle also stay in a waking nightmare. Tall Australians coming at them in neverending waves through machine gun fire. 'Bulletproof vests,' his men shout. Leather vests, they find when they thrust with their bayonets. We cannot lose this, he thinks, even now reliving it. We are too well-entrenched, and reinforced, our minefields impenetrable. They mow them down, but the Australians still come to kill them.

Filippo, his friend and fellow lieutenant, lost his platoon, every last man, and has not been able to wash the blood from his hands. The guilt of survival overpowered him, or the shame, or something Giuseppe said or failed to say. In the POW camp, Filippo painted faces that delighted with their likeness, but shocked in their exposure of the soul, the sitter's and the artist's. His own face was the most interesting. His hair was limp and fair and straight and beneath it shone grey eyes of such warmth and faith. His cheekbones showed the angles of his sensitivity.

'What do you know, Giuseppe?' he would ask.

'Nothing at all, Lippo.'

'I will tell you something.' And he would remember something his grandmother had told him. '*Sarebbe bello aver amici anche all'inferno.*' It is always good to have friends with you even in hell. It wasn't hell, more like purgatory to Giuseppe, but it was good to have Lippo there. Or he would tell Giuseppe about an artist unknown to him: Kokoschka, de Chirico, Tuculescu. He x-rayed personalities with scientific disinterest, but he leaned close when they spoke in order to know their ways and wants. He bought grappa with his sketches. He was taken to hospital with food poisoning. The doctor called it alcohol poisoning. A concoction of alcohol and rat poison is still an unpleasant death, even when plenty of alcohol is ingested before the poison is added. One long night, after two years in this camp, he tried it and it worked.

Earlier that evening, they had sat shoulder to shoulder smoking outside their hut, Giuseppe thinking, stupidly, that Lippo was a little happier. But then he said: 'You're smart and you're a good man, Giuseppe. Learn a few more things and you'll have a good life.' It sounded like goodbye, but they often had this kind of conversation. So he probably answered as he had done before. Who can remember now? 'You are the one with all the talent, Filippo.'

Giuseppe wanted him to feel his responsibility to share, the duty of the gifted. It was not the moment to deliver a sermon. Why should Filippo not paint for himself, every brushstroke invented by and for him? His death was another work of art. Now his paintings face the wall beside Giuseppe's bed. He smells the rich oils. They used to nourish him with ideas. He does not want to look at them any more. From his pillow, he can see the ends of the colours lapping around the edges of the boards, and they accuse him. It is the man he thinks about. He wants to sit with him and hear him say things that penetrate the anaesthesia of a day in camp, to draw him into his thoughts and expand his life, to make him laugh. Giuseppe had thought his friendship would keep Filippo safe. He is teetering now. His blood is drying in his veins.

The barbed wire disease that killed Filippo has come to Giuseppe. It has been incubating for two years. The camp is an airy cage surrounded by serviceable army-green Australian bush and exposed to a broad sky. But to him it is like being suspended in a bell jar in space. He has stopped sleeping. He watches the obsequious white dawn hesitating at the high louvred window of the hut. He has longed for it, but he panics that another day of waiting is before him. Nausea squats in his stomach and his throat aches as though he has been punched. The only cure is release into the world. Not knowing how long he will have to wait is eating at the framework of his optimism like cancer at a bone. They are slipping into another bleak winter where no leaves die a brilliant death to make way for the pale shoots of spring. No snow cleans and softens the landscape.

He stands in a metallic cell of loneliness outside the commandant's door. An inconsiderate wind flattens his trousers against his legs. It does not comfort him that the commandant, who is rotund and good-hearted, reminds him of his grandfather; it makes him sad. They are both veterans of the Great War. Like his grandfather he has few words but plenty to say. And though he tries, he cannot talk Giuseppe out of volunteering for farm work.

'The working men's quarters on these farms can be primitive. You could be lonely. These people are often prejudiced. The Geneva Convention absolves officers from work. You'll have to work with other ranks on equal terms. That could mean problems for you, Lieutenant.'

It is Giuseppe's fellow officers who make problems. They do not like his lukewarm enthusiasm for fascism and Mussolini, so they've stopped speaking to him. He sits listening to the commandant but not looking at him. He stares out the window at the grey corrugated iron huts. From behind these, a streetscape of Bologna protrudes a few metres. Arches and pillars of ochre and cream and their grey-green shadows are painted on a line of huts. Even the Australian guards admire and wonder at it. Filippo. He could have been a great Renaissance artist. Filippo Lippi. Not locked in a stone palazzo but a barbed wire compound. He drags his gaze back into the hut. 'I must work. I must get outside this barbed wire.' When he speaks he feels a surge of warmth through his body as though his blood has thawed. Surely this is right. Surely life is good and death is bad.

He goes out into the wind and back to his hut where Filippo's bed is yawning at him like a grave, mattress folded in two under a neat pile of blankets. He picks them up and flings them at the wall. What comfort did they give his friend? He slept hardly at all. If they could have their last conversation again, then maybe it wouldn't be their last.

Giuseppe is given a place on a farm. A gleam of freedom breaks the surface of this lake of tedium. He begins to look forward and plan. He asks to be placed at a farm with Vincenzo Stanghieri, Enzo, because he likes people who laugh. Giuseppe is addicted to laughter. Enzo is an energetic man, a man of common sense and goodwill, not tall, but seeming taller than he is because of his upright athletic bearing. He is always in a group, playing soccer or cards, and everywhere he goes shouts of laughter burst forth.

Giuseppe cannot remember one note of laughter in his father's house. Without his grandparents, his childhood would have been empty of it. He saw little of his father. Giuseppe's summers were spent in mountain forests with friends, and winters with his mother and sister helping with chores. Later, he went down into the valley to live with his grandparents in winter and to go to school. He was glad that he was not Rosa. His sister was kept at home to help their mother.

But this country, his prison, is a new secular world. Probably as ignorant and superstitious as his own older world, but here he hopes to find a life without need of holy vision, without relying on the help of the dead who, being blind themselves, want to make others blind also. If it is a place without heaven or hell, perhaps then it will not always fall short on promises, because it makes none. He hopes to find more than he expects and tries not to expect too much in order to be pleasantly surprised.

The place Giuseppe will call home for the next two years is not what he would have thought to recognise as a home. He will travel towards a vast, flat dryness, every leaf, every blade of grass, struggling against desiccation and death. He will think that the people who work there must be unaware that their work is nothing in such a geography. He will find farms carved out on the very edge of the known world, in an obstinate battle against nature. When he arrives and the wheels of the control centre truck toil through the thick gravel of the driveway he will feel that he could be at this place with some peace of mind, that he could try to understand a life like this, a home like this and its people. What he will discover is that his thoughts might expand here into the void that is occupied by noise elsewhere and for the first time he might learn the power of silence to heal and not deaden.

THE BREAD WITH SEVEN CRUSTS

His *paesani*, his countrymen who come here to *guadagnare il pane*, to earn their bread, the 'bread with seven crusts', the hardest crust they will ever earn, had told Giuseppe that on the coast it rains as much in a year as it does in Milan but the sandy soil lets the water drain away like a colander. Summers are entirely dry. Seeds germinate in late autumn. The growing season is winter and spring and then nothing more grows until the next winter, except bitter weeds that contrive to exist on a rogue summer storm. Here summer is for hibernation, not winter. There are no bears.

The Italian prisoners designated to work in Western Australia board a ship in Melbourne and in Fremantle are disembarked and marched through the streets seven miles to a temporary camp at Karrakatta. The first thing Giuseppe sees on the wharf is a statue in bronze of a man on a tall stone pedestal, the engineer who designed the harbour. This is encouraging. They think highly of engineers in this country. The column of soldiers without weapons, wearing Australian army uniforms dyed an offensive shade of magenta, draws stares from civilians as they pass, but there are some who call out and wave greetings. At an ornate Victorian railway station a train is getting up steam. They march on past a row of old stone bond stores. It is a stolid town, set aside like an unloved child. Unlike any port he has seen, this one is clean. The streets are swept at dawn. A gentle ozone breeze lifts the waxed leaves on the eucalypts and lets them trickle back into place. Sailors from four nations, yet to discover that life is elsewhere, stride about the streets or stand undecided in twos and fives.

The prisoners cross the bridge over the river at a narrow bend before it straightens out into a slow wide estuary. The ripples reflect the sun in an exchange bright enough to blind the eye. Through quiet suburbs with lush gardens and neat lawns they march towards Perth and it is good to be in a street again, a European street, clean and orderly. There are shops. Now and then they pass an evil-smelling place called a fish and chip shop. Giuseppe knows what fish is, but not chip. The smell of rancid fat loads the air and he remembers the wisps of roasted coffee that drift above the streets of Trieste. Karrakatta is almost entirely a cemetery. A city of dry bones and headstones that fights for space with rose beds and stonemasons' workshops. Here is an industrial approach to death, efficient business practice steadying any drift towards the maudlin. Life is determined to go on in spite or even because of all the death it involves.

And then east by truck through Northam, a country town astride a modest river of nesting swans, enfolded in yellow grassed hills and dense uninviting forests. Uniformly straight tree trunks, burnt black in last season's fire, darken the road with their new-grown canopies. Beyond them, hills turn purple before they become horizon. Giuseppe, Enzo and a third prisoner, Carlo, are going to a farm two hundred miles east into what they expect to be total desert, on the back of a truck with sixteen other prisoners bound for other farms. A tarpaulin over the truck keeps sun off and dust in. The air inside is thick, stagnant with suspended dust. The prisoners sit along the sides with their legs stretched into the middle and smoke, and the air becomes thicker. The dust from the road and the smoke from the cigarettes combine to make the twelve hours' travel toxic. Discomfort does not dampen the optimism Giuseppe is enjoying for the first time since his capture.

Until this moment the night of the battle had never left his mind. In the endless early morning darkness Australian soldiers kept coming towards the Italian bunkers, fearless, or so it seemed. Not wild madmen, but ordinary men in leather vests who had walked miles across stony desert with heavy packs but who seemed to have more energy than the entrenched Italians. Inside the trenches, bullets and shells ricocheted off concrete walls. The occupants had no hope of survival. Giuseppe and most of the officers had known at the time that the Italian push to the east towards Egypt had been fatally slow. They could have taken it all before the allies had assembled troops, but instead they built a railway line across the top of Africa and a sealed road and concrete trenches.

Giuseppe finds himself a place to sit at the front near the cab of the truck. There he can lift the tarpaulin away two or three inches and see the brittle landscape rush towards him and away. To the eye of someone who has lived on the border of Switzerland, it looks like a place that has never seen rain. There are trees, so it must have rained, and there are dried stalks from last season's crop, but there are no rivers and no lakes, only dried salt pans. Once or twice they see a dam, but it is always empty, the clay bottom exposed and crazed into shiny patches. Sheep graze on what looks like nothing. Towns are forty or even eighty miles apart and villages are three or four stone or sheet-iron buildings squeezed onto the side of the road at the edge of a patchwork of red cultivated or black burnt fields. There is always a general store with a double front and verandah, a hall, constructed of orange stone, a one-room school house and a tennis court. One or two mud houses accompany these amenities but not in sufficient numbers or well enough situated to provide a sense of community. It is all bleak and disparate.

The winds of war have blown them to the farthest corner of the earth. They were hoist by their own gunpowder, into the sky to rain down here like fish on the desert. Giuseppe is pleased to have Enzo with him, but Carlo has a strong admiration for Mussolini and a resentful nature. Giuseppe understands what resentment can do. He has seen it among the troops. It starts in the brain and runs down the spine and into the arms like molten lead. Carlo calls farm work slavery. He could have gone to a camp in the south and worked at timber cutting instead. Giuseppe suspects he has chosen the farm because timber cutting is arduous and dangerous. They are the last to arrive at their designated farm. Their destination is the most eastern outpost. Prisoners have been left at six other farms, each one isolated and dry.

'This is the end of the earth. We are the last and this is the last place God would ever love,' Carlo growls, as the truck slows and changes down through gears to drive in at the gate. He has drawn this conclusion from the other farms he has seen. He cannot know what this place is like since he can see only shadows and shapes in the dark.

They can make out farm buildings and a house with a high pitched roof and verandahs, set in a garden with a picket fence. By moonlight it has a comfortable presence. It has softness. Giuseppe at least is not unhappy to be here and perhaps is even a little determined to like the place. After hours of the howl and roar of the truck engine, the silence is like an ocean. It runs at them like a wave sloshing down into their ears and making their eardrums ring.

A young man comes out of the house to meet them. He is tall and wide-shouldered. They recognise him. He is like every second Australian soldier they had seen in North Africa. He smiles and speaks to the prisoners without contempt, in fact with friendliness. Giuseppe makes polite replies to his questions about the trip, and cannot help thinking that they might have been normal travellers at the end of any journey. Enzo does not speak more than a few words of English, Carlo knows a little more but chooses not to use them.

The prisoners are surprised to find that they will sleep in the house. That the farmer expects them to behave in a civilised manner, and that he does not expect them to offer him any harm or attempt to escape, is both comforting and demeaning. But where would they go, to the barren desert? They have no maps and no idea of how to look for water. Max, they are to call him Max and not signor Nash, shows them where to put their bags, in a large bedroom at the front of the house, and where to wash, in a bathroom constructed as an afterthought on the verandah, and invites them to come to the kitchen for tea as soon as they are ready. Tea, a disappointing drink.

In the kitchen they meet Mrs Nash, Max's mother. She is probably not sixty but the weight she carries robs her of agility. She has a mass of grey hair swept into a bun and a sweetness in her look that echoes youthful beauty. They sit down to a large meal of roasted meat and vegetables. This is not just a cup of tea. The prisoners have the sort of hunger that only a journey into the unknown can excite. Hunger for the comfort of a full belly more than for the replenishment of energy. Carlo bends his head over his food and eats without stopping and without looking up.

Mother and son are interested in where the prisoners are from, how long they have been in Australia and when they were captured. Giuseppe tells them he was captured at Bardia, Carlo and Enzo at Benghazi.

Max turns to his mother and says, 'You know Jimmy was in that.'

'No. He was captured by the Germans.'

'Bardia was before Greece. The British won this show.'

Giuseppe does not like to ask who this person is. It might be Max's brother.

'Jimmy lives next door,' says Max.

'And he has been captured?'

'By the Germans, in Crete.'

'That is not good.'

'They are supposed to be your allies. You should be pleased.'

'Yes, they won a battle for Greece that we Italians had been fighting for some time. I think if Britain had stayed out of it, maybe even Greece would have won against us.'

Max looks at the prisoner with sudden interest. 'You don't have a lot of faith in your own army.'

'Faith, no. I am not a person for faith. But what I have seen and know in my heart is that as much as we want Italy to be great, we don't want it enough to lay down our lives.'

'That's honest anyway.'

There is silence while Max and his mother digest the horror of his lack of patriotism. Giuseppe, out of the corner of his eye, thinks he detects a sneer developing on Carlo's face. 'You will not find all Italians think this way,' he adds. 'My friend here,' and he nods towards Carlo, 'is very patriotic.' Carlo lowers his head and goes on eating. Giuseppe suspects that Carlo has a better knowledge of English than he allows.

For Giuseppe, this meal is the most enjoyable moment of the last two years. Emotions drain into his chest and throat each time he swallows. The evening had grown cold and dark as they travelled and the kitchen is bright and warm and smells of roasting mutton. It is a large room dominated by a central table laid with a blue and white floral cloth and in the middle a glass vase of yellow flowers that give off a sweet peppery scent and a blue and white striped jug of milk. Metal bins labelled flour and sugar stand beside a work table in the corner, a shelf above it holds a wireless attached to a large battery. A green enamel stove squats comfortably at one end of the room like a benevolent fiery gnome. On the hob beside it a large wooden salt pig is perched alongside a stoneware jar sprouting wooden spoons. Above the sink on the window sill stands a row of small green herbs for cooking. The room is filled with the wholesome ambience of femininity. Everything in it makes him breathless with the need for comfort, and worried that he should be so susceptible to a few simple signs of a home. He wallows in the knowledge that he will come to this table every day until the war ends and it will be to him like a gentle hand laid on his shoulder. He can't believe his luck.

After a pause Mrs Nash speaks. 'Mr Er . . .'

Max interrupts. 'His name's Giuseppe, Mum.' He pronounces it with a hard G and it sounds strange to the Italians. 'That's a bit of a mouthful, what do they call you for short?'

His mother and sister always call him Pino, but that was his childhood name.

'My name is the same as Joseph in your language.'

'Doesn't sound like it. How do you work that out? Anyway that'll do me, we'll call you Joe if you don't mind?'

'Well then, Joe,' the signora says. 'Your bedroom belongs to my daughter.'

'Where will your daughter sleep now?'

'Oh, she hasn't lived here for years.'

'She's up in New Guinea at the moment at the army hospital,' says Max. 'She's a nurse.'

He gets up and goes to the bench under the window and returns with an ashtray and a tobacco pouch. He takes some of the fine brown strands from the soft leather pouch and then offers it to Giuseppe, Enzo and Carlo. They refuse and bring out their own cigarettes.

'Yes,' says Mrs Nash, 'and what I was wanting to say is, if you'd please be careful in there with the furniture and curtains and things, since it is her room.'

'Of course.' Giuseppe thinks she probably expects the worst sort of barbarity from them in the same way that so many of his own soldiers were expecting from Australians.

Max tells them that the rain is late this year and that he is waiting to start seeding as soon as it arrives, which means that the three men will need to learn the ropes as quickly as possible so that they can take over the farm chores and leave him to sow the crop.

Remembering the empty dams and dry lakes they have been driving past all day Giuseppe asks him about drought.

He says, 'Some years we have less rain, but it always comes. If we are ready for it, we can grow a crop.'

The bedroom is large and high-ceilinged. French doors lead onto a verandah. The walls are painted cream and from picture rails hang two prints too small for the wall — Vermeer's *Girl Reading A Letter*, an unhappy Dutch scene of pregnant widowhood, and facing it on the opposite wall an unhappy Australian scene of a small girl feeding hens under a threatening sky called *Tea Time* by Charles Conder. A photograph stands on an oak chest, three rows of army nurses looking out of a silver frame. Giuseppe wonders which of them is the owner of the room. Two nurses on the right end of the front row are more photogenic and slimmer in the ankles than the others, but he settles for one in the centre of the picture, somewhat resembling Mrs Nash, blonde curls escaping her veil and double chins escaping her collar and a softness of expression that speaks of caring.

'British nurses, big bones, little eyes,' sniggers Carlo.

There are two strong beds with oak bed heads and one simple bed with a metal frame. Giuseppe predicts a problem if Carlo does not get a good bed, and he does not want him lording it over Enzo so he announces that he will take the metal one himself, since it is away from the others against the opposite wall, and seems to provide a separation and some privacy.

When Carlo goes to the bathroom Enzo says, 'You must sleep in this bed beside Carlo. I will take the small bed.'

'No, I have decided.'

'Carlo is the one who has decided and he knows and knows we know. This is not good. He will be trouble if he feels he has power over us.'

Enzo is right. When Carlo returns, Giuseppe tells him that they have devised a system of changing beds every week.

He looks at Giuseppe with a contemptuous smile and says, 'That is a stupid idea.'

'Nevertheless, it is what we will do,' Giuseppe says, in a tone he hopes does not invite contradiction.

Giuseppe gets into the metal-frame bed and stretches his travel-cramped legs between cold sheets. He looks at the ceiling with its ornate plaster cornices held in place with batons picked out in black. He extinguishes the oil lamp and falls asleep without noticing the lumps in the horsehair mattress. As he drifts off he registers a floral scent in the room. He doesn't know what it is, but he has smelled it many times. Lilac maybe, or something more astringent. Whatever it is, it comforts his release from consciousness.

IL CONTADINO

He was up at first light and out through the casement door onto the verandah and into the crisp morning. The sky was white and the still air was clean with the fragrance of eucalyptus. The sweet, clear silence was pierced at intervals by a rooster's crow or a magpie's conversation. He walked around the house through a dew-damp garden and a whining gate into a parched farmyard, crunching the coarse glassy soil under his boots. He halted at the barbed wire of the first fence and looked out and across to the distant line of trees that marked the opposite fence line. Here was a landscape as wide as silence. Unlike the Sahara Desert, there was enough of life here for it to be an inviting kind of treed nothingness. He felt free for the first time since he had been drafted into the army.

He turned and leaned against a heavy strainer post, folding his arms against the sharpness of the air and surveying the farmyard. The house dominated it like an old duchess in a crinoline. A faded, red painted iron roof swept down, dipping gracefully before it reached out across a wide verandah that wrapped all the way around the house. Dark-green painted timber and glass french doors opened at regular intervals onto it. Grape vines and rose creepers rambled about verandah posts. The walls of the house were red-brown like the earth. The garden was a maze of neat gravel paths separating beds of flowers and shrubs and vegetables and fruit trees. An overgrown doormat of a lawn between the kitchen and the back gate was the only sign of formality. Beside this, a mound of earth above several steps leading down to a door indicated the presence of a cellar. Large deciduous trees created a circle of protection around the garden and were in the process of covering it with tawny leaves. Beyond the house in a depression near the dam he could see a sizeable orchard, netted against the birds. All this cultivated verdure contrasted strongly with the dry spread of the land around it. He circled the farmyard looking into sheds and pens, introducing himself to eight or nine pigs and half a dozen horses and a black and white dog tied up to a kennel. He turned back to the house as the late autumn sun began to push at the horizon of the new day.

The prisoners spent their first morning in a ploughed paddock picking up the roots of mallee trees that had recently grown there and piling them up for burning. It was heavy, dusty work. When they stopped at the sound of the cow bell that heralded lunch Carlo said, 'So, Lieutenant, what would the other officers think of you now?'

Giuseppe knew that Enzo and Carlo thought he'd been brought up in the brocade of the city and he was not going to shatter the illusion. At the control centres they made the same assessment and put them together so that Enzo and Carlo could make up for his lack of brawn. He did not want Carlo to know that he was the son of a peasant, a *contadino*.

'I hope they don't waste time thinking about me at all.'

'You are right,' said Carlo. 'This is donkey work. They might mistake you for one.'

'Is that why you have taken to it so well?' asked Enzo and he and Giuseppe laughed.

'You think it is a joke to do filthy work for these peasant people. You have no brains.'

'It is honest work,' said Giuseppe. 'And better than idleness.'

Giuseppe was wiry rather than slight, taller than the other two prisoners but not as tall as Max. He had an open, receptive face from which he knew his thoughts could escape and on which he knew his feelings were often instantly apparent. It was fortunate that he could not see his own face for more than a few minutes a day because it often showed the disappointment we all feel when we are finally honest with ourselves.

In the bathroom before breakfast he could hear Mrs Nash talking to her son as she clattered about the kitchen.

'That Joe,' she said, 'doesn't look like an Italian.'

'What does an Italian look like, Mum?'

'Swarthy.'

'Carlo's not swarthy.'

'No, I suppose not. But Joe is different. I mean he seems to know things.'

'He should, he's an engineer.'

'He'll be able to fix the machinery.'

'I already tried that one. Structural not mechanical.'

'Why is his English so good?'

'I expect he's a spy.'

'Very funny.'

'Some Australians speak Italian.'

'Do they? I've never met one.'

'Neither have I.'

He heard them both laugh and laughed too. They were light-hearted together, he thought, more like friends than mother and son. He had never exchanged banter of this sort with his mother. He was not too clever to miss the irony that gives leavening to a day or an hour. He was always ready to exchange a moment of laughter for one of contemplation. It made those around him willing to talk to him. Did Mrs Nash see it as an advantage that he did not seem Italian? She thinks he knows things. She has only met Italians who work with their hands. The immigrant class. She has separated him from them. He was ashamed to be pleased at this.

He was a proud Italian, but not in a political sense. He was loyal, but not a campaigner. He had not escaped unscathed from his two years behind barbed wire. His confidence was a little tattered by the experience. If someone were to ask him what he wanted, he would be hard pressed to answer or even remember how he had felt or where he was heading before the war. Until Filippo died, he was like a motor idling in neutral. Then he was made to look around and see what he already knew, that he disliked his fellow officers and that he was beginning to dislike himself.

Enzo was more like the Italians that Mrs Nash knew. Enzo was brawn but he was not a mule, not stubborn or stupid. He was strong-willed and deliberate. His home in the Abruzzi mountains was renowned for these qualities in its people. Although it was only one hundred and twenty kilometres from Rome, until he was drafted Enzo had never been there. He had piercing brown eyes that never missed an absurdity or an incongruous sight, and hair as black and oil-shiny as a rooster. Away from the strictures of the camp he felt safe to make fun of Giuseppe at every opportunity. Giuseppe did not mind that every joke was at his expense. At least there was laughter. Simple slapstick much of it, as he was a true incompetent as a farmer, but he was willing to learn. His skills were slight but he had been brought up to work. Enzo's presence threw down a challenge. He was still whistling after five hours stacking bags of staggeringly heavy superphosphate. After chopping down hardwoods all day his hands grew callused without blistering. And when the prisoners were left overnight on the hill under canvas to listen to the dingoes in the dark, he would howl back at them and they would grow quiet while the blood of the other two would stay chilled until the dawn.

Carlo came from a small town in Umbria. His father was a school teacher. He did not show any signs of wanting to follow him into this profession. He was young and angry and had no interest in books. He had been conscripted from school at eighteen. He affected a perpetual look of indifference and sloped about the farm as though he might be about to fall down in a deep sleep. His eyes were half closed even when the smoke from his cigarette was not spiralling into them and a lick of straight dark hair fell between them. There was a certain lethargic beauty about his face that gave rise to gossip in the camp. His first days at the farm set a pattern that did not change. He appeared to have no other object than to offend everyone. He was afraid of large animals and refused to handle cows and horses. There was plenty of other work to do, but he resented being sent away to dig post-holes or scrub water troughs on his own. When Giuseppe was asked to accompany him, Carlo attacked him for volunteering to work. Giuseppe responded as patiently as he could. He explained that he preferred to live in the country. He did not want to admit to any depression that might have been the real reason for his needing to leave the camp and give the younger man fuel for attack.

Halfway through the second year in camp Giuseppe had felt the indolence of depression creeping up from his gut to his throat and he was afraid. He watched Filippo sink and could do nothing. They had been constant companions through officer training, in North Africa and in prisoner of war camp in Australia. They shared a laugh at every incident of pomposity or incompetence. Then one day Filippo stopped laughing. When once they had relied on each other entirely, in the end he could give his friend nothing that he needed. Filippo had been one of the few officers who had something real to do. He had taught the other ranks to draw perspective and they had painted a whole townscape on the side of three huts. But he could not withstand the forces. The structures of his mind had not enough resistance and he crumpled. Without him, Giuseppe became less resistant to the pressures. It was like the principle of moments. A structure exists because it resolves all the forces that act on it and has material in the right places to withstand those forces. Without Filippo he had lost some of those materials.

They buried him in a lonely corner of the local cemetery away from the civilian graves. A truckload of prisoners stood under the cool white limbs of the tall gums and listened to the priest. A chill wind slipped across the road on the south and whipped at the lace on his alb and swirled away the words of his prayer. He stood above the grave looking down over the mound of his stomach at the poised coffin as though he owned life, not only this life but the next one as well. His chasuble, his lace alb and most of all his tasseled stole was his passport. For Giuseppe the pain of loss came with betrayal, by Filippo and by himself. He had been of no use to his friend. He blamed his own heart and soul and at the same time he doubted the very existence of them. His human worth had disintegrated into a tangled heap. There was nothing left to weigh.

Carlo showed no deference to Giuseppe's rank or respect for Max and the signora. After a week Giuseppe was so tired of him that he asked Max not to send him to work with Carlo. At the end of the second week Enzo made the same request.

Because of his family story Giuseppe had no Arcadian fantasies about rural life. The mountain was a cruel home. They had few animals there. Families kept some pigs or hens, a cow if they could, but it was crops that were important, vegetables, corn and vines. But in this dry place, growing abundant crops and fat animals was a constant challenge. Here he was expected to handle horses, pigs, sheep and dogs and to drive four cows in to be milked.

Because Enzo and Carlo were strong, they were to keep working in the fields while Giuseppe went to the cows. He tried to chase them home, but the paddock was large and they kept doubling back behind him. On the first evening it was dark before he had them in their bails. They never did it again. He was convinced they knew he was a rookie. After that they were always waiting at the gate. In the mornings Giuseppe gave the separated milk to the pigs. They lived in a yard fenced with railway sleepers. He poured it into their feed trough and watched them squeal and push and grunt and slurp to get as much as possible as quickly as possible.

One enterprising individual always stood in the trough while the others drank around his feet. He made Giuseppe laugh. Pigs were so like people.

The milking was a gruelling process. His wrists ached, his shoulders too and the bucket from the first cow was only half full. La signora Nash guessed he was in strife when he took so long, and came with the lantern to help.

'In two weeks this will be so easy you'll laugh.'

He didn't believe her. She filled three buckets and he one. His cow was insulted.

She bellowed and kicked and let fly with her dung before he could move the bucket. Then she kicked it over his boot and the warm contaminated liquid seeped through his laces and drenched his thick woollen Australian army-issue sock. At that moment, his imagination failed him. At home on the mountain, to lose a bucket of milk would not have been considered a joke, but here at the dinner table everyone, especially Enzo, enjoyed a great laugh. As Giuseppe was the entertainment, he found himself obliged to smile.

'I can see you'll stop at nothing to win this war, but torturing cows is going a bit far,' said Max.

'It was not torture. It was a battle and she won.'

'You chose the youngest, the worst-tempered.'

'I like her. She has spirit.'

'I'd get your skills up before you tackle her again. You'd better leave her for me to milk. She obviously doesn't agree with your politics.'

He could laugh at this too. Fortunately Enzo took some months to learn English well enough to understand this sort of joke. He was still something of a fascist, disillusioned with Mussolini, but was not so fast to become a republican. After all, he had fought for the glory of fatherland and king. He did not want to fight the Germans with the allies. He wanted his own country for itself and not for the communists. He was wise enough to keep his thoughts to himself.

At night, sitting on the side of the bed or on the verandah smoking, when Carlo was not around, Giuseppe would try to draw him out, but Enzo knew Giuseppe was not, and suspected he never had been, a fascist and that it was sticky ground for them. What he loved to talk about was his family. Married for two years before the war began, a son had been born at about the same time he was taken prisoner and now would be more than two years old. Few letters came, and when they did it could be up to ten months from the time of writing. Once he received a photo of his son and he did not speak for hours. He had to bear a sadness they could not share.

No one needed to draw out Carlo. At any moment when only the three prisoners were present, he would start up again about Mussolini and the greatness of Italy. He was convinced that with Hitler on their side they were bound for glory. When it became known that Il Duce had been rescued from his place of arrest, a hotel in the Abruzzi mountains, by a Nazi glider squad and taken to Germany, his triumph was complete. Giuseppe and Enzo could do nothing but walk away from these outbursts. At such times Enzo never spoke a word. He seemed to go into a dream when Carlo began to speak.

On 9 July 1943 the allies landed in Sicily. Two months after the arrival of the prisoners at the farm, on 25 July, Mussolini was deposed and arrested. July 29 was Mussolini's sixtieth birthday. Carlo, who had become sullen and defiant at the news of his leader's demise, announced to the other two prisoners his intention of staying in bed all day. He said he was having a national day of mourning.

The signora became quiet and stern. 'No one stays in bed all day in my house unless they are seriously ill and under doctor's orders.'

She looked shaken, as though someone had threatened her. She had never heard of such a thing in all her life. It was to her a most dangerous precedent.

Giuseppe was sent to ask him to get up and go to work. Carlo laughed and called him an enemy sympathiser. Giuseppe returned to Max and apologised.

'He is a foolish boy. He does not seem to understand that he has volunteered to do this work.'

'Why did he come?' asked Max.

'I have asked the same question. I know he was not popular in camp. Even his fascist friends were growing tired of him.'

While saying this to Max, Giuseppe was nagged by a feeling that he was being disloyal to his fellow national, but he knew that he already had a loyalty to Max based on rapport and respect that was stronger than any national bond he might have felt for Carlo. The more sullen and defiant Carlo became, the more admiration Giuseppe felt for the way Max handled him.

The following morning he turned up at the breakfast table as though nothing had happened. The signora did not sit at the table after she served the food. She went off to begin her chores. Breakfast was eaten in silence.

'You'll have to make up the time on Sunday, Carlo, a full day. This isn't a resort,' Max growled, and stood up to look for his tobacco pouch.

Carlo leaned back, balancing on the back legs of his chair, and sneered a smile.

At six on Sunday morning Max knocked at the bedroom door and entered. Before Carlo could argue the point, the farmer had him on his feet and pulling on his clothes. Max drove him to the farthest corner of the farm, a distance of almost five miles, and left him for the day at the camp of a Montenegrin timber-clearing team in the middle of the bush. They were contract clearing for the farmer next door. He had arranged for them to teach the Italian to cut down trees.

Carlo was not comfortable in the bush and had no confidence that he could find his way back to the house, nor was he fond of Yugoslavs, with whom the Italians had been disputing territory for most of the century. The eight clearers stood together with their arms folded watching with contempt while the leader showed him how to use the axe. English was their common language and none of them knew much of it. It was a long day of blistered hands for Carlo, a good lesson to the young prisoner that his employer meant business, but any change of attitude was short-lived.

Before dinner next day, Monday evening, the signora announced with pride that she had cooked macaroni for the prisoners. Good news. They had not eaten Italian food since leaving prison camp. When she brought them each a plate of mutton chops and vegetables Giuseppe began to think he had misunderstood and started his meal without questions. Carlo was not so docile. He asked for the macaroni and was told that it would be ready soon. He refused the meat and vegetables and sat sullenly waiting for the macaroni.

'Not hungry, Carlo?' Max asked.

The signora served the macaroni in bowls with cream. She had baked it in the oven with milk, sugar and egg. Two of them ate it and were twice surprised. First, that anyone would think to do this with pasta and second, that it was not entirely unpleasant. Carlo took a mouthful and spat it onto his plate. He stood up from the table, pushing his chair back with such force that it fell over, and marched out, leaving the kitchen door to slam.

Giuseppe caught up with him at the end of the path and stood between him and the gate.

'The signora was trying to be kind. You should apologise.'

Carlo swore and called Giuseppe a traitor.

'Mind your words,' Giuseppe snapped. Carlo put his fists up and offered him a fight.

Giuseppe walked back to the house shaking his head. He turned at the door and said, 'You will soon be back in camp.'

He heard the younger man spit at the ground as he walked off into the trees. He went back to the table and apologised for his compatriot.

'Well,' said Mrs Nash. 'If those are Italian manners, I can do without them.'

'They are not,' said Giuseppe. 'He has no manners.'

'I thought you Italians liked macaroni.'

'We cook it differently.'

'How do you cook it?'

'We do not make it with sugar.'

The signora creased her brow and looked at him sideways, only half understanding. He could see she was trying to work out how they make dessert in Italy without sugar. He did not know how to explain without seeming ungrateful.

'Well, perhaps you could get me a recipe.'

'Of course. I will even cook it, if you like.'

The signora looked perplexed and possibly, thought Giuseppe, a little under siege.

Some evenings Giuseppe risked Carlo's contempt further by playing the piano. The signora encouraged him. She would have liked it played every night, but he sensed the others did not feel the same way. Now that her daughter was gone to war the piano stood silent. Untuned for many years, some high notes didn't sound. Their hammers needed straightening. Giuseppe was able to do this, but his skills did not include tuning. He was disgusted to hear himself playing hideously on a flat piano, but as he practised he improved and became used to the deviant sound. The more delicate the passage the stranger it sounded. Beethoven, Mendelssohn, deranged, dislocated. German music from another century and another culture, capable of mystical heights in art. A culture grown deaf, whose descendants now laid waste to the rest of the world, and as a result Giuseppe fingered notes carefully on an old dried instrument at the farthest reaches of the western world. Absurdity played into notes. It felt good to sound it out on the piano. Beethoven is so expressive of opposites. It is difficult to say in words two things that simultaneously contradict. Absurd. But absurdity can be played on an instrument or sung in a song. To love the culture that is the means of your destruction is perverse and human and can be played on the piano. To suffer and enjoy, love and hate, yearn and reject. Music can palliate like a skilled physician. Inside the piano stool he found sheet music of Noel Coward and Cole Porter that amused the others as well as himself and was more appropriate to the instrument, and perhaps also the times.

To bring music, however jaded, to this house was a pleasure. In the paddocks he was not so able to be of use. Unable to lift full bags of wheat at first, he had to leave them half empty. Gradually he could carry more weight. He never became strong enough to lift a full bag of superphosphate on his back like Enzo. Unlike Carlo, it was a matter of pride for him to do the job well.

Max, he guessed, was in his late twenties like himself. He had an easy temperament but expected hard work from everyone. He always worked the hardest and longest. He rose from his bed every morning in the dark and came home after the sun had set and the dark had folded in again. His hands were large and callused. The tips of his fingers were so thick that he had trouble turning the pages of the newspaper he read each evening after dinner. However late he came home, he would dip water into the bath from the copper lit by his mother, bathe and change his clothes before he sat down to eat. Over the top of the paper he would eye Giuseppe and ask something like: 'Where's Brindisi? Your king has gone there. Is it a big place?' Giuseppe would give him a brief history, starting with the Romans.

'Yeah, I've heard of the Appian Way, Rome to Brindisi? Like the Old York Road.'

This made everyone laugh. The Old York Road ran along the south fence of the farm. It was the one man-made, historic ruin in the district. Miners and prospectors had pushed their barrows and camel trains had wended their way along this track, three hundred and fifty miles. Granite outcrops contained natural wells that provided one of only two or three sources of fresh water along the way. Now relics of a former age, they were less than seventy years old in settler history, in Aboriginal history perhaps thousands.

'Not as long as the Old York Road.'

'How long?'

'Five, six hundred kilometres.'

'About the same, I'd say.'

Max would ask the prisoners' opinions about the state of the war in Europe. They had no more information than he did. Few of their letters received answers and when they did the news was too stale to be meaningful. Giuseppe found more in common with Max than he had with most of his own officers in camp. So if under these circumstances, at the farm, they could share a joke from time to time, that was as much as he could ask. Although it took six months for Enzo to have enough English to communicate well, Max and his mother always showed him respect. With Carlo they did what they could at first, but he would make no effort to return their friendship and as time went on and the incidents of his antagonism accumulated, Mrs Nash became cold and withdrawn in his presence and when they were all together he threw a rough blanket of hostility over them.

EDDY

Her return, by way of a huge coal-stinking train, filled the empty night with such light and sound, such fire and bulk, that she thought her memories might have been wrong. Nothing so fierce and foul could be found in a place so utterly insignificant. But of course, when it slid away, downing the hill, galumphing and coughing the hill, it left a disgusting hole, the size of itself and bigger. It left less than nothing and signalled its contempt by an acrid smell which in ten minutes would be gone.

Silence lives and moves and has its being in empty spaces between sound. The science of silence confounds. It doesn't exist except in space and how many of us have been there? Here silence is not science, it is thought, prayer, birdsong, wind in grass. When Eddy thought of home she thought of these things. But like silence, they could take away words and leave their imprint, dark shadows, half-formed ideas without names, that isolate and contaminate.

Coming home after four years of service as an army nurse was like falling overboard from an ocean liner in the dark and watching it steam heedlessly away. She could not take solace in its offer of calm solitude. Instead she fretted that the silence of this place could be so empty, so far from the war that it seemed stupid, leaden, oafish. She reminded herself to take care, to keep the kit bag at least half packed and not to let the safe smell of vanilla in her mother's kitchen peel away the carapace, her means of survival, and embalm her in need.

And she expected that everything would look unimportant now that she was back. Tedious, flat, yellow paddocks behind meaningless miles of fences. Monotonous summer tones. Sighs of heat from trees drooping their tresses, still gasping for air after a hundred summers. And daily, weekly, the same, without the renewal of a cooling night. The screaming vermilion of every summer evening's red imperative to stop everything and look, even though you know it will be there again in a repetition of tomorrows. And when you stop, you think about God and dust. Night, so simple, so predictably tattooed with starlight easily defined without interference from landlight.

She watched the stupid red dot of the train tail diminish and diminish and become nothing. Its cargo of newly drilled recruits was better out of sight and mind, especially mind. A mixture of rough men, conscripted fodder for cannons from the bottom of a deep and derelict barrel. Fortunate that her rank and gender made it unnecessary for her to share a dog box with them. She could not see them as the train drew away in the dark, except for the red tips of their chain-smoked cigarettes. She had seen what could happen to them where they were going. It was an effort not to see. She never stopped seeing. Mutilated arms hanging loose, faces blown away, whole stomachs missing and row upon row of stretchers of stoic, soon to be dead, heroes. But this train was not bound for glory, this train. These heroes were unwilling indeed. Heroism was for those who could afford it. They had no reason to stand up against the enemy, nothing to fight for, nothing to come back to. But their chances of coming back were good, compared with thousands of volunteers, eyes bright with starvation, sitting alone behind barbed wire, holding their bony knees.

In the black, on the silent siding, she listens to her own breathing and then gradually to the putter of the motorbike with the sidecar. And there will be Max and with any luck he will have left Winston at home so that she can have the sidecar without dog-share dog-hair ... and she is right about that too. She can see only one outline aboard the old bike. She will run over to him calling his name. He will give her a hasty, dusty hug and pile the luggage on her lap in the sidecar and she will wait while he scrabbles around by starlight looking for parcels, goods, things brought by the train, ordered with coupons from the city.

Not so. She stands quite still while the headlight of the bike glares at her, blinding her. She shades her eyes. A man, not Max, gets off the bike and approaches in silhouette against the light. Max would have looked good after all this time, the same of course, wearing his hat even at night. Where the hell is he? She picks up her small leather case, ready to bring it down on the head of this motorbike man should she need to. A tactic successfully practised before, on an unfortunate Arab in an unlit Jerusalem street.

Unusual for her, such a lapse of discretion. June air at midnight in the garden of the King David Hotel was heavy, decadent, languid after the busy heat of day. They sipped Armagnac at the bar after dinner. There was dancing and flattery from an English officer, a latter-day T E Lawrence, desert man, speaker of Arabic, and strolling in the garden arm in arm, stopping in shadows for close talk and time-slip. Her party had gone without her. He read it wrong and assumed she'd wanted it that way, conceit coming off best against sense. He offered his bed, himself. She did not accept and he became angry and left her standing in the lobby in mid sentence, her reserve fuelling his misunderstanding. There was, of course, no room at the inn, no transport in the curfew and no dignity in sitting the night in the foyer without leave.

The walk to quarters was not far, taking short cuts, relying on the curfew for safety through narrow stepped streets. Folds of a flowing gelebieh caught the moonlight and her eye. A tall Arab terrified her with an offer of assistance in rounded English vowels. Swinging, flailing her small leather case, she glanced his chin and bolted in panic. He was only chivalrous, apologising for her violence. Worse was meeting him next day in the officers' mess wearing a suit and a bruise on his chin. Nothing was said. He made a slight bow and an expression of pleasure at their reacquaintance.

A man of little more than medium height without a hat comes towards her and stoops to pick up her kit bag. He swings it over his shoulder before speaking. This irritates her, taking liberties with her belongings, some hanger-on of Max's. He speaks. She doesn't understand.

'What did you say?'

He repeats. 'Are you Max's sister?'

This time she understands. 'Yes. I'm Max's sister.'

'I am Giuseppe Lazaro. At the farm they call me Joe.'

'You're Italian.'

'I am a prisoner.'

What the bloody hell does Max think he's doing sending a POW to fetch her from the train in the middle of the night?

'They let you drive?'

'Only on the farm.'

'This is not the farm.'

'Max says in the night there are no police.'

She has been away so long and she will have to go away again for who knows how long and Max cannot come four miles to fetch her from the train at midnight. He sends instead an enemy prisoner who might have fired the gun that caused the fatal wounds of a soldier she had tried to keep alive. If not him, then his brother, his cousin.

He places the bag under the front cover of the sidecar and touches her elbow ready to help her in. She pulls away from his fascist sting.

'I can manage.'

Hot air becomes cool as they speed through the night. The headlight of the bike whitens the trees into rows of cauliflower stalks. She remembers them this way as a child, at night in the headlights. In that world, her father brought home a pony with a blond mane and a head too large for its body that filled her childish years with friendship and a practical means of transport. The same world where her father worked all night to save the pony's life and she ran back and forth in the dark frost bringing boiling potions to the stable and where they cried together at the dawn death. In that world, school stopped without the blond-haired pony because there was no way to get there now, and no money to buy another one, and her father went away to find work and never wrote a letter back. But sometimes in that world she would come home from a dance on the back of

Karl Fischer's truck with Max and the two Fischer boys lying on wheat bags, heads in the middle, and they would sing loudly and out of tune and she would see the cauliflower trees.

She stares hard into the dark to make the cauliflower stalks go back to trees. Her mind casts about for a wisp of comfort from remembering. It is there but she does not take it. She wants to leave behind childish enchantments. It was not a comfortable childhood. Not after her father left. And this is war. Why let contorted memory concoct pretty histories? There is more comfort in finding the strength to face things as they are now. She has her family and her friends to think about. Where are the Fischer boys? Where is Hal?

If anyone had taken the place of her father it was Hal. Eight years older, a leader, an organiser. Her supporter and her critic. He taught her to patch up a hole caused by a fight and to apologise, and the thing she found hardest, to accept apologies and allow others to patch the hole they had made. She had learnt both of those skills, not perfectly, but to a level of competence. His greatest success was in the area of kindness. He found this quality in her and nurtured it. A quality others had failed to see, hidden as it was under layers of opinionated defiance. His mother had given birth to twins at the age of forty-two, when he was twenty-four. Eddy expected his interest in her to wane, but it didn't. She could see now that he had just added them to his course designed to teach her how to be a decent human being. He took them about with him on farm errands and still stopped to pick her up as he had always done. A boy, Billy, and a girl, Cat, they were naughty children because their mother coped by ignoring them. If it hadn't been for the attention of Hal they might have run completely wild. They would be ten years old now.

There had been no letters from Singapore since it fell. Her old world back here would have no centre without Hal. Coming home threatened to be a formality, an empty gesture.

Her mother waits for her in the kitchen, making iced coffee without ice, without coffee, spreading grape jam on bread. She is crushed to her mother's old linen dressing gown. Her face presses into a fleshy shoulder of tight pink buds with purple stems. There is a certain amount of crying to be done now. She will leave it to her mother to do. She has no tears. She knows about exhaustion. It causes floods of tears at wrong moments for no reason and when they are needed they are gone, dried up heartless, like a mirage. The prisoner walks past them with her kit bag on his shoulder, and disappears into the house. He is familiar with the geography of it. He wears what looks like army uniform in a bizarre purple red colour. He has not been invited to enter the house. He has not asked. He has walked past the tears of her mother in her girlish rosebud gown and desecrated their privacy and it could eclipse the emotion of their greeting.

She had seen and done dreadful, bloody things in foreign places these last four years, but this was the farmhouse, the homestead, the inner sanctum. A private place. Here the working men did not fraternise. There was the house where they came for meals and instructions and there were the men's quarters where they lived and there was a distance to be kept. The certain distance of ownership, however meagre. Not master and servant, but free enterprise and labour for a fair wage. Something had broken down. War changes things.

While her mother is speaking she watches the interloper, the enemy alien, walking back through the kitchen. He has an open sensitive face and an air of confidence. He nods slightly and says, 'Good night signora, signorina,' and walks out into the night. Her night on her farm.

Her mother calls after him. 'Joe, go and tell Max his sister is home.'

He does not speak. His feet on the gravel crunch away to silence.

'Where's Max? I thought he'd be at the train.'

'Fixing the harvester.'

'At midnight?'

'We need the early start. It's hot, there could be storms. How was the train? You look tired, but you look good.'

Her eyes begin to swim. She holds her daughter's face between her hands. They are warm and smell of bread and jam.

'You look very good.'

What her mother means is that she looks a lot better alive than dead, even though thin and grey. But she will not say that. She will not speak of the time of loss. Real then, but shadows now. She will not speak of the sinking of a ship and a telegram with condolences. For three months her daughter was dead. Then came a second telegram. In the twenty seconds before they opened it, the mother and brother re-felt every feeling of the first one, but this one was quite different and they didn't trust it. If it had been wrong before, it could be wrong again. Things happen in war, confusion, names out of order, left off the right list, put on the wrong list.

Her mother says, 'Jim and Hal Fischer are missing.'

Missing is dead. Hal and Jimmy can't be dead. Eddy hardly has enough breath to speak. The component bits and pieces of her life are getting lost. Her friends. Herself. She blurts out, 'I was dead for three months.'

'You were alive.'

'But if you and Max thought I was dead, then I was.'

Edith has her own definition of death. In her work the breath leaves a person and they do not change. If you are in mid-conversation you go on talking until the subject is exhausted. They are still there. It is a long time before a dead person becomes a body, if ever. So there must be another definition. If the people who want you to be alive think you are dead, then you're dead. That's the definition.

Her mother is shocked. 'No, what about you, you knew you weren't dead.'

'Yes, and when I'm dead I won't know that either. So I don't count, but you knew, you suffered.'

She is not thinking of her mother, but herself. She must not think of Hal as dead. Missing but alive. Like other army balls-ups it was an ongoing muddle, not an end. She will not picture it, will not think of a grave. She knows what her mother felt. An ocean of loss laps at her brain, threatening a marooning flood.

Her mother now suffers no loss, but there is the memory of pain. It is better to talk about the wheat crop and about the clearing of the land and the yields from the new land. Economically, her mother tells her, the war is good for them, but they work so hard now, harder than ever before. They have no men to work except the three prisoners.

'We moved them out, so you could have your old room.'

They've been sleeping in her room. She would have asked about the prisoners, why they'd been in the house and not the men's quarters, but she couldn't speak. Words didn't form. Why were they not rotting in Burma or dead like so many of the men she'd patched up? Her friends. More than friends. Men who need you to be mother, sister, all the women they cannot see any more or maybe ever again. If he looks at you like a brother or even a lover undressing you, you allow his eyes to do that, and it is more contact than any encounter in one of a thousand shuttered Tel Aviv rooms complete with sagging bed and sultry ceiling fan. Her mother, her brother, knew nothing. They had even lost sight of who was the enemy.

Max, swinging a hurricane lamp, arrives from the shed and hugs her to his greasy work clothes. The imagined hug was better, this one is marred by her concern about dirt marks on her uniform.

'We'll have to get you onto a better pasture while you're home. Got the best vegie garden we've ever had. Vince looks after it. He's a gift. Can grow anything and twice the usual size. You're about half the size you were when we saw you off at Fremantle.'

She thinks he probably wants to add, 'and twice the age.'

'Who's Vince?'

'Vincenzo. Itie prisoner. Works like a demon.'

She is beginning to wonder whether her mother and brother have read a newspaper or seen a newsreel in four years. Perhaps the wireless is broken. Her stomach tightens, her gut straining to contain the gall.

'Have they been using my room?' She tries to sound casual.

'Yeah. We had to bring them in until we got time to fix the hut. The windows were out and rain was coming through the roof.'

'It's summer now.'

'Yeah, well, they're company for Mum. Chop the wood, do the garden. I haven't got time any more.'

'Don't they work in the paddocks?'

'Of course. Do a lot of clearing. Sometimes they camp out, on the hill.'

'That'd be a bit rough for them, wouldn't it?'

'They don't seem to mind.'

'I'm glad to hear it. Only Australian soldiers, Hal and Jimmy, at the front fighting Germans and Japs and Italians, don't forget Italians, should have to put up with canvas and latrines. I don't see why enemy prisoners should have any inconvenience to their comfort.'

'There's nothing to get upset about, Eddy.'

'No. No all right. Fine, I won't mention it.' Her sarcasm is shrill.

He looks at her sharply, astonished. Her mother is worried.

'You must be exhausted, Edith, sit down and have some coffee.'

She can't sit in the kitchen and be confined. She prowls out onto the back porch and slumps into a deckchair. Before the war she would have kicked off her shoes, but her uniform and rank have taken away ease. She has unlearned how to be casual. She has also unlearned how to be compliant and tactful. Max follows her and leans against the door frame.

'Eddy, I've got to have these blokes here. I can't do it on my own.'

'Do you have to be so chummy?'

'They're all right.'

'Why wouldn't they be? They've got it laid on here.'

She gets up and paces around looking for something she doesn't find and slumps back into the chair.

'How do you think I should treat them, torture, solitary confinement?'

He is silent and is sorry he has spoken to her like this.

'I shouldn't have said that, but you know Italy has surrendered. Mussolini has fled. The Italians are now fighting against the Germans.'

She is not impressed. 'All of them?'

'Enough. Most.'

'These two don't need to fight, they've captured a little corner of the wheatbelt of Western Australia. Not bad for a couple of Mediterranean peasants.'

'Ed, calm down. Calm down.'

'Don't tell me that!' She is shouting at him. 'Don't tell me anything, not anything about them, not anything. You want me to be calm, or comatose like you?'

'Bloody hell, Ed.'

Max gives up, takes his Tilley lamp and heads back to the shed. She can see him shaking his head as he leaves the circle of light from the porch.

She sits in silence with her mother. She could be asking all manner of questions, catching up on home trivia, but their worlds will be separate for a while yet. Eddy can't afford to let herself be absorbed by this world too quickly. As soon as she is rested she will be off to New Guinea again. Her uniform is absurd alongside her mother's floral gown. The tightness in her stomach is at odds with the wide sky and the scented air. Her exhaustion is having a cheap champagne effect. Light-headed and queasy. She is remembering Hal, sitting here with them, his long legs stretched out, hank of blond hair over one eye, bragging about the runs he would make at cricket next Saturday. His voice rises in pitch and volume with each new six and with each wild catch. She can keep him alive with her thoughts. He can keep her thoughts alive. She will shed no tears, make no sign of mourning. What does he think about, over there in the jungle not dead?

Finally her mother says, 'We wrote about the prisoners. You knew we had prisoners working for us.'

'You didn't tell me you'd adopted them.'

In bed she lies staring into the dark, thinking about the prisoners. They could come in the night and chop her up with the axe. Shoot her with the .22 rifle. Or she could shoot them. She was capable of that. Were they? She despises their lame compliance.

She sleeps until the evening of the next day when the sky is getting ready to colour up red again. Her room is dark, cool, cooler than anywhere else, at least, and still smells of lavender. They haven't taken away the lavender and replaced it with garlic, she thinks. She lies with leaden limbs in a waking dream where she holds the image of Hal from her sleeping dreams.

'You should sign up, Hal. They'd make you an officer.' She could hear herself sounding as though she were chief of staff of the armed forces. She didn't mind being a little absurd in front of Hal. It was one way to get a rise, and she did.

'Rubbish, Eddy, you don't know that.'

She got a laugh out of him too, unexpected bonus.

'I do. They'd have to be stupid.'

'Who says they're not?'

'We're all in a great deal of trouble if they are.'

'Our track record isn't great. Look at Gallipoli. You don't think it's going to make any difference to the course of the war if Australia gets involved?'

He liked to be right, to guide and patronise her, so she fell into the role of child and pupil. She knew he was having one of those devil's advocate arguments with her but she couldn't help herself.

'All those deaths in the Great War were for nothing, I suppose.'

'The last war was about a bunch of old blokes feeding a much larger bunch of young blokes to the cannon.'

'Or defending themselves against the Hun.'

'They could have managed without us.'

'But we have to help them, and if we're threatened they'll help us.'

'Why?'

'Because we're all one. Same people. Just separated by a lot of water.'

'You sure they see it like that?'

'Your father's German. You have a different perspective.'

'You think I'm a Nazi? My mother's English. Even if I wasn't in a reserved profession they wouldn't want me on the first intake, I'm nearly thirty.'

'I'll miss your birthday.'

'I'm coming to the city.'

'I thought this was to be our farewell.'

They rode up and through a strip of gravelly breakaway, the highest point for some miles, thickly wooded with a mixture of white gums, pines and the tamma trees that gave their name to the farm. The dark green pines, the soft she-oak needles of the grey tamma and the tall white gums made this the family picnic spot. Perfect Christmas tree pines decked the air with incense. They'd stopped over the other side of the ridge in what Max called 'heartbreak country', sandplain, to sit among the morrison. Fluffy heads of white and yellow were finishing flowering on low woody bushes, cerise heads burst into view between them. It was like a planted garden. Elizabethan. Knee-high bushes spaced between scatterings of delicate blue orchids and faded pink and yellow everlastings. The whole place seemed everlasting, like it had been there for ever and would go on being there. *There's rosemary. That's for remembrance.* Ophelia, in a lapse of latitude, might have wandered past. It gave the farm a history, a point on a time line, a connection with a period otherwise unknowable. Always at this place Eddy was in wonder at its quiet beauty. There were signs of sheep pebbling the pale earth between the plants.

Hal frowned at the idea of getting off a horse to sit when there was work to be done.

'What are you doing?'

He watched her tie her horse to a branch of York gum and sit in its meagre moving dapple.

'You can only do justice to this place with your head three feet above the ground. You must sit.'

'On sheep shit?'

'It's old and dry, it doesn't smell.' She stood up and scraped aside the droppings with her boot. 'Here's a clean place. Sit and dream.'

She was confident he would humour her. After all, it was her work they were not doing. He was on a social call.

Here, she had read the Brontës. Lying low, protected from wind that wheezed through the tops of the warm bushes in much the way it did across the cold rocks of Penistone Crag. On a neighbouring farm there was a family as brutal and drunken as the Earnshaws. But the sun and absence of ancient stone buildings would not allow the Gothic to complete the picture. There was no one of propriety and breeding to match the Lintons. At fifteen, Eddy had found Catherine a bit of a disappointment. She starts out a good strong heroine, not a simpering Jane Eyre, but marries a man who is a friend in preference to one she passionately loved. If she'd been raised in this country she'd have shown more courage. If she'd been raised in this country perhaps the sun would have bleached away her passion. And perhaps here, as in any hemisphere, the middle-class aspirations of the ignorant socialite would have suffocated her passion in its universal starched linen. It was something to watch out for. This was a new-settled area, away from more established places where class was a daily exercise. One or two recent arrivals from England affected the role of country squire, but no one took any notice of them unless they refused to shout their round at the pub.

A travelling library came to the store at the siding and offered mainly popular English novels, celebrating the adventures of a series of cads, bounders and debutantes at spiffing weekends in the home counties, chasing foxes and tennis balls. In parts of Australia they did that sort of thing but it seemed as far removed from this life at Noonalbin as England itself. At Alberts in Perth, Eddy could buy any number of books, even Australian publications; in fact, she did most of her reading at the city library, which she joined for a small annual subscription. She worried that there would not be enough books to read when she was sent overseas, but then perhaps there would be no time for reading between long shifts and whatever else the war saw fit to dish out, air raids, shelling, blackouts.

But these bushes were scented and could remind you of an experience you'd never had. Of the herbs and flowers of Shakespeare. A picture of Anne Hathaway's cottage in the village of Shottery near Stratford hung beside the telephone in the front hall of the farmhouse. The three or four acres of wild garden here looked like the tiny garden there. Eddy had never thought to ask her mother where this picture had come from. It had always been in their house and when she looked at it England no longer seemed far away. Before the war she had begun to save her salary in order to make a journey back there, to where her family had originated, so recently, in terms of history.

'You love this place.' Hal broke the silence.

Did she? She supposed so. In the way you do your crippled child, because it is yours and because you pity it. She resented it for not being more and admired it for not caring less.

She tried the question on him. 'Do you?'

'What?'

'Love your farm, this district?'

'Don't know. Never thought about it. It's a place to make a living, to survive. I've no doubt there are plenty better.'

He was doing his sang-froid thing again, displaying no feelings, no attachment. She took it with a grain of salt. She stood up and stretched her cramped legs and wandered over to a collection of dry bones, the remains of a long dead sheep. Its skull had disappeared, carted off by a fox or a dingo. She squatted and began sorting through them. She stood up when she had found what she was looking for and turned back to Hal.

'Here,' she said handing him two small, white bones. 'For Cat.'

'She's not quite up to playing knuckle bones yet.'

'She soon will be.'

Occasionally a taller wattle, grevillea or mallee punctuated the area. The sheep sheltered in these wild gardens on cold nights. They were not here now but grazing at the bottom of the paddock. Two or three ewes had stayed behind to care for the lambs resting further up the slope. 'Sheep may safely graze,' sang Hal.

'Not any more,' Eddy groaned. He was always so out of tune.

They met in the city four weeks later and he seemed different. A double-breasted suit made him look even thinner and taller. His old-fashioned shoes were a bit of a giveaway and they, with the hank of pale hair hanging across his forehead, stamped him rural. And gentle, she thought. You can see he is gentle. She was waiting for him in her uniform in the foyer of the Esplanade Hotel. Well-to-do farmers stayed in this Victorian iron-lace birdcage overlooking the river. Graziers stayed at the Weld Club, a few doors and levels of society up the road. He never stayed in either place, but used the Esplanade like all country people did, as a meeting place, to have a drink, see a familiar face. If he looked different to her, she was completely transformed for him. Here was no girl to be spoiled and protected. She was causing a mild sensation. Several people had approached to talk to her. Few women in uniform were visible at this early stage of the war.

Their greeting was awkward for being out of its usual environment. There seemed to be a need to shake hands, which was too formal, or kiss cheeks, which was too familiar. Hal had booked a table at a restaurant. A rare place in this town. A rare adventure for both of them. Its lacquered timber door opened straight off a tiny street with no footpath, squeezed into the middle of the city. Gentle rain was making the steep street shine in the lamplight.

'Like Europe,' Eddy said.

'I know.'

Europe, where they had never been. By contrast, the rest of the isolated capital city was a shambling country town. He held the door for her and she stepped inside onto a half flight of stairs with no landing, descending straight into the dining room. Patrons were obliged to make an entrance like actors on a stage.

She placed his present on the table in front of him between the *entrecôte* course and the *tarte aux pommes.*

'It's your birthday,' she said, when he raised his brows at her.

'So it is.' He sighed with what she hoped was not sarcasm and leaned back in his chair and folded his arms. She had seen him look like that when he was about to give her a roasting. She couldn't think what she'd done.

'What?'

'I'm thirty.'

'Only thirty?' She shook her head, feigning ignorance.

He laughed. 'How old did you think I was?'

'Oh, I thought at least thirty-two. Maybe not as old as God, but easily as old as Christ.'

He didn't smile. 'I'm no saviour. I feel like there's no future.'

'What a thing to say.'

'I thought I'd have done more by now,' he said and twisted his damask table napkin into a rope.

'You're way behind,' she said, with concern. 'You still haven't overturned any money-changers' tables, and what about the forty days and forty nights? You keep putting that off.'

He gave her a half-hearted smile and they fell into silence and then she said, 'I think you and Max are wonderful staying home to grow crops while everyone goes off to war and to see the world.'

'I don't want to be in a war,' he said, lifting his hands from the table to show they were empty.

'It's not a war, it's *the* war. You make it sound a million miles and years away.'

'I wish it was. I curse this war,' he growled. 'I don't see what's so bloody exciting about it. People get killed, you know.'

'I do know that.' She was beginning to wonder what they were talking about.

'Yes, I suppose you do. It's just that I thought when the Depression ended I might be able to get somewhere, do something.'

So that was it.

'Medicine?'

'The only way I'd want to go to war is as a medical officer. I'm not keen to be killing,' he said.

Wine had loosened his tongue. She had never seen him affected by alcohol although she had seen him consume it in quantities at times. Being like a rock at the farm and secretly wanting to leave all the time was shocking. He and the farm went together. The Fischer farm and the Nash farm, alongside each other, inseparable. Neighbours entwined completely in the welfare of the other. And not wanting to fight. Almost a conscientious objector. Even more shocking. He shrugged and smiled his nice, leathery brown face, but not his eyes, dark and sad. His eyes were not smiling. She didn't like it when they got that look in them.

'The war won't last for ever. There's still time,' she said.

'I'd always felt there was time until this bloody war came along and now who knows what will happen?'

There was no answer to that. She waited for him to speak again. Eventually he reached out and picked up the small rectangular parcel and shook it.

'A cigar. Havana? I'm trying to give them up.'

He tore off the white tissue paper and lifted the lid of the small box. Inside, lying in stately velvet like a corpse in a coffin, was a tortoiseshell fountain pen with gold trim.

'Is this a hint?'

'You've only written me two letters in the four years I've been in Perth. I think there's room for improvement.'

'The wheat is ripening, the lambs are growing, the dams are empty, the sun is burning. You could write it yourself.'

'I don't care what you say, as long as you say it on paper and send it to me when I'm alone at the war and homesick.'

'It'll be dull.'

'Think of it as your war effort.'

'That's about the size of it, a few scratchings with a pen.'

'Not scratchings with that pen. Beautiful clear arcs and circles describing clever thoughts.'

'Such an optimist.'

'And you're a pessimist. I've never seen you pessimistic before. You always scorned self-pity, "the lazy way out," you used to say.'

'You think I'm self-pitying?'

'I think you're not happy. It's unlike you.'

'It's not unlike me, but until now you were too young and self-absorbed to notice.'

'Was I?'

The waiter brought the tarts and settled them into place with a flourish. Why, she wondered, did waiters in expensive restaurants flourish? Being a waiter was not, after all, like being an actor or musician who was expected to flourish. Such a strange little job of no importance, reserved for women and men who were refugees. Like being a nurse really. Maybe she should introduce a few flourishes. Place the scalpel in the surgeon's hand with deft flick of the wrist and the pan under the patient's bottom with an obsequious bow.

'The waiter is attentive,' she said, holding back a smirk.

They watched him at the next table dipping and fluttering about his diners like a dinner-suited moth and Hal peeled off a slow grin and they were able to laugh together.

'You are the least dull person in my life,' she said.

'I know.'

'And the most conceited.'

'If you don't include yourself.'

He hadn't been particularly grateful for his expensive pen. What with the money she'd put into the farm account and this present, she had no money at all to last until next month. Anyway, no one knew when they might have to pack their kit bags and head off to Europe.

He drove her through the drizzle to the hospital in his Ford Prefect. 'Don't forget to write,' she said as he pulled on the handbrake.

'Oh shit!' he said, patting his jacket pocket.

'You haven't lost it already?'

'Must have left it at the restaurant.'

The hair began to stand up along her arms. It was such a bad omen.

He started the car again. 'We'll go straight back.'

'No, you'd better let me out, it's almost curfew.'

At the door of the nurses' quarters they hugged goodbye and she wondered for an instant why she had enlisted so readily. Right now it seemed a vain and stupid thing to do. When he released her she looked hard at his face in order to memorise it. The moon emerging from the fast-moving clouds and the pale light over the door had turned his skin green.

'You come back.' He began to clear his throat.

'Of course,' she said and kissed him briefly on the lips and turned to go and heard him sigh, 'Oh God.'

'Any pen will do,' she said smiling at him around the door. Then she closed it and was gone from his sight and his night and was mounting the well-polished stair to her shared room on the first floor. She pulled the blind away from the window an inch to watch the cream Prefect snail away. A forlorn speed. All night she'd been fending off his dark mood, but the sight of his slow-retreating car made her throat ache and her breath shallow. She pulled a handkerchief from her pocket and blew her nose.

Her roommate sat up. 'You all right?'

'Did I wake you?'

'I didn't know you had a boyfriend.'

'I don't.'

'Not what it looked like from up here.'

She might have known that they were being watched. Was there anything about this night that had actually gone well?

'You can't see those sort of subtleties at this distance in the dark.'

'Sorry.'

'It's okay. He's like a father.'

'Young for a father.'

'Brother then.'

'Does he know that?'

'Yes, he does. He's always ticking me off.'

'Brave man. Got more nerve than anyone around here. Poor devil.' She lay down again and pulled the sheet over her head. 'Turn the light on if you want, it won't bother me.'

'Good night, Shirley.'

'Good night, girl. Don't know who to feel sorry for, him or you.'

'Go to sleep.'

'If you're throwing him back, throw him this way. What does he do for a crust? Surgeon, barrister, film star?'

'Good night, Shirley.'

Lying in bed watching moon shadows move tree shapes across the blind, she thought about what he'd said. He was right, war was frightening and no one knew what it would bring. He was the only one who seemed depressed about it. It was not unusual for him to be out of step. He was smarter than most. Everyone at the barracks was excited about going to Europe to fight Jerry, to teach him a lesson. No one had any intention of being a casualty. Poor old Hal, always there with his kindness and scoldings, trying to turn her into a silk purse. Since she'd been away in the city he'd had few opportunities and, she liked to think, less cause. It had been some time since she'd found herself on the wrong side of his good humour. Although tonight no one could say he was happy.

Things should go right for Hal, a person so right in every way. Clever, good, energetic, he should have been able to make things go his way. He was one of the few people in the district who had made it all the way through secondary school. He'd passed his leaving certificate and matriculated and been something of a star at boarding school. You'd expect a boy like Hal to end up as school captain. You'd also expect him to go to university, but the Depression put an end to that. Grasshoppers had changed the course of his life. When he was not much more than a kid, during the Depression, he engineered the survival of his family's farm by selling mutton to butchers at the satellite gold mines that sprang up around them in the early thirties. He had a truck and plenty of feed and never stopped working. Then the grasshoppers came and ate everything, including his opportunities. All his savings disappeared between the mandibles of millions of hoppers.

In view of what he'd said, she felt guilty at her excitement about the war. But for the moment she wanted to do something useful, to be part of something important. The war was an opportunity beyond her wildest imaginings. She would apply herself to it like a test and she would pass with flying colours. She wanted what so many of those now enlisting wanted, to see what the rest of the world was up to and be part of it. It was more than a chance to leave the backwater of the world, the most forgotten and insignificant place on earth, it was time to see what she could do. She wanted to work beside people from other nations and see how she measured up. She wanted to measure up, in truth, she wanted to be better, if not in skill and knowledge then in hard work and dedication. She wanted them to know that there are serious people living in the antipodes, not just kangaroos. It did not occur to her to question why that should be important.

WAR IN THE WHEATBELT

The timbers on Grey Tamma Farm were hardwood and some of them tall, fine trees. To the prisoners, they were strange-looking trees, with names they learnt slowly, except for the salmon gum, easy to remember with its trunk the colour of the fish. Pink trunks and shiny leaves the shape of peach leaves, but stiff and waxy with strong eucalyptus scent, different in every way from the softwoods that grew on the mountains of Giuseppe's home on the border of Switzerland, where three kinds of larch clothed the slopes along with silver birch, beech, chestnut and hazel and beneath them grew wild strawberries and bilberries. Here, the understorey of the open woodland was treed with the slim shiny limbs of what he came to know as mallee. Between them scrambled bushes of quandong, tea tree and wattle with brittle branches and sharp, defensive leaves. They grew in red loam beneath a layer of shiny large-grained sand. Low rainfall created so little humus that the soil smelled clean.

Clearing the land was cruel work. During the first week their hands became so sore from the axe that they could not sleep at night. Carlo was not able to bear the discomfort quietly. Max showed him how to get to sleep by placing a bucket of water on either side of the bed and dangling his hands in it. Carlo at first scoffed at the logic. Water made hands soft and useless. But as soon as he was asleep he would turn over, and in doing so take them out of the water. They all suffered the pain of rubbing their palms with methylated spirits to harden them. They did harden, but at first Giuseppe and Carlo had to wear bandages while they worked.

A team of horses pulled the trees into a pile so they could be burnt. The worst part of the job was digging out roots. Some were so large that Max used gelignite to blow them out of the ground. It was a week before Eddy's return that Max discovered he was short two sticks of gelignite. After making a search, he asked Giuseppe if he knew anything about it. Giuseppe's stomach fell to his boots. He did not think it was beyond Carlo to try to blow up his employers, or even perhaps all of them. War in the wheatbelt. Carlo's last stand. Giuseppe searched the hut and helped Max search the shed. Finally he decided to consult Enzo.

'Have you seen Carlo doing anything secretive, going anywhere?'

'I try not to see him or hear him.'

'From now on one of us must be with him all the time. Tonight I will stay awake until two and then you can take over and let me sleep.'

Enzo groaned. Giuseppe felt sorry for him. He worked harder than anyone and was tired.

This arrangement was never kept. Soon after midnight Carlo rose from his bed without a sound. Giuseppe followed him through the gate and down into the dam paddock. The only sign of moonlight was a silver rim around a ceiling of dark cloud. It was not easy to keep

Carlo in sight and avoid giving himself away by standing on sticks and bark. At the dam he could not see him. He began to circle it thinking Carlo might be behind the bank. He heard a footfall a second too late. Before he had time to turn, Carlo sprang on him, putting him in a headlock and wrenching his arm behind his back.

'Let me go,' Giuseppe shouted. 'You are crazy. I know what you are up to. Everyone knows. Give it up.'

It was bravado. Giuseppe was at a disadvantage and had no idea how to get out of it. The next moment he was face down on the ground and trying to get out from under Carlo. He struggled to his feet to see Carlo's dark form running into the trees with someone in swift pursuit waving a shovel and shouting a string of Australian swear words. Giuseppe heard a crash and a cry of agony and caught up with them to see Max standing over Carlo with shovel poised. Enzo must have woken Max. Max had come up behind Carlo and hit him between the shoulder blades with the flat of a shovel while he was busy restraining Giuseppe.

Giuseppe drove with Max forty miles to deliver Carlo to an army officer at the control centre, who was not pleased at being pulled out of bed in the middle of the night. He roused the police sergeant and arranged to hold Carlo in the town lockup until he could be taken back to camp. All this he did in a plaid woollen dressing gown and a pair of felt slippers, his uniform cap on his head and his service revolver in its holster around his waist.

At daylight Max and Giuseppe returned to the dam in search of the gelignite with Carlo's curses ringing in their ears. *Traditore, collaboratore, schiuma.* They skirted the paddock and criss-crossed it but found nothing.

'Could be anywhere,' said Max, hands on hips surveying the landscape. 'He says he didn't take it. Perhaps he really didn't.'

'I think he lies more than he speaks the truth. We will be better now without him,' said Giuseppe.

They were standing at the far fence line bordering the uncleared land. The pale limbs of the mallees were picking up the early light. A low-pitched drumming broke into the noise of morning birdsong.

Giuseppe looked at Max. 'What is that?'

'A bird.'

Giuseppe looked up into the tree tops.

'Not a flying bird. Come with me.'

Max climbed through the fence and made off into the bush. They walked about twenty yards. He stopped and squatted down.

'Malleefowl. That's his incubator.' He pointed to a mound about four feet high and fifteen feet across.

Giuseppe squatted beside him.

'You'll see him if you stay still, he's never far.'

After five minutes the malleefowl cock came through the brush scratching some leaves with his feet, adding them to the line of sticks and leaves waiting beside the mound.

'What is he doing?'

'He gets the leaves and grass ready and when it rains he puts them in the hollow of the mound to make compost heat and then she lays eggs. Great big eggs, lots of them. They check the heat with their beaks and keep it at the right temperature by taking the soil off or putting it on.'

'He is small. From his nest I thought large like an emu.'

'More like a hen.'

'They are industrious. They build. I like them.'

'So do I. They never give up. There are three more nests over there, but I don't think they'll be there much longer, the foxes are so bad. Wait a bit and you'll see the hen. They never make that noise unless there is another one nearby.'

Before long the other one showed up and began scratching among her treasure.

They headed back through the fence and past the dam. At the gate Max said, 'Thanks for the help. Take the morning off and get some sleep.'

'The cows will not like that.'

'I'll milk them,' said Max.

'No. I can do it. It is my job. I am beginning to see their good qualities. How do you say? They eat out of my hand? I am for them *simpatico*.'

'Yeah? I've got to see this. I'll come down and give you a hand.'

Once Carlo was gone, the work became easier for the other two prisoners. Even the continual struggle with the notorious mallee root became a challenge instead of a curse. It is said that the mallee tree has more root area underground than branch area above it. In paddocks cleared for many years it was still necessary to follow the plough and pick up the roots it exposed. These were collected and used for firewood.

Chopping firewood was Giuseppe's job. He heard this order the morning after their arrival with some relief. This was a job he could do, having done it for his mother as a boy. He took the barrow and went to find the woodheap. It did not take him long. Ten metres high, twenty metres wide and thirty metres long, it looked like a spiky hill, large enough to have its own climate pattern. The final resting place of the ubiquitous mallee root. He walked around to the lee to where someone had been cutting wood before. There was a large log covered in dried blood. He became alarmed that his predecessor might have slipped and cut off his foot. Later he discovered it was where chickens were executed for Sunday lunch.

His struggle with the mallee root became a favourite dinner-time joke. Learning to chop these mysterious pieces of wood was an infuriating process. The roots were large, twisted, knotted clumps. It was impossible to find one straight line. At the first stroke the axe bounced off without making an impression. He couldn't believe his eyes. He reached down to feel the root to make sure it was not ossified. It was warm and smooth. It was wood. He chopped and chopped and made only chips that flew off perilously in all directions. He went searching for more amenable lumps. They all reacted the same way. At length he abandoned the axe and spent the rest of the time looking for small pieces that didn't need cutting. He knew there was no future in that. He would have to learn to do it eventually. Neither Max nor his mother bothered to explain the characteristics of the mallee root and the skill needed for cutting them.

Whenever he had a spare minute, he would go back to the woodheap to practise chopping. Thwack, thwack, the sound resonated among the corrugated-iron sheds and aroused the interest of whole brigades of marauding pink and grey galahs, inciting them to shriek and chortle in ear-shattering response. And with each stroke of the axe, the farm turkeys gobbled out a short protest as if remembering a recent execution at that place. Eventually he learnt to find the grain and use a sharp blow to split the root as many times as he wanted. As if in acknowledgement the galahs finally abandoned their perches and flew away, but the turkeys kept up their vigil. There was some satisfaction in his accomplishment, but he still had to put up with teasing. Stories were invented about him spending so much time at the woodheap that he must have been meeting a lover there.

Perhaps it was not such a funny joke to be three years without female company. He had become the custodian of an imaginary world and was susceptible to the slightest glance from a young woman. He had had no special girlfriend when he left Italy for North Africa, but there had been many in the past. Some were simply formal, conventional friendships and others more casual, more purely physical. He thought about them all at night in bed. In camp, sleep often eluded him because he did not have enough physical activity to exhaust him and the frustration would build. The physical deprivation was an obvious problem but what was not so obvious was the need for a woman's presence, for her talk. He had become heartily sick of the sight of men. La signora at the farm was not young, but she was a fine strong woman with a nice face. She was kind to them, which he found good but curious. They were enemy prisoners. He was grateful for this attention. She arranged for the neighbours to take the prisoners to mass every second Sunday. Giuseppe had not had a faith since he was twelve years of age, but he attended mass because there he would see young women.

Church was an opportunity to meet fellow prisoners from other farms. Some felt uncomfortable about Giuseppe's rank and were stiff and unfriendly. Giuseppe was more interested in conversing with the daughters of the Women's Guild who offered them sandwiches and tea. They were surprised at his English and glad to spend a minute or two in conversation. Most of them were shy and of few words. Some would not have been averse to striking up a friendship with a prisoner if their parents had not been glaring at them. It was strictly against rules for prisoners to fraternise with women. If a liaison were discovered, the prisoner was sent back to camp and placed in detention for anything up to six months. Sometimes the sight of a pretty girl would make Giuseppe think it was worth the risk. In the end he chose his fantasies, preferable to being sent back to camp. That would drive him mad. Here he had freedom and a family life of sorts. It was more than he could have expected.

THE SWEET YOUNG DEAD

She passed out over a baked dinner. Leg of mutton, tomato pie and three veg. The sort of dinner she had eaten so often as a child as to become bored with it. The sort of dinner she'd have given anything for when she was in the Middle East and New Guinea.

'Max took a couple of hours off to kill a wether so we would have a nice dinner when you got back home.'

'He's kind.' Her voice was faint.

Perhaps she shouldn't have shouted at him last night, but it needed to be said. Max was still on the harvester using up the last of the day's warmth. They could hear the old MacCormack from the table, the two women and the two prisoners. She couldn't speak to them. They didn't attempt to speak to her. The warm Velvet-laundry-soap smell of the two men hung about the table parasitic like clumps of mistletoe. The sound of their breathing syncopated with the kitchen clock. The prisoners spoke to her mother from time to time, organising the trivia of farm chores. They did not speak to each other. She noticed that there was nothing rough about their manners. They passed things politely about the table and stood up to help her mother serve and clear.

But still their presence jarred. Sitting in their stupid red uniforms as though they had been born here. Even the smooth tan on their forearms indicated that they had acclimatised too much. The older prisoner, Enzo, had dark hair and his skin had gone nearly black. The younger taller man, Giuseppe, looked like he belonged here, might have come from a neighbouring farm. He had curly brown hair the top of which had started to bleach in the sun. The ordeal of having to eat with the enemy, combined with the malaria, caused a powerful reaction. She could see the roasted pumpkin coming towards her, bearing down on her, and was powerless.

She came to in time to prevent the local doctor from becoming involved. He would have her back in the military hospital at Northam. She had plenty of Atebrin. What could they do for her, except keep her away from her home? Perhaps she would die before she had the answer to this question. Feeling like this made her want to die. She had seen so many sweet young dead and there were nights and early mornings after long nights when she had ached to lie down with them and be still and become dust too. And at other times she had thanked God, Mr Lucky Stars or whoever it was, that the pale, passive face did not belong to her and that she was alive.

Two weeks passed while nothing at the farm changed except the knowledge that there was a young woman asleep in the house. She awoke at intervals to take a little food, drink and medication and then slipped back into a heavy sleep. The first day that she did not need to sleep all day marked the beginning of her recovery. She walked about in the darkened cool of the house. She sat in an old morocco chair. She remembered sitting in it with her father before they moved from the city. 'Oh she is, yes she is, sweeter than marmalade,' he would sing on a tuneless half whisper. She would take his watch out of his fob pocket to feel its smoothness on the palm of her hand, happy for a moment of his attention and thinking that marmalade could be as bitter as it was sweet.

She sat on the floor and opened the piano stool to look at her unplayed music. Chopin on top. She'd rejected him at age seventeen as too sentimental. Her favourite, a waltz, op. 64, no. 2, dedicated to the Baronne de Rothschild. So much yearning and so much energy together. So many not published until after his death. He might have rejected them for sentimentality too. When she played music which made her feel longing and loss and passion for everything or nothing, she could see how easily things might get out of control. Ten years later, seeing the sheets of manuscript started her thinking about that. Skulking around was an idea of herself that looked different from the one she saw in the mirror.

She placed her hands over the keys of the piano but didn't strike a note, not wanting to break the fizz of silence that gave her healing. The feared and wanted silence. The giver and taker-away. Gradually she was able to sit on the verandah and finally to do a few things in the kitchen. She avoided meals at the table because contact with the prisoners agitated her. Her mother's reassurances made it worse.

'They are surprising, these boys, except for the language, they are just like our boys. They could be the Fischer boys.'

'They are not the Fischer boys, Mum,' she said and turned away from her mother on the bed to where she could look out the casement doors into the garden.

'I know they're not the Fischer boys,' her mother continued, 'but if Jimmy and Hal are prisoners somewhere, then I hope they are meeting with kindness. By showing kindness to these two, then perhaps somehow the kindness will get to our friends' boys.'

'I doubt it. They're prisoners of the Germans and the Japanese. It's not the same thing.'

'Maybe not, but treating these prisoners like we would any other worker seems to be the right thing to do, and they're responding.'

Eddy was amazed at her mother's lack of understanding. 'Mum, you are not treating them like any other workers. More like family. You seem to have given them the run of the house. They sit with you after dinner. No working man ever did that here before.'

'But they've had a terrible time. They've been prisoners for so long.'

'As terrible as our men stuck in the jungle with the Japs?'

'I know. It's not good up there. But these are good men. We've grown to like and respect them.'

Eddy lay still, looking out the doors away through the picket fence past the line of kurrajong trees to the constant taupe of summer. She let her gaze fall back into the dappled light on the grass under the trees. A garden of spirits. Playmates of a solitary childhood. Wafting in the green shadows, sliding through the pickets, out of the gully of eucalypts to play under the cape lilacs and then slip away when she was called into the house. Sometimes wild, teasing, scouring her fair skin, whipping through and away with a willie willie, dealing out punishments, and then on gentle days as though nothing had happened she would find them there waiting, kind again. They would not be ignored. When she perched in the trees with her books they would become jealous and try to trap her high in the leafy tops, so high once that she couldn't get down. Finally Hal had come from the paddock and stood beneath the tree and spread his dusty hands.

'Why do you want to get down? Monkeys live in trees.'

'I need to feed Toby.'

'He's got grass, he'll survive.'

'He needs hot bran.'

'Where's your father?'

'Gone to the city.'

'He only just came back.'

'He's gone again. Get me down, Hal, please.'

'You can get yourself down.'

He talked her down to a place where she could safely jump into his arms. The safety of the arms were paid for by his teasing and game playing when she was in the utmost anguish. Struck by a fear much more powerful than anything she could think. Something felt and not thought was running her and more than embarrassment at being found out, she was mortified that she could not rely on herself, that she was nothing to herself. There were times when she knew she was of little importance to those around her, but to be nothing to herself, to abandon herself, that made her panic for her future, made her blind to her future.

There were definitely things unseen that saw me in that garden, she thought. She still felt their presence. She had never mentioned them to anyone, not even Max. They were there like watching friends. One day she might call on them. Until now they had kept this house safe, this oasis green, cool, sturdy. But nowhere is safe any more. Perhaps that's what it is to grow up. To understand what a dangerous world it is. Without Hal, how could there be a safe house?

'Vince, the older one, is so good-natured,' her mother continued, 'and has a wonderful sense of humour. He misses his family. He has a son he's never seen.'

Ignoring Eddy's cool silence, she said, 'And Joe, his mother must miss him so much. He's well-educated, his English is excellent. He's been to England.'

'That's great, Mum.'

'Oh Eddy . . .'

'Look, I don't want to talk about them. I've heard enough.'

'All right, you haven't been well, we'll leave it. You're well enough to come to church tomorrow though. People want to see you.'

'I don't go to church any more.'

'I think you should this once. Everyone is proud of you. You have to show your face. You can't just skulk around here.'

That is how it comes about that Eddy opens her wardrobe the next day to take out a suit she has not worn since the war began, that she has been looking forward to wearing again, and sees that it is not there. A crimson linen jacket with pinched-in waist and wide lapels. There are other things missing. Blue crepe de chine dress. Cream fine wool coat. Navy jacket. A ball gown in grey silk satin. All gone. She searches her mother's wardrobe and her brother's. Nothing. The sounds of breakfast, knives scraping egg onto forks, the whistle of the boiling kettle, are beginning to drift through the house with the aroma of toast. She cannot go to the kitchen and ask her mother where her clothes are without coming face to face with the prisoners, so she continues to search. Drawers, cupboards, linen press. She spends half an hour searching. She pulls out a deep drawer under her mother's wardrobe and finds a framed photograph of her father on top of her mother's folded clothes. When she hears the whine of the back gate and the click of its latch she decides it is safe to proceed to the kitchen.

'Sleep well, Eddy? Like some breakfast?' Her mother is sweeping the floor.

'No thanks. Mum, have you seen my clothes? My suit and coat, my evening gown?'

'Oh, wear your uniform to church, everyone would love that. That's what they really want to see, you wearing your uniform.'

Her mother goes outside to empty the dustpan into the garden. Eddy pours tea and sits at the table to drink it. She traces the grain of the scrubbed wood with her thumbnail and waits for her mother to return.

'Where are my clothes?'

Her mother frowns and hurries about the kitchen inventing tasks.

'Mum?'

'Yes, all right.'

'Well?'

'They were such fashionable styles, they would have gone out of date.'

'You gave them away.' Pause. 'Mum?'

'Well, when were you going to get an opportunity to wear them, and Gretel and Sophie unable to get anything with coupons the way they are.'

'Gretel! She's four inches shorter than I am, and who's Sophie? I don't even know her.'

There's another pause while her mother takes up her gardening gloves and goes outside again. Eddy follows her to the vegetable patch and watches her pull up carrots and radishes.

'When did you give them away?'

Her mother goes on pulling and weeding as though she has not heard.

'Mum? When did you give them away?'

Her mother stands up and taking the basket of vegetables walks back through the vines and the roses, Eddy following, talking to her back, her voice rising in volume and pitch the faster they walk. The talking becomes crying and shouting.

'You gave them away when you thought I was dead. Expunged all trace of me. Let the prisoners sleep in my room. Have you cleaned out my bank account? Is there anything of mine left anywhere? How could you?' She screams and cries after her mother, following her to the laundry where she will wash the vegetables.

In the laundry, the Italian prisoner who fetched her from the train is washing the milk buckets and the separating equipment. There is a strong smell of bleach. He looks up alarmed, trapped. Eddy is at the door sobbing and shouting at her mother who begins to wash the vegetables with maddening deliberation. She is brought up short when she sees the prisoner.

He says '*Scusi*' and looking down at his feet steps past her and leaves. She stands aside to let him pass.

Her mother shakes her head and says quietly, 'Eddy.'

Eddy is shaking with anger.

'Get them back. Telephone Gretel and whoever this Sophie is and ask for them back.'

'Eddy.'

'No. Don't say that, as if I'm to blame.'

'I can't.'

'Yes you can. Just explain that I'm not dead. I've come back and the clothes I saved so long to buy are needed again. That gown, you know, came from Paris. I saved for a year to buy that. I love those clothes.'

'I can't. They've altered them to fit. Cut off the hem and the sleeves.'

'I don't believe it,' she howls.

She runs out of the laundry and out of the yard and away across the paddock to the south, wading through the wheat, full heads slapping at her thighs. She becomes exhausted and goes to the edge of the dam to sit in the shade.

War heightens emotions and cheapens them too. Minute new-hatched feelings of desire or connection get enlarged, distorted before they have time to mature. They become unwieldy and burn themselves out, wither with instant blowtorch morbidity. Hourly issues of life and death combined with months of dreary routine and inactivity leave the brain unable to relate to the normal things of life. Issues of loss and reconciliation to a helpless situation render the brain inactive. Desire becomes a function, more than ever, of the possible.

So fast to get rid of her things, of what was left of her, after they thought she had died. The comfort of knowing that if she died in some terrifying war zone, she would leave a family at home that would love her and mourn her and never forget anything about her and remember her by treasuring her things was now gone. If she had known how easily she would be forgotten, going into the war zone would have meant something else altogether. Perhaps she wouldn't have volunteered to stay in Greece when the German army was closing in fast. No one needed to volunteer. Everyone did. To be taken prisoner as a woman. The violations were not discussed. Eddy wanted herself to know that she was rock solid.

When the strafing began and with it the Luftwaffe bombings of the slow line of traffic heading south to Piraeus, the truck in front of the one in which she was travelling was hit and overturned into a ditch on the side of a mountain. She made soldiers from a passing transport help her lay the wounded out in the grass until they could be taken away. She turned and walked away for no more than two minutes to find transport for them and the bombing and strafing started again. She sheltered on the mountain covering her ears with her shaking hands against the screaming of the Stukas. They flew away to rearm and refuel. She tried to find her way back, but there were only craters, gaping holes.

She searched while the streams of trucks and cars drove down the rough mountain road hour after hour in slow procession. She could not recognise the terrain. The place where she had left them had been completely altered by the bombing. It was not a place any more, it did not exist. Light rain began to fall and with the drizzle came the cold down through her coat into her bones. She stood on the edge of a crater, she claimed it and she stood and wailed at it. She didn't care if anyone noticed her. No one spoke to her. Finally in the dark she accepted a ride on a truck with some troops who were silent with retreat and chilled with hunger.

Then she was once more with her fellow nurses and they did not have to stay but were evacuated to Crete where they waited for a ship while the Germans started to come out of the sky. They hid for one freezing night among the headstones in a graveyard. And finally on board ship the sight of Alexandria and the coastline of Africa felt like coming home. The Australian nurses and physiotherapists stood on deck as the port came into focus watching the comforting business of its day. No one spoke except to thank their God. All were bound together in a tight sisterhood that never unravelled.

When she was a child she would come to sit beside this dam when things had not gone well. When loss and sadness seemed to be piling up around her. The things that grew and flew about here were constant, oblivious to the human tailings of grief and loss. Even the tiny shiny grains of sand gave comfort. A nice strong stick, a fallen nest. A miniature hill, inside it a city of ants. The comfort of industry. Bees collecting nectar from flowering bushes. The gentle sound of wind in grass. She sits here now to remember this comfort, but recalls not comfort but pain. On a grey, moist, west-wind day she might be here alone. The wind cutting a line between her senses and the world, wrapping her tight in its invisible blankets, healing, dabbing, sponging the wound. An escape from thoughts of a kind, good mother unable to rise from her bed not for any physical cause, not for any cause at all to the eyes of a child. A small horse, dead for no reason, but that did not mean from no fault. A father gone away for the sake of survival. Leaving with promises and foreboding sadness. Days, weeks and, afterwards, years empty of letters and full of empty promises. Hard days of subsistence, physical and spiritual.

To this place she would come, trailing a long bag of sadness and yearning. Learning here, being taught by these natural things their arts of survival. The working cure. She could do that herself without help. She could go from here with something to do if not with something to please. She would do it now if she could summon the energy to stand.

She is sweating and starting to feel weak. She is too far from the house, perhaps half a mile. Her mother and brother would have left for church by now. Her heart is pounding and she is afraid that she will faint, so she lies down in the shade trying to avoid a trail of ants but losing focus and finally accepting any piece of ground with or without ants.

She is aware of being carried, cradled like a baby in strong arms. She can hear a conversation between two men. She tries to understand but cannot. She is being handed from one man to the other; he walks on, carrying her, panting slightly. Then understanding and horror seep into her consciousness.

'Let me down,' she tries to shout but her voice is barely audible.

The prisoner who is carrying her says, 'Yes, soon. We are near the house. *Enzo. Apri la porta. Grazie.*'

She begins to struggle and he says, 'It will be better if I carry you.' She feels his grip tighten and wishes she had a knife to stick in his ribs. He releases her into a chair in the sitting room and asks, 'Can I get you something? A glass of water?'

'No. Just go, please.'

Before she falls back into sleep she thinks with dread of her mother's and brother's return from church. The prisoner comes back with a glass of water and places it on the table beside her. She thinks about tomorrow when her mother will say: 'You were so lucky Vince and Joe just happened to be trapping rabbits in that paddock or you might have lain there all night, or heaven knows how long. Everyone asked after you at church.'

And then she will have to listen to her mother waxing lyrical about how good the prisoners were to have brought her home. To have carried her no less. What fine men they are. She will be forced to think about the fact that she had been unconscious in the arms of the enemy. She will then have to get over her revulsion and admit that she should feel some gratitude. In truth she never will say thank you, but they won't miss her thanks as they will be repeatedly thanked by her mother.

PORRIDGE AND POLENTA

She makes the same movements. The same shape, the spoon an extension of the arm, stirring. It is six a.m. He has crunched across frosted grass to stand in this wide windowed kitchen in the cold of the new day and watch the signora stirring into the pot from the muscles of her back. Porridge made of oats ground last night has been on the stove all night. And while the fire grew cold the porridge cooked slowly and became creamy. She lifts a jug and pours milk into the pot and cinnamon in a pinch between forefinger and thumb and returns to the action of stirring with wooden spoon. Rhythmical, reassuring. He has seen them before, these movements, but heavier. Shoulders moving over the stove. But here the movements are lighter, more willing. She moves with impatience, eager for the day to begin. She believes in life. She has faith in its potential for good as she would a religion. Watching as a child, standing in the cramped dark stone kitchen full of smoke, he saw slow movements resisting the day. Polenta, sustenance, corn from his father's fields, essential calories. She moved her spoon with the weight on her shoulders of generations that used the same recipe for survival.

At home his mother takes her joy and her life from the spiritual world. The world of the dead. The son of God who died for us, His long-dead mother and all the dead saints since. Here the saints are alive. They play football and tennis. God is a cricketer. A great batsman with many runs on the scoreboard. The Holy Virgin is nowhere to be found. *Joie de vivre* here is *joie d'esprit* there. It comes via the Virgin from heaven, never from earth. Earth is a shackle to hold you in endless toil, repetitive movements through hours that knit together visits to the shrine.

Like her mother before her, she makes her way down the mountain, small steps fighting the steepness of the slope, to kneel in the basilica in front of the shrine. She enters through the side door lifting her crocheted shawl over her head. Three fingers dip gently in holy water, sign the cross. Elaborate organ pipes in wood reach up to a carved stone ceiling. She genuflects and signs the cross again before the altar. Above it is a painting in oils of the Blessed Virgin. Santa Maria, hair sprouting golden light, appears to the young Marco, a clean-faced shepherd. Good choice. If She'd appeared to one of the middle-aged women here in the chapel making novenas to Her, no one would have taken any notice. She requested a basilica be built in this place. A basilica, more important than a church, more blessed than a cathedral. A Romanesque structure, no clearstory, no light. Enlightenment of any kind strangely missing in a valley where eyes are constantly lifted up to hills and to mountains for help. Help promised by the beauty but not delivered. It could have been yesterday, not five hundred years ago that the Virgin made her request. The story has been retold aloud and in silence every day since, by the people of this blessed town.

She turns, head bowed, and moves silently to the back of the basilica to the shrine. Such a thing of pride, the Virgin stands in gold two feet above the altar of the shrine. The face of beauty sublime. Who on seeing it would not know that absolute beauty is holiness? Who would not know that if the Virgin hears a prayer it will be answered and that the one who prays is not alone, need never be alone? His mother prays silently on her knees to be with the dead mother of her mother and the dead mother of God, both enjoying eternal life. The afterlife lived by the good after this life of living death.

As a small boy he would go with her. He remembered her face and the faces of the other women at the shrine. A different face from the one that watched the wooden spoon stir polenta, golden, gritty, until it stood up in the stiff paste. At the shrine a softer face, separate from him. A face that forgot about him. There were people in heaven she loved much more than him. He thought the dead must be very greedy. They had a great hunger for the prayers of the living. Where the child accepted, the adult judges. Thinking of his future child, should he be fortunate enough to have one, in a world wearing the soft white wisps of peace, he would want it to have a mother who was present here, now, who worshipped life with her activities. And a father who had time to watch with care.

At the age of nine he stopped going with her. He no longer wanted to sit in the side chapel of the shrine with the women. Whatever their age, these women were not young. Their lives on the side of the mountain had bent them into age. They looked at him but did not see him. They did not smile. Praying was about the dead and, like death, serious. What could he do to compete with these dead, who had been sanctified by libations? All the honour and importance which had escaped them in life was now thrust upon them in death. He was on slippery ground if he wanted to compete with the unction that gave comfort only to the dead. The priest saw him and he smiled. He sat at his desk in the middle of the basilica writing words in large books like ledgers. He smiled too much. He conspired with the dead, and those who took comfort from them.

Giuseppe stopped going with his mother and went to his grandmother's house instead. Nonna smiled often, never too much. Nonna was alive in this world, not waiting for the next. She did not need the shrine. When she looked at him her eyes said she saw him and the sight gave them a sharper focus. She gave him sweet things to eat and made him read to her from the books she never opened unless he was there to read them to her. Her favourite was Manzoni's *I Promessi Sposi.* He must have read it to her three or four times over the years. It was the beginning of many interests for him. History, politics, law. His grandmother had a piano she could not play and sent him to lessons so that he could play it for her. He would rather have played the trumpet. When his grandfather came home from the sawmill he would take his grandson up to the loft to feed the pigeons and tell stories of their courage and endurance. The boy liked the pigeons for these great qualities and his grandfather for admiring them. He was a large man with hair grey as the swirling river. His white brows collected flecks of sawdust and he smelled sharply of pine wood.

Now, watching the movements of this Australian woman, the signora in this kitchen stirring porridge, a waft of nostalgia swept across his face like a silk scarf. He did not mind. He knew nostalgia for what it was. A charlatan in fancy dress pretending to know things it doesn't. He preferred to keep reminding himself of the facts. The community he was missing he had willingly left with no intention of returning. At the prison camp there was endless talk about loved homes in town, city and country. Cool houses with history. Churches and cathedrals with flying buttresses. Lines of soft, green poplars twisting around hazy summer hills. Walls painted to blend with the earth in which they nestled. His mountain home was a cool beauty, frozen for long months, with no care for its sons and daughters. He had no need to let his throat and chest tighten. Emotions seemed to want to invent themselves after years of imprisonment.

In this strange dry land there was no danger in seduction by beauty. There was no beauty. His home on the side of the mountain looking into the valley was the Garden of Eden, more beautiful, the most beautiful. You could die from the love of it. A slow, unseen wasting away. The tyranny of winter matched the fecundity of summer. Subsistence was hard and grated daily, hourly, against the powerful elegance of the mountains. The lake reflected the beauty in an echo that made fun of the mountains, copying, taunting I can do that too. The great dumb river rushed and stumbled through the valley, opaque, heedless. Gushing grey, foaming down past vines around drooping lavender buddleia on mid-stream islands to retire, changing to become one with the clear blue of the quiet lake, to be swum in, sailed on and admired by the rich and the fortunate.

Giuseppe's grandparents spent two weeks every summer on the lake. One week they would have him with them, the other week his sister Rosa. They were the only ones among their friends who enjoyed such a privilege. No one in their village had ever taken a holiday. No one spoke the word. Their mother had been taken as a child but since her marriage she stayed home with her husband. Giuseppe's father was pleased for them to go, but could not afford to go himself and would not accept the charity of his wife's parents. He knew that he had a son of some intellectual ability and that it was his passport to a better life. Nonno would take him sailing and fishing. The landlady spoke only the dialect of the lake. Her voice was a rasp and her orange hair curled loose over her shoulders. In the evenings she sat on her balcony and smoked cigarettes from a long holder. None of the women in his family smoked. It was a man's pastime. On Sunday evenings in the tiny square outside the church, men would sit on stone benches to smoke and talk, but mainly to smoke. The boy could not understand much of what their landlady said, but her worldly habits made her an exotic and abandoned creature. Her daughter, four years his senior, served at table. She was dark and sullen and he knew it was because her mother did not behave like a normal mother. In his childish mind she did not really have a mother and he never saw her father. She was the same age as Rosa and would ask Nonna about her as soon as they arrived. She would not bother to speak to him, though he could understand her because she spoke not only dialect but also *lingua italiana*, the language of school and of the cities. Rosa made friends with her. His sister had no taste in friends.

Nonno taught him to sail a small wooden boat. He was forward hand, taking care of the headsail. The flapping of the sails as they luffed up into the wind to climb aboard at first worried the boy. It was wild, reckless, ignorant. But once they were in the boat with the sails pulled on, tacking upwind, they sailed with tight control. 'The wind in the sails is working like the water on the keel,' Nonno said. The air became tangible, something to push against or slice into to give speed and movement, Nonno shouting, 'Get ready to go about, mind your head,' and swinging the tiller ferociously. The first time they turned across wind on a shy run the little boat heeled over and Nonno shouted, 'Hold on, lean out, hold on!' the boy thought he would burst with fear and exhilaration. The first time he was trusted to ride a horse alone, galloping across brown fallow on this flat Australian farm, he felt a similar exhilaration. A gentle canter home downhill on a loose rein, into the sunset, is like a square run home with the wind behind and a red spinnaker billowing in front. Wind puffing the sail proud like a pigeon's breast.

It was on a Sunday that Giuseppe learnt to ride.

'We need the ewes and lambs down from the top paddock,' Max said at breakfast. 'Pity neither of you can ride.'

'I would like to learn,' Giuseppe said.

'How about you, Vince?'

'*Forse, più tardi.*'

'He says he is not quite ready to learn yet,' translated Giuseppe.

Giuseppe watched Max catch MacGillacuddy's, the old mare, by whistling for her. She had been a fine-looking animal. Chestnut with a blaze and four white socks. Now she had grown a barrel of a grass belly. They were friends, this man and this animal. She lowered her head for him to put on her bridle and lifted her feet for him to inspect and clean. She was not so gracious about the saddle. For tightening the girth, she blew out her stomach. She showed no interest in her new rider. She stood next to Max nuzzling into his side while Giuseppe flapped his legs to get her moving. To Giuseppe she looked like a brown hairy mountain.

'How tall is this horse?'

'Mare, she's a mare, a horse is a stallion. She's just over sixteen hands. That means sixteen times four inches. You know how they do it in the American westerns? Well, we don't do any of that,' said Max, watching the Italian flicking the reins to get her moving.

She was a patient old girl and all her resources of that rare commodity were needed this Sunday. Max's patience lasted for about half an hour. Fortunately, his student was a quick study. Max saddled his own gelding and they trotted out to the sheep. This was uncomfortable for Giuseppe who found himself bouncing around the saddle alarmingly. A canter he could do better, but the mare managed to put him neatly on the ground after about two hundred yards. She shied at something she imagined she saw and instantly there was nothing between the rider and the ground where he found himself in an ignominious heap before he knew how.

Max caught the mare and brought her back laughing. 'You're off to a fine start. You've got to have ten of those before you call yourself a rider.'

Giuseppe was covered in dust, his teeth felt shattered, his hands skinned and his bottom numb. He climbed back on and as he did the mare lunged her head around and snapped at him.

'You said she was quiet,' accused Giuseppe.

'She's the quietest ride on the farm. Unless you'd like to try this one.' Max's horse was dancing, turning and sidestepping, anxious to be off again.

'Kite is a good name for him.'

'Yeah, on windy days he gets so excited he hardly puts a foot on the ground.'

The trip home was more sedate. Ewes and lambs travel slowly. The old mare knew all about it. She ambled along behind them half asleep.

'Give her a loose rein and she'll take you home nice and easy, unless it's dinner time,' said Max. 'You come from the country, how is it you never learnt to ride a horse?'

'The peasants are too poor for horses, one or two have a plough horse, but mostly it is cows that they can also milk, and in the towns and cities it is all cars and trucks. It has become a sport for the rich.'

'You'll be fashionable when you go home. You can join the upper classes.'

'I do not want to do that.'

'You a communist?'

'Not officially. My father is. My grandfather is not. I am a sympathiser.'

'Pink.'

'Pink?'

'Not fully red, just a tinge of pink. I'm a bit pink myself. Don't see that this mighty capitalist system has done us much good so far. But the commos have got a few problems. They're not strong on personal freedom.'

'Like the fascists.'

'Like the fascists. You're not a fascist, are you? It must have been hard to fight for them, to put your life on the line.'

'Yes, and so we are prisoners. Even the ones who did not go to war. They are prisoners in our own country.'

'You believe in right and wrong in war?'

'Of course.'

'It sounds as though we were both on the same side.'

'But the English have not been right in every war. The First World War was not so clear. We were on the same side then. Perhaps we were both wrong.' There was a pause in their conversation while Max turned his horse back to round up some straggler lambs that had become separated from their mothers. 'Communism does not suit this open free country. People can own land and cars. There is so much plenty,' Giuseppe continued.

'I'd probably never have thought of it if I'd stayed on the farm,' said Max. 'But working for the station owners, guarding the wool that made them so wealthy, guarding it against blokes like shearers who work so hard and have so little. I didn't like it. And then I ended up shooting someone, poor bugger. Thank God he didn't die. That shocked some sense into me. After that I worked as a stoker on a ship and there were people from all over the world on that ship. That's where I came to understand what communism meant, or at least what it set out to be.'

'It is about what is put in someone's hand when they reach out.'

'What do you mean?'

'My father had little put in his hand, my grandfather a lot. My father is a communist.'

'People can be better than that.'

'They do not choose.'

They talked for the two hours it took to walk the mothers and their babies to the home paddock. Giuseppe had never known a man like this. He was a landowner, but not arrogant because of it. He worked the land himself, but he was not a peasant. He read books on every subject, but he was not an intellectual. Most of all, he didn't seem to look down on Giuseppe as a prisoner.

At the stables they dismounted. Max handed Giuseppe the reins of the gelding.

'You unsaddle and rub them down, I'll get the water troughs working.'

Unsaddling had to be easier than saddling a horse. All he had to do was take everything off. He tied the mare to the rail by the reins and attended to the gelding who pranced and whinnied to his horse friends. While he was having the sweat rubbed off his coat he became agitated and stood on the prisoner's foot. Giuseppe shouted. The horse took fright and flung up his head, and rearing, snapped the reins and flew off across the paddock sending clods of mud high into the air. Seeing the futility of chasing a galloping horse Giuseppe set to work on the mare and turned her without incident into the paddock.

Max returned leading his steaming horse. 'I should have taught you how to tether a horse,' he said and grinned and shook his head. 'You'll be needing a hot bath to soak out some of that stiffness.'

He never mentioned the broken rein, but next time Giuseppe went to the stables he noticed it had been mended, bound tight like a wound with a leather bootlace. The prisoner's toenail took longer to mend. It went black and fell off.

He limped back to his hut as though he had been in the wars again, wondering if he had broken a bone in his foot and how long it would take to grow the skin back on his hands and whether he might have broken his coccyx. He had sustained injuries, but was pleased with his day. During the course of his imprisonment, Giuseppe had found himself growing increasingly intolerant of his fellow men. But here was a man he could get on with and who laughed when he saw how painful it was for the prisoner to sit down at the table for dinner.

FARMING WITH NOTHING

Every time Eddy looked at the prisoners she thought of Harry Simms, killed at Bardia by Italians. She cried when she read his name on the list of dead and missing in action. He was twenty-one. Her head ached for three days. Thirst consumed her body. The web of sorrow that spun itself around her child-heart when she knew her father was not coming back tightened again. She definitely didn't like losing Harry. She'd been in the Middle East for some months when she met him.

Things were hotting up in Palestine. Rumours were flying around about a 'show' in Libya. Eddy and her friends saw that it was starting to get serious. On the other hand, there still seemed to be time for a fair bit of mucking around. Everyone was always on for a shindig whatever the excuse. There was plenty of partying — a special race meeting for the troops at Barbara, and always the King's birthday. No one seemed to know when it was, so the celebrations just went on and on. Nurses were invited to the officers' mess for very polite cocktails and small talk. It was just a matter of being the only women in sight. The local women were definitely not in sight. She preferred the spontaneous dances and sing-alongs down with the other ranks.

June 1940. The night she met Harry she'd been dining with some officers at a restaurant in a resort hotel at Beit Meri in the mountains above Beirut. Beside them was a table of top brass and one young lieutenant. He looked no more than a boy and he looked as yellow as a daffodil. She noticed him getting lower and lower in his chair, joining in the conversation only when he was directly addressed. She watched his senior officers drink coffee and brandy as if there were no tomorrow. Harry's tomorrows were looking precarious, and when he slipped from his chair to the floor semi-conscious, she could see that he had gone into a hepatic coma.

'Find our driver. We'd better get this young fellow back to camp,' the colonel bellowed at whichever of his henchmen happened to take it personally.

Eddy was disgusted at the insensitivity of the man. The young lieutenant was seriously ill. It was plain to her that he had hepatitis and was in a dangerous condition.

'I shouldn't move him, if I were you, sir, he may not last the journey.'

'And who might you be?'

All colonels are the same, she thought. Unless you are wounded in action, you can't possibly be in a dangerous condition. No mere illness is about to be dangerous. And they all seem to grow a moustache the minute they rise to the rank. After she explained who she was, the colonel became amenable, and then after she explained why the young lieutenant could not be moved without endangering his life, he became compliant and by the time she finished her explanations he was thinking of asking for her hand in marriage. He watched fascinated while she coerced the hotel manager, who was pleading full house, into providing a room and a doctor. They shook hands, the best of friends, and the colonel went out into the night in search of the man in search of his driver, and she supervised the carrying of her patient to the suddenly available bedroom and stayed with him all night until he could be moved to hospital by ambulance.

He spent the next three weeks in hospital. From time to time she would stop in at his ward. Someone had lent him a copy of *Anna Karenina.* He wanted her to read it.

'It's a large book,' she said, weighing it in her hand. He'd covered it in brown paper like a school book.

'Not as big as *War and Peace.*'

'What's it about?'

'Love, I think.'

A book about love. Well, most fiction is, love or the lack of it, unless it's crime. However, she was always looking for something to read.

'I'd better go.' She was always having to rush off somewhere. 'The girls are nagging me to get off my backside and go scavenging.'

She didn't want to stand in the ward discussing love with this boy she hardly knew and besides she had to go hunting for wood. The nurses were provided with baths and bath heaters, but there was never anything to burn. Anything that wasn't nailed down was fair game. If the colonel had put down his swagger stick that would have been in the furnace too.

The hospital catering was all British. Food was not abundant nor was it delectable, so she bought him sweet Jaffa oranges through the fence from Arab boys, even though they were told not to deal with the locals. She enjoyed contact with the children. They seemed unaffected by the war, except to take advantage of an expanded market.

'I washed them in Condy's crystals,' she said, lining up the oranges on his locker.

A blush spread across his freckled face and up between the roots of his white-blond hair. He looked around to see if they were observed by the other patients. Eight faces were looking from their beds to his end of the ward. A female visitor, even if she was an off duty nurse, was a rare thing. She could see that her gift, such as it was, her small show of kindness, embarrassed him.

She introduced a new subject. 'The bombing bothering you?'

'No. Not really,' he stammered. 'They're aiming for the sweet-water canal, not us.'

'Yes, but their aim's not too hot.'

'I know. I suppose I would rather be on my feet when they come over, smaller target area. What about you?'

'Never think about it,' she lied.

She took him to Gaza Beach when he was well and he met her friends. It was wonderful at the beach. They had surf lifesavers there, from Sydney. Even awkward, intense people like Harry had to unravel a bit among the bare arms and legs and the sand. He let it slip that he played guitar and they made him promise to give a recital. Eddy felt sorry for him. He was so shy. He was no performer, he was mathematical. It turned out he was in Intelligence. She hoped they wouldn't keep him to his promise. One of the physios had a gramophone and a collection of classical records and used to hold desert concerts. Her guests would sit out in the evening looking into the desert listening to *Sheherazade*. Harry played Rodrigo's *Aranjuez Concerto* for her, or parts of it, without any sign of stage fright and made everyone weep. No one had heard it before. Eddy had never heard anything that so inflamed her soul.

They all went to Jerusalem. Jerusalem. Mystic, frozen in time and a patina of biblical dust and with air cool and crystalline clear. Could the enemy drop bombs and make rubble of the pale stone walls? But the Germans had owned Jerusalem as much as everyone else, except the real owners, whoever they were. She and her friends walked on the wall until they staggered. While she walked she tried to think how it might have affected her if she still had the gift of faith. She even allowed herself a moment of faith when she stood in the Garden of Gethsemane. Harry said it was unlikely to be faith, but pity evoked by a story of trust and betrayal. He said it was an Arab city. Muslims. They had a beautiful mosque from where Mahommed had ascended into heaven. They stood at the gate and listened to the call to prayer.

'So authoritarian,' whispered Eddy.

'Or else permission to rest for a moment in the presence of their God,' said Harry.

He took photos in the evening and morning, light angles accentuating built angles. His mother sent them to her in New Guinea. By then she'd forgotten a time when war was exciting. His photos from his camera. He wasn't in them. She was. Death hadn't stopped his conversation. He reached back from wherever it was that death had taken him to say, 'I am now out of the picture.' She searched and searched the small black and white photos for any sign of him and at last found a shadow on the ground in front of her in front of the Wailing Wall, head bowed to look into the viewfinder, elbows out to hold the camera steady at his waist. For a moment she understood why so many cultures worship the dead. The dead can be so powerful. He was more with her now than when he was alive. In life he had given her thoughts a wide berth. She knew how easily he was embarrassed and took care not to be too outspoken around him. Now he knew them as she thought them and she knew he could not always approve. She didn't always approve of her own thoughts.

His mother intimated that he'd been in love with her. She used old-fashioned euphemisms like 'special place in his heart' and 'so little time together'. They seemed to be about two other people. What had he written to his mother? She must know that in war desperate infatuations were commonplace. But why should she apply that to her son? Eddy could taste the alkaline remorse of someone not entirely guilty but of someone who knew too late she should not have been so friendly, so casual. Perhaps he fell in love easily. She wasn't sure what part of her life she had lost with him, but she knew that the mother of such a boy had lost the whole world.

In the end, everyone was reading *Anna Karenina* and talking about it. He was right. It was about love. Tolstoy had penned a banquet of loves. Anna's destructive love for Vronsky and her love for her son. Dolly's love for her children. Kitty's for Vronsky and Levin. Levin's for Kitty and for his brother. Karenin's for Anna. All so different, all a kind of love. And friendship also as a kind of love. And betrayal in deed and in the heart. What a complex and dangerous place, the world of the heart. Life took a lurch in a magnificent direction with Harry around. Then there was Bardia and then there was nothing, and the world became drab, too drab, more drab than it had been before. And clever, shy, young Harry was rotting in the ground, if he'd been lucky enough to receive a burial. For nights she couldn't sleep. She shut her eyes but no sleep came. She found out about the cubists. When she closed her eyes geometric shapes superimposed on the pictures in her head. Severed arms and mutilated legs in squares, triangles, rectangles. She was going mad. It was the sort of thing she could have asked Harry about. He'd have known of other cases.

Three years of war had been fought since then. At Grey Tamma Farm with the Italian prisoners on board, times had never been so prosperous. The war had changed everything, even the farm. It was still isolated and swinging violently in the course of the year from luxuriant green to desolate brown. It still depended on the Kalgoorlie pipeline to bring water and the train to bring everything else, but the government had set a fair price for wheat and was encouraging the production of wool. Perhaps at last there was a small profit to be made.

Eddy remembered how four years ago on 3 September 1939 war was declared and everything in the world changed. And how at Grey Tamma Farm everything had changed on a warm Wednesday morning early in October of the same year. It was a clean spring day revving up for heat and giving off sweet smells as it cooked the yellow paddocks while men and women sweated and grew sour at their chores. Eddy had been working the separator when her mother came through the door as quickly as her bulk would allow without letting in flies. Flies laid waste to whatever was civilised, whatever had taken hours of work and dedication. The land making its last desperate stand against the invaders after failing to blast them out with heat, wind and dust. A moving, buzzing net to find its way down your throat when you breathed. Inter-species pariahs, looking for shade like everything else, not wanting to drown in the sweet butter patted into ribs any more than anyone wanted them to.

The road past the farm gate was straight for the last five miles. You could stand in the middle and look down it until it became a pinpoint. An approaching vehicle would make a puff of pale dust for ten minutes before it emerged pupa-like from its airborne chrysalis. Mrs Nash had noticed the dust out of the corner of her eye after she shut the gate to the cows and, not expecting anyone, hurried to the cellar to make butter. Feed was low, hay was nonexistent, and if she didn't look back she wouldn't see the cows following her with hoping eyes.

Because of the gentle whine of the separator as it turned, they heard the motor of the bike later than they might have. What they heard was not the wide apart, almost syncopated putting of old Duke's motorcycle, but one they hadn't heard for so long that they'd forgotten the sound.

The heels of Eddy's hands started to tingle. She looked to see if her mother had registered anything but the older woman was not romancing with hope, she was filling the churn with cream. Eddy leaned all her strength into turning the handle, intense as she had always been, even as a child. It was not until the crunch of his boots on the gravel and his silhouette in the doorway that she could prepare to acknowledge his return. No one thought of the flies he let in. Mother and sister clung to him and cried. It had been four years. They walked arm in arm towards the kitchen and the mother saw that the grey handkerchief her son took out of his pocket to wipe his eyes was unrecognisable as one she had boiled white so often in the copper.

'We had your last cheque by yesterday's mail, you could have brought it yourself.' His mother's first words to him were a gentle reproof.

'I didn't know I was coming home till yesterday.'

'You staying?'

'Yes, I'm staying. The war's changed everything. You know there's a war on, you know that?'

His mother turned from the hob of the stove where she was pouring boiling water from a heavy black kettle into a brown teapot.

'We know. We thought you'd enlist. Go overseas. Get killed.'

'Yeah well, they wouldn't have me. You got the rest of the money, didn't you?'

Eddy looked at her mother. There was no expression on her mother's face that Max would be able to read. She knew that 'don't question me, you won't get answers' look.

'You've been using the money, you didn't lose it? Mum . . . Eddy?'

'Eddy's joined up. She's only home for the week.'

'Yeah?'

Max was hiding any envy he felt, but Eddy was fairly sure that he was feeling some. The way she saw it, going to a foreign land and risking death was easier than trying to make a go of the farm in its present state without money. Money. She wondered how long her mother would be able to keep the story of the money under her hat. He would find out eventually. Typically, he was already questioning decisions made without him even though he had been away almost four years.

'You're not making butter in this weather? In this heat and no green grass? Mum, why're you doing this? Where's all the money I sent?'

His mother offered no answer. He stood up and walked over to the stove and spoke almost inaudibly.

'I've a right to know, Mum. I had to race every weekend, drive miles, to get enough to live on. I've a right to know.'

'I put it in the bank.'

'Why? Why'd you do that? If you didn't want it, you could have bought Eddy some clothes. I wanted her to have . . . Why'd you do that?'

Eddy could not bear to hear his distress, knowing that when he knew the whole of it, there would be so much more to distress him.

'I had enough to live on, Max, my pay, and we live in quarters.'

'I didn't know how long this Depression would last,' his mother said. 'We've had enough to survive.'

'Bugger it, Mum. I may as well have been home here. The Depression's over now. There'll be an industry boom. They told me I had to come home and grow wheat and wool. Australia's got to be self-sufficient.'

'How you going to do that? This place has only ever grown horses. There are no men, they've gone off to join up. If you're going to grow wheat you'll have to clear land. I can't chop down trees any more.'

'No one's going to make you chop down trees, Mum.'

'You can't do it on your own. The war'll be over before you get anything planted.'

Max sat listening to his mother worry and fume and let it wash over him as he used to as a boy. Just for an hour he wanted to enjoy being at home. The smell of the stove blacking and a wisp of recent baking hung about. Three sleeping tabbies lay tangled on the step outside the wire door. Timbers in the roof space were creaking as the galvanised iron expanded in the sun. He watched the whirlpool of his tea after he'd stirred it. He'd ridden all night. If he'd been passed fit, he'd have been kitted out and in a training camp by now, polishing his boots. He might never have seen this farm again, or his mum or Eddy.

His mother stood in front of the stove staring sadly at him. What was she thinking now? She was always thinking, planning. She never stopped.

'You've got wide shoulders now. But you're skinny.'

'All the running.'

Eddy suspected it was more than running that had worn him to sinews and bone. He'd probably been lumping bags of superphosphate off trains onto trucks. Everyone knew it was a mug's game, but when you were pushed to the limit, that's what you did. He wouldn't tell their mother. It made Eddy sad. Max was smart and good-natured and dedicated to keeping the farm for the sake of the family.

'Wish you'd written more often, Max, told us about your wins. You were winning?'

'Had to. Most meetings I could win a tenner. Beat the state champion earlier in the year. Got an offer to play for Subi after that.'

'Have they ever seen you play football?'

'Don't know. Anyway, the war's on and everything else is off.'

'And what about that nice girl you wrote about. Alison?'

'Alice. We called it off.'

'What a shame.'

Max stood up and went to the door.

'How you going to do this clearing, Max, on your own?'

His mother didn't expect an answer and he didn't offer one.

The two women went back to the cellar to make butter and Max stood on the back verandah. He could smell the warming grass and see that it was too thick, too tall around the house fence. Snake territory. Should get some sheep in to eat the grass. His mother wouldn't like it. All night bleating, the flies, the smell. Solves the snake problem though. Sheep were on the top of his shopping list. A dead tree spread bleached branches over the shed as it always had. It was decorated with pink and grey galahs shrieking like an Indian raiding party in an American western. Won't see much of them this year, he thought, no plunder here this summer, no crop, no spilt grain. Their clamour was dispersed by the puttering of Duke's motorbike. Duke wore his flying cap and leather jacket to ride the bike, even in summer. His daily six-mile journey to the siding was his only outing. He'd been a pilot in the Great War. It was assumed that he was a hero. He had the goggles and the cap and most of all the deafness to prove it.

'Gidday, Duke.'

Duke stared for a few seconds before he recognised Max and swayed along the gravel path on bow legs to shake his hand too vigorously.

'You home for good, Max?'

'Yep.' No use making a more detailed answer as the old man would miss most of it.

'Give you a hand if you like,' he said, heading down the steps to the cellar.

Max laughed and nodded his thanks. How old was Duke? He wasn't young, everyone knew that. Max went over to look at his sidecar. He was going to have to find a tractor and some sort of truck. He could use what his mother had put in the bank from the money he'd sent home as a down payment and take out a promissory note for the rest. Find something secondhand. And this time, with any luck, the war would keep the prices up and they wouldn't be repossessed.

Duke reappeared and indicated for him to hop in. So he took a spin four miles to the siding with Duke's red dog and the butter. He had to run along the platform and give the butter to the guard as the train was pulling out. Butter from Grey Tamma Farm was asked for by name at the dairy counter of Boan's department store in Perth. After the train had gone, Max walked across the singing lines, past the grey corrugated-iron silos hunched beside the track waiting for harvest. Dan was standing outside the store as if he'd been there like that for four years. Feet wide, rolling a cigarette, red hair over one eye, the other squeezed tight against the glare.

'Max, you bastard. When'd you get back? Not joining up?'

'Won't have me. Too many old injuries, too short-sighted.'

'Yeah? Lucky bugger.'

They both knew he meant the opposite. Max was a reject, and there was nothing more to be said on the subject.

'We're going to sign up tomorrow, Wally and I. Going out tonight for a bit of shooting. Why don't you come?'

'Rabbits or foxes?'

'Rabbits. We can hang around a bit, see if we can get some foxes if you like. Foxes are bringing in a quid a pelt. Emus are two bob a beak now. They're everywhere.'

'Rabbits are fine.'

'I'll pick you up on the way past. Mum'll lend you her rifle.'

'I've got one, just needs a bit of oil.'

'Oh . . .'

'What?'

'I think your mum might have sold it to Wally.'

'Don't be silly, why would she do that?'

'Said she didn't need it, or you didn't, or something.'

'Jesus.' Max took off his hat and rubbed his head with the heel of his hand.

Duke dropped Max back at the farm gate. He was starting to feel sick. Losing his rifle and lack of sleep. He walked into the kitchen letting the door slam and leaving his boots on. Eddy was up to her elbows in flour. She noticed the boots but didn't say anything. She could sense his anger.

'Has she told you?' she asked.

'Who? Where's Mum?'

'In the nut orchard. Has she told you?'

'What, that she sold my rifle?'

'She sold your rifle?'

There was silence while Eddy thought about what she would say.

'Look, Max, sit down.'

He stood there, not budging. He wasn't going to be very pliable, she could see that. She began to speak quietly, finding her feet.

'I want to thank you for the money you sent. It was our only cash. We could never have done without it. I couldn't have gone nursing. I didn't have the train fare to Perth or money to buy uniforms. Mum couldn't have employed a man.'

'Good, that's what I wanted you to do. So why's she struggling along making butter in this heat?'

At that moment Mrs Nash came into the kitchen bringing two cats with her.

'The nuts are setting so well. I thought maybe we didn't get enough rain, but the flowers were thick and I'm going to have a bumper crop.'

'Keep the water up to them. All those flowers are a last-ditch stand because they've been lacking water. Mum, why'd you sell my rifle?'

'Oh well, darling, you know, I can't shoot.'

'I'll have to get it back. Have you got that last cheque I sent? I'll buy it back. How much did he pay you?'

'Oh, he didn't pay at all.'

'You gave it to him?'

'It was after Eddy went away and before Sam came to work. Wally came a few times and chopped wood and fixed the roof and a few things. He was so good. I gave him the gun. You didn't seem to want it.'

It was just an old .22 rifle his dad had given him for a birthday, his eleventh, when things were still going well. It was secondhand then. Nothing very smart about it, but he needed it. It looked like his mother thought he was never coming back.

'If you'd gone to the war, they'd have given you one,' she said, with a disarming lack of logic.

Max had given up a lot in the last four years. Eddy had taken money from him and gone to the city to get a profession. And with the money she earned she had not repaid him. She had been to cinemas, to galleries, museums, concerts and had shopped for clothes.

She could hear a truck outside and went to meet it to get a little air on her hot face. It was Dan and Wally. Wally put his arm out the window and banged on the door and shouted, 'Hey! When did you get home? Don't come and see us, do you?'

Wally was a square-shaped man. He had turned square when he'd moved out of boyhood. He had wispy blond hair and a moth-eaten beard. He manufactured endless energy from his thick muscled body. Too much energy. His exuberance was overwhelming anywhere but in a wide open paddock. He slid out while the truck was still moving and ran over to her.

'Ed, you look pretty fit. Home for good?'

He used to put his arm around her shoulders and give her a squeeze when they were younger, but he didn't do that any more. He shuffled his feet in the dust and stood beside her, not in front.

'No, I'm off in a few days. I joined up.'

He started to laugh. 'Yeah? Infantry or submarines?'

'Hospitals. Wally, did Mum give you Max's rifle?'

'Yeah. I told her not to, but she said he didn't want it.'

'Can I buy it from you?'

'No.'

'Whatever it's worth, I'll pay more, just name a price.'

'Can't. Sorry.'

She couldn't believe he would be such a bastard. She wanted to do this before Max came out of the house. She needed to do it.

'Look, Wally, I know you were good to Mum. She had no one to help her. I'm sure a rifle was not enough to pay for the work. I want to pay you properly and buy the gun back. All right?'

'No,' he said, grinning.

She stood still and looked at him, stared at him. You think you know someone and then find you don't. Her father used to say you had to eat a bag of salt with a bloke before you really knew him. How many years did it take to eat a bag of salt? More than fourteen it seemed. Max appeared at the gate and began to walk across to the truck. Dan was fiddling around under the bonnet setting up a spot. Wally turned away from Eddy and walked towards Max. They shook hands and Wally held out the rifle.

'Yours I think, mate.'

'No, it's yours, Mum gave it to you.'

'Nah, I was just minding it for you. She never gave it, she just lent it. I've cleaned it for you, running like a charm.'

He turned, walked to the truck and jumped on the back. 'They'll give me another one where I'm going, and it'll be a darn sight smarter than that old piece of ironmongery. Are we going shooting or is this country week?'

As the truck drew away, grinding its gears and wheezing its motor, Wally turned to wave at Eddy. Eddy lifted her hand over her head and waved back. It didn't take that long to eat a bag of salt. Funny fellow, Wally, you could never tell what he was thinking. He and Dan were outgoing and charming. They had never been away from the Noonalbin district, except for a week in Perth once or twice, but they were not shy and introverted like so many of the other young men here. She was sure that they would do almost anything for her, as she would for them. She wished she could have paid for the rifle.

She would draw her savings out of the bank and leave them for Max. At least she could do that. She'd be paid in the army and she wouldn't need much anyway. Poor Max. Saturday's child, destined to work hard for a living. He was so good, and strong. Why did that mean he had to draw the short straw? All his friends were going off to war, seeing the world, joining in the excitement. He had to stay and make a farm from nothing with no machinery or money. She didn't envy him. As for the other money, her mother could tell him about that.

Max had developed an aura. He'd come back looking brown, from hair to boots. Skin, eyes, hat, shirt, everything brown. He was taut and muscular. He didn't look unfit for anything, let alone the army. You couldn't see his poor eyesight, his asthma, his old shoulder injury. Raw energy flowed in his veins, as though he had taken on the land and the land had taken him on in return. If anyone can do anything in the world, then he can, Eddy thought. And at the same time she was sorry for him. So much to do here. No one had grown rich out of this country yet. He'd have to get a team of horses together. The purchase of a tractor was far beyond him. He would find out that the purchase of anything was beyond him.

Next morning he came through the wire door to the kitchen, letting it slam, and threw a brace of skinned rabbits on the table.

'Make a nice casserole, these.'

'Lovely, dear.'

Distracted today, his mother was tripping in and out to the fowl yard, the vegetable patch, all corners of the house. Every time Max tried to converse with her she was somewhere else. This time he attempted no preamble.

'Mum, I'd like you to come to the bank with me tomorrow and make that money available so I can buy stock and machinery.'

It was a straightforward proposition but she was making excuses — couldn't be tomorrow, she was baking, the next day ironing.

'For crying out loud, Mum, this is crucial, those things can wait.'

She made no answer and disappeared into the belly of the house. He sat down at the table to make a list. He couldn't blame his mother if she was a little difficult at times, she hadn't had an easy life. The last four years, apart from occasional visits from Eddy, she had spent on her own. In fact, her entire married life had been a story of departure and separation.

She wasn't a resentful woman, nor was she a victim. She had a knack for keeping her own equilibrium, a status quo of mental strength she always maintained in the same instinctive way you maintain body fluids. When you sweat, you must drink more water. When someone she loved went away, she erased as much of them from her daily life as she could, so she would not miss them, and then she set about finding replacements. Like everyone, she had a need to love and be loved. A jinx seemed to have settled around those she loved, that kept sending them away from her, until finally they stayed away altogether. It had a lot to do with geography. She lived a good distance from any other place and especially from the cities of the world. But plenty of other husbands and sons and daughters in the area only went farther than the railway siding if they needed to attend a funeral, and often then it was their own.

In the case of her husband, when he left and forgot to return, she behaved for many years as though it was one of his normal trips, extended. She invented an itinerary for him. Not an elaborate one. Wangaratta, Canowindra,

Toowoomba. Mysterious eastern states locations. Just enough to be able to answer the polite questions that gradually dwindled away. No one accused her of being deluded, but they did accuse her of manipulating the facts. They could not prove this of course. No one except the man himself knew the facts, but they could gossip.

Maisy Spry, postmistress and wife of storekeeper Ernie, worked the small switchboard that comprised the entire telephone exchange for the area. She sat in the post-office-designated corner of the store and connected every telephone call in and out of the area, and sorted every letter, parcel and telegram. She knew that old Charlie Nash had not written or telephoned since Guy Fawkes Day 1930, a week before his wife's forty-eighth birthday, and a week after he had left. She sat among the dusty boxes of camp pie and Horlicks engrossed in a life full to the brim of things written and things wrapped. That they passed her by did not disturb her. That they had come her way at all gave her life more colour and variety than she had ever anticipated.

Her years at the store taking orders and tying string around brown paper parcels and at the exchange pushing plugs into the twelve-point switchboard went on. And they did go on — she was there for twenty-five years before Ernie died and she was forced to sell at a pitiful price. As these years came and went, she became as empty as the boots that swung by their laces from the exposed rafters of her shop.

The lady herself was unaware of this. She had a friend in Sybil Kelly, wife of Kel the stationmaster. Sybil was a wonderful woman, a real gem. No one, including herself, was in doubt about that. She took Sunday school classes and played the piano for church, and for any other occasion that required the edification of music. Indeed, she had been Eddy's first piano teacher and being the only one in the district she had been almost every little girl's first teacher. She grew roses in front of her small mud house on the railway line, and waved to the barefoot children crowded into the other tiny mud houses on the line, and she had afternoon tea, which always included the famous Sybil Kelly scone, on a regular basis with Maisy Spry. This was the conduit, the funnel through which morsels of local tittle-tattle poured out to the rest of the world.

Sybil was always worried about someone, for instance the Johnsons' poor boy — 'I'm sure he wouldn't mind me saying ...' — she was only being concerned and sympathetic, of course. Didn't she cook things for the afflicted? Soup, chickens, cakes and, of course, the scone. She had no children to fuss over and not being on a farm meant that she had fewer chores and worries than the other women in the district. It showed in the smoothness of her brow and hands. She was a pivot for this isolated and flung-about community. She was the only one who had time for anything other than survival.

In spite of the fact that everyone in the vicinity knew about the fecklessness of Charlie Nash, no one, including Maisy Spry, showed Mrs Nash any disrespect. She had presence. Although disappointment and years had faded her beauty, she still had a fine, intelligent face and a genteel demeanour. She was not aloof like the wives of the English settlers, and she had poise and good dress sense. After eighteen months, no one asked her about Charlie, no one dared.

People would rather condemn than understand that it was difficult to be a man with ideas about himself and his family's position in the world. A man who dresses impeccably to buy the best horse flesh, and who relishes the kudos afforded by purveying fine animals to discriminating buyers, cannot easily admit to the failure of his business. Motors replaced horse power. Drought and the Depression took away the market for farm horses. He was fifty-eight when he left, too old to think of ways to change, but probably at twenty-eight he would have found himself afflicted in the same way, bereft of ideas.

In order to keep the equilibrium, Mrs Nash needed to replace Charlie. She gave his entire wardrobe of three-piece suits to Sam, her right hand and the only one slim enough to fit into them, and began to look around. He had been a sometime-never sort of husband and it was necessary, therefore, to have only an intermittent replacement. So she put herself on the Women's Guild of the church and once a month when the parson came to conduct a service, hers took precedence over all other invitations to luncheon. He came willingly and diffidently and if she had expected spiritual counselling or close friendship she'd have been disappointed. The Reverend Albert Cole was always famished by one-thirty on a Sunday and wanted sustenance. Even a parson had to take the occasional step along the way of all flesh. Mrs Nash was delighted to be able to add to his already generous proportions of it. Sometimes his wife accompanied him to the small service in the fragile creosoted timber hall and she too was welcome at the Nash luncheon table with daughter Sophie, small and wan and, at the age of sixteen, still fussy about her food. Mrs Cole could not always resist patronising Mrs Nash and her geraniums. A deserted wife was not, after all, entirely respectable.

The good-natured Reverend Albert Cole was unperturbed when he sat at table with Max who, straight from the paddock and in a hurry to eat and be gone, had not taken the morning off work to worship and give thanks for the bounty of the Good Lord. He was even happy to talk rain, pests, fertiliser and cricket. He had a practical side too. After Max left, seeing Mrs Nash helpless in a place unsuited to a woman alone with no farming skills, he encouraged her to grow an orchard. First, soft fruits about the garden, and then a nut orchard near the dam. He brought her seedlings from his retreats in the city and manuals on their cultivation. He gave her an active role within her capabilities. She was no longer a fish out of water, a marigold in a mallee forest. In the years when Max had been away, this touch of male company at the table once a month was better than nothing to a woman who had been left. Left to hold onto a place that, in her opinion, if habitable at all was suited only to men. She stayed to keep the bailiff from the door, not for her own sake so much, as in hope of a day when she could gather her family again.

If it hadn't been for the orchard she might have learnt to truly hate the place. She missed the smooth edges of the suburbs. She loved to catch a tram to the city and look down as it crossed the causeway, into the shallows at the pale slim fish. She loved alighting on the footpath in front of a limestone office block and walking down a street alive with men in suits and women in pretty hats. She loved to wander in department stores among the gloves and handbags and about the public gardens and rest on a bench beneath a willow and watch children throw bread to the ducks. She loved to climb the wide steps to the art gallery with its Streetons and McCubbins, and the museum with its rows of shells and rocks all labelled and neat, and its sad dusty animals caught in suspended animation.

When Eddy left for the war Mrs Nash was more bereft than when it had dawned on her that her husband had absconded. For him there was always hope of return, but Eddy had thrown herself into the way of danger. Rather than go mad with worry she cleared her daughter's room by giving her clothes to Gretel, daughter of the neighbour, and to Sophie, daughter of the parson, and replaced her in her thoughts with her niece, Gracie, who had sensibly nested in a quiet suburb with an accountant and three offspring. Gracie's mother, Mrs Nash's sister, was philosophical about having to share her daughter and grandchildren.

Max proved harder to replace. He sent home monthly cheques and if it hadn't been for the Depression, he wouldn't have gone away at all. But she had no great faith that he would return. She gave his .22 rifle to Wally. Wally was not a suitable replacement for Max, he was too wild and noisy. Both Hal and his father, Karl, from next door were often there to lend a hand and between them and her Sam Pole she got along as best she could. Sam Pole, a dusted miner, had opened up land four miles east, granted in compensation for his ailment. He'd taken it gladly for his sons, but his ailment began to take his strength and his sons needed him less and less.

Two days a week he came and did things that Mrs Nash thought she was unable to do. He wore his face as happily as he could, considering that it was a series of deep grey lines running down to his jaw with almost no flesh on it. His bony bald head was fringed with a jagged border of steel-grey hair, and the sound of his breathing was like the wind in the grey casuarinas that clustered at his farm gate. He was a withered man, but he showed willingness. Willingness to clean the grease trap from the house drains and empty the pan from the lavatory, and other unpleasant and leaden chores like mucking out the milking stalls and cleaning the green scum from the sheep troughs. The day he climbed on the roof to nail a lifting sheet of iron, Mrs Nash wondered if she had taken advantage of his willingness once too often. He took so long to climb the ladder, and once on the roof, so long to recover his breath, that she worried that he would never come back to earth. Sam's wordless presence was his most important contribution. Without him Mrs Nash was alone.

She was a woman of duty. She had learnt to sit at a sewing machine turning sheets and collars. She came from a house where worn articles were given to the poor and needy. In her own house she cut thin sheets down the middle, sewing the outer edges together, and the sleeper had to put up with the join. She unpicked worn collars and turned them around and sewed them back on again, doubling the lifespan of the shirt. She was a stoic. Getting up at any hour, staying up till any hour, never speaking the word tired. Max knew this and was her greatest admirer, but she had a way of avoiding what she didn't want to talk about. At lunch she could not escape.

'So that's settled, Mum, we'll go to the bank tomorrow.'

'It's not a good time for me. There's so much to do just now.'

'This takes priority. I've got to make a start.' A certain amount of irritation had crept into Max's voice.

'Well, I can't and that's that.'

'Mum, this is crazy. What's the matter with you?'

His mother stood up and hurried out of the room on the verge of tears.

Max looked at Eddy, astonished. 'What's the matter with her?'

Eddy picked up her plate and began to wash dishes.

Her brother was starting to grow agitated. 'You know, don't you?'

Eddy said nothing, so he repeated, 'Don't you?'

'Yes.'

'Would you mind telling me?'

'I think she should.'

'Why? What's she done? She hasn't got it, has she? She hasn't got the money.'

Eddy came back to the table and sat down. 'No, she hasn't.'

Max stared at her without expression. Eddy forced herself to go on speaking.

'I didn't tell you before because I thought she should tell you herself.'

'Well, that's all right. I sent it for her to use. Why didn't she just say so?'

'Because she didn't use it.'

'She lost it?'

'As good as. Last time I was home, about a month ago, she was really happy. Dad had been home. She gave him the money, Max. He said he had a bright idea, something to do with his horses. He needed a bit of capital to restart his business. She hasn't seen him since.'

Eddy had become flushed. She put her elbows on the table and cradled her head. Max breathed as though the air had turned to treacle. He rose from the table and pushed in his chair. His face was stone white. He walked out onto the verandah, took his greasy felt hat off the peg near the door and slapping his leg with it walked in the direction of the shed.

Eddy waited half an hour and then went to look for him. He was mending post and rail fences in the sheep yards, drilling holes and hammering in nails. He saw her arrive but didn't look up.

'I'm sorry, Max. It's disappointing.'

He went on working while she stood watching. Wanting to help, she picked up a plank to hand to him.

'I can manage.'

The whack, whack of steel hammer against steel nail resounded through the timber rails, like angry barks.

'Old fool. There's been no money in horses for twenty years,' said Max.

Eddy stood in the yard, dust settling on her boots and halfway up her trouser legs, sun burning her dark hair on her hatless head, wondering whether to tell him about the old man's plan to train racehorses and decided against it. She felt angry for her brother. What kind of man turns up after ten years and takes away the sweated savings of his son? A man who is too ashamed to see his children. A man who has nothing at all to lose. At that moment, her father was all monster and her brother all angel. It was a passing wave of hate, but it was strong while it lasted.

Max stopped hammering and walked to the corner of the yard to get a short length of timber, lined it up to reinforce a post and said, 'I shot someone you know.' Whack, whack, whack. 'When I was carting wool in the Murchison on the camel trains. A shearer.'

She stood and watched and didn't speak.

He resumed belting the nail into the wood and then leaned over for another handful of nails. 'Didn't kill him, but that was just luck. I'm no great shot. The station paid him off and he told the hospital it was an accident.'

'Why did you shoot him?'

'Well, I had a loaded rifle. They jumped us when we camped on the way to the port with the camel train. When we were sleeping. They jumped Kev, one of the Abos. Stuck a knife in him. It was dark. I shot at him by the light of the campfire. I thought I'd killed him. After that, when we got the bales loaded on the ship I just walked off. I told the Afghan to take his camels back for another load and to tell them I wasn't coming back. Left without getting paid. Talked the captain into letting me work my way back to Perth.'

'What did you do in Perth without money?'

'Nothing. I had to get back on the boat and work as a stoker going up and down the coast. I went back to the station after a few months and collected my bike. Fletcher's not all bad, he paid me in the end. I had a bit of fun in Perth then.'

'With Alice? I'd like to have met her. What happened, Max? Your letters were full of her and then nothing.'

Some minutes went by with Eddy thinking and Max whacking the rail.

'I came back to Perth one time and she'd gone and her aunt wouldn't tell me where. So I went to her father's farm and he chased me away with a rifle. Silly bugger. She was there, but she wouldn't talk to me. He wouldn't let her. Arrogant drongo. I got the message, loud and clear. He didn't leave me in any doubt.'

'She never wrote? Never explained?'

'Not a word.'

There was another minute or two of silence until Eddy said, 'I've got some money. I was saving to go to England. I won't need it now, I'll be going anyway.'

'How much?'

'A hundred pounds.'

'Yeah?' Max stood up and let the hammer dangle by his side. 'If it goes into the farm you mightn't see it again. On the other hand, I might make a fortune.' He smiled and scratched his head through his hat with the claws of the hammer. 'Unlikely, but you just never know. They're talking of setting up a marginal lands reconstruction scheme, there could be a bit of money in that.'

He squatted down and resumed whacking the fence rail while Eddy looked on. Eddy tried not to shake her head, not to be pessimistic, but she knew that the government was discouraging wheat-growing, putting quotas in place. When he finished she helped him pick up his tools and as they carried them back to the shed he said, 'Poor Mum.'

DANCING IN THE DARK

Christmas Day, 1943. Max has bought Giuseppe books. 'The only Italian books I could find that haven't been confiscated were at the University Book Shop and all they had was poetry. Hope you like poetry.' Enzo is not a great reader, so he finds himself with a new hat.

Max has been to the city, two hundred miles, and come back with an ancient car. A 1925 model T with a fabric hood. 'It's not exactly a fine-looking piece of machinery,' he apologises, but they can see he is pleased. 'Took all my bloody petrol coupons to get it home.'

When the harvest is in, he'll convert it into a charcoal-burning car. He has bought a gas producer which he will attach to the car on a trailer and make a pipe to take the gas through to the manifold of the engine. He is a good amateur mechanic. Giuseppe is learning about engines from him.

For his mother, Max has bought a scarf of red and pink flowers and for his sister, a blue shirt. She wears the shirt to the dinner table. It reflects the colour of her eyes and makes them shine like a slice of the sky. Giuseppe is finding them mesmeric. His gaze creeps back from time to time and withdraws when he realises he is staring. She likes clothes.

He sees that. Her new acquisition lightens her mood, not so that she is happy, but it changes her manner from brusque to reserved. Her dark hair is loose, rolling across her shoulders in large curls formed by the tight knot she usually wears. For the first time, Giuseppe notices a sensuality. He has wished for it and there it is, like an answer. Enzo creases the crown of his new hat and rolls up the sides. He puts it on his head and makes his hands into six shooters and walks like a cowboy with bandy legs. Even Eddy lets a chuckle escape, a clear, low series of notes, like a sound from another person in another world. It transforms her. For one brief moment she is spontaneous.

Enzo has made things for his employers. A cigarette box for Max, a small dish each for the women, carved from local wood.

'You got this wood from here, Vince?' asks the signora. 'I've never noticed any nice wood around here.'

'It is good,' says Enzo, 'interesting,' and not knowing the English word for grain he uses his hand in a snake action, '*grana*.'

'Interesting grain,' says Giuseppe.

Giuseppe has bought chocolate and scented soap from the control centre canteen for his gifts. After three years in Australia he is used to sweltering his Christmas, but he hasn't celebrated a family Christmas for five years.

For Giuseppe, two books of Italian poetry. Leopardi and D'Annunzio. He will not tell Max that Gabriele D'Annunzio was the warrior poet. If the Australian government confiscated all Italian books from shops because a book is a dangerous thing, it would not want to know that this was the man who gathered an army about him and marched into Fiume to take it back for Italy. Everyone knew about how d'Annunzio stood in the city square, making speeches and rousing the crowds to fever, while Mussolini, occupying a factory in Turin, became jealous. The politician learnt from the warrior poet how to sway a crowd. He learnt from D'Annunzio that there is more glory in nationalism, more fervour in imperialism in Dalmatia, than in occupying a factory in Turin. His early poetry was lyrical. Giuseppe could enjoy it because he was so dislocated, far from what was familiar and comforting.

Han bevuto profondamente ai fonti
alpestri, che sapor d'acqua natia
rimanga ne' cuori esuli a conforto
che lungo illuda la lor sete in via.
Rinnovato hanno verga d'avellano.

They have drunk deep at alpine springs,
so that the taste of native water
may remain in exiled hearts as a comfort,
to charm their thirst far along the way.
They have renewed their staffs of hazel.

His father taught him that. To make a hazel staff, leaving the strip of bark to twist around the rod and up the handle like a Christmas peppermint stick. To soak it until it agreed to bend and then let it dry to become strong. He had never been a shepherd but he had known many boys who were. In the summer holidays he would seek them out in their mountain huts and play cards with them. Thirteen- or fourteen-year-old boys, already earning a small living by minding sheep. They would watch smugglers weaving the secret mountain tracks to bring cigarettes from Switzerland.

Shepherd boys did not often suffer long hours of solitude. Their friends would walk up the mountain to entertain them. It was an easy job. Others, the same age, were carrying soil up the mountains on their backs in baskets from the valley where it had landed after rain, stopping to rest on stone seats, there for the centuries of peasants who carried their soil back up the slope every year to make a new crop.

Good to remember that work. Giuseppe remembers pain in the muscles of his back after a day carrying soil up the mountain and he remembers futility. The idyll of making hazel staffs fades to nothing by comparison. The selectivity of nostalgia is deceptive. Nostalgia is endless rows of vines climbing the mountainside with ease, no struggle there, dripping scented fruit, leaves greened deep by a mellow sun, and tree after tree of apple, peach, pear, glowing, opulent.

Leaving to go to Trieste to become an engineer had felt like a betrayal. He wondered if the harm to those he left behind would be lessened by the trees and the mountains, the streams and rivers, the valley below. A nurturing beauty he would have to exchange for cobbled square and busy harbour quietening into the Depression years. He would be set adrift in the Hapsburg elegance of the city, with a few words from his papa running around in his head: '*L'è bel viv iglioga su, ma l'è trop fadiga fa quadra 'ldisnà cu la scena.*' It is beautiful on the mountain, but it is too difficult to eat both lunch and dinner here.

The son offered to come back in the summer to work, but his father did not want that. He considered the work on the mountains a waste of time. The only way to make money on the mountain was to — *luarà de sfros* — work at fraud, become a smuggler. You could smuggle bread and cheese and salt and always cigarettes. Because of currency values these items were more expensive in Italy. For an energetic walk across the mountains from Switzerland with a bag on your back, a good profit could be made. But his father had an answer for that too: '*L'è mei stüdià che bricòla purtà.*' It is better to study than carry a knapsack of contraband. His mother's advice he did not follow: '*Laurà, pensà, urà e tasè, a nigügn ga po fa dispiasè.*' Work, think, pray and keep quiet, and nothing will go wrong. She did all that herself and nothing in her life had gone right.

Giuseppe is a communist in all but execution, in all but the barbarity it takes to enforce a view. There are many communists like him in Italy. They have been exposed to a smattering of Marxism by the writings of Labriola and Mondolfo. They had a gentle leader, Antonio Gramsci. A sickly, romantic man whose whole life was a struggle. Like the socialists he did not want war. Wasting lives for national pride.

And now this life, in the bush of Australia. He turned the page of D'Annunzio and read 'To a Torpedo Boat in the Adriatic'. '*Guizzante, bello come un'arme nuda, vivo palpitante.*' In this flat brown place it reads like pornography. 'Shining, lovely as a naked weapon, alive, quivering ...' Giuseppe wonders if there is an Australian poet writing words like this. D'Annunzio had taken his warmongering ways to the grave, ways that seemed inappropriate to Giuseppe now, except for the phrase, '*Sara' dunque eterna la vergogna?*' Will the shame last for ever? Giuseppe understands its meaning very differently from the way its author had intended.

The poet died before the war, but he and his followers wanted war, to prove that Italy was great. Giuseppe worries about his family. His father would be strong, he would help the communist resistance. It was from his father that he had learnt to be a communist. But his grandfather showed him how life could be lived and enjoyed, showed him it was possible to employ people without grinding them into poverty, abject and exploited. In Australia, it is possible to have the right to proper payment for hard work. He has read in the paper that the unions are angry that the Italian prisoners do not receive the wages that free men would receive and that they are undercutting the market. Eight shillings and ninepence a week does not amount to much, but they have food and shelter and an allowance of two and sixpence from the control centre. What he is pleased to have, the friendly acceptance of his employers, has nothing to do with money. He expected to be treated as a peasant. He saw too much of that in his childhood.

The evening of Max's return, Giuseppe sits in the dark with Vincenzo, smoking. It is late but he is not sleepy. They discuss the things of the farm. How they will make a pit to burn wood for charcoal for the new car. Vincenzo goes to bed and Giuseppe sits on in the dark, listening to the sky's dry crackle. There is no moon but starlight sifts silver onto leaves and fence posts. He walks out across the paddock and stops in the middle of its wide spread of stubble. The slow shape of an owl drifts by. The earth is holding its breath waiting. Only in the early morning cool will it be ready to exhale. He stands still holding his breath. Nothing. Thick sweet aching air. He breathes and walks on. Sheep run in front of him, silent except for their padding feet. They swing away and allow him to walk past. They sense he has no business with them.

He walks on in the dark, disembodied. Haphazard tree shapes and shadows come towards him. He wants to arrive at the stand of trees but once he is there regrets the loss of starlight. He sits on a log, not for rest but because he must do something to mark his arrival. A few quiet animals fly about or scurry at his arrival. It is like falling asleep. The rest of the world still functions but this world has stopped and you are unaware of any other. Sounds disturb the reverie. The snap of a twig. Scuffling. He is paralysed. Frozen in the hot night. A spot whips across the sky and down into the trees. A shot, another shot and another. Lights, guns, shouts, running. He has heard it before in the desert.

The shelling began as they had expected it to some day, but from the wrong side. Suddenly awake at five-thirty in the morning, he was confused, disorientated. People were shouting, running, there was panic. A few machine-guns were heard between the shells. Filippo was stunned, unable to move. Giuseppe shouted at him to put on his boots while he scrambled into his own. Then his friend was all frenzied action, as though their survival depended on him alone. Giuseppe realised that there were tanks, British Matildas, shelling from the wrong side, from country the Italians had already occupied.

They had come without warning. They had taken Italian outposts and fortifications without the encampment knowing, driving swiftly across the dark desert without roads. They took up positions in the slit trenches that had waited for action. They resisted with Bren gun and machine-gun. Resistance was futile, immoral, even one death was wasted in a defeat so final. They had been outplayed. His war was over. He was now an animal in a cage. They were kept behind wire, under canvas, waiting. Some were taken to work on the roads. The rest waited and dreaded the Khamseen, sand-laden winds that reduce a world that consisted of very little to nothing at all.

Finally they were marshalled into two carefully chosen groups. One would go to India, the other would remove to a larger ship in India and continue to Australia. The group chosen to continue to Australia comprised those with surnames starting with a letter between L and Z in the alphabet. Those at the A to K end of the alphabet would go to India and no farther. Giuseppe heard complaints that the voyage to Australia was too far and too dangerous, that they would be forced into the hold of the ship and not allowed out, that this mysterious land was full of barbarians. He knew that however bad Australia was, India would be worse. He had heard about the soldiers who would be their guards in India. They were made up of the dregs of British cities. Thin, starved petty criminals and worse who were bound for prison had they not signed up, and were made more brutish by the power that came from wearing a military uniform. He knew about the heat and squalor in India and had no doubt that it would be part of a prisoner's life there too. He preferred to risk a dangerous journey and the airless crush of a ship to Australia.

As soon as they had boarded the small ship in the canal that would take them to Ceylon, they were in Australian hands and the atmosphere changed. The Australian guards were more relaxed than the British. They tried to learn a few words of Italian and laughed at the prisoners' attempts to speak English. Nights were filthy. They were kept in the dark. When a light was on, the windows had to be shut, and much of the journey was through the tropics. Many of the prisoners were poor sailors and there was the constant stench of vomit in the overcrowded cabins. Latrines were gutters built over the side of the ship at the stern which channelled the effluent out behind the ship. The only place to sleep with any comfort was in the open on deck. Because Giuseppe was an officer he was permitted to do this. An unfair privilege, but he took it anyway. At Colombo they boarded *Queen Mary* and everything changed. Optimism was in every heart.

The shooters move away and Giuseppe stands up. He had slipped down behind the log to save himself from stray bullets and the necessity of explaining his presence and had landed on a clump of doublegee prickles. He is painfully picking them out of his knees when a truck drives up. He watches them load three dead foxes and a kangaroo. Perhaps the kangaroo, like him, has been unhunted quarry, a bonus. A spotlight slashes through the darkness cutting angles out of the black and comes to rest on him.

'Jeez, there's someone there.'

'Where?'

'Over there, in the trees. Hey, who's there?' A rough voice makes the question sound like a threat.

Giuseppe is not comfortable to be showing himself to these tough men with rifles and the smell of blood in their nostrils. He strolls out of the undergrowth and stands in front of the truck, blinded by the spot. He is not aware that his palms are sweating.

'What do you know?' The rough voice is now gleeful. 'Bullseye, we caught Mussolini.'

'Finish him off, don't let him suffer,' says a joker and they all laugh.

Giuseppe calculates there are six or eight men with guns. It would be easy for them to shoot him and say it was an accident.

'Well, how were we to know he was sneaking around here in the dark up to no good. Just a very sad accident.'

There is no laughter after this statement. Giuseppe is thinking about escape, of running back into the bush. He sees a vehicle approaching across the paddock, its headlights bobbing up and down as it drives over the ruts in the stubble.

'Come here, dago, we want to see the whites of your eyes before we shoot you.'

'You'll have to shoot me first.' It is Max. He is out of his car and walking towards the truck. When he gets to it he pulls the spotlight out of the battery. The darkness provides a blanket of safety. 'You blokes had better call it a night, I think.'

'Just a bit of fun,' says a voice in the dark.

'For who?' asks Max.

The conversation finishes there. The men pile onto the back of the truck.

'Don't forget to shut the gate on the way out,' Max yells at the driver as he turns the vehicle around.

The quiet and the dark close in again. The starlight takes back the night in peace. The two men stand in the dark and watch the truck disappear down the road.

'What made you come out?' asks Giuseppe pushing his shaking hands into the pockets of his trousers.

'I dunno. Just got sick of listening to the shooting. It was keeping me awake. I don't mind them shooting here, it saves me the trouble, but not all bloody night.'

'Thank you for coming. Do I owe you my life?'

'Probably not, but I like the idea of being in credit, maybe you can return the favour one day. Want a ride?'

'No. I will walk.'

He walks back across the paddock, where all is quiet now, his head buzzing and rattling with gunfire. He lies on his bed sweating, not sleeping until the creeping grey dawn releases him from his waking nightmare. At breakfast the conversation turns to the shooting party. Max says nothing about Giuseppe's humiliating night. He never mentions it at all.

ROST DE PULASTRU

She has tied back her hair with a red scarf like a Russian peasant and pushed her hands into rubber gloves, one of which is reaching into a headless, featherless rooster and dragging out its gizzards, its crop, its liver, stomach, kidneys and lungs. Giuseppe has beheaded these two creatures for Sunday lunch. He hung them on the clothesline to drip their red blood into the red soil and brought them to her in the laundry where she dresses them for the oven, plucks their feathers into the concrete tub, pulls out their entrails.

He offers to help.

'Ever plucked a chook before?'

'Of course, as a child, but we did not call it chook.'

'It's your day off.'

'I will do it.'

'If you insist.'

She picks up the second rooster by its scaly yellow legs, toes curled stiff, copper feathers ruffled downwards, and hands it to him.

'What did you call it? Chicken cacciatore?'

'*Rost de pulastru*, roast chicken.'

'My mother calls it roast fowl.'

'But foul also means wrong.'

'Just another English word with lots of meanings, running around like a chook with its head cut off.'

Her humour is heavy with aggression. She adds repulsive images to unpleasant tasks. It is like being splashed by mud from the wheels of a passing motor car. She is efficient, businesslike.

'I thought you'd gone to mass with Vince.'

'I do not believe.'

'You're Italian.'

'I do not have to make a leap of faith to be Italian.'

She smiles. 'But it goes together, Italy, the Pope, all that.'

'Not for all.'

'Don't you want to meet with other prisoners after the service? Have a chat?'

'I am content.'

He has not been accepted into the group of Italian prisoners who meet after mass. They feel constrained by the presence of an officer. His efforts to put them at ease have not succeeded. He prefers to speak, have a chat, with her. Probably she guesses that, and makes sure the conversation stays away from idle chat. She shakes her head and looks down at the 'chook' she is preparing. She washes it under the tap inside and out and says, 'If you pour boiling water over the feathers they come out more easily. I'll bring you the kettle.' She cuts the feet off her rooster and crosses the verandah to the kitchen with it. She is neither hostile nor friendly. She is cold. She returns with the kettle and pours boiling water swiftly over the bird and waits to see how easily the feathers now release their shafts from the flesh. He pulls feathers fast, not wanting to look inept. They smell dank and sweet with the hot water and stick in clumps to his hands.

'You see? It works.'

'It is a bad smell.'

'But it's faster.'

'The patented method of Edith.'

'Eddy.'

'Benito Mussolini's daughter is called Edda.' His attempt at conversation sounds lame to his ears.

'You share your name with Joseph Stalin,' she snaps.

'Yes, and with the husband of Mary, the mother of Christ.'

'Does that make you a Christian or a communist?'

If Eddy is like most Australians, she believes that communists eat babies. He does not want to disavow his beliefs nor does he want to become an eater of babies.

'Communism is very complex, especially in my country. I cannot tell you about it in less than many hours. Perhaps we do not have that long.'

'What about fascism, how long does that take to tell?'

'Fascism tells its own story. It does not need me.'

'So why did you mention Mussolini's daughter?'

'You read, you are interested in many things.'

'I'm not interested in fascists.'

She goes back to the kitchen with the empty kettle and prepares a baking dish for the birds. She examines the one he has dressed and without speaking adds it to the other. She presses onions, sage and breadcrumbs into them and covers them with mutton dripping and puts them in the oven. It is time for him to leave.

He takes the feathers and offal and buries them. As he walks to his hut she comes onto the verandah with two enamel mugs of tea. She holds one up and calls, 'Like some tea?'

The edge of the verandah is a good place for drinking tea. It takes away the sitting-together-in-chairs intention and allows a small sliver of ease between them.

'Thanks. For the help.' She says it quietly, sleepily, sun on her shoulders and head, winding her fingers softly around a tuft of grass that is creeping up the verandah post.

'You needed no help.'

'I hardly ever do.' Pause. 'But I hate it, that job. I do it because I eat it. You shouldn't eat meat unless you're willing to kill it.'

'Or unless someone is willing to kill it for you.'

'Not what I mean.'

'I killed it for you.'

She looks at him and grins. 'So you did. Only you can eat lunch with a clear conscience.'

'I do not like it.'

'You will. It'll be delicious.'

'I do not like killing animals.'

'What do you like killing?'

She never misses an opportunity to point out his brutality. As though she wants this talk of killing to take him back to somewhere in the desert where men died — some from his efforts — and it does. For reasons of her own, she decides not to persecute him.

'For pudding there's raspberry jelly and angel's food.'

'Strange for one who does not believe in God to make food for his messengers.'

He picks up her change of tone as it swings about. He tries not to lag behind even though the changes are like lightning.

'It's only my first line of defence.'

'What else do you have in your armoury?'

'That I don't really absolutely not believe in him. If I did, I don't think I'd find him in a church. He's not that biddable.'

'But his messengers come to your table, and you know the recipes they prefer.'

'Yes, custard whipped into air bubbles.'

'Zabaglione. I like zabaglione and I do not have to kill it first.'

'You can't live on custard with air bubbles.'

'You do not know that.'

She laughs. Again he is surprised by her. He laughs back. Headless roosters are not things to bring people together. Milky sweet tea, though unpalatable, is better. But this is a shiny rivet of time pinned between the dull sheets of days and months. They look out through the house fence across the pale stubble and the red fallow ridged by sun and shade. Lines that push the rest of the world away to where it cannot be seen or heard. He hears her sigh. He is sure it is a sigh. Now he hears the motor of a distant car. It is the model T. He stands up.

'They are coming. They are early from mass.'

'Not mass. Old Lizzie Harmer has just landed another of Mum's legendary cakes. She manages to get hold of some sugar and then gives it away.'

'Your mother is good.'

'Isn't she.'

'You disagree?'

'Of course not, but it's not exactly heaven living with an angel.'

'We are back to angels. Well, you have food for her. Perhaps you are right. Heaven I think is no place for the living.'

'You mean earth is no place for an angel.'

'No. That is not what I mean. Your mother makes life better for her friends here, now.'

'Old Lizzie is not a friend of my mother, she is one of her people. Someone to care for.'

'She needs care. Her history is sad.'

Wally and Dan were Lizzie's sons. They were born during the First World War, the youngest, Wally, while her husband was away in France, getting killed. She was told of his death when the baby was five days old. She brought them back to the farm, raised them and by the time this war began they could not wait to be gone. Perhaps they looked for adventure, perhaps escape from drudgery. She kept farming as she always had, in poverty, ready for the boys' return. Wally will not return. He is buried in Syria. Dan is in New Guinea. It is difficult for her to think about him. What is left if he dies there? The signora sends Giuseppe across the paddocks to help her sometimes. He chops wood, fixes things. Max helps her with her crops. She is no longer young.

Eddy jumps to her feet and snatches his empty cup.

'Go. Go round the side. They're almost here.'

They have spoken of nothing personal, of none of their own concerns. She called him to sit with her and drink tea. He is pleased. If she senses this, he hopes she does not pity him.

'Thank you for the tea.'

'*Tea and Sympathy*,' she says and laughs.

He looks at her, horrified.

She raises her eyebrows and shrugs. 'It's a play.'

He walks around the house and out the side gate through the trees, like a trespassing cat who has had a bucket of water thrown at him. The breeze is winding ribbons of bark around branches and trunks like a plantation of maypoles. The leaves stay on the branches, while the bark is shed in strips like the skin of the reptiles that move silently beneath them. It speaks of difference, opposites, upsidedownness. This is temporary, he thinks, he will be home in a time not too distant and things will make sense again. Trees will lose their leaves not their bark, and a woman he likes who likes him will smile at him.

Part Two

L'Infinito

Sempre caro mi fu quest'ermo colle,
E questa siepe, che da tant parte
Dell'ultimo orizzonte il guardo esclude.
Ma sedendo e mirando, interminati
Spazi di là da quella, e sovrumani
Silenzi, e profondissima quiete
Io nel pensier mi fingo; ove per poco
Il cor non si spaura. E come il vento
Odo stormir tra queste piante, io quello
Infinito silenzio a questa voce
Vo comparando: . . .

This lonely hill was always dear to me,
And this hedgerow, that hides so large a part
Of the far sky-line from my view. Sitting and gazing,
I fashion in my mind what lie beyond —
Unearthly silences, and endless space,
The very deepest quiet; then for a while
The heart is not afraid. And when I hear
The wind come blustering among the trees
I set that voice against this infinite silence . . .

GIACOMO LEOPARDI

L'INFINITO

. . . e mi sovvien l'eterno,
E le morte stagioni, e la presente
E viva, e il suon di lei. Così tra questa
Immensità s'annega il pensier mio:
E il naufragar m'è dolce in questo mare.

Giacomo Leopardi

And then I call to mind Eternity,
The ages that are dead, and the living present
And all the noise of it. And thus it is
In that immensity my thought is drowned:
And sweet to me the foundering in that sea.

He sat on the bed in his hut in the eastern wheatbelt of Western Australia reading poetry while his own faraway country was having its heart and tongue torn out. It had now been occupied in the south by the American liberators and in the north by the Nazi murderers where all of those he cared for lived. Were they prisoners or fighting in the Resistance and in grave danger? He was in a raw emotional state. He spent many nights by the oil lamp reading

Leopardi, someone who knew what it was to be stifled. '*A me la vita è male*' — To me life is evil. The poet's solution was to take pleasure in nature. The prisoner would try to do the same, with what resources were at hand. Where Leopardi envied the contentment of the moon, Giuseppe wondered at its indifference. Where the poet was ruined in health and hope through intense scholarship, the prisoner had no such excuse for restive melancholy. Even so, there was much in his words that comforted.

On Sunday afternoons he sometimes wandered across the fence to where Fischer's Rock stood. Low, but by contrast with the slow undulations of the local topography, an obvious hill. It was a place to go, a place to arrive at. An outcrop of granite, that is all, but it had an ambience that attracted. Aboriginal tribes passing through would have gone there for water and shelter and perhaps for rituals. They did not go there now. Max believed that Aborigines never stayed long in the area, but came for ceremonies and then went on their way to other places.

'Too dry,' he said. 'They didn't have tin roofs to catch the water into tanks and there was no pipeline from Mundaring then.' When Giuseppe asked if most Aboriginal tribes were not wanderers, Max shrugged and said, 'I suppose so.'

'Where are they now?'

'Just wandered off, most of them. When we first came here, there were a few working in the area, but they all left to go to Kalgoorlie, more work there.'

'And someone like me would never know they'd been here.'

'Further west in the old settled areas, better rainfall areas, there were some bad fights. Last century. Lot of natives killed. There are some rock paintings about fifteen miles in that direction.' Max pointed to the northwest.

'I'd like to see those,' said Giuseppe, and then the conversation dried up. It occurred to him that Max did not see the need to know the history of his home. His family had been here for twenty years and that was the scope of his knowledge. What had happened before that was no longer relevant. It was the view of someone raised in a new world. Giuseppe was attracted to the freedom of that, and yet he had an uneasy feeling that it was an excuse for ignorance.

To the Italian prisoner sitting alone on the rock, centuries of tribes coming and going, having sacred ceremonies, had infused it with spirits. When he had been visiting the rock for a few months it began to take on a character for him too. Its permanence spoke to his transience and comforted like a parent.

'*Va bene*,' it said, '*Io sono sempre lo stesso*.' It's all right, I am always the same. In a world where two small men, one with a moustache and the other a bald head, no more remarkable to look at than a pair of clerical assistants in a bank, can change or destroy everyone's lives permanently, completely, speaking to a rock did not seem so strange, especially when it spoke back.

If Enzo did not accompany him, on Sunday, his day off, he would take Leopardi and sit on the shaded south side of the rock in a moss hollow and read and understand in a way that he had never done at school.

Ma sedendo e mirando, interminati
Spazi di là da quella, e sovrumani
Silenzi, e profondissima quiete
Io nel pensier mi fingo;

... endless space
unearthly silence
the very deepest quiet.

He was not alone here, so far from home with these thoughts and feelings intensified, reduced in this place to a concentrate. In Italy, at the beginning of the nineteenth century, the poet could have known nothing of this kind of space and silence. But from his distant time and place he wrote: '... *ove per poco/Il cor non se spaura*' — ... and then for a while/the heart is not afraid.

Leopardi had known what it would be like. He had imagined and felt what the prisoner was now experiencing. With Leopardi in his hand, Giuseppe could look about and absorb, like the poet. This landscape was not conducive to voluptuous verse. Compared with the opulence of the lakes and mountains, it was a negative place and he could see only what was not. No mountains, no rivers, no lakes. By coming to the rock to sit and look he gradually began to see. Wide, wide horizons, unobstructed, unconstricted, free. At first he felt uneasy with them, abandoned by everyone and everything he knew, but with the passing of time they taught him freedom of a sort he had not before experienced. Day upon endless day of blue skies, clean of any wisp of cloud. Ultimate, pure, infinite.

In the deserts of Africa there had been no peace of mind to appreciate the openness and there was the Khamseen, the blinding brown and white sandstorms, summer and winter. In Australia, the summer dust storms were red. In Africa, sandstorms could bury you alive and strip the skin from your body. Here they closed your lungs and left stripes of red along corrugated-iron walls. More frightening to see coming, because it looked like the sky had begun to bleed, but when it arrived it was gentler, being dust and not sand.

When he saw his first dust storm approaching, he was two miles from the farmhouse bringing in sheep on the horse. He noticed a red line diffusing upwards from the horizon. He rode to a stand of trees and dismounted, walking in as far as he could. Horse and prisoner put their backs to the wind and waited for it to pass. Trees swung wildly above their heads and he began to wonder if he'd made the right decision when branches came crashing down about them. The mare was not happy. She showed the whites of her eyes and turned circles about him. Five or ten minutes and all was silent again. He mounted and went to look for the sheep thinking they would have run in every direction. He found them exactly where he'd left them. They'd seen this many times before. They simply turned their backs to the wind and stood it out. There was something to be learnt from them. He gathered them together and went on his way. The temperament of the mare had changed. She was prancing on her toes and reefing at the reins, impatient to be home.

Seasons changed suddenly here. The land was so wide and flat, there was no protection from the fierce winds that blew from the southwest and swallowed everything.

Giuseppe woke in the night to see the dark shape of Enzo at the louvred windows, trying to close them the last two or three millimetres.

'Tira vento fortissimo. È un tempo da cani.'

It was his way, to announce the obvious. Their small weatherboard hut shook on its timber footings. They were in danger of being blown away inside it. Sheets of tin on the roof were prized up and flapped with a furious noise that permitted them no sleep for the rest of the night. At dawn the wind subsided. Whole trees had been uprooted, branches snapped off and thrown about. Boxes, bags and sheets of iron had landed in untidy heaps around the farmyard. Telephone wires sprawled across the road. At breakfast, Max announced that the prisoners might be needed at Noonalbin siding to help clean up.

He was right. Trees littered every clear space and where normally one or two cars were parked at the general store, today there were at least twenty vehicles of every description. Men stood in groups murmuring to each other. There was a hollow quiet all around. Leaves and branches shredded from the trees carpeted the ground and gave off a pungent odour of eucalyptus. There was no shade. The birds that had survived were silent. The men were talking about the community hall, where all denominations worshipped, where every meeting, wedding and funeral took place, where the school produced its Christmas concert. A large structure with a high pitched iron roof and creosoted timber walls, it had been blown over onto its side, complete, leaving its timber footings stuck firmly in the ground, like an elephant that had taken off its feet and was lying down from fatigue.

Almost every farmer in the district dedicated the next two days to reestablishing the focal point of their community. Max asked Giuseppe to assess the situation and give his opinion as an engineer. He squatted on his haunches mirroring the stance of the farmers and drew lines in the dirt. They gathered around to watch. Some were uncomfortable having an Italian prisoner give advice, and laughed and joked about getting it back upside down, or with hooks around the walls for hanging salamis. Doug MacDonald, policeman and self-appointed leader, scorned

Giuseppe's plans and complained of not being able to understand his accent. 'It's just a matter of common sense. We built it and we can get it back up.' The priest and the schoolmaster were equally convinced that they knew what to do and began to talk about winches. Giuseppe could hear all this and tried not to take it into his mind. The project was overrun by experts and prejudice. In the end, it was the farmers led by Max who solved the problem.

Eleven prisoners from surrounding farms, all wearing magenta uniforms, stood to one side diffidently until they were given instructions. There were those who did not welcome their presence. They could be tolerated as manual labourers, but as people with knowledge and experience they did not exist. The children stared at them and did not speak.

Cables, ropes, tractors all appeared at the scene. Giuseppe advised them to erect temporary trusses inside the building before they began to pull so it would not tear apart. He explained how it could be done so that the harder they pulled the stronger the structure would hold together.

'Yeah well, what works in one country doesn't necessarily work here.' Policeman Doug argued against it without logic for a while until the farmers stopped listening and, under Max's instructions, went ahead and did what was needed.

Giuseppe noted that policemen in this community had less influence and authority than he was used to seeing. In Italy, the *carabinieri* were not there so much to keep the community safe as to enforce the policy of the ruler. They were an arm of the fascist government. They had the ear of every citizen. Here, Doug was listened to with polite indulgence and then ignored.

At midday, more vehicles appeared bearing women with baskets of sandwiches. Billies were boiled and tea was made. Eddy arrived in the model T with her mother and a mountain of cakes. She was the only woman not wearing a dress. She wore her tropical army nurse's uniform: trousers and boots. She did not stay in the mill of women setting out food on trestle tables. She lit the fire and organised tea. She looked for Max who was still nutting out strategies with Giuseppe.

'I thought you'd have it on its feet by now,' she said with a grin.

'Joe here tells us that we have to brace it before we start pulling and pushing it about or it'll fall to bits.'

'You know about these things, do you?' she asked, archly dismissive.

Giuseppe smiled and made no attempt to reply.

'Modest too, I see.'

Max gave her a warning look that said, 'don't stir,' adding, 'He's an engineer, we can use his knowledge.' She shrugged and walked away without further comment.

Soon Giuseppe noticed her pack the car and drive away, leaving her mother to fuss and socialise with the other women. She took Enzo home with her and most of the other prisoners went to their homes. There was nothing for them to do at this stage. Eddy was not part of the men's world. She could be part of it on her family's farm, but not in the community. Giuseppe, also, was not part of any community. He did not fit with the other prisoners. And, like Eddy, there was a place for him within the fences of the farm. Nowhere else. The enigmatic Eddy, her incisive stare and critical eye. It was as though she could read him. He didn't congratulate himself on having a complex personality, but he did not want to be read, even by her. On their first encounter at the railway station she had taken the high ground and maintained it. As prisoner/employee it was something he was powerless to change.

At sundown everyone stopped work. On some invisible signal they all started walking in the direction of the pub. Max and Giuseppe were relying on neighbour Karl Fischer to take them home since they had come with him. There was nothing for them to do but go to the pub until he was ready.

'Come on.' Max nodded in the direction of the pub and Giuseppe followed.

'Prisoners are not allowed in bars,' said Giuseppe.

'Yeah,' said Max. 'Stupid rule. None of them have got enough money to do any harm. Follow me.'

They walked into the noisy pub and the talking started to peter out. Soon everyone at the bar had turned around to stare, beers poised. Max behaved as though nothing were amiss.

'This way,' he said and led Giuseppe to a corner where Karl sat on a stool.

The barman, a ruddy, muscled man, walked over slowly and shook his head. 'You can't bring him in here,' he said, eyeing the prisoner.

'Bert,' said Max, 'this is Joe Lazarus. He's an engineer, been helping on the hall this afternoon. It's bloody thirsty work.'

The bar was now quiet enough for everyone to hear what Max said.

'It doesn't matter,' said Giuseppe, who was beginning to feel uncomfortable. 'I will wait outside.'

'Why?' said Karl. 'Be buggered. Give the man a beer, Bert, he's earned it.'

'I'll lose my license,' said the barman, but the resolve in his voice was beginning to fade.

'Who's going to take it away?' asked Max. 'Doug here? You wouldn't do that to Bert, would you, Doug, when he's saving poor bloody Joe here from dying of thirst?'

Doug grinned and turned away and began a conversation about cricket with a fast bowler who had lost a foot in the Syrian campaign. A detail that Doug in this moment of pressure had forgotten. The barman raised his curly eyebrows and shrugged his hefty shoulders and pulled two schooners of beer with perfect little heads and set them on the bar.

Max drew five shillings out of his pocket and laid it on the bar. 'Appreciate that, Bert. Have one yourself.'

He picked up a beer in each hand and gave one to Giuseppe. The drinkers were only half as noisy as usual. The intrusion of the prisoner had taken the wind out of their tales.

'Think we're going to be able to sit her up again, Joe?' asked Karl.

By the time Giuseppe began to answer, the conversations were flowing again and the noise level had risen to its normal thunder.

At dawn the next morning six tractors were attached to the building by ropes, three on one side and three on the other. It took some time for the tractors to assemble, one had to come from thirty miles away. Winches were nowhere to be found, so half the tractors were needed to lower the building slowly and gently onto its footings to avoid an impact that might smash it to pieces. When upright, the building looked ragged in a way it had not when on its side. Lying down, the wonder was that it was in one piece at all. It seemed intact, but standing up, the sheets of iron gone from the roof, the shattered windows, ripped-off doors and missing weatherboards were apparent.

The next step was to ensure that it would not blow over again. Everyone began to talk at once about how to prop it up, and how they had propped up their farm buildings, and where to find the timbers to make props. However Giuseppe knew that what it needed was tying down, not propping up. But tying down depended on the use of steel cables, not in ready supply, so they decided to mount an expedition into the bush to get some tall timbers. For this Max used his team of horses. His flat top cart was longer than any of the trays on the trucks.

Enzo stayed behind to ply his trade, fixing broken windows and doors and replacing boards and sheets of roof iron. Max and Giuseppe stayed out in the bush overnight. They lit a fire in a clearing and cooked damper and chops and boiled a billy for strong sweet black tea, a taste Giuseppe felt he might acquire after about a thousand years and only if he were finally convinced there was no coffee left on earth. Max succeeded in getting Giuseppe to drink a small amount, just palatable when hot, but as it cooled fast in its enamel cup, he found it necessary to secretly fling the last half on a grateful bush.

Max rolled out his swag under the cart, but Giuseppe chose to ignore the dew and sleep without cover so that he could look at the stars in the clear southern sky, where all his favourite constellations were in different places and facing different directions. Max sat for a while smoking by the fire while Giuseppe lay on his back observing the infinite. He looked across at Max and wondered whether this practical man ever noticed the skies.

'The Southern Cross I can see now, the pointers, the cross, but I did not expect it to have another larger cross so close by,' Giuseppe said.

'Centaur. The Aborigines give them equal importance in their stories. You can see a man and an emu, if you look in the right place. The man is sitting beside the Southern Cross. The emu's beak is the man's neck. The emu is running. His neck stretches out through the Milky Way.'

'Of course. We see a sky full of beasts and heroes, so would they.'

'With just as much mythology too. The emu up there was being hunted, chased out of the spirit world and his running frightened a spirit who flew up through the tree tops to the sky to rest beside two waterholes. The emu ran up there too and keeps on running.'

'A sky that we share is as strange as the different parts of the world from where it is viewed.'

'Gold was discovered at the town of Southern Cross by prospectors who were told about the quartz- and gold-bearing rock — "money rock" — by Aborigines who showed them how to use the Southern Cross as a guide.'

'Were you taught the Aboriginal mythology in school, as we were taught the Greek and Roman?'

'Afraid not. Most people don't know about it at all. I heard about it up in the Murchison. The black stockmen would tell me the stories if I was the only white around. The other whites thought it was kids' stuff. I liked it. I like stories, I suppose. See those two clouds not far from the Southern Cross, they're the two waterholes.'

'Magellan clouds.'

'Winter's the best time to see that story.'

'Did you make friends with the black stockmen?'

'When we were out mustering we did. The Yamagees were in their own camp back at the homestead.'

'What about the women?'

'That's another story. It's getting late, I'm going to bed. If we get time tomorrow I'll take you to see those rock paintings, they're only a mile or two from here.'

The cave was detached from the main rock, round and hollow, like a small, cosy house with openings at intervals in the perimeter. They ate their lunch, even lit a fire and boiled a billy, beside the cave in the granite outcrop, a much larger, higher landmark than Fischer's Rock. Giuseppe thought they might be committing sacrilege, like taking a packet of sandwiches into a European cathedral or museum. He wondered how long these works of art had been there — forty years, four hundred years like Michelangelo, four thousand? Was this art or inventory? Hands in groups and alone, an echidna and what might be a stream or a spear, or the line between heaven and earth. A cave with a corner blackened by fire. He wondered at it, but he did not know what to make of it. Where were these people or their descendants? In Kalgoorlie? Dead?

'What was life like here, for these people?'

'Hard. Hot. Cold. They didn't wear clothes or skins. Not like the people further south,' said Max. 'There was an old bloke who used to be a shepherd out here before they opened it up for cultivation. He said that the Aborigines used to have scars from burns they got from rolling into the fire in their sleep. Their only way to get warm.'

Max seemed to like the place in the way a parent likes the artworks of his child. They were amusing, curious, but not part of the adult world. He was preoccupied with securing the hall and getting back to work on the farm.

They brought in six lengths of timber and placed them at equal intervals along the external walls of the hall like raw and insubstantial flying buttresses. They served the same purpose as those built in stone to support gothic cathedrals.

Several days of being away from the farm and the two prisoners were looking forward to a bath and to washing their clothes. They set the fire under the copper in the laundry on the back verandah of the house. The place sprang to life with the presence of the two men. From the kitchen sink as she peeled vegetables for dinner, Eddy could hear them talking and laughing. Good-natured laughter. She could not understand a word of their conversation. She scrubbed and scraped and chopped, absorbed in their fun and a little envious.

Her mother burst into the kitchen with a tray now empty of tea and scones with which she had been entertaining her neighbour. Yvonne Fischer was affronted to hear Italian spoken at such volume so near the house.

'What a racket those young men are making. You'd think they'd have more consideration. You don't have to allow them to use the copper. I know Dotty Case won't have them anywhere near her laundry.'

The mood was broken. Eddy sighed and agreed that they were a little boisterous. Her mother murmured something about boys and high spirits. Just then they ran out of the laundry and headed for the line with their washing in baskets, charging the gate like schoolboys to see who could be first through. Giuseppe turned to close the gate and noticed Eddy looking out of the window and acknowledged her with a nod and 'signorina'. They had taken off their shirts and wore shorts and no socks. Eddy had seen thousands of men in her nursing career in various stages of undress. The two older women turned away from the sight in modesty. Eddy stared at the tanned, muscular backs of the men. She smiled down at the potatoes leaving mud in the sink. Whatever she thought of the prisoners their obvious companionship was beguiling. If she had not left the farm to go nursing, she may never have made friendships with women.

Out here women were kept apart. Distance made it difficult for them to form strong bonds. Children were equally isolated from playmates. Max had been her only friend for their first few years at the farm. He had learnt to trust her on an epic journey that proved to him that she was no sissy. It was a watershed for her, and from then on she was not left at home when he went rabbit trapping or fox shooting. There were dark mornings when the grass was white frosted and she would rather have stayed in her warm bed than milk cows or feed horses but she was either a sissy or she wasn't. If she wavered she was gone and in the women's camp for ever. She lined up the potatoes and chopped them into cubes. She could remember every inch, every second of that journey. It had worked an independence into her character and made her self-reliant.

PONY AND SULKY, 1924

'I'm not going unless I can take Silvie.'

'I'm not paying for her to go on the train.'

'I'll ride her then.'

'Ride her then.'

That was the sort of conversation Max sometimes had with his father. It was possible to get your own way but you paid for it. Old Charlie Nash everyone called him, although he had just hit fifty-two. He was thin and tight, not enough flesh to be called muscular, just enough to hold his bones together. Food was something he took if he thought his energy needed stoking, not for pleasure or comfort or because there were sounds from his stomach like an orchestra tuning. He was always sending horses from one place to the other by train. One small pony would not have made much difference, but there was no profit in it, so it would not be done.

The decision to sell the house of the finely turned finial, the bay window, the five chimneys and the circular drive was his alone. Like everything else he did, whether or not it concerned others, there was never any consultation. No one knew about it until he came home after six weeks away bringing a strange man with extravagant black sidewhiskers and a briefcase from which he took a pencil and notepad and who, after bowing slightly to Mrs Nash, began to walk through the house writing things. He walked from room to room putting first his head through a doorway and then following it with one side of his body, standing angled in the doorway as if ready for a hasty exit. The two children followed him silently until he could ignore them no longer.

'Hullo, kiddiewinks,' he said, with the sort of jollity that makes adults sound silly, and with the word 'winks' he winked. The children turned and ran out onto the verandah where they fell on top of each other, laughing loudly enough, they hoped, for him to hear. In the kitchen, Charlie offered the man tea, which he did not get because it relied on Mrs Nash to brew it and she was too shocked to speak, let alone to brew.

'It's a solid place,' said the sidewhiskers.

'I built it myself,' said Charlie.

'Very nice. Very nice, I'm sure.'

Neither of these men were what you would call 'men's men'. They were alike in this, so should have hit it off. But men like these, who could not befriend men of the elbow-on-the-bar variety and who even had trouble befriending themselves, were in no position to make friends with each other.

'Not too many modern homes like this out here, eh?'

'Not many at all, very nice, very nice.'

It was. It was a wonder and a miracle. After the cramped urban semi-detached, this was everything. It was fields and fresh air. It was a pony in the backyard and a garden with flowers as well as vegies. It was a new school full of languid barefoot kids. Boring kids for Max, not like Keith and Tommy. Max hardly saw Keith and Tommy any more. They were his city friends and he missed them a bit. The three of them used to be able to think up anything. Do anything. Go anywhere. There were shop girls to be distracted while the glass stopper of the boiled lolly jar was eased off and a dirty hand put in to extract one or two of the contents that would never be missed. There were garden walls to be jumped for peaches and bulbous figs browning in the heat, and trams to be swung on and off before the conductor came. There was catching the old paddle steamer *Duchess* across the wide river from the city to the lagoon to trap crabs and sleep overnight in a tent. And everything, absolutely everything, to be climbed if it rose into the air any distance. He missed his two friends, but Eddy was a pretty fair sort of companion. She preferred tadpoling in the creek to dressing up to go to town. She loved it here. All the space, the river right alongside and their dog, and Max had his pony.

Here, home was also work. This was where their father kept the horses. From here it was Max's job to herd them across town, through the city streets before dawn to the saleyards, and bring the unsold ones back at dawn the next day. He, and whoever else his father could find in the way of casuals, had to wade the horses across the narrow part of the river and for a few yards they would have to swim and always for these few yards he would hold his breath in case a horse panicked. He had heard of horses drowning in a strong current. It was man's work but Charlie would never pay a man to do a job Max could do free. It was the children's job to care for the horses while they waited for the next sale. He was eleven years old and Eddy was almost ten. The children were only fifteen months apart.

The agent with the black sidewhiskers went away and it was now clear that their residence at this place would soon end. Charlie had ideas of becoming a squire, part of the establishment. He wanted to sit on the verandah of his house and watch the sheep grazing in the sunset. His land was well situated at a staging post between the city, two hundred miles west, and the gold mining town a hundred and seventy-five miles east.

It had started as one of Charlie's clever schemes. Soldier settlers began to take up new land in the area after they returned from the Great War. Charlie bought a block right beside the Agricultural Bank which had opened its doors to see to the needs of the settlers who were given money and land by the Industries Assistance Board to get started. When the bank manager handed over their start-up money he would suggest that they invest in a good horse that could be bought at a reasonable rate from Charlie Nash next door.

There was no agreement between Fergus MacFee, bank manager, and Charlie Nash, horse dealer, but the trade-in the financier received for his fourteen-year-old swayback gelding was very favourable indeed. In fact no money changed hands and a Welsh mountain pony for his daughter was included in the deal.

After the rush of soldier settlers it became a place where those in a hurry on their way to the goldfields could trade a poor horse for a good one. He was not a sharp dealer. A horse from Charlie Nash was a first-rate animal. Horseflesh was probably the only thing he knew about, the only area in which he was reliable. He could not be relied on as a companion for his wife, or as a father for his children. He spent most of his time sailing back and forth from Victoria trading horses. When Charlie Nash had a new shipment of horses, that was the time to go to the saleyards. They were not cheap, but they were as good as you could get.

There was a germ of pride waiting to be nurtured in Max and Eddy. No one could train a horse like their father, but then they had lived in the city where many fathers had never ridden a horse. Those fathers came home from work in the evenings and went with their rods to the river to fish with their sons. They chopped wood in the backyard and dug the sandy soil for rows of carrots and cabbages. They re-paned broken windows and oiled rusty hinges. They read the paper after dinner by the fire while the washing up was done. In a street of such fathers it was not a thing of pride to have a father who could do none of these things. Perhaps he could do them; they had no way of knowing because he never did them. When he was doing well there was always someone to come and do them, when he was not, the house waited patiently for repair.

All this was forgotten when the children watched him handle a horse, especially a youngster. He could break in a horse in an hour. He could teach a horse to count, to answer questions yes and no by nodding and shaking its head. He could get a horse to lie down, to bow and to dance. He was a man of some magic. All this he would do while wearing a three-piece suit and carefully chosen tie. He dressed like a doctor or a lawyer, like a man of property. And that was his plan now. Not to save to buy an established farm near the city, but to go to new land that was cheap and build a house and start a dynasty. Some of the soldier settlers didn't stay. He bought from one of these. A thousand acres with two hundred and fifty cleared. Max tried to imagine his father ploughing paddocks and shearing sheep. Do men plough paddocks in three-piece pinstriped suits? He didn't want to bet on it. He supposed a boy could learn to plough. On a farm someone must plough. Eddy worried that she would be left in the city with her mother. Left behind while all the world opened up.

And so it was decided between the boy and his father that he would ride his pony the two hundred miles to the new farm.

'You'll ride with him,' his mother said.

'Two hundred miles?'

'He can't go alone.'

'He wants to.' His father reached along the dinner table and ruffled Max's hair. 'Don't you, boy?'

Max didn't know what to say. He liked the idea of an adventure on his pony but was not really able to think about being all alone in a strange and wild place.

'How long will it take?'

'Silvie can do thirty miles a day easy. She's a good little mare.'

'Charlie, he can't do this. On his own for a week.'

Charlie was silent for a minute and then stood up from the table. 'Nothing can hurt him in the bush.'

As it turned out, Max did not go alone, Eddy went with him. She was able to do this only because her mother did not know about it. Mrs Nash had been taken to hospital with nervous exhaustion. The sudden collapse of her domestic situation had proven too much for her. Since Eddy was left in her father's care, which he found inconvenient, he saw no reason why she should not go with her brother. He found them a sulky so that they could ride behind the pony together. He took her to the barber and had her hair cut short, back and sides, and fitted her out in her brother's clothes and, for the journey, she became a boy. She was delighted. To be out in the world like a boy was wildly exciting. She was ten years old.

On the first day of the trip they had to get up the escarpment into the ranges without tiring the pony too much. As the ground began to rise the two children piled out of the sulky and walked alongside. Silvie was dappled grey. In winter she became woolly and the dapples disappeared under her coat, but in summer she was washed and brushed and rinsed with beer to make her shine. The dapples stood out darkest on her withers and chest, fading gradually across her flanks towards her rump. Her silver mane stuck out and away from her neck unruly, no matter how much it was brushed. She loved sugar, boiled lollies and peppermint stick. She would sniff and nibble at the pockets of anyone standing near. She liked to blow hot air down the back of whoever was leading her on a loose rope. Silvie was a good friend, the best one they had.

They had some thick mutton sandwiches for lunch and cold pasties for dinner for the first day. From then, it was mainly apples and bully beef out of tins. The bread ran out after two days. On the second day the hills became steeper. Going up was no problem, but coming down with both children and Silvie's feed in the sulky was hard on the small pony as the weight of them pushed her on and Max was afraid of the sulky getting out of control. After the first hill Eddy jumped down and walked while Max held the brake on to slow the sulky and Silvie took the weight patiently. The children and the pony rested at the bottom before tackling each rise. This was slow progress and at the end of the third day they camped just outside Northam beside the river only sixty miles from Perth, nowhere near halfway. They had been meeting the river from time to time as they made their way along, but they knew they would have to rely on pipewater from now, as the river swung away from the road.

In the morning they bought bread, milk and cheese on the way through the busy town.

The fourth day ended with the sulky bogged. The road, rough most of the way, now dissolved into sand. Both children had to keep off-loading to push. Finally, exhausted, they decided to stop early for the night at a point where, as they rounded the bend, they saw an open car with five people in it, spinning its wheels, spurting sand six feet into the air behind. Afraid that the noise and dust would unsettle the pony, Max decided to wait before he unharnessed. The driver of the car at length stopped the futile spinning of the wheels and four of the passengers got out to push, leaving one in the driver's seat who, from the look of the hat, was a woman. The children could hear the men cursing and arguing. They wondered what sort of men would say such things in front of a woman until they heard the woman shout. 'You lazy buggers, put your bloody shoulders to it would you?' Until that moment they had never heard a woman swear. They did not know that women actually did swear. It worked like a charm. The men fell silent and pushed together while she revved the engine. When the car leapt out of the bog at speed they all shouted and began to run after it.

One of the men did not follow. He walked off the road and began to unbutton his flies. He sensed someone looking at him and turned to the children standing about fifty feet away. 'Well, what are you looking at?'

Max and Eddy busied themselves with the harness, embarrassed that he should think that they would watch him relieve himself against a tree. He soon joined the others as the car progressed in fits and starts in and out of the sand until it disappeared over the horizon.

On the fifth night they stayed at a hotel in a small town with a general store, a railway siding and a post office that served the farming and mining community around it. The town was a handful of tiny houses dotted either side of the railway line for fettlers and workers at the pumping station for the pipeline. Eddy had never been inside a hotel before. It was a two-storey brick building with wide timber verandahs and cast-iron balustrades. Inside, a polished timber handrail curved around the carpeted stair to the first floor and the bedrooms. Max went into the bar to ask for the manager, Mr MacNamara. He had a letter for him from Charlie. There were about ten men in there, elbows on the bar and feet on the brass rail.

One of the drinkers caught sight of him out of the corner of his eye and turned. 'And what are you doing in here, young nipper?'

He had dark wavy hair plastered to his forehead by the sweat that had gathered under the hat he'd left on the bench at the door. He put a callused hand on Max's head and gripped it. 'You better skedaddle before old iron britches catches you.'

'I've got a letter for Mr MacNamara.'

'You mean Mrs, don't you?'

'No, "Mr" it says here.' He held up the letter.

The man drew in his chin, raised his brows and under a breath forced out on a belch said, 'Yeah, well whoever wrote it doesn't know that Mr's been gone for nearly five months and I don't reckon he's coming back.'

'Why's that?'

Max was disappointed. This staying in a hotel idea of his father's wasn't going to work out. It was turning embarrassing. A kid couldn't just book a room at a hotel.

The man opened his mouth to show a row of gaps between tobacco-stained teeth and wheezed explosive bursts of laughter.

'You won't ask why after you've met Mrs, I don't reckon.'

And he continued the explosions until a tall woman with grey hair in a bun and sharp brown eyes which she pinned on Max stalked through a door behind the bar.

She sighed as she folded up the letter, looked down her bony nose and shook her head. She took the coins from the envelope, slipped them into her apron pocket, already dragging from its heavy contents, and turned away with a brusque, 'This way. Hurry along. I've got a lot to do.'

She led the children up the sweeping stair along a corridor, down a few steps and then around to the side, not to the main part of the hotel, but a weatherboard extension that looked older than the rest. They arrived at a small room with no mat on the floor and no curtain at the window.

'Tea's at six. You two'll need a bath and some clean clothes before you come to the dining room. Come down when you hear the gong.'

Max knew he ought to say something, probably thank you, but he didn't like to speak to this woman. She didn't invite talk. When she left, her brown laceups clomped angrily along the creaking floorboards until they faded into the soft carpet.

'I'd rather be camping,' he said.

'I wouldn't.'

Eddy was looking in drawers and cupboards. Each one she opened filled the room with the musty citrus of dressed oak. She began pulling the cord that hung from the ceiling, intrigued by the pang pang as she switched the electric light on and off. Seeing his sister enjoying herself made Max feel a little brighter. He sat on the bed thinking about the tea they would have. Eddy was thinking much the same thoughts.

'You think there'll be jelly?'

'Bound to be,' said Max.

'And custard?'

The bathroom across the hall was one large room with several cubicles, each with a bath. They filled two baths until the hot water went cold, and even though they washed with plenty of soap and made a brown line around the bath, they muddied their white towels, with *Commercial Hotel* printed on a red stripe down the middle, with leftover dirt from forgotten places like the back of necks and knees.

The gong sounded from the bottom of the stair. Four notes played up and down the scale three or four times. They wondered who had played it and wished they'd been watching this musical performance. The dining room was already full when they arrived. There were six tables of men and one table with four men and a woman who might have been their mother. Max straight away recognised them as the people bogged on the track last night. He hoped the man who peed on the tree would not turn around. Vain hope. Two such young lads helping themselves to a meal in a hotel dining room were a rare sight.

The talk faded as they stood inside the double swing doors with two circles of opaque class in the top. Mrs MacNamara let them stand there and be stared at for what seemed like hours. She beckoned them by crooking her index finger once. She sat them on their own at a small table with a stiff white cloth so close to the kitchen it was almost inside. A partition in front of the kitchen door prevented the diners from seeing in. The two children were seated almost behind it. A young waitress helped Mrs MacNamara to serve. With some relief they watched the waitress come towards them with her thumbs in two bowls of vegetable soup. She bumped the swilling liquid in front of each child and said, 'Where yez from?'

'Perth.'

'And where yez going?'

'Noonalbin.'

'Where's that?'

They didn't know what to say. Max knew it was along this road somewhere and that they should get there in another two days. They were to ask at the general store where Grey Tamma Farm was, that was all they knew. So they picked up their heavy silver spoons and began to eat the warm, salty soup. At the same moment Mrs MacNamara strode over to the waitress.

'Daisy, plates on table three, if you don't mind.'

Mrs MacNamara was a frightening woman. Her creased brow said either that she was perpetually offended or suffering from eye strain or both. She wore a navy blue dress to just above her tree trunk ankles and a black apron. Her long nose lengthened her long face and her large jagged teeth, more often seen behind a sneer than a smile, were dark yellow like the bone handles of the knives on the tables. The waitress was soft and round. Wisps of curly brown hair escaped her white cap. Her forearms were white and smooth like bread. She could have been a nurse or someone important in her blue dress and white apron. She didn't smile either, but that was probably because she had to work for Mrs MacNamara.

She brought them two plates of stringy roast mutton, baked potatoes, pumpkin and boiled cabbage afloat in a dark brown gravy swamp.

Max said, 'Thanks, Daisy.'

'Cheeky,' she said, but he thought he saw a tiny smile as she turned away.

Escaping at last from the dining room after finishing their filling but disappointing marmalade pudding, the man from the table with the woman turned and called to them.

'Hey, boys.'

Max went over to their table, Eddy hung back.

'That your pony out there in the yard?'

'Yeah,' said Max and he couldn't help a grin, he was so proud of that pony.

'Nice bit of horse flesh.'

'Thanks.'

'Where'd you get it?'

'My dad.'

'Where'd he get it?'

'Victoria, I think?'

The man laughed. The others all laughed too. They'd heard plenty of fibs from kids before.

'Oh yeah? Where's your dad?'

They all laughed again. The man asking the questions was the man who had peed on the tree. He had a thin face and very red lips and a nose almost as red. Max became uneasy. He didn't like this stranger putting him through these questions. Just because he and Eddy had wet hair sticking up in a cocky's comb and dirty shoes didn't mean they were orphan runaways, stealing horses. They all stopped laughing at once. The man turned in his seat and pinned him with a hard eye.

'Last time I saw a little horse as good as that it belonged to Charlie Nash.'

'That's my dad.'

'What?'

'Charlie Nash's my dad.'

'You don't look like him,' the man said, drooping his eyelids and leaning back in his chair to look him up and down.

Max started to back away.

The woman took pity and said, 'Leave him alone, Vic, he's all right.'

'What's the matter here?' Mrs MacNamara demanded, not looking at the children but at the man.

'Don't know yet.' The man shrugged at her.

She turned to the children, 'You boys run along, I'll deal with this.'

Max looked at her, hesitating.

'Run along I said. What are you waiting for?'

As they pushed through the swing doors of the dining room they caught a glimpse of Mrs MacNamara talking to the man with her hands on her hips, nodding her tight bunned head at him. They raced back to their room as fast as they could, taking the carpeted stairs two at a time. When they reached it Max shut and locked the door. She wasn't such an old bat after all, Mrs MacNamara. Max didn't say so to Eddy but he was worried about those men. What if they took Silvie?

He lay awake long after Eddy was asleep. Finally, he rolled out of bed, bare feet on a cold floor, pulled on his jumper and boots, and went to check on the pony. The front door was locked so he went off towards the kitchen, with only the reflection of moonlight in window-shaped squares on the floor to help him see. The kitchen door was locked as well. No key. It would be in the bulging pocket of Mrs MacNamara's apron. He climbed through a half open window onto the verandah and ran quickly across the moonlit yard. The five or six horses in the yards were all peaceful. There were a half dozen more in stables, you'd have to pay extra for those. Silvie was standing in a corner, asleep. Her pretty head drooping, her ears relaxed and pointing to the side. She was a tired little horse. He didn't wake her. He stood for a while looking around. No one was stirring. The hotel was in darkness. They had turned off the engine of the electricity generator. He didn't know what time it was. He had been lying awake so long worrying about Silvie that it seemed like two nights in one. He made his way back across the yard, boots noisy on the gravel in the silence of the night, feeling silly at being so worried.

On the verandah he found the window closed and locked. He tiptoed along trying all the doors and windows. Around the front, everything was locked. He could climb up to the first floor verandah but it didn't go past his room. There was a drainpipe but it wasn't close enough to his window for him to get in. A tea chest on its side outside the kitchen had a dog in it, long-haired like a border collie but not. He was friendly, used to a lot of people coming and going. He didn't mind, in fact he seemed quite pleased when Max gave up trying to get into the building and curled up with him in the box under one of his smelly chaff bags to keep off the cold.

The cook woke him at five, fumbling with a ring of keys. She was a round woman, shapeless under layers of coat, cardigan, apron, dress and a petticoat that looked like it was being squeezed down towards her ankles under the weight of the outer garments. She even had a squashed hat on her head with a fraying flower held on by a thread. Over her arm she carried a basket inside of which was an apron folded neatly on top of a pair of felt slippers. She was the first to start work and didn't seem at all surprised to find a boy asleep in the dog kennel. Max went in through the kitchen and up to his room. He woke Eddy and they packed. The cook made porridge and fried eggs and let them eat it early in the kitchen so they could be on their way. She gave them some cold meat and bread and butter for their lunch.

They spent much of the morning pushing the sulky while Silvie pulled. The track was still sand in patches and for the first hour they kept getting bogged. They had a waterbag tied to the back of the sulky and a bucket to fill for the horse. They had well and truly drunk every drop by the time they reached the tap at the waterstand beside the next rail siding.

That night they camped away from the road so that they would not be seen from the track. If the men who had questioned Max at the hotel were gold miners then they'd be coming this way. The gold was all in this direction. It was better to be in the bush than at a hotel, however smart it looked. Nothing can hurt you in the bush. Eddy pitched the tent and lit the fire. Max had fallen asleep in the sulky. Next morning, as soon as they started, they could hear the clack clack of a loose shoe as Silvie trod the harder ground. They spent two hours in a large farming town getting her reshod. It took a while, as the smithy wasn't used to shoeing ponies. As they waited outside the blacksmith's shed they saw the open car with the four men and one woman speed past. It was a relief to see the back of them.

'Where do you think they're going?' Eddy asked.

'Mining, I expect.'

'I'd like to have a gold mine.'

'So would everyone.'

On the evening of the eighth day, the brave little horse struck up a trot as they turned into the track to the house.

'Where's the house?' Eddy asked.

Max didn't answer, but his eyes were on something that looked like a shed with a chimney sticking through the roof. Shed or house, they'd seen a few of these along the road from Perth and had pitied the people who lived in them. Smooth gimlet trunks stuck in the ground acted as the main structure. They were still shiny with green streaks through the brown. Around them for walls were hessian bags that someone had whitewashed. The flat roof was sheeted with corrugated iron. From this, a downpipe fed water into a square rusty tank.

There were stables nearby constructed the same way, except that these had walls and a roof of brush from tea trees. They sat away under some elegant salmon gums, looking like dishevelled hairy creatures come to rest. Silvie didn't care. She was happy to be unharnessed and given a feed. Waiting for them in his three-piece suit was Charlie who had arrived on the train that morning with another load of horses. Demand was strong. The Agricultural Bank inspector had been around after the February burn and was handing out the fifteen shillings an acre for land cleared and burned. Many were up to two hundred and fifty acres cleared and had been given their grant to buy horses and machinery.

'You made it,' was Charlie's less than effusive greeting.

His attention was on the pony. He lifted her feet and felt her legs, slipping his hands all over her body looking for galls while the children took off the harness. He nodded to the rusty tank and said, 'Get some water in the bucket and wash her down. She's pulled up pretty well.'

This was a relief to hear. Life would have been difficult for Max and Eddy if she'd been in any worse condition. Now that the children had arrived at the farm they felt exhausted. While the trip was still in progress they had a level of energy to solve problems and keep their wits about them. On arrival all this disappeared and they could hardly lift an empty bucket. There was no negotiating with Charlie, especially about the care of a horse.

Eddy picked up the bucket and stood gazing vacantly about. Max took the bucket and filled it at the tank and began to rub the horse down. Any other horse would have objected to the fuss. Silvie stood patiently nuzzling at his pockets. She'd done most of the work. If she had enough energy to trot the last few yards the least they could do was make her comfortable.

Inside the shed/house were two rooms, a kitchen and a bedroom. In the kitchen was a stove with an oven and a chimney made out of flattened kerosene tins bricked in. The floor was bare earth. It did not need to be packed, it was already hard as rock, and could be swept clean and the dust settled by sprinkling it with water. Charlie hadn't lit a fire or cooked a meal. It hadn't occurred to him. The children had smelled cooking as they passed through the village. They were starving. They sat on boxes around a crude table made from raw timber boards that bristled with splinters and ate tinned dog, as Charlie called camp pie, and bread and onion. The rations they had carried had been more palatable. Eddy looked about. Her mother would never agree to live in this hessian place. She would have to go back to the city to live with her and miss out on all this.

Charlie told them all the things he wanted them to do tomorrow. The children were too tired to listen. But that didn't stop Charlie. He was still talking to them when they were asleep in their swags on the hard kitchen floor beside two bundles that Charlie had brought up on the train for them. When they woke in the frosty morning they could see these were camp beds that they could put together for a more comfortable sleep the next night. It was four-thirty and Charlie was still talking, this time in rhymes. 'Edith Frances, Maxwell John, get up and put your trousers on.'

There would be no rest. From now the daylight hours were only for work.

THE INFERNO

The evening of the seventh day of 1944. A new year that brought hope for an end to the war and a return home for the Italian prisoners. Giuseppe walked across stubble to milk the cows after a long day of stacking bags of wheat under a pitiless sun. Heat shimmered off yellow straw while they worked. He was becoming used to it, but he would never be used to the way people worked through the heat of the day in this country without respect for the climate. They thought they were still in England where no midday was ever too hot for work. This was the first summer on the farm for the Italian prisoners. Giuseppe had suffered sunstroke once, with several days of headache and nausea.

In high temperatures, dry heat is easier on the body than humidity, but Giuseppe was used to moist summers. The dryness here was life denying. Still, hot air draped across your face and ears like a poultice. Sun-heat absorbed by the earth burnt back up through the soles of your shoes. Sunlight bleached the straw on the ground, the leaves on the trees and the ether in the sky, relentless except for the startling contrast of shade. In a stand of gums, under the verandah and especially in the garden under the European trees, shade was darker than in places where the sun is not so bright. Deep shade, cool by contrast, could be a greater comfort here than in more inviting landscapes. Winter birds, plover and willy wagtail, gave way to crow and galah. That there was some life in the trees was a comfort.

In Lombardia, when a fold in the landscape creates a chasm or a valley, there is always a stream. Here the land barely undulates and in the shallow valleys it is dry. To someone from the mountains it looks completely flat. Overnight, heavy rain will create a temporary creek spreading wide like a lake across the flat. For a few weeks the land will transform. Every kind of duck, goose and long-legged waterhen will appear to nest and breed. Gradually it will dry up, the birds will make their formations in the air and fly to another wetland. A new line of saplings will emerge from the soil, the seeds having been washed into lines at the edges of the temporary lake.

In summer, you must take your canvas waterbag with you into the paddocks. In the mountains of Giuseppe's home, water is everywhere, flowing, spurting and rushing out of every pore, around every corner and through every opening. Melting snows. The source of everlasting life. The sound of gushing water is all around. The river splashes, bounces, gurgles, sometimes even thunders through the valley. In the town, every street has its own perpetual fountain, an excuse to embellish the townscape with gargoyles carved in stone, lion heads or mythical monsters gurgitating pure, icy water. The Virgin sits on a pedestal in the centre of the fountain in the square of the basilica. Near his grandparents' house is a fountain many centuries old. In the middle is a stone obelisk with an acorn carved into the point. There is only one fountain in his village. Source of water for every house and animal and a place to do the washing, and of course to meet with neighbours.

Here, water does not create a community. It is an industry. It makes no sound. One enormous silver pipe snakes its way two hundred miles from the coastal catchment area in the hills and then on another hundred and seventy-five miles to the large goldmining town. It is a lifeline, utterly depended upon by households, stock and industry. Mending the large main pipe and the smaller ones that lead from it is neverending. Occasionally, a geyser is created by a weakness in a joint and a telephone call quickly brings old Howie Spinks on his bicycle to the scene, to plug the hole. No one envies him. There are frosty mornings when he is immersed up to the top of his rubber waders fixing a submerged leak.

There is enough precipitation to grow a winter crop if the farming is done to precision to take advantage of the moisture when it falls, and enough to grow natural grass for grazing and to fill the dams in the winter, but not to keep them full through the summer. Fishing is not a favourite pastime here, neither is sailing.

Giuseppe had been at Grey Tamma Farm eight months when, in the dusk, walking home from milking, he saw the line of smoke rising from the horizon. He brought the milk to the cellar to begin separating. Max put his head around the door.

'I'm going to lend a hand with the fire. I'm taking Vince.'

He walked over to Giuseppe and stood in front of him.

'I'm not worried about Mum and Eddy if you're here, Joe. I know you'll take care of them. You think you'll be all right?'

'Yes,' said Giuseppe feeling both flattered and concerned. He had no idea about bushfires in Australia. He could see that he was about to learn. Max and Enzo filled the watertank on the back of the old truck from the waterstand at the railway siding and took off into the night.

The fire was twenty miles to the east. The signora was nervous. Fire was her greatest fear. Fire had taken her family home and every possession when she was a child. She told him at breakfast it could travel fast and be at the farm in a few hours. She spent most of the next week making sandwiches and pies and flasks of tea. Trucks would pass on the way from filling up with water at the siding and drop off bread and pick up her hampers and take them to the firefighters. Different farmers came by, sometimes in the Nash truck, but she never saw Max. He was the captain of the bushfire brigade and could not leave the scene of the fire. She worked faster than was her usual style, crashing and clattering pots about the stove and sink, slamming through the wire door to stand on the edge of the verandah to check the size and direction of the smoke and muttering under her breath. She was hardly recognisable as the benign and confident matriarch. She took the fire as a personal attack. She might have been Joan of Arc. She had reason to be concerned. Wind was gusting hard from the desert, blowing the fire towards them. They needed to get the crop off before the fire came.

Giuseppe rose at four to feed the horses. Eight horses had to be harnessed and hitched to the harvester. He had never harnessed them before. Horses are happy creatures, easier to handle than cows. It was a welcome change. They whinnied low and soft in the dark when he came with the feed — chaff, oats, bran and molasses mixed with water.

They took an hour to eat. Good food for hard, hot work. Heat sat about in lumps like dough in the early hour. Usually the dry air carried sweet odours and filled the emptiness with a city of smells. Now every smell was ash. In the dark, the east horizon glowed a long horizontal line of orange-red fire. Hell was on its way.

The cows were waiting at the gate. He let them into their bails and gave them hay. Eddy arrived with buckets and her usual scowl and they began milking. He could keep up with her now. They milked silently. When the signora helped with the milking they talked, discussed the health of the animals, their dispositions, and such technical things as how much cream each cow gave for butter and how much longer they would be in milk before they were made dry by the summer.

Eddy was silent. With the prisoners she was usually silent. She had been home for two months and, with rare exceptions, remained as reserved from the prisoners as ever. He was surprised when she said without antagonism, 'Take these two buckets to the house and stay and have breakfast. I'll do the rest.'

When he made to protest she snapped, 'Just do it, please.'

She did not want consideration, not from a prisoner. She no longer had malaria. She could work, she did work, so did her mother. But she still had hate. For the enemy.

It took the two women and Giuseppe an hour to harness the horses. They were in the paddock just after dawn. The sky had become sulphurous. The end of the world. L'Inferno. The sun was a small red ball suspended in a wall of grey. Perhaps the smoke cover would make the day cooler. Perhaps not. Through the long morning, billow after billow of smoke was driven across by the wind. Pernicious easterly. Even without fire it dried the land until it crazed like a mosaic, bent trees, peeled skin off faces, and dried washing in ten minutes. It lifted the earth and shook it in fine powder over the leaves of trees, roofs of the houses, the blades of grasses. It closed the white-lashed eyes of the sheep. It tumbled turnipweed along tracks like a line of dancing Cossacks, and dammed up red dirt uselessly against fences. It picked up oaten dust and whipped it about in sheets slipping down between skin and shirt bringing the madness of irritation, an itch that became a pain. It breathed into lungs like coils of wire and it brought hellfire.

For five days they did not stop to rest in the hours of daylight. They harnessed before dawn and harvested for as long as the horses had the will to pull the machine. Giuseppe discovered a joy in working with these strong, brave animals and in the skills of driving them in front of the harvester. While the horses rested and ate from their nosebags they flew about on the motorbike, Eddy driving, Giuseppe piling the bagged wheat into the sidecar and grinding the old bike slowly back to the shed, hoping the corrugated iron would be a protection against fire if it came. There was no truck to take it to the silo at the siding.

On the sixth night, the fire was behind the nearest hill. He fancied he could hear it crackle. A comforting sound in the grate on a cold winter night, but in the paddock on a hot summer night it was the sound of impending destruction. By night, the horses were exhausted with courageous toil. They fed them and let them go, leaving the gate to their paddock open. After milking they did the same with the cows. The chickens and ducks were left to the mercy of the foxes. At midnight, the prisoner was still climbing ladders to clean leaves out of gutters, plugging and filling them with water. They placed hessian bags in drums of water on each side of the house to be used to beat out flames if they came. The fire had gone past them to the south and burnt the telephone wires as it crossed the road. They had no contact with the world. They could see the flames getting closer, moving around to the north, heading for the Fischer farm. Eddy piled the sidecar with wet bags and Giuseppe had to run after it to leap aboard before she roared away along the north road.

Fischer's truck was standing at the gate loaded with furniture and suitcases. A pink and grey bird squawked in a cage. Mrs Fischer was sitting in the cab crying and Gretel was behind the wheel revving the engine and sounding the horn. Cat was running about with a box of kittens trying to find the mother. Eddy found her asleep in a basket of dirty clothes. Giuseppe wrapped her in a towel to stop her from scratching and handed her through the window of the truck and then lifted the children onto the back. Eddy ran across the yard and lifted them down again.

'They can't sit there,' she snapped.

She opened the door and loaded them into the cab on top of their mother with the box of kittens. Billy scrambled out to get his mountain devil and came back with it sitting dazed inside a straw hat already lightening its camouflage to match. Yvonne Fischer was so close to hysteria she hardly knew what was happening.

Giuseppe walked around to the driver's side of the truck to speak to Gretel.

'Where will you go?'

'I don't know,' she said, 'out of here.'

'Go to Noonalbin siding, that is away from the fire, and then go to the hotel and stay there. We will find you there,' he said. 'Don't try to come back.'

As soon as the truck had gone, Karl Fischer, Eddy and Giuseppe set about filling the gutters and placing drums of water and wet bags around the house. They filled three metal knapsacks with water and went on the motorbike to try to stop the blaze from reaching the sheds to the north of the homestead. There was a terrible heat coming from the blaze. A tongue of fire had licked south at this point devouring a clump of trees and was now eating the stubble. They drove to within fifty yards and went forward on foot with the knapsacks. When they ran out of water they used wet bags to beat out the fire. The wind had dropped. They were beginning to make an impression when they saw that the fire had swept around behind them and was destroying the homestead. The eucalypts around the house were ablaze, flames leaping high above the roof of the house, enveloping it like an incinerator.

'Oh God,' Eddy screamed.

From the hill at the edge of the black stubble they saw the house disappear in flames and could do nothing. Karl Fischer stood watching motionless, speechless. It was eloquent enough. What could be said? Eddy dropped her gaze and started kicking the stubble with fury. Fischer's fury was there too in the tightened muscles of his face, but he did not speak. To Giuseppe, only the dying men in the battle in the North African desert had been so terrible. War with nature is inexorable, more than machine-gun and tank. Nothing can fight it. Except the wind. The wind changed direction and burnt the stubble fire back on itself putting it out.

Fire in the wheatfields beyond the house to the west was burning back and putting itself out. They walked the old man between them back to the sidecar. Coming down the hill they could see that sheds and animals had been spared. Flames were still leaping all over the house. Why Grey Tamma Farm had been spared no one even thought about. Danger had passed. There was nothing for the fire to burn, no link for it to get back. The change in wind direction to northwest was bringing the outer reaches of a cyclone, banks of cloud and cooler temperatures.

Eddy found sedatives for Karl and put him into her room to sleep. She brought Giuseppe a cup of tea on the verandah where he sat slumped against a post. He was thinking about Enzo and Max, but he did not want to say so and alarm her.

So was she. 'I'd like to see Max . . . and Vince.'

'You are worried. I am worried too.'

She snorted a little, derisive.

Normally he would not offer his thoughts. She did not invite it. He stayed out of her way. Her heavy dark hair and brows were a roadsign on a perilous scenic drive. Beware. He liked to look at her, but had given up trying to converse. Exhaustion and her contempt for his feelings broke his reserve. His anger at her arrogant ignorance exploded. 'You think because I am an Itie dago I have no feelings? They are good men and I have learnt to value them, love them.'

She snorted again. 'You have no right.'

'No one can dictate anyone else's rights about their feelings. That's what the Nazis and Fascisti do. You are supposed to be fighting against it, but you are as bad as they.'

'You can talk! Not so long ago you were one yourself.'

'I was never a fascist.'

'Not a member of the party maybe, but you were in the crowd cheering Il Duce.'

'You know nothing about Italy. I do not support evil and many, most, of my friends are the same.'

'I don't think so.'

'You can think what you please.'

'You're in no position to speak to me like that.'

'But you are in position to speak to me any way you like. That is why your self-respect should stop you from taking advantage of it.'

'And you're bloody rude. I can have you sent back to camp tomorrow.'

A powerful weapon. Camp was a battle he could die in. Killed in inaction, by torpor. He wondered if she resented the pleasure he got from working with her family. She would have liked him to be lazy and insolent. She wanted him to rise to the bait now and tell her he did not care, to say, 'go ahead, send me back, I am tired of it here.' This might win the argument, but it would not be a victory for the prisoner.

'You are right, I should not have said that. I apologise.'

'You're pathetic,' she growled.

'Yes.'

'Don't bloody agree with everything I say.'

'*Va bene.*'

'And don't speak Italian. Enemy talk.'

'We are now your allies. We are fighting the Germans too.' He thought it better not to continue the argument. He stood up. 'I must go to bed before I fall over.'

'You can go to hell for all I care.'

'I have no doubt that is where I will end, but I hope not for a little while.'

He thought he heard her laugh. This was good, he had made a joke and she had responded. In the half light he saw she was not laughing, but silently crying. Tears flooded in muddy runnels down her ash-powdered cheeks like a river bursting its banks after drought. He was shocked by the sudden show of emotion. Struck by the instant wilting of aggression, he felt that it had been brutish of him to argue with her, especially as he now could see that she was not as tough as she wanted everyone to think. He tried to guide her to a chair on the verandah but her limbs were stiff and unable to move. Her mother appeared and put her arms around her.

'Time for bed,' she said leading her daughter inside. 'You should sleep too, Joe.'

He did not know whether he envied the mother or the daughter. He would have liked to weep in his own mother's arms. More, he wanted to be the arms that were wept in.

He stepped off the verandah heading back to the hut and bed at last and felt the first drops of rain on his face. Even the worst times eventually end. He sat on the bed to take off his boots and decided against it. In the shed he filled a can with petrol and covered it with wet bags in the sidecar of the bike. He filled a waterbag, and headed out on the road north. After six miles he came to a T-junction and turned east along a narrower road. He splashed through muddy puddles beside blackened paddocks for five miles, but noticed there were no tyre tracks on the road. The fire had swept through leaving a ghostly forest of black trunks and limbs with no leaves. Without warning, the road stopped at a dam with a set of charred sheepyards and a most shocking collection of burnt and dying sheep. Giuseppe could not imagine a more gruesome scene in hell.

He was seized with panic. He must find Max and Enzo before the same thing happened to them. He turned the bike around and rode back. He had never been out this far north before. He sat at the junction of the two roads trying to figure out the geography. He set out again the only way he could, west, even though he knew that the fire had come from the east. Gradually the narrow road swung north and slowly round to the east. Not everything was burnt. Patches of bush and crop were untouched. The sight of it gave him hope. But his hopes soon faded when he could see beyond, the fire raging towards him. It had not rained here. The atmosphere was humid but the paddocks were still crackle dry. He did not like riding towards the fire.

He rounded a bend and there was the truck abandoned in the middle of the track. He ran over to it and stepped onto the running board and looked in the window, heart heaving, breath out of rhythm. It was empty. He circled the truck calling, looking under it, in the bushes beside it. He climbed on top of it to gain a vantage point. The fire was coming fast and only half a mile away. Then he saw what he wanted to see. In the distance two figures were walking away to the south across a paddock of pale stubble. He brought the bike alongside the truck and parked it in the ditch at the side of the track. He covered it as best he could with the wet chaffbags and took the jerry can out. By this time he imagined he could feel the heat of the fire, he could certainly see it. He levered the top off the can of petrol and it popped like a champagne bottle; but it wasn't champagne, it was petrol and one spark, one piece of hot ash, and he would be an incendiary bomb. He poured it into the petrol tank as carefully as he could in his panic, trying so hard not to splash it that he did not breathe until he had the cap back on the tank. Then he climbed into the cab and pressed the starter. It made so little response that he thought it must be the battery. He tried again. This time the engine kicked over and then sputtered out. He looked back at the fire. It was two hundred, three hundred yards away. He tried the starter again and the motor came to life.

He took the truck along the track looking for a gate into the paddock. The two figures had turned around and were walking back towards the truck. There was no gate. Giuseppe turned the truck towards the fence and put his foot down hard and drove straight through it. When he got to the two men they looked ready to pass out.

Max said in his usual understated way, 'Joe. I thought you'd show up sooner or later. Everyone all right? Mum, Eddy?'

'They are sleeping.' Giuseppe's hands were shaking. 'The Fischer house is burnt.'

Giuseppe turned the truck and retraced his path back across the paddock in the direction of the fire. At the hole in the fence he pulled up.

'I will go back for the motorbike.'

'Not on foot. In fact, not at all,' said Max.

Giuseppe opened the door and slipped to the ground.

'Bugger it, get back in, we'll drive back,' said Max.

The fire was close now. It was a risk to be going into its path. They drove back to the bike, Giuseppe ran to it. He definitely could feel the heat of the fire now. He had never been so afraid, even in battle. While the truck was turning around he got the bike out of the ditch and followed the truck back along the road at full throttle, putting as much distance between himself and the fire as he could.

They stopped to look at the Fischers' place and feed the animals. A red kelpie appeared, trotting towards them. Giuseppe put him in the sidecar. Nothing was left of the house. They had only what was on the back of their truck. A few sad flames flicked around the charred footings.

Enzo was embarrassed when signora Nash hugged him. Eddy shook his hand. She cooked eggs for them before they collapsed into bed. They were both red with sunburn and fire burn. Max had lost his eyebrows and lashes at some time during the last week. They had not slept except to snatch forty minutes or an hour a day.

Max was proud of Enzo. 'We ought to make you an honorary member of the fire brigade. You are a good firefighter,' he said to the Italian. Enzo went off to bed hardly able to raise a smile.

Max came over to Giuseppe and put his hand on his shoulder. 'You saved our lives.'

'I don't think so.'

'I'm sure of it. We're one–all now. I'm not sure I liked the gung ho way you went back for the bike, could have got us all killed.'

'I saw some sheep that are all burnt but still alive.'

'Our sheep?'

'No. I found them out on the east road when I was looking for you. They were in some yards there. The fire had been through. There are a lot. Maybe two hundred.'

'I'll go back when I've had some sleep and shoot the poor buggers.'

'I will come with you.'

Giuseppe had gone beyond sleep. He went about feeding animals and shutting gates. Everything had changed. Rain was coming down hard. The air reeked of wet ash sweetened with wet straw. It would damage any crops that had been spared. In the stables he found Eddy moving about, feeding the horses, murmuring to them. She looked up briefly at his silhouette in the doorway and kept on with her work.

Together they milked, churned butter and took it to the station on the motorbike. The rain had stopped and the sun was burning away the clouds. The sun, insensitive as ever to the need for one cool day. The stationmaster frowned when he saw the prisoner driving. Eddy laughed as they drove away. Her laughter, so rare, was almost as startling as her tears.

'Old stuffed shirt Kel,' she said. 'He'd rather I drove, but he's never seen me drive,' and she laughed again, finding it a huge joke.

He thought she might be a little delirious from fatigue.

Giuseppe pulled off the road a mile south of the farmhouse, climbed through the fence and stood on the bank of the dam. No clear blue lake with reflected mountains, but it was water. Eddy followed.

He turned to her and said, 'I am going to swim.'

She looked at him nonplussed. 'In here?'

'Of course. You do not swim?'

'Not in the dam.'

'Why not?'

'Well . . . it's for the sheep and ducks. It's not clean.'

'I will survive it.'

He took off his shirt and boots and waded into the creamy water. Cockatoos on the edge flapped away into a tree. He swam to the middle, treading the deep cold water. The water at the top was warm and below that freezing cold. The line between the two temperatures was precise.

There had been nothing to stir it until he swam across it. Eddy sat on the bank and unlaced her boots, peeled off her socks and rolled up her trousers to her knees. She stood up and tiptoed to the water's edge to cool her feet. Clay as pale as skin squeezed between her toes. Giuseppe swam over.

'Swim. You will feel better.'

She squatted on her haunches and stirred the water with her hand.

'Good,' he called, 'you are nearly in.'

'I'm not going in. And if you could hurry, I'd like to get home.'

She turned to walk up the steep bank and slipped on a rock, lost balance and toppled into the shallow water and sank into the clay. 'Bugger!' she swore, struggling onto her elbows.

Giuseppe was instantly beside her. He tried to lift her but it was difficult to get a foothold.

She shook off his hand. 'Leave me. I don't need help.' He pulled her to her feet in spite of her protests and she lost balance again and grabbed at him and pulled him over with her.

'Just leave me alone,' she said unfairly, since it was she who had grabbed him. She was behaving like a child.

He lay back in the mud-churned water and laughed at her. He had no idea how she would react to this provocation and in his current state of exhaustion was past caring. He did not have to wait long to find out. She crawled to where he lay and taking a large handful of clay, slapped it on his forehead. It took him by surprise. Normally he would have retaliated, but he was so shocked he just put up a hand to wipe away the mud. Meanwhile she had gathered another handful and slapped it back where the first one had been. Then she took another handful and smeared it through his hair. She wanted to play.

He said, 'I will not do that to your hair.'

'Do it! Here,' she shouted. She slapped a clod of clay into his hand. 'Here.' She lifted his hand to her head and rubbed it into her hair.

'Your hair is too beautiful,' he said.

'Your air ees too bitiful,' she mimicked, rubbing more clay into his hair.

He looked at her in astonishment.

She looked back defiant, shook her head and said, 'Love thine enemy, but I find you a disappointing enemy. You were angry enough with me earlier, wouldn't you like to pummel me with clay?'

'Yes.'

'Well, now's your chance.'

'Thank you, for your offer.'

'You turning me down?'

'You change too fast.'

'You went to look for Max and Vince.'

'Of course.'

'Why?'

'*Perchè? Perchè perchè?*'

'Speak English.'

'Don't speak anything.'

'Tell me.'

'Why do you ask?'

'You're the enemy. One less of us is one more of you, isn't it?'

She was back in character and as objectionable as ever. He stood up and waded into the dam to splash water on his face.

'We are not monsters.'

'You are,' she laughed. 'You look like you just crawled out of Loch Ness.'

'I am not a fascist,' he said.

She came to stand beside him. He was washing his eyes with hands full of muddy water.

'We'd better get you home, this murky water's not going to do your eyes much good.'

She dived in and stayed under so long he thought she had drowned. He waited until he began to panic and dived to look for her, but the milky water made her invisible. When he surfaced she was scrambling up the bank. His eyes were beginning to sting and bite at the corners. She drove the bike home. He sat in the low sidecar too tired to blink. She was right, he thought, he was pathetic.

She stopped outside the hut. He got out and walked away without speaking, without looking at her. Enzo was sleeping like a dead man. He envied him. The taste of clay hung on the back of his tongue. His lips fizzed from sunburn and fire. He showered and lay down on his bed, too tired to climb between the sheets. He drifted at once into a troubled sleep of swirling red and black and grey smoke. He'd been asleep for about forty minutes when there was a hand on his shoulder. It was Max.

'I'm going out to finish off those sheep. You said you wanted to come. I hate to wake you, but I could do with a bit of support.'

Giuseppe pulled on his filthy clothes and his boots and they sat in silence as Max drove the truck out along the east road.

'This is the worst job you can ever do on a farm,' said Max.

Rain had moved north, extinguishing the fires there. At the burnt-out yards the sight was as appalling as the prisoner remembered it. About fifty charred and dying animals were still standing or staggering about, some bleating in pitiful cries. Max loaded his rifle and leant it across the top rail of the fence and began to pick them off, one by one. After twenty or so shots he dropped to his knees and regurgitated his breakfast onto the ground with such violence that it splashed back up at his face. Giuseppe took the rifle from his hand and loaded it and finished off the job while Max dry retched. Afterwards, they walked around to see that they had killed them all. Giuseppe had begun to feel nauseous too. He drove home.

They said not a word for the first few miles. Then Giuseppe said, 'Why were they left in yards to get burnt?'

'Old Jock, the old bastard. He's only half a farmer. He was probably loading them on a truck to take them out and left it too late. Bloody shocking. But they would have got burnt if he'd done nothing, so I dunno.'

'If it is only stock who die, then that is not so bad,' said Giuseppe.

'But it's not. Old Stan Fowler copped it. Poor devil lay down on the ground to sleep, he was so tired.'

'He was killed?'

'Yeah.'

Nothing more was said for the rest of the journey. At the farm they climbed down slowly, wearily, and Max took up his rifle.

'Thanks, mate,' he said. 'Thanks a lot.'

Giuseppe nodded his acknowledgement and they both went off to their beds.

THE MONDAROO GIFT

If Japanese POWs had been allowed out to work, Max wouldn't have applied for them. And he would have hesitated to have Germans, but Italians were a different story. There had always been a few Italians around. He knew their ways a little and liked their sense of humour. He admired their ability to work. Some Australians didn't. They worked too hard for too little pay. Italian timber-clearing teams were all over the new farming areas. They worked fast and for very little. There were several Italian families farming in the area. They kept to themselves most of the time. Considering the suspicion from the rest of the community, this did not surprise Max. Their social events consisted of getting several families together, usually relatives, for a christening, a wedding or the making of pork sausages. On the whole they stayed away from organisations like the Farmers' Union, but there were times when they were forced to rub shoulders. At the wheat silo, at the siding, at church and in the event of a bushfire. Gradually they became conversant with the Australian way of helping neighbours. Max considered that he had been lucky to get Vince and Joe. They were hard working and of good character and were becoming good friends, especially Joe.

All he had to do now was to make sure that he had enough money to pay their wages. Sometimes that could be a little nerve-racking.

It occurred to Max that making money, though difficult, was nowhere near as hard as hanging on to it. He didn't seem to have much luck entrusting his hard won cash to friends and family, much of which was won fair and square at country track meetings. Max had gifts. If ever he'd been in a war he'd have been called a true Anzac. He stood just six feet tall, well muscled and square shouldered. Anything he set his mind to do, he did with above average competence. One of the things at which he was better than average was running. Simple running.

Max's last race had been the Mondaroo Gift, an open two-twenty flat race. He remembered not so much the race itself, but the getting there and the coming away. The getting there was a bumpy twenty miles of dirt road by motorcycle that wasted a good spurt of valuable adrenaline. They'd spun on some loose gravel and been off-loaded onto a bank of thick grass, full of seeds. Phil got nasty, cursing Max for not slowing properly at the bends and cursing Jasper for saying bloody silly things like 'bollocks' and 'raving lunatic', his Pommy idea of swearing. Phil and Jasper had a few grazes, but Max, being at the front, just had a fright. They straightened the mudguard and went on their way, Phil driving this time and Max on the pillion with Jasper, finding out how uncomfortable it was riding three on a bike.

At the track there were people everywhere. Blokes in braces and no collars, blokes in suits, waistcoats buttoned, and women in their too-early-for-the-weather summer dresses gathered under the trees to drink tea at small tables, or lined up for lemonade. No time to look at them now. In front of a crush around the two bookies, their pencillers called out the odds, matching and bettering each other in turn. In the middle of the arena a brass band was playing marches while kids improvised formations and rolled about on the grass. The atmosphere of shared anticipation made Max's hands fizz and lose their strength, starting with the thumbs. He had to stop it from going to his stomach. The wanting of this race was powerful, pressing down on him. If he let it, it would take away his speed. The trick was to get the wanting to stoke the speed, lighten him, not weigh him down. A few boys spotted him and ran over circling.

'How ya' gunna go today, Max? How ya feeling? Legs strong, are they? You on form, Maxie? Running quick today, are ya?'

He grinned and shook them off as fast as he could.

Phil took Max's quid and went to get the best odds and Jasper strolled with hands-in-pockets nonchalance to suss out the opposition. In the pavilion with the others Max was distracted. He needed quiet, so he used an empty show stall to get ready. He had to quieten down and listen. Like praying, only not sending messages, waiting for them to come to him. They always did come. It didn't matter where from. Probably thought of them himself, but they always seemed to just crop up in his mind as if put there from outside. After he'd listened to the message, he'd slowly, always in the same order, change into his string vest and strides and put on his spikes with a rhythm that matched his breathing, a rhythm that became more marked with the final knot of the final lace. Then, with head bowed, he'd jog and shake his feet and try to remember the feel of the last time he won. He had to keep happy, and think in a long straight line.

Jasper came back looking nervous. Talking too much and smoothing down his already smooth and shiny cap of blue black hair with the palm of his hand. In the other hand he held a number five for Max's arm.

'Bloody hell, Jas, I always wear eleven.'

'Not eleven in the race.'

'Doesn't matter, go back and tell them if they won't give me eleven I'll wear my own.'

Jasper had a quiet stubbornness about being sent on errands. But Max was insistent. Eleven was his football number, his mother's birth date and the age he had learnt to drive a car and left school for good. Eleven felt strong, plain, two strong legs, two pillars. Definitely his number.

'Don't think they'll like it. You're not the only drawcard today.'

'Doesn't matter.'

'You don't want to get disqualified.'

Phil ducked around the hessian curtain hanging across the door of the stall with a fistful of betting tickets.

'Disqualify him? Don't be silly, Jas, the odds have been too short, there's a heap of money on him.'

Max started to fret. 'Damn, we should have got here earlier for the longer odds.'

'Earlier would have been worse, they just went up again. You're eight to one.'

Phil sounded upset. Max was alert.

'Why, what's going on?'

Jasper took off back to the marshal's tent, forehead creased and the ends of his heavy black brows darting up and down nervously. Phil went quiet, tidying Max's things, folding his clothes with clumsy hands.

'Christ sakes stop fussing around, Phil, what's the matter with you?'

'Nothing. Ronan's here.'

The fizz in Max's hands leapt to his stomach. He let fly a few words about bodily functions and then went silent, trying to pull himself together. He'd met Albie Ronan a few times over a hundred yards, but this was two-twenty. Would that make it better or worse? Ronan was the state champion at both distances and Max had never beaten him. This was a bush meeting with a small purse. Why'd he have to come all the way out here from the city to take their money?

Max didn't want to start thinking about money. It was for the money he did this. It wasn't worth it for the glory. He'd won over a hundred pounds this year. At home on the farm they thought he was earning it. But jobs only came along now and then. This purse was ten quid and he could win eight on the bookies. He'd send the ten home. The rest he'd need to get to the Murchison. Two years ago he'd left the farm to go twenty miles away to do seasonal work, and then he'd followed the jobs wherever they took him. He got more work than most who wandered the bush, and plenty did. He was strong and had skills. He knew horses, could hitch up a team of sixteen in the dark as fast as anyone, shear sheep and fix machinery. As many as twenty would turn up for one week's work stacking bags of wheat into a shed or onto a cart. There was a certain pride in being chosen while others were turned away. But then he was the one who had to work like a pack horse while the others loafed about. He got the sunburn, the blisters, the aching back. He was twenty-two and had been working on the farm from the age of eleven. It was five years since his father had left. He was the breadwinner for the family, no question.

There wasn't more than a second between him and Albie Ronan, and nothing was ever certain. The odds were saying the city kid was a sure thing, but Max wasn't going to lie down yet. He must be calm, he must sit a minute and listen. He asked Phil to make sure no one disturbed him and then sat down to be quiet. Nothing came to his mind. He waited. Nothing. He couldn't seem to clear his mind. He kept thinking about the start. He could hear voices outside. A woman was speaking to Phil, arguing. He didn't sound happy. Alice. Max would know her voice anywhere. What was she doing here? He didn't want to talk to her or anyone. He needed to be quiet. He'd been seeing Alice a bit lately, but not much, because he could never afford to take her to a dance or the pictures. It was just a matter of catching her in the street when she needed her parcels carried or at the tennis club. They'd met when he was lumping super on her father's farm. The old man didn't like to see them together, didn't like her talking to a labourer. He gave up trying to hear anything, but he felt calmer.

Alice was standing near the start in a red dress and a big straw hat perched over one ear that looked like it was about to slide off the side of her head. She was with three other women. She was taller than the others. He knew she was watching him, but he didn't look at her. He didn't look at anyone, especially not Albie Ronan. He'd seen it all before. Ronan had a ritual set down to put the wind up the opposition. His trainer always came right onto the track with him, all dressed up in his waistcoat and trilby, and Ronan would arrive with a long white gown over his shoulders and a white towel around his neck, looking like a boxer, and he always wore his socks pulled right up like a boxer. He wanted his opponents to make the connection and they did. He'd wave and smile to the applause of his beloved supporters. Then he'd turn his back on them and walk up and down on the spot shaking his feet and pulling his knees up to his chest, breathing deep. And then, and this was really bad, he'd go into the group and shake hands with the other starters and slap them on the elbow or shoulder and wish them luck. Max knew it was bullshit, especially when the trainer, with great ceremony, took off Ronan's gown and towel for him and kissed him on both cheeks like some French pansy. Then Ronan would do a pious praying act crossing himself two or three times, as though God was his special friend. For all anyone knew he wasn't even Catholic.

What a performance, he might as well be a Hollywood film star. But he didn't have the looks for that. He had the lean grey look of the city about him. He was dark and although clean shaven, always looked a bit blue around the gills. Deep lines ran down his face like poverty lines on a horse's rump, only this bloke wasn't poor, he was rich and all muscles. A bit short though. The other boys looked golden and red and new born, almost new baked, compared. Some were in bare feet, some tennis shoes, only the ones who'd had the odd win could afford spikes. Most of them had a good-natured admiration for Max. He was a hero to the younger runners. They all waited in a group behind the line moving around swinging their arms, away from him and away from Ronan who was like some mythical God dropped in from another planet.

The band was playing, the bookies shouting and the crowd was making a noise like a hive. He shut it all out and started to stretch and get ready by thinking about breaking the tape at the end. He lined up to the start and it came to him. The start. That's it, that's his edge, that's what gives him an even chance. His other two races against Albie Ronan were in the city where they started on blocks. He wasn't used to blocks and had got away slowly. But Ronan wasn't used to a standing start. He didn't know about starting thinking you were in the middle of the race like Max did. He probably didn't have a mouthful of dry bones and a howling dingo tearing at his belly either. It didn't matter. He was all right again. In his head. Keeping happy.

And after that it was all blank. He heard the 'on your mark', he saw the starter raise his pistol, and then nothing until he felt the tape taut on his chest. Jasper described it later at the winners' party given by the mayor.

'It was a great race, exciting. You got away well, but you didn't win the start, the redhead kid Bluey Bonner took off like a rocket, but it only took Ronan about twenty or thirty yards to wear him down. At the halfway, the rest of you seemed to be all bunched up about two, even three, yards behind him. He must have been feeling good and going easy and he stayed that way until about the two hundred when you came round the outside like a train and the crowd started up a roar. The women were screaming and pulling at each other.'

'I didn't notice.'

'I don't think Ronan knew what had happened. He thought he had it in the bag. He was on the rail and you were on the outside and you got your chest to the tape before him, just. It was whisker close. The crowd went really quiet for a while until the marshal led you to the middle of the track. And then there was a hell of a noise. You had a few supporters here today, Max.'

All Max could remember was throwing up his guts on the grass in the centre of the field and not being able to see anything or hear anything except blood pumping through his ears. And then Phil started pounding him on the back and rubbing him down with a towel.

'You bastard, you beat him. You beat the state bloody champion, you crafty bugger.'

'I won eighteen pounds.'

'Holy hell.' Phil was looking almost as white and excited as Max.

'What's the matter? Where you going?'

'To the bookies, to collect. Where you think?'

Max was still doubled over trying to catch his breath when Alice came out stepping daintily in her red high heels and red dress to congratulate him. He felt embarrassed that everyone could see her standing beside him in the middle of the track in front of the stand. Then he realised she wasn't there for him, but in an official capacity. As the daughter of the chairman of the Mondaroo Athletic Club she was to present the trophy. Max was too excited to be embarrassed when she kissed his cheek, but when she did, a few wolf whistles came out of the crowd leaning over the fence.

They were standing in the mayor's marquee having drinks with the VIPs. Jasper liked that sort of thing, he was born to it. He was holding forth, describing every inch of the race for the third time, when Alice's father condescended to approach and give what he clearly thought were congratulations. His hearty growl of a voice was too loud. The group around Max disintegrated.

'Well, you've got a nice purse this time, young fellow. Alice will have told you about the job.'

'Job?'

'She was going to tell you before the race. I need a leading hand. Abel's left me in the lurch. I thought I'd give you a trial. Strictly one month on half wages until you prove yourself. So I'll see you bright and early in the morning.'

He had to be desperate. Every possible alternative applicant must have had a better offer or gone to the goldfields. Old bastard was so afraid of a hard day's work, he'd risk his daughter seeing Max every day. Max wasn't thinking of marrying her, but her father was obviously scared to death of it, and the whole district loved to gossip and blow every friendship up into something it wasn't. Well, he wasn't going to put the old bugger's mind at rest.

'Thanks, Mr Anderson, I appreciate your offer, but I'll be otherwise engaged.'

You couldn't read the older man's face, but his body stiffened and his chest pushed out.

'I wouldn't let this little victory go to your head. Resting on your laurels isn't going to put food in your belly. You're not likely to get a better offer.'

'I don't know. I think full wages, no trial period and on the job training's a pretty fair offer.'

'Who's offered you that? Bloody Ferguson, isn't it? Is it?'

'No, not Ferguson.'

'Not someone from around here then?'

'No, not from around here.'

'Where then?'

'I can't tell you that. It's not in my interests.'

Max wasn't the sort who went looking for quarrels, but he wasn't a pushover. He had a sharp mind and a tongue to match and if he thought someone was having a go he'd pull him up pretty smart. This old geezer thought he owned the district. His father had left him a nice big grazing place and a house with wide verandahs, and that made him important. Max didn't see it that way. He had a small farm and a mud house with narrow verandahs. But Max was a reader. He'd kept up with what was going on in Russia and it didn't seem such a bad idea. Things could do with a bit of levelling out. People needed to understand that however rich they were still animals, and if they understood that it would make them more human. Max didn't think that being pushed around, especially by this bully type, was going to do him any good. He had nothing to lose. So when Anderson raised his chin and narrowed his eyes and said, 'Young peanut, how would you know what was in your interest?', Max said what was on his mind.

'I probably wouldn't, but I know what isn't, and working for you isn't. And telling you where I'm going isn't either.'

'Who do you think you're talking to?' Anderson's booming voice grew louder.

Things were getting heated when Alice, having eyed her prey, stalked it gracefully across the tent and slid her arm through Max's, probably with the intention of cooling her father's obvious irritation. He was wagging his head and swaying in indignation like an emu. Max thought of pulling away, but he liked the feel of her arm on his. He wasn't sure about the idea of her attaching herself so openly to him. She acted as though she hadn't noticed the antagonism in the air.

'So have you two settled it all? I must say, Max, I don't think much of your friend, he was positively rude to me before the race.'

'It wasn't his fault. I asked him to keep everyone away.'

'I'm not everyone. Am I? I needed to tell you about Daddy's offer before the race.'

'Why?'

'I was . . .' She stopped to choose her words.

'You didn't think I could beat Ronan.'

'Well . . .'

'That's all right, neither did I.'

'I thought if you knew you had a job to go to you wouldn't be so disappointed. So when do you start?'

'Never.'

Archie Anderson scowled through the curls of his overbearing brows. 'Alice, I'm leaving in five minutes, get your things together.'

He turned into the crowd to look for a refill for his sherry glass. Max wondered if the tight politeness of the social occasion had not had a hold on Anderson his manners wouldn't have disappeared altogether. Alice watched him go.

'He doesn't like "no" unless he says it himself.'

Someone collided with Max making him spill his glass of beer down the front of her red dress, splashing a mark like a map of New Zealand.

'For crying out loud, Phil, look where you're going.'

'Ah sorry, mate . . . mates.' He snorted an inebriated laugh and slurred: 'Jeez, sorry love, 've I ruined your beeoodiful dress?' and rocked back and forth in idiotic mirth.

'Phil, you're drunk, mate, get lost. Wait at the bike. We'll all get out of here in a minute.'

'Yeah, but which minute, eh? Which minute?'

'Go on, shove off.'

Max turned him and walked him to the door and gave him the shove he'd recommended and watched him wobble off through the trees talking to himself. He half expected

Alice to flounce away in a fury, but she was waiting where he'd left her. He pulled his handkerchief out of his pocket and offered it to her. She looked at the colour of it and turned it down.

'Yeah, don't blame you.'

He grinned. She grinned back.

'Why don't you take the job? You scared of me?'

'Course not,' he lied.

She was a bit frightening. Self-assured or something. He wasn't used to that in a girl her age. And with her dad being such a hard case.

'I'm going to ride shotgun on the camel trains up north,' he blurted out, probably to prove that he wasn't scared of anything.

'Wool?'

'Yeah. Keep it under your hat.'

'That's dangerous.'

'Yeah, but the money's good.'

'Don't get shot. Don't shoot anyone. I can't blame you for going. I'd prefer to die in a shoot out with the shearers than work for Archie Anderson too.'

He laughed. It was good talking to her. She was funny. He shouldn't have told her though; if anyone found out, like the unions, he'd be a goner.

'It has to stay a secret.'

'I'll tell you a secret, Maxwell Nash. I've applied to train as a teacher, in Perth.'

'What for?'

'Get away from Daddy, what do you think?'

When she laughed she threw her head back and her hair fell over the collar of her dress in a soft pale wave. He could see Archie Anderson pretending not to stare at them over the heads of the cocktail sippers. That's why he'd offered him the job. Alice would be a hundred miles away.

'I'm glad you didn't take the job,' she said and touched his arm.

He picked up a brisk pace walking back to his stall past the scrap ends of the punters straggling through long shadows of slim morel gums towards the gate. Discarded tickets confettied the ground. A few dusty-booted kids ran about collecting them and shouting, pretending to have found a winner. The muscles of his thighs were beginning to harden, but he was floating excited, just off the ground. Probably about riding up north tomorrow and starting the rest of his life. And about Mum and Eddy getting the money, and being able to send them regular cheques from now on. And maybe, but this was silly really, but maybe he'd enjoyed that last conversation better than he'd enjoyed any other before in his life. What if he stayed a couple of days and took Alice to the pictures. He had eight pounds, nine shillings altogether. They could have tea at the Blue Lagoon beforehand. He wondered if she'd be willing to get on a motorbike. She might. He was feeling brave, exhilarated.

She was leaving the tent with her father when he got back there. He grabbed her arm and pulled her back into the crowded tent before old Archie striding ahead knew she was gone, and she did say yes. He didn't have to worry about the motorbike, she would go to her aunt's house in town, and meet him at the café. Bloody hell, what a day. Now it was more than exhilaration. It was euphoria.

Phil and Jasper weren't waiting for him at the bike, so he rode down to the post office before it closed and bought a postal order for nine pounds, nineteen shillings and ninepence. He needed the threepence for the postage. He couldn't spend it now. It was safe. His mother relied on these funds, and his winnings would make his life almost normal, for a while anyway. Things were going well.

Back at the showground Jasper was wandering around sipping sherry out of Max's trophy, his black-fish brows raised in a permanent look of astonishment. Phil was curled up asleep on the floor of the stall. Max pushed him with his foot. Apart from his endless repertoire of swear words, you couldn't really say that Phil had the gift of the gab, but explaining to Max that he didn't have the eight pounds from Max's bet on himself was the hardest string of sentences he'd ever tried to put together. It turned out that when he'd seen Ronan at the track he'd lost his nerve, and put the money on the state champion to win.

Max was knocked for six. It took him a minute to comprehend. Then through clenched teeth: 'You bloody great drongo. Don't ever ask me to lend you money again.'

The worst of it was the money. Not having the money. He didn't care that Phil hadn't shown faith in him. That was nothing. No one thought he had a chance against Ronan. He hadn't thought that he'd had much of one himself, but he got some hope at the last minute that gave him the boost he needed. He needed the money more than Ronan. He gave Phil a sour stare. He wanted to punch him.

'I meant to, to put it, the money, on you. When I saw you were eight to one. I saw A Ronan, evens. They should'a given two or three to one for you. But they were giving you no chance at all. And the odds for a place on you were so bad. They had you pegged for second. They oughta know. It's their business. I knew your money was important, so was mine. I lost my money too. I'm an idiot now, but before it seemed sensible. If it'd worked . . .'

He wasn't going to apologise, that was clear. Max had heard enough.

'Oh shut up, for Christ sakes. As if you knew anything about it. You couldn't run a message. Bugger off, I don't want to look at you.'

Phil picked up his jacket and hat and turned to go.

Max growled, 'Find your own way home. You're not coming on my bike.'

It was only twenty miles. He'd be home by morning. Wouldn't hurt him to do some thinking while he walked. He'd never noticed before what a weak mongrel Phil was.

Max had one and six to take Alice to dinner and the pictures. Forget it. He'd meet her at the café and explain. What a pathetic sight he'd make. She'd think he was a complete drip. He'd go to her aunt's house and leave a note to say he was needed up north a day early. He couldn't get a loan from Phil or Jasper. Phil had lost all his money on Ronan. Jasper hadn't had enough to make a bet.

Maybe it wasn't such a great day. He hadn't told them he'd arranged to take her to the pictures and he never would. Jasper made a lightning return to sobriety and started muttering things about sow's ears and inherited imbecility and was almost weeping over words like loyalty and comradeship. Poor Jas could get quite soft, even sentimental, over things like money. He didn't have any. The nearest he ever seemed to get to it was by sticking with Max.

Max's friendship with Phil grew less vital with every dark, dusty mile of the ride home; in fact he'd be bloody pleased to be out of this place altogether. It might be wrong to bust unions, but it was wrong to have to live like a swaggie on a neverending hunt for employment. He was getting tired of busting a gut at these races to support his friends as well as his mother and sister. If things would only pick up a bit he could go home to the farm and get on with his life. It was all getting to be too difficult bashing around the bush like this. He felt like a gypsy without the violins and the songs.

If he was disappointed with Phil, Jasper was never more than he seemed. It wasn't possible to be disappointed in him, because he never gave signs of being any better or even understanding the concept of trying. A remittance man from England with a kind nature, a bit of a pansy, but that was his upbringing. Well-educated. That appealed to Max. He could talk about books that Max had only heard of and seemed to know a lot about the world and its history. Apart from that and a good laugh now and then he was pretty useless. He began to wonder why he attracted such unreliable friends. It was time he started to mix with people who had a bit more going for them. People like Alice, strong-minded and capable with definite ideas about things, even things she knew nothing about. And she had those tall, fair, Scandinavian looks he liked. He was not good enough for her, by her father's measure. He guessed that most would agree, but he knew he was up to her and she seemed to know it too.

Alice had another aunt in Peppermint Grove she stayed with while she was going to the teachers' training college. It was from there that she wrote to him after the disaster of the Mondaroo Gift Day. He'd thought she might have been browned off and given him a miss. Typically, she didn't pull her punches. She came right out and said she'd heard what happened.

The word got around that Phil was at one of the pubs and cursing you to everyone, saying you were a rotten loser. No one could work it out because you hadn't lost. So I took the car and drove out to Ferguson's to see him. He was ashamed by then and told me the story. I hope you were able to travel without starvation and with enough petrol. I'm sorry you didn't ask me to lend you five pounds. I'd have liked the opportunity to be your friend.

He never found out how she came by his address. But he now had hers. He replied that after the wool was loaded in June he was catching the boat down from Carnarvon, and would come to see her.

ALIENS

Every other Sunday, Karl Fischer, his wife Yvonne, daughter Gretel and ten-year-old twins Billy and Cat, brought Enzo home from mass and stayed for lunch at the Nash farm. They had been living in their shearers quarters since their house was destroyed by fire. Mrs Fischer, always sick and depressed, was at a loss. On her own, she could do nothing about her family's accommodation. She must wait for her husband to say that he could spare the time and money to rebuild. Many suspected that he was in no hurry to spend hard-sweated money on such an unproductive item as a house. Meanwhile, she must wait, and she had no idea for how long. During lunch they would soon arrive at the subject of the dreadful ashy place where their house had been and Max would say, 'After seeding we'll have a working bee. Help you rebuild.' And Karl Fischer would go on eating, distracted, as though the subject did not concern him.

Nine of the ten people at the table were hoping that Mrs Fischer was not crying again but they knew that she was. Even the twins had stopped whispering and passing things under the table to stare at their mother. They sat still and pinned their sharp brown eyes on her, waiting for a volcano to erupt. They had seen it before many times. She took a large handkerchief from her sleeve and wiped her nose. No one paid her the attention she felt she deserved. So many tears had been shed so often by her, and so many words of comfort given, that they had become meaningless. After listening to her sniff for at least a minute, Mrs Nash spoke the needed, the waited-for words.

'It's dreadful for you, Yvonne, but we'll help you. Everyone will help. You have a good cry.'

These last were words of magic. As soon as she heard them she stopped crying and asked how her friend had got hold of jelly crystals for the pudding. Like most people she could be consoled by trivial pleasures not the least in proportion to her sorrows. But she must find solace where she could. She had a weak resolve and an unsympathetic husband. He was a good neighbour but not easily moved by other people's emotions, especially it seemed by those of his wife. He was a survivor in a hard land. It had made him hard or perhaps it had attracted him because he was hardy. Everyone acknowledged that he deserved success. Apart from the Nash family, he had few friends.

There was no doubt that everyone would rally around and help them build a house. The sort of cooperation Max spoke of was different from the cooperation at Giuseppe's home where traditions were in place. In the mountains where he lived and the valley beneath, there were families that had been there for as long as man. Many families had the same surname and were identified by extra surnames, *soprannomi*. Families were tight-knit and helped each other without question. Sometimes this did not help the community to come together as it did here where cooperation was born of isolation. Here, most people's parents, aunts and uncles lived far away, either in a distant city or an even more distant country. They made their family from among their neighbours.

'What will you build it from, this new house?' Giuseppe asked.

'That's his big problem, materials. You can't buy anything even if you have coupons or money,' said Max.

'The war has taken everything,' said Eddy.

'What will you do?'

'Ah, well,' said Karl, 'Max here has the secret, from an Italian too. Mud.'

'Max built his own house from mud.' Gretel, eager to praise, makes two arcs in the air, fingers spread. 'All this.'

'He learnt from an old Italian bloke from Calabria,' her father continued.

'Gino,' said Eddy. 'Whatever happened to Gino? Clever man.'

'He was interned down south somewhere,' said Max. 'We could do with his help.'

'Well, it's better if those sort of people are safely put away for the war at least. We don't want to take any risks. There are enough odd bods about as it is.'

Yvonne Fischer was in constant demand by her own feelings, but knew nothing of the feelings of others. Giuseppe understood what she meant. Enzo, unfamiliar with the idiom, was saved from the insult.

Max, not swift to anger, was showing a little annoyance with his lady neighbour. 'He's not interned any more. They let them all out when Italy surrendered to the allies.'

But it was no use and it was true, she did have grievances.

'I hope they appreciate the humane treatment they're

getting from our government. Our own boys are not so lucky,' Yvonne sniffed, warning of more tears.

In the silence that followed everyone thought of the two boys, one missing in Malaya presumed dead or imprisoned by the Japanese — they did not know which of these options to hope for — and one in Germany, a prisoner of war.

Karl Fischer had made an application for Italian prisoners of war to work on his farm, but he did not qualify as an employer. His parents, now dead, brought him to Australia from Bavaria when he was three years old. He was classified by the government as an enemy alien and considered a security risk.

Giuseppe broke the silence, tentatively addressing Max. 'It must have taken a long time to make the bricks and build the house. It is not a small house.'

'During the Depression. Took about eighteen months. There was nothing else to do. Grain prices were so low we couldn't afford to grow it. Everything we did grow was taken off by hoppers.'

'Who are hoppers?'

'Insects, grasshoppers, we had several years of them.'

Karl sat shaking his head, remembering things he would prefer to forget.

'They stopped the trains,' Gretel chirped. 'So many hoppers on the line the train couldn't get up the hill, too slippery. We all had to cart sand to the rail line and pour it on the track to get it going. And they ate the garden. Every time I went outside they'd get all through my hair.'

Yvonne pulled out her handkerchief again and seemed to be going to dry her eyes, but instead thought of something to say.

'So many couldn't honour their promissory notes. They walked off. The banks just took over the land. It was wicked. They more or less gave it away to the Italians.' She pronounced it Eye-talians. 'Our people opened up the land and it broke their hearts and then they had to walk off with nothing and these foreign immigrants took it all for free. Just got off the boat and took it all on a platter. It's a shame. Why would the banks treat their own people so badly?'

There was a tight silence. The air in the room had been pressed by the vice of her resentment. As part of the despised race, she seemed to need Enzo and Giuseppe to take the blame. Soon she was talking again: 'No wonder they had all those riots in Kalgoorlie. Poor miners. All their jobs given to foreigners . . .'

If there were others at the table who wanted to agree, their sensitivity to the feelings of the prisoners might have stopped them if Max hadn't broken in on her monologue.

'I could spare Vince or Joe if you want a bit of help with the fallow, Karl.'

'It'd be breaking the law. They'd throw me in a camp.'

'How's your ploughing going?'

'Slowly.'

'Didn't think I could see much happening.'

'Had a few breakdowns.'

Giuseppe did not want to work at the Fischer farm. Enzo looked interested when Max said, 'I'll have a word with the control centre. We're going to need Vince's skills when we start building your house.' Giuseppe decided not to tell Enzo what Yvonne Fischer had been saying.

The prisoners had eaten Sunday lunch with the Fischer family many times before. It was a time for them to be quiet and listen, but Gretel wanted to talk to them. She was a pretty girl of eighteen and liked to be admired. Her hair was a curly brown mop framing a face that, with its pert turned-up nose, was all freckles. She had none of Eddy's intelligent intensity or black humour. She was a bright untidy girl, flirtatious. She was eager to involve Eddy in a conversation about coupons and dress fabric. An innocuous subject that caused Eddy to become angry and red in the face and storm outside muttering about needing to bring in the washing. Most of the diners at table knew of no reason why Eddy should behave in this way and were puzzled. The children saw it as an opportunity to leap up from the table and run out of the room after her. Those who did know, like Mrs Nash, chose to ignore.

Giuseppe wondered at the tactlessness of Gretel and Gretel did not for one moment suspect that her being the recipient of Eddy's expensive clothes had anything to do with it. After watching her friend's departure in astonishment, she turned to Giuseppe.

'Why weren't you at mass, Joe?'

'Thank you for asking. You are worried about my soul?'

'Of course not,' she answered, looking quickly at her mother.

Everyone stopped talking to listen. They all wanted to know the answer.

'We thought you might not be well. There's a nasty bug going round, the change of season. Dreadful.'

Mrs Fischer was so interested in ailments she was able to forget that she'd been glancing sly blows at the Italian prisoners and drop into her other persona, solicitous and saccharine.

'I am well, thank you.' Giuseppe was not going to make a disturbance by announcing that he was not a believer, and any other reason he had for remaining at home was his own and would be kept to himself. 'I was a little tired and needed to rest.'

'It's a pity not to make use of the Catholic service. There was no priest at all here until all the Italians moved in. One good thing to come out of it I suppose,' she said smiling, pleased with her own willingness to give credit where it was due.

Max continued talking to Karl. 'I'll come over after lunch and have a look at your tractor if you like.'

Max had the looks they liked in Hitler Youth. Except for the blue eyes, it was hard to see where he and Eddy were brother and sister. He was a man of kindness. His personality spread into the voids of the small and scattered community to give it substance. Without him, time spent at a meeting of the Farmers' Union, the fire brigade or the tennis club would become flaccid and resolution might be at risk, might become elusive. Max was the sort of man who never wasted time, and people were loath to waste it for him.

After lunch he will follow the Fischers' truck on his motorbike. Gretel will make a fuss until she is allowed to ride in the sidecar next to him. They will work until midnight servicing machinery. Fischer has a generator for electricity so there will be light to work by in the shed. He has a tractor capable of pulling a plough, and a plough of a much later vintage than Max's. A more successful farmer than Max, he has more cleared land, and with the work of his sons has survived the Depression better.

Gretel was an unpredictable element at the table: although she looked at Max every possible moment, she directed more of her questions and notice to Giuseppe. He suspected she thought that she would awaken some sort of feeling for her in Max by flirting with him. But Giuseppe showed himself to be a very dull sort of prisoner who did not like to be used for flirtation. Max discussed wheat varieties and superphosphate ratios intently with her father and Giuseppe sat thinking about this bright, bare country with so little rain and such difficulties in cultivation. He wondered whether the hardships of the land made the people more resentful of the newcomer or whether it was the same here as everywhere. His thoughts went back to university days in Trieste. A city colonised by the Austrians. He did not like the Austrians for their habits of invasion but he had many friends who were of Austrian race. These problems of race here seemed trivial to him when he considered his own country, invaded from the north and the south. A few foreign farmers were nothing compared with a whole German army and a whole American army.

After lunch, Enzo headed off south to walk to a neighbouring farm to visit three prisoners who lived there. He would stay into the evening and have a meal which they would cook themselves. Spaghetti and a sauce. The sauce would be left to cook all afternoon while they played cards. Giuseppe, not invited and only half wanting to go, set off north to the rock at Fischers' farm, feeling the icy hand of loneliness clamped about his shoulder. A dark bank of cloud had blacked out the sun and an occasional drop landed on his nose or hand. He would go anyway, and dry off later. There was no comfort in sitting in his hut on a wet Sunday afternoon. He walked past the cluster of corrugated-iron sheds. Someone was in the grain shed. He could hear the scuffle of bags being dragged and the grunts occasioned by the effort required. He went in and found Eddy wrestling with a bag of grain.

'Can I carry that?'

She stopped and looked at him a second. 'Yes. I can't find the trolley.'

Carrying a full bag of grain was a skill he had recently acquired. He could do it, but always with some effort.

'Where do I put it?' he asked, trying to sound nonchalant as he heaved the weight onto his back.

'Chook yard,' she said. 'But we'd better wait, it's setting in.'

He hadn't heard the expression but she had nodded to the open door, and he saw the rain. It was coming down hard on the tin roof and he could hear it as well. He set down the bag and went to the door to watch it fall. He was beginning to understand the meaning of rain in this place. There was no orchestra that could play music to lift the heart like rain played on the roof in a place where only ten inches fall in a year. Coming now, at the start of the season, it made perfect music.

She stood beside him at the open door and took a deep breath. She sniffed the sweet air like a hound. She found the trail and was gone in her mind to the land of plenty. It was the force of life, or the promise of it. He had never seen her so happy and so calm. She was giving off no hate. She seemed content to have him there with her. They stood together at ease, like two old friends. She turned to him, her eyes shining.

'Rain is nothing to you, is it?'

'I have seen a lot of it.'

'I'm sorry for you. You have never felt what I'm feeling now.'

'Perhaps we feel the same when the thaw starts and the trees bud.'

She nodded slowly and looked back to the rain, giving it

her full attention. He would have liked to turn his head and watch her watching the rain.

So this is what it was like, not to be hated by her. To be her friend, what would that be like? Friendship waits for the next joke, for the next shared activity. But he wanted to know the shadows of her soul as well. He could only watch from the corner of his eye the rise and fall of her breasts as she breathed, the pulse at her throat, the moisture drifting from the rain, glistening on her cheeks, and stop himself from telling her how these things affected him.

Across the fence the horses turned their rumps into the wind that bore the rain, their stringy, sodden tails blowing at their sides.

'Do they put up with this weather so patiently because they know it brings green grass?' he said, trying to get his mind onto something else.

'The green will take some days. They'll have forgotten by then. If people aren't good at connecting cause and effect, how can we expect horses to?'

'Always thinking of consequences can stop us from living life well.'

'And never thinking of them makes us stupid.'

And so they stood for half an hour and then together took the grain and poured it into the self-feeders in the chook yard. The smell of wet fowl dropping and feathers was sickly and heavy. The chooks came out of their shelter and pecked officiously at the cracked wheat. The rooster pecked and strutted, pecked and strutted. He couldn't keep his mind on his food.

The twins came running from the house holding two hefty sticks and a tennis ball. 'Play with us, Eddy, please, Gretel won't. Please.'

Eddy was washing her hands under the tap that supplied the fowl yard. She turned to Giuseppe. 'We need four. Can you play hockey?'

'I don't know.'

'Well, here's your chance to find out.'

She threw him a stick, picked one up for herself, and he spent his most enjoyable half hour since he had come to the farm, playing bush hockey between the trees with two ten-year-old children and one irascible nurse. Eddy ruthlessly stole the ball from the children and dribbled it up the field and just before she hit it between the goal trees would allow one of them to steal it back and run away with it. Giuseppe would wait until they needed help and run in to tackle Eddy. A fierce battle would ensue with the children screaming encouragement.

The game ended when Cat fell and skinned her knee and elbow. She was a tough little girl, holding back tears so as not to show weakness to her brother. Eddy took her to wash the wounds under the tap which made them sting and caused a certain amount of dancing about by Cat. Giuseppe produced an almost clean handkerchief from his pocket and helped her to remove the dirt. She was happy again when he bound her knee and secured it with a knot. By this time the wounds were beginning to stiffen and burn. Eddy had gone to take the washing in and Billy had found an ant nest, so the prisoner carried the child into the house on his shoulders and deposited her on a chair beside her mother, who was almost overwhelmed by the horror of it all, and it was only then that Cat shed a few tears.

Mrs Nash stood up. 'Where's Eddy? Why isn't she attending to this? Get her, will you, Joe?'

He stood at the laundry door.

'Your mother has sent me to ask you to come and attend to Catherine's injuries.'

'It doesn't take a trained nurse to apply Mercurochrome and Elastoplast.'

'She will feel better for your attention. You have the power because you are a nurse. She will believe herself cured.'

She put down the washing basket and turned to the first-aid cabinet. She took out the bottle of bright pink liquid, the Elastoplast and the scissors. She walked through the doorway past him giving him a mock scowl as if to say, I don't believe a word you say but I suppose it must be done. He smiled at her back as she disappeared into the shadows of the kitchen. He had been sure that she had a better nature, but until now had not known that it was possible to appeal to it.

SNAPSHOTS

Sunday. Winter. Gloves on for morning frost, sweaters off for midday sun. Giuseppe was at the house mowing the lawn and pretending, even to himself, that he wasn't hoping to see Eddy there. Vincenzo had gone Sunday visiting. Max and the signora were at church. Eddy was sitting on the porch at the oak table poring over books.

'Good morning,' he said and began to oil the mower. She made no reply. Perhaps she hadn't heard him.

The small square of lawn between the porch and the gate was long and straggly and the mower had no motor. Even when he began the rhythmic ratchet ratchet of the mowing she showed no sign that she knew he was there. He had to admit that he was being ignored. After a while she disappeared into the house, ending any possibility of a conversation.

He was raking the cuttings when he heard her scream. He found her in the kitchen surrounded by flames spreading across the floor. He picked up a newspaper and beat at them. They took some time to go out. In the middle of everything the cuff of her trouser caught fire. He stripped the cloth from the table and slapped it on her leg.

'I was filling the fridge.'

'You should have turned off the flame.'

'I hardly need you to tell me that.'

'You are lucky it was kerosene and not petrol.'

'Yes, bloody lucky,' she said angrily.

She was trembling with agitation. He didn't expect thanks for his help and she gave none. He led her back to the porch to sit down.

'No harm has been done.'

'I know, I know.'

She put her head on her arms on the table covered in photographs and howled. He felt alarmed, embarrassed. He wanted to stroke the back of her neck where the hair had fallen away to reveal delicate skin. He decided against that. Instead he would walk away and leave her to her private tragedies, whatever they were, something in the past by the look of the photos. He moved them away from the moisture of her tears and closed the albums.

'I'm sorry,' she sniffed.

'You make a lot of tears for a tragedy that didn't happen.'

'It's not the kerosene. Look.' She rifled through photos spreading them across the table again and picked out one. A small girl was riding on the shoulders of a nearly adult boy. They looked pleased with themselves. 'Max's twelfth birthday. Hal and I won the cock fight.'

He nodded and sat down slowly. Just when he wanted to leave she was ready to talk.

'I don't know what I'll do without Hal. He's not dead. He's missing.'

'You love him very much,' he said, feeling more wretched than he had expected to today. Everything he had said so far had been inane. He knew it, but he couldn't help it, inanity seemed to be the order of the day. She threw him off balance with her acid tongue.

She looked up at him, sniffed and wiped tears from her chin with the back of her hand.

'After Dad went, he was here every day. He did everything, taught Max the farming skills that Dad should have. He's good at everything, smarter than anyone. He wanted to be a doctor, but there wasn't enough money to send him to Adelaide. Such a waste, rotting in the jungle. He's my best friend. The only one I need.'

And getting better all the time, because he was away and in desperate circumstances. It occurred to Giuseppe that there was no one at home grieving for him in this way. His sister had a husband to mourn. His mother no doubt had a contract with the Virgin whereby he would be saved and go to heaven, so the sooner he was dead, the sooner his salvation would begin. There was no point in being jealous of him, this man of perfection. What claims could he ever have, this prisoner of many faults?

'Are you going to marry him?'

'What?'

She jumped up, stung, gathered her photographs and went into the house. He remembered the kerosene on the kitchen floor and went in search of a bucket and mop. The green lino was now patterned with brown and blistered creekbeds. He mopped and listened to her slamming drawers and cupboard doors, making small howls and groans like an animal caught in a trap. She was wild, perhaps a little mad. She was someone who felt everything. He was not permitted to be involved except to clean her kerosene mess. He was embarrassed to have invaded her privacy. He had been stupid to say such a thing but she was a tightly fastened bundle of emotion and anger and he felt the need to strike a match and see if she would go up. Then he could peel back the layers and see what was inside.

'What are you doing, Joe?'

The signora stood in the doorway of the kitchen. He could think of no way of explaining that came out well for Eddy.

'She knows not to do that. Bloody silly.' Max was not impressed. He didn't believe in accidents. He often lectured the men about carelessness. Giuseppe was tempted to try to explain that she was upset, but thought better of it.

The signora said, 'Good thing you were here or it might have been a disaster.'

She stopped him as he went through the door with the bucket. 'What were you doing here, Joe?'

'Mowing. I was mowing the lawn.'

'That was good of you. I didn't ask you to, did I?'

Her voice was taut, high-pitched. She was still holding her handbag and had not taken off her hat.

'It's your day off, Joe, you should take advantage of it. Read, have a rest.'

'If you're so keen, you can give me a hand to draft sheep after lunch.' Max was not happy. He examined the marks on the floor and shook his head.

Giuseppe felt responsible even though he was not. He was guilty of a much greater crime. He thought he might be a little in love with Eddy. Call it 'in love', it didn't have to have a name, nothing would come of it. More accurate to call it obsession. He could be obsessive. His mother didn't like that about him. His father said it would help his work, and he was right, but having an obsession about a person wasn't a good thing. He could handle it though, he thought.

He wasn't about to embarrass anyone. Eddy was a cross between a poisonous snake and a hedgehog and although he was fond of animals some were better kept at a distance.

Lunch was quiet without Enzo and Eddy kept to her room. Halfway through the meal they heard her walk down the hall and let the back door slam behind her.

The signora went to the window and called, 'Eddy, what about your lunch? Where are you going?'

Giuseppe could hear her answer but not catch what she said.

The signora sat down and shook her head. 'She's going for a walk,' she said, as if she were going to the moon. Why would anyone expend energy on walking when there were so many chores to be done?

There are two skills in sheep drafting. Both take time and practice. First, there are the split-second reflexes needed to move two gates between three openings while not stopping the flow of the sheep. Sheep follow each other like a string of beads slipping off the edge of a table. If the gate is not smoothly operated they stop and turn back and it is difficult to set them moving again. At that point they become intelligent. There is never any good to be had at the end of a race. They will be robbed of their coat, their gonads, their young or even their very flesh. Suddenly they know it all, they have understood and will go no farther. But one is undecided, it hesitates. The dog notices everything. He rushes in barking in a frenzy of determination with his mouth on the leg of the sheep, teeth an eighth of an inch from a bite. The sheep can't match the resolution of the dog and it is gone. They all become stupid and forget what they knew for one moment and run to their fates. The second skill necessary for drafting is to be able to train a dog to chase the sheep into the run and hold them there, so that the gate can be shut. It is a two-man job, but it can be done with one man and a good dog.

This cool in the shade, warm in the sun afternoon, they separated ewes from lambs to be weaned and ewes from old ewes to be sold. Max was fast and accurate on the gate. The still air above the yards became clotted with bleating, barking, whistling and shouting. They worked together easily: Giuseppe moving the sheep along the race, calling instructions to the dog who had no trouble understanding his Italian accent, Max concentrating on the gate, looking up occasionally to see that Giuseppe was managing the dog. Max was not stupid, he was bound to pick up something of Giuseppe's penchant for Eddy sooner or later, though it was a matter of pride, as well as survival for him as a prisoner, to hide it from everyone, especially Max.

'You'd better knock off now. It's your day off,' Max said as he closed the last gate. 'The truck will be here at six tomorrow morning. I'd be glad of a hand then.'

Knock off. Sunday afternoon should be knocked off. Knocked off the calendar. Sunny Sundays were the worst. When the sun is shining people have a moral obligation to nature to enjoy it. The sun, bright like this on his idleness, seemed to spotlight him, searching him out to examine him. What it found was a displaced person. He should not be able to like this place, it was his prison, but he felt himself beginning to. A bit like the way he was beginning to feel about Eddy. Maybe the two were linked. Harsh, extreme, inconsiderate. It was all about waiting. It would not last for ever in spite of the thousand-year Reich promised by Hitler. When he went home, after the war, he must pick up a half-baked life he'd fallen into before the war, no longer a student but not yet building a home and family, or he must return to the village. His father would lock him out of the house. He belonged nowhere and to no one. He'd have been happy to spend the afternoon with Max working, but Max had sent him away. Well, he would walk across and see if old Lizzie Harmer had something for him to do.

'I'll go to Lizzie and chop wood.'

'Check at the house to see if Mum wants anything taken over,' said Max as he headed off to the machinery shed.

Plovers swooped low along the fallow screaming in long notes and looking for their nests that had been ploughed away. Giuseppe sank into the moist tilled soil up to his ankles. He was not alone on his journey. He had with him a fine, shiny, black rooster in a bag. The signora was lending it to Lizzie, whose rooster had died, and with luck there would be spring chickens. A rooster in a bag. Just like me, he thought, and trudged on while clay built up on the soles of his boots.

The flywire door was open, swinging in a light breeze. He laid the rooster on the ground and called out. No answer. He could hear someone moving about on the timber floor inside. He called again and turned to survey the farmyard. A white duck was shaking its feathers, settling itself over half a dozen eggs under the steps to the shed.

'What are you doing here?'

Eddy was standing at the door holding death between finger and thumb like a dirty rag. A yellow piece of paper. He knew at once that it was a telegram and in wartime a telegram is death.

'Since you're here you can help. Go back to the farm and ask Max to bring the car. Then ask Mum to phone Doug and tell him we'll take her body to town. I'll stay here with her.'

'Is there nothing I can do here?'

'There's nothing anyone can do now. She was an efficient woman. Got this job done well and truly.'

'Are you all right?'

'Me? Of course, why?'

'You could be shocked.'

'Yes, I'm shocked, I'm horrified, but I'm not in shock. I've laid her out. I'll sit with her until we can get her to the undertaker in town.'

'It is a long way. There is not one here?'

'Where? Where would there be one here? There's no cemetery.'

Giuseppe had to think about that. To live in a place with no cemetery. To live in a place that could not receive your bones when you die, is truly barbaric. How can you attach yourself to a place that will not receive your body back to dust, to make more dust for the future? This place was nearly all dust, blowing in from other places, resting like a red veil over everything. What is not eaten and breathed must stay aloof, ready to blow away to another place. He thought of Filippo's funeral near the camp in Victoria. He had never felt so bare, so alone, standing that day in the cold wind waiting for the coffin to fill the hole in the ground as though that was a job done instead of something precious undone. Not only was Filippo, the most important person in his life, lost to him, but he was lost to himself. Foreign burial. How many soldiers think of that when they go to war?

The hour's walk back seemed like two. His haste made heavy work of the fallow that pulled at his feet like quicksand. There was no hurry, she was already dead, but he hurried anyway. She was dead, because of the telegram.

He wanted to know how she had done it. Did it make any difference to know that she was calm at the end? He thought he was lonely sometimes. Her loneliness had been absolute. Her death was more shocking than the death of her sons. They had died for people like her and when they died she had nothing to live for, so they died for no reason. Bleak world. Cold as the dark side of the moon. The sun was slinking beneath the horizon but the sky was still clear and pale. The new shoots of germinated wheat were pale. The late afternoon air was pale and sweet and cold. Everything was vast and light and washed, except Lizzie's tiny darkened cottage, untouched by abundance and ease for its twenty-five years.

She had been awkward and suspicious with him, but after only two or three visits she looked for him to come. It was easy to like the small wiry woman for her courage. He had never seen her laugh and never heard her complain. She had a mean shrivelled exterior covering a good heart. Her eyelids had folded into a hood that gave only occasional gleams of light from her eyes. She would wriggle on her stomach under her house to get eggs until once she got stuck. He found her and dragged her out by the ankles.

She wanted news. He told her all the news he could remember of people in the district and she filled in their histories for him. It made him listen more carefully at the table and take more interest, because he knew he would have to relay the information. Two outsiders coming together over talk of people for whom they were nonexistent. She never asked him about Italy. His enemy prisoner status was never mentioned. She spoke in a nasal voice that flapped its Rs and squashed the life out of its vowels. She remembered Afghans from her childhood, selling goods, and native girls working as housemaids for her mother, and Chinamen with pigtails, selling vegetables. She remembered a wide dusty street of hotels in the desert gold town where she was born. He sat at her table and drank her weak milky tea and ate her oatmeal biscuits. Nothing was out of place, and nothing was clean. Cotton print curtains hung on wire above the kitchen sink stiff with smoke, dust and grease. Whatever colour they had started life, they had been brown for most of it. If she had been a man, this would have gone unnoticed, but a woman, even a woman who worked in the paddock like a man, was expected to make an effort in the house. To have more delicacy than to eat at a table that had weeks perhaps months of accumulated tannin teacup rings. She enjoyed none of the meagre conveniences of the Nash farm. No refrigerator, no telephone and apart from a passing swaggie, no company. If he had come upon her before she committed suicide, Giuseppe wondered what he would have said to convince her that life was worth living.

Giuseppe and Max carried old Lizzie, now stiff with rigor mortis, down the timber steps of her house and laid her along the back seat of the car. Eddy had wrapped her in sheets from the bed, the only ones she could find. She was a package now without a face. Giuseppe went with them the seventy miles to the town. All three jammed into the front seat. Hardly a word passed between them. They met the policeman and gave him the story.

The trip home was silent except when Eddy said, 'Death is terrible when there is no one to mourn.' She turned to her brother. 'You're a Christian, at least you can believe she's with her sons in heaven.'

'Yeah, but I don't know whether I believe that.'

'Why can't she be buried on her farm?' asked Giuseppe. 'It is so cold to take her away, to put her among strangers.'

'Who would do it? The undertaker won't come,' said Eddy.

'We could do it,' said Giuseppe.

'She's dead. She'll never know. We've got better things to do.'

Irritation, probably due to having seen so many young healthy men die, thought Giuseppe, she didn't like a fuss to be made about dying.

'I know what you mean,' said Max. 'When old Sam Pole died I thought about that, but his sons didn't seem to care where he went.'

They dropped back into silence and Max started thinking as he drove, about Sam's funeral in late 1941, before the prisoners came, before Eddy returned and just before Hal signed up.

Max found himself a pallbearer at the old man's funeral. His two sons and Hal and Max carried the coffin. Except that the shape of a coffin makes it necessary to have four bearers, the weight of Sam's could well have been borne by one. He was a grey wisp of a man by the time of his death. His sons went to his tent to wake him when he hadn't risen to light the fire for breakfast and he was cold. He must have died early in the night. Max didn't write to Eddy about this. He thought she had enough death to worry about. His mother was upset. She stood at the graveside forlorn. The only woman present. Counting Sam, and the clergyman, there was a total of eight to send him off. The shortage of mourners was more noticeable in the church than at the graveside, and more noticeable still at the pub afterwards.

In the flat grassing field and the red shifting dirt of the cemetery no one expected to see a lot of people. Apart from about ten goldrush years in the 1880s when the town had countless hostelries and a daily newspaper, there had never been a lot of people at this place. The graveyard had fifty or more weathered, lopsided headstones bearing the names of young men in their twenties who had died in an epidemic of typhoid fever, and rows of unmarked graves, and of course the children who had died of various infantile fevers, including typhoid. The more recent graves looked pathetic alongside the old. At least the occupants of graves from the goldrush had seen some excitement, had lived in Southern Cross when it was known all over the world for large quantities of gold and the promise of civilisation. One old mine still beat on with its battery like a metronome set to count the time of the past, producing just enough ore to stay open. And the town clung to life by a thread, to service farms being carved out of the heartbreaking bush.

Max couldn't help thinking that, in wartime, the death in his sleep of a decrepit dusted miner, although he was no more than sixty, was not a sad occasion. His wife had run off twenty-three years before, leaving him to bring up the boys. The boys, now in their thirties, showed no emotion on the day. The mourning of their father affected them no more than it caused them to take half a day off work and dress themselves in stiff collars and uncomfortable suits and go to the pub afterwards for a farewell beer. They did notice the absence of their father at the pub. He was not a big drinking man, but all three of them had always drunk together. As with many a bush father, Sam had been taking them to the pub, passing them off for twenty-one since they were no more than fifteen.

Mrs Nash didn't go into the pub. It had no ladies' bar and even if it had she would not have ventured into it. The line between the women who did and the women who didn't enter a pub was as uncrossable as the Great Sandy Desert. Max had a quick drink with the boys while his mother waited in the tearooms and greeted passing acquaintances. She had invited the boys home to dinner that night, but they did not accept. Max could see that such an invitation would embarrass them, even frighten them, where his mother assumed that they wanted privacy for their sorrow. She did not see any incongruity in the fact that she was now inviting to dine in her house the sons of the faithful retainer who had never once been invited to set foot in it. She had felt a fondness for the man even though he had always had his afternoon tea served to him on the verandah. She had suspected that he was illiterate. His way of speaking, though gentle, had been quaintly ungrammatical. He had carried with him the stamp of the labourer, whereas his sons, who had come by their land through their father's generosity, were now landowning farmers — land he had slaved in a mine for and then quietly died for. To many, including Max, the father was worth in intellect and decency ten times more than both sons together.

By the end of the day he had changed his mind about the nature of Sam's death. It was just as tragic as any soldier in the field because no one seemed to be going to miss him, except his mother, and he knew very well that she would soon find a Sam replacement. Since then, the undertaker had left the wizened town of Southern Cross, and the nearest one was a hundred miles in the other direction.

They drove into the farmyard and got out of the car in silence. As he walked away, Max said to Giuseppe, 'I think we should do it.'

Giuseppe knew what he was talking about. Eddy stood listening to the conversation.

'I've got a place in mind,' said Max, 'a little rocky outcrop with tamma, she-oaks. It's our land, but it's better that way because her place is bound to be sold.'

'That is very good. I will help. What shall I do?'

'I'll give Doug a call in the morning and find out what we have to do to get permission. Then I'll phone about a coffin. And when we get a minute we can start digging.'

Both men felt pleased with themselves, and with each other, elated, as if doing this would do the poor woman some good, almost as if she were no longer dead. They stood talking in the cold of the night under the trees. Two fingers of light from the bathroom on the back verandah and the kitchen beside it reached out along the ground towards them.

Eddy waited for the moment to be heard. 'Why are you doing this?'

The two men turned and looked at her. To them the reason was obvious. It was the sort of thing that Max would have done years ago for others, if anyone else had been there to do it with him. The minds of the locals did not move in this way. It was something he could do for Wally and Dan. He had promised to keep an eye on their mother, and if she were brought back here, he could go on doing it.

'It'll be good, Ed. She was such a poor old thing. She loved her land.'

'She hated it.'

'Don't be silly.'

'She stayed on there only for the boys. She had a life of loneliness and slavery. It was a tragedy.'

'I think you're overdoing it a bit.'

'Am I?'

'If her life was not good,' said Giuseppe, 'that is a reason to make her funeral good.'

'You can't believe that it will make a difference.'

'It will make a difference to us,' said Giuseppe.

'Isn't that a little selfish?'

'We should be buried where we belong.'

'Why?'

'I don't know. Something about going back to the dust we come from, like they say in the funeral service, and something about the spirit.'

'Sounds medieval to me.'

Giuseppe couldn't disagree. But was medieval necessarily all bad?

'Don't forget,' Max called as they parted, 'six in the morning, and we'll get busy marking those lambs.'

Marking lambs, relieving them of their tails and testicles, only one step better than the worst job on the farm, killing for meat. It would be a day of knives and blood.

The Reverend Albert Cole didn't bother with a cassock for the occasion. He stayed just long enough to officiate and was on his way as fast as he could go. After the coroner had made his report, Max, Giuseppe and Eddy had gone to town to collect Lizzie from the undertaker. He had been less than friendly at having a customer whipped out from under his nose.

'There she is.' He'd nodded to a blond-wood coffin on a stand in the corner of his preparation room and had gone into his office and closed the door.

The two men had lifted the coffin between them and carried it outside. While they were loading her on the truck,

Eddy had knocked on the undertaker's door and spent a few minutes trying to placate him.

They were sorry Lizzie had to suffer the indignity of travelling on the back of the truck roped down tight in her coffin and covered with a tarpaulin. Max drove as sedately as he could out of respect for his load.

'You succeed in charming the old buzzard any, Ed?' asked Max.

'I felt sorry for him,' she said.

'He's got a monopoly, needs a bit of competition.'

'People like us are a real threat. He doesn't get any corpses for weeks on end sometimes. He relies for his business on the fact that live people are squeamish about dead people.'

The pallbearers had to include Enzo and Eddy. Mrs Nash was the only other mourner. When she saw Eddy prepare to lift the coffin she said, 'You shouldn't be . . . It's not respectful.'

'I feel no disrespect to Lizzie,' said Eddy.

'Well,' said her mother, and then said no more, because there was no man to do the job.

Enzo offered to carve a cross out of a piece of wood. Giuseppe had never seen any signs that the woman was a Christian and the Reverend Albert Cole was behaving in a way that indicated he felt himself greatly put upon. Especially when he had to walk half a mile across a muddy paddock with clay building up under his shoes. The coffin had to be carried across the paddock too, since the ground was too boggy for a vehicle.

The day before, Max and Giuseppe had gone up there to dig the grave. Giuseppe suggested a place under a grey tamma tree. Max pointed out that it was too rocky. Another place was rejected as too damp. Finally, one was chosen sloping down the hill with a view of her farm.

'What a nice view,' said Mrs Nash when the Reverend Albert Cole had finished his prayer. 'Lizzie will be happy here.'

Everyone nodded and murmured in agreement and no one believed it, not for one second.

They walked in a slow shoe-clodded procession down across the paddock towards the house and lunch. Eddy fell in beside Giuseppe at the back. After five minutes she said in a voice only loud enough for him to hear: 'She hanged herself.' As if to make him aware of the full horror of it, that this was not just a picnic day. He did not understand the meaning in the tone of her voice and so did not take the rebuke.

'That was bad, for you.'

'Not for me, for her.'

'She chose it.'

'You never choose that. It's not a choice. It is the only thing left to do. She didn't want anything, could not give anything. She had finished.'

'You think we should not have made this special grave?'

'You know I do.'

'Why?'

'Because she wanted nothing except death. She would not have wanted this.'

'You are so sure?'

'I have seen so many young men, like Wally and Dan, who wanted life and wanted everything so passionately and had so much to give, die for no reason and have no grave, no funeral.'

'Does that mean that Lizzie should not have one?'

'Have you ever seen someone who has been hanged? Do you know what they look like? Do you know what happens to their eyes, their tongue? It is a very angry way to die. If you had seen her, you wouldn't have done all this.'

'You would not let me see her.'

'Now you know why.'

'You wanted to spare me the sight?'

'I wanted to spare her your gaze.'

She walked a little faster and turned her head to look across at Lizzie's house. She was so interesting to him in her contradictions. He was impressed by the level of her understanding and he felt chastened in a vague way. He could not be sorry for the funeral they had given Lizzie, but he knew now why Eddy had opposed it. He didn't entirely agree with her view, but he agreed with how she'd arrived at it and he admired her for it.

MAKING HAY

Inside his head, Giuseppe was a mess. How no one could see that was a miracle. He went on working, talking, eating, with it emblazoned on his forehead. Carved deep into the flesh, E D D Y. He had developed a fixation with a woman whose sight he dreaded and whose absence made him anxious and nervous. He was making an acceptable situation into an agony.

What sort of girl was she? She was not a girl. She had served in army hospitals at the front. He didn't stop to consider that perhaps it didn't matter what she was like, soft and sweet or tough and bitter. She was smart, good-looking in a taut, muscular way that spun his head. She didn't have the even temper of her brother. She worked on an edge of ill humour driven by her intelligence and if she slipped from it into a more settled frame of mind, it was remarkable and didn't last.

The desolation of this place, its long-suffering olive-grey bushes and heroic pink-limbed trees no longer seemed strange. There was nothing to impinge on his thoughts. They were free even though he was captive. There was room here to spread out, lay yourself out like a map and see the pathways. He had never done this before.

He could feel a need for it developing where he had not known of the possibility before. A glimpse down an enticing lane foreshortened by a bend and promising much if he dared to open the gate. There was nothing here by the standards of his birthplace or even the standards of the North African desert. No caravans passing in the distance. No black-shrouded Bedouin community on the way to a place unknown to all but themselves. Where were the nomads here? And yet he did not want anyone else. He wanted space. Instead of becoming larger to fill the emptiness he seemed to diminish to nothing.

He found it was impossible to hold on to the neuroses of a built place. A person must let them go or leave. This place did not want them and they did not want this place. Perhaps without looking for it he had found a place that demanded the spiritual, or at least where the spiritual was possible, or where it was not impossible. Where the personality was pushed out to the margins in favour of the physical which was constantly tested and, after the exertion, it was the spirit that survived. Visitors came from the city and could not bring themselves to step outside the house. A journey to the edge of the verandah tested to the limit delicate and conceited minds. They scuttled away, enraged at being invited to the barbarity of the nothing, eager to the point of hysteria to know that they did not have to stay. He thought it fortunate that he had no choice but to stay.

Just as he was beginning to understand these things, he had allowed his thoughts to fix on this young woman. Her beauty was obvious but everything else worked against it. And it did not. A tough, outspoken young woman was a novelty. At home, women spoke out only in old age. Did she understand meaning, or did her brusque manner describe only strong emotions? Perhaps she really lived to a purpose, when everyone else just shambled along until events overtook them. If so, he wanted to comprehend the purpose. It had something to do with the greater good, the community, morality, selflessness, but she showed no interest in community gatherings and contempt for anyone who didn't measure up. Where he came from these sorts of intense emotional commitments were couched solidly in tradition which usually meant religion and superstition. But she dismissed such things. What was her mythology?

Being a prisoner for so many years threatened to make him abject. He might be pathetic in her eyes, even in his own, but he wasn't soft, and he was in need of a quest, something to counter any saccharine compliance he might be tempted to exhibit. It was a novelty to be the rejected one, unsuitable in every way. But to her he was more than unsuitable, he was a threat. This mystified and amused him. Unless he had the enemy in the sights of his rifle he had never thought of himself as a threat to anything. The two prisoners working for her brother meant her no harm, but they were part of a larger, more dangerous picture. She had her own peculiar honesty. She was not overtly rude to Enzo, she chilled him with formality. He accepted this without comment. It would have been no different at home where his father and grandfather were blacksmiths and he was a carpenter. There he would not have been the social equal of the daughter of a landowner.

Enzo had thrown himself into his work on the farm and earned respect. He was fearless. Much of what they did each day involved some danger, working with explosives, sharp tools, machinery that chopped and sieved, and large fractious animals. Summer threatened sunstroke, winter chilblains. He enjoyed the life. He was good with horses and when Max was too busy, he was the one who drove the team that pulled the machinery.

The prisoners and Max were working a mile from the house, making hay. A warm morning was being polished by a light breeze. The wooden blades of the binder swept mown hay from the ground into a machine that made it into sheaves. It swept the dust through the rays of the sun at the same time. From the back of the machine came neat bundles that flopped to the ground making passive shapes of fodder for the future. Enzo attempted to climb down from the machine before the horses had stopped moving. They had not heard his 'whoa'. His foot slipped on the edge of the step and became caught in the binder. Giuseppe turning to see what in the corner of his eye had moved through the air. Max responding to the cry. Enzo trapped. Max at the front of the horses, backing them, backing. Giuseppe pulling Enzo free and lying him down in the mown rows of stalks with any snake that might have come out to lose its skin. The foot inside the torn boot looked broken at the instep and the flesh deeply lacerated. Enzo's eyes already starting to glaze with shock, his mouth uttering nothing through parted lips. Giuseppe cuts away the boot. Max takes off his shirt and ties it round the foot and the blood pulses through bright red. He pulls it tight to slow the bleeding. Enzo doesn't flinch. Max sends Giuseppe with Enzo back to the house on the motorbike and stays with the horses. The bike crashes and bumps across the pitted ground of the winding track. Quail scatter through the crop and sheep lift their heads and run away. Enzo is grey beneath his tanned face, not making a sound.

Mrs Nash hurries through the house with a saucepan of potatoes she is about to cook, through the garden, calling for Eddy. Eddy runs into the kitchen taking off her gardening gloves. She leaves her large straw hat on her head and orders Giuseppe: 'Put him down here,' and moves the vegetable peelings from the kitchen table to the sink in one movement. 'Bring a pillow,' she says to her mother like a surgeon asking for a scalpel.

She unwinds Max's bloody shirt from Enzo's foot. It is all but severed across the arch, a gruesome wound. Giuseppe's stomach turns. Eddy has seen worse. She dresses it, applying pressure and makes a temporary cast by bandaging a folded newspaper on either side of the foot.

'Put him in the car, on the back seat,' she says to Giuseppe. Seventy miles is a long way to drive in a very old car with an injured man. Giuseppe offers to go with them.

'And what possible use do you think you could be? Are you a doctor?' she snaps.

In contrast, she is reassuring to Enzo, placing her cool hand on his forehead and giving him a clean shirt to wear to the hospital. Her voice has no edge. Giuseppe watches, fascinated. She has transformed herself into nurse and Enzo into patient with no other status.

Five hours later, followed by the policeman on his motorbike, she returned. Enzo stayed at the hospital to be stitched and set in plaster. It would be a week before he was home.

The policeman was a cricketing friend of Max's, not from his team but the umpire. He was better at that. He was a large man in his early thirties with red hair and no visible eyebrows or lashes. Giuseppe remembered him from the hall reconstruction, when he opposed everything Giuseppe suggested. He made no sign of recognising the prisoner. Mrs Nash introduced them. The policeman pressed his lips together, nodded just a little and grunted. He turned away rather than shake Giuseppe's hand. It was fortunate that he had not offered it.

The policeman stayed for dinner and made a meal of it. He ate deliberately as though each mouthful chewed was a duty performed. He picked around his plate, taking equal amounts of each vegetable until he had his fork laden with layers in different colours. Between bites he splayed his knife and fork out each side resting the blade and prongs on the lip of the plate. Giuseppe had never seen someone make a meal into such joyless work. He noticed the policeman look at Eddy often and become nervous when she spoke to him, though it should have been Eddy who was nervous. He had followed her through town when he saw the car speeding erratically all over the road. When he caught up with her, he decided to escort her to the hospital and then home again. He knew she was unlicensed, because to get a licence she had to apply to him. During the meal he asked her if she had gone for her licence while she was away in the army. It would have been better for him if she had lied, but she simply smiled at him, raised her eyebrows and shook her head.

'No, Dougie. No licence, sorry.'

'Don't you think you should get one?' He was too diffident to suggest she was in need of a few lessons and a danger to other motorists.

'Never needed one before.'

'Laws are tighter now, you know. Come over to the station tomorrow and I'll give you a test.'

'Oh come on, Dougie, you know I can drive. Just write me a licence.'

He was embarrassed. He blushed. His fair skin hid nothing.

Max took pity on him. 'I'll bring her over in the morning. All right?'

Eddy muttered under her breath that it was a waste of precious time.

'Joe can cope for an hour while we're away,' said arbiter, problem-solver Max.

Once Eddy had been the family driver. Charlie turned up from one of his trips with something quite unexpected. An Oldsmobile. He had been driven all the way from the city to the farm by the dealer. Only Charlie was able to get that sort of service. When the young man, who had never been outside the city except for a Sunday drive, saw he would be accommodated for the night in a tin and hessian shed house he was aghast. He asked over and over for the timetable of the train as though he kept forgetting the answer. There was one train a day to the city and it always came at the same time. He was up before anyone in the morning, anxious not to miss it. Then he left, having taught Eddy how to drive him to the station. She was ten years old. From then, she was the official driver of the car. No one could understand why Charlie had felt the need for a car that he would not learn to drive. Max learnt soon after, but it was always Eddy who could be spared from chores to drive her father and occasionally her mother as well. She applied at the police station for a licence and was issued with one without a test, as was the practice then, but at the age of fourteen, when testing came in, was obliged to hand her licence in and since then had never got around to having a test. By that time the Depression had begun to bite and Charlie was forced to sell the Oldsmobile along with all other moveable items on the place.

The conversation moved on to the state of Enzo's health.

'I can't see why he shouldn't make a good recovery. He's fit and healthy,' said Eddy.

'Lucky he didn't lose that foot,' said Max.

'Inexperienced, some of these prisoners, don't know a thing about farms,' the policeman sweepingly stated.

'Vince is the best worker I've ever had, I'm sure Joe won't mind me saying that,' said Max, and looked at Giuseppe for agreement.

'It is true, he is much better than me.'

'Well, now that he knows the language, he is. He's smart and he's got more stamina than I've seen in one man.' Max would have gone on praising him if he hadn't sensed that everything he said seemed to work against the prisoner in the eyes of the policeman.

Mrs Nash had seated him in Eddy's usual place to avoid putting him next to Giuseppe. Eddy now sat in Enzo's place beside Giuseppe. Doug paused, holding his forkful of food ready for his mouth, and breathed heavily through noisy nostrils. The rest of the company waited to hear what he would say next.

'Didn't show much stamina in North Africa.' And he pushed the food into his mouth and continued chewing as though he had spoken about the weather.

Max threw a glance at Giuseppe to see how he had taken it. Giuseppe stopped eating. He turned his head and looked directly at the policeman, who would not meet his gaze but smirked down at his plate as he refilled his fork. Eddy and her mother behaved as though they hadn't heard.

'They've got eight nurses at the hospital now, extraordinary,' said Eddy, without making it sound extraordinary at all.

When she stood up from the table and began clearing plates, the policeman watched from under his invisible lashes, unaware of how pitiful he looked. He was no match for her. Giuseppe would have been, in another place at another time. He thought so anyway. She was a challenge that he felt equal to. It was futile to think about such an impossible event, but to think about it clothed the naked hours. He rose from the table shortly after Eddy and excused himself. Everyone except the policeman said good night. Giuseppe was astonished to hear Eddy say, 'Doug, Joe is going now.'

Doug looked up sharply from the crumbs on the tablecloth. 'Yes, good night,' he said and looked back down again.

If Eddy and her mother had not been present his hostility might have been unleashed. Giuseppe might have felt angry if the man had been more intelligent.

Mrs Nash moved to the door. 'Wait a while, Joe. We'll go into the lounge room and you can play for us.'

He knew the others wouldn't want him to stay, especially in view of their visitor's hostility.

'Please excuse me tonight. I'm very tired.'

He had not played since Eddy had come home, so this was the signora showing him special consideration. Eddy played often but not for general consumption. She never played popular tunes, nothing light-hearted. She could be heard at it on Sunday afternoon or before the evening meal, when she thought she was alone. She often played scales and exercises in repetition, arpeggios over and over, and then Bach, the even calculation of notes. Where the exercises were intense and aggressive, the Bach was gentle and controlled. He heard it when he came to stack the firewood on the verandah by the living room door. He stacked quietly so she would not know he listened. It was impossible to make the mallee roots into a neat pile the way he was taught with firewood as a child. While he worked he listened and her music seemed to bare her contradictory soul to his eavesdropping ear.

He sat on the verandah pulling on his boots and he could hear the policeman speaking in the kitchen.

'Max, why do you have the wog at the table?'

'He's OK. He works hard. He's a good bloke,' said Max.

'He's a wog and a Nazi.'

'You mean a fascist,' said Eddy.

'The control centre asks us to have them at our own table,' said Max.

'That's unreasonable.'

'I'd have had him here anyway, like we do any working man.'

'Bloody dagos. Wouldn't treat our boys like this, over in their country.'

As he rose to walk away, the prisoner thought he heard Eddy speak. He thought she said, 'Doug, you don't know what you're talking about,' or perhaps she said, 'There's nothing we can do about it.' Sometimes he wished that his English was not so good.

DANCE

'You've been home a year and hardly shown your face. People are beginning to think you've got fancy ideas.'

'I don't care about that, Mum.'

'You may not, but I do. You'll go away again, but I live here and I don't want people saying you're not interested in your old friends.'

Once there was a dance every Saturday night with a three-piece band, piano, saxophone and drums, to thump out the old favourites, flirtation barn dance, pride of Erin, foxtrot and the modern waltz. Twenty years ago when male settlers outnumbered females by ten to one, men would dance with each other. Young men weatherbeaten into middle age, often obliged to dance in workboots with the dirt rubbed off and freshly oiled. Now such giddy evenings were rare.

'Max, you must take her to the dance. I'm going to Perth to help Grace with the baby.'

Mrs Nash never needed help. She gave it. She had spent a good part of the previous year caring for her sister while she died, watching the cancer suck the flesh from her bones and the light from her eyes. Until the illness, she had envied her sister, whose only hardship was the giving up of domestic staff during the manpower push of the war. Now she could not remember ever having wanted her slim figure and affluent widowhood. All bounty seemed now to be turned in her direction. She spared no effort in making her sister's last months comfortable. Now she would give up her time and energy to her sister's daughter who was about to give birth to her fourth baby while her husband fought in New Guinea.

On the night of the dance Eddy was running late. She was in the kitchen, keeping an eye on the oven. She had her foot on a chair and was drawing a line on the back of her leg with an eyebrow pencil to represent the seam of the stockings she wasn't wearing. She kept stopping to wet the end of the pencil with her tongue. She had plenty of bulletproof army issue but silk stockings were a blackmarket item. Drawing a straight line from heel to back of knee asked for skill. She'd had to scrub it off once already, leaving red streaks on her skin.

At times like these, she remembered what an abiding disappointment she had always been to her mother. She had never developed the culinary art of the supernaturally weightless sponge cake. As a result she had planned to provide some cold poultry for supper at the dance. And because she was putting off the moment when she would finally admit she was going to the dance, she had started the cooking too late and now she and Max were standing in the kitchen waiting. From time to time she took it out of the oven to see how easily its leg moved. It was a tough old bird. Max, always on time or early, was trying to be patient. Finally he headed out the door.

'You've had all day to cook that bloody chook. I'm going to get Joe.'

When he returned with the prisoner Eddy had the bird carved and on a plate surrounded by parsley and was wrapping it in a teatowel. She looked a little odd. The lines on her legs ran out at a rakish angle as they travelled towards the back of the knee, added to which she was wearing one of her mother's dresses, a georgette wraparound number in flesh pink. Not Eddy's colour, nor her size. The wraparound design made it possible for her to keep wrapping until the fabric ended, when she could fasten the tie. She looked bandaged, like an Egyptian mummy. She noticed Joe looking at her as if trying to find the thread that held it all together. No sense in worrying, she had nothing else to wear.

Joe followed them out to the truck and when Eddy, who was sitting on the passenger side, did not look likely to make room for him, he put his foot on the hub of the wheel and jumped onto the tray.

Half a mile down the road Eddy asked, 'Why are we in the truck, where's the car?'

'Couldn't get it fixed in time.'

'Where's Joe?'

'On the back.'

'Why's he on the back?'

'He's coming with us.'

'To a dance?'

'Not allowed to leave him at home on his own.'

'Why on earth not?'

'The officer from the control centre has been going around threatening to take prisoners back to camp if farmers leave them unattended.'

'What's he going to do? Raise an army and capture the railway station?'

'Yeah, well, somebody must think so.'

'Stop the truck.'

'Eddy, we're already an hour late.'

'I know. Stop the truck. Please.'

Max slowed, grinding through the gears. Eddy jumped out and walked to the back.

'Joe, come and sit in the cab.'

'I am happy here, the air is cool.'

'Yes, but you must ride in the front with us.'

'No, this is fine.'

'For heaven's sake, man, you can't arrive on the back of the truck like a sheep or a cow. Everyone will think we mistreat you.'

'It is dark, they will not see.'

'You want to bet? In a place like this everyone sees everything.'

Max stuck his head out the window and shouted, 'Christ sakes, Ed. If you don't bloody well get back in, I'll go without you.' He started revving the engine and engaging the gears.

Frustrated by the intransigence of both men, Eddy was in danger of losing her temper.

'All right. Go. It wasn't my idea to go to this rotten hop.'

'Don't be silly.' He'd seen a few volatile moments when they were kids, but since she'd been in the army she flew off the handle at the slightest provocation. 'Get in, don't be daft.'

'You think it's daft, do you? I'm going to this stupid dance so that my mother can listen to everyone sing her daughter's praises and be mother of the year.'

'What are you raving about?'

'Just so long as she's happy, everyone else can go hang.'

Max groaned. 'Whatever you say. Now get in.'

'She prefers the prisoners. They're a cause.'

'Eddy, cut it out.'

'Yes, I think I will. Go on your own. I'll walk home.'

'Suits me. See you later.'

She turned and stepped out along the unmoonlit road on her high heels trying not to break an ankle in the potholes, angry and foolish, and wondering why she could not bear the thought of this harmless dance. Perhaps because there would be so many old friends missing. Hal, Jimmy, Wally, Dan. Wally and Dan dead, Jimmy a prisoner of the Germans, Hal a prisoner of the Japanese. He was worse than dead. She threw back her head and bellowed like a calf caught in a fence. When her voice faded she heard a boot on the gravel. She turned and could see only black. Whoever it was slowed his pace.

'Eddy, it is Joe.'

'What are you doing?'

'Max did not wait for me.'

'He thought you were sitting on the back.'

'I climbed down. I was waiting to get in the front. Waiting for you to get back in.'

'I can't believe it. You caused an argument between Max and me because you wouldn't get in the front and then you changed your mind, and didn't say anything?'

'It was not easy to interrupt the argument.'

To hear him say the word argument was infuriating to Eddy. 'You could have tried. Max'll think you've fallen off and come back for you.'

'You are not afraid to be here on your own?'

'What can hurt me in the bush? There are no tigers in Australia.'

'There are people.'

'What people? You?'

'You are never afraid?'

'Not out here.'

He walked to the side of the road and sat on a log.

'What are you doing now?'

'If Max is coming back for us, there is no need to break our legs on this dangerous track in the dark.'

She stood on the road. To walk on would be pig-headed. She did not feel pig-headed. She groped her way across the ditch and sat on the other end of the log. The darkness hid an odd sight, he in his Australian army uniform died red, she in her funereal winding cloth dress. They stayed silent until Giuseppe said, 'Are you all right?'

'What do you mean?'

'You were upset.'

'No, I was angry.'

She didn't regret what she'd said, but she did regret that she'd shouted. She couldn't remember if she'd shouted to be heard over the engine or from ill temper. 'I didn't mean to shout,' she said.

Giuseppe laughed.

'You find it funny?' she asked.

'I find it surprising.'

'That I can be angry?'

He laughed again, unconcerned by her irritation.

'That you are so angry with your mother.'

'My mother?'

'You think she is too good to the enemy prisoners.'

It was the truth, but admitting it made her look mean. 'Yes,' she said, but that was not the truth either. 'No. I mean, everyone should be well treated.'

'You cannot think she likes us, prisoners of war, better than her daughter?'

'I don't know what she likes.'

'She was not happy when you were away.'

Here on a log in the dark with a prisoner of war she was discussing her mother. What business was it of his? They sat in silence again. After some minutes she began to see the joke. It really was quite funny. Max was right. She was raving. What was the point in being bad-tempered? In any case, the feeling had passed.

'I'm not angry with her. She wants people to be happy. She sometimes forgets that I am people.'

'How many people?'

'Me? Quite a few. There's me the nurse — professional, dull, funny hat. There's me the concert pianist — artistic, difficult, famous. Me the farm worker — argumentative, muscular arms, funny hat.'

'Which one is really you?'

'One I haven't mentioned. Me the gaoler. Keeper of prisoners of war.'

She could hear him breathing. She could hear a distant sheep bleat, a few willy wagtails colonising the trees across the road, and the night silence left by the other birds. She had been holding her breath and let it out on, 'Sorry,' and wanted him to hear it, but could not say it loud enough to make sure he had.

Then they could see the headlights of Max's truck returning. They stood apart and the lights picked them up in the middle of the road. With all three of them in the cab, Max turned the truck around and drove back towards the community hall muttering things about it hardly being worth going at this hour.

They walked into the hall together. Max spotted some friends and disappeared out a side door with them. Eddy, aware of standing with Joe inside the door with everyone staring, scurried off towards the kitchen with her plate. When she returned to the hall she saw a colourful row of prisoners sitting together at one end in their burgundy uniforms, chatting and laughing and swaying to the music. Two of them jumped to their feet and danced a few steps, springing about on bent knees, and sat down again to the cheers of their friends. Giuseppe stood at the end of the row. Occasionally he turned to one and spoke a few words. Eddy sat next to Yvonne Fischer and watched the dance.

A hotchpotch of sizes, shapes, colours and rhythms shuffled and bounced along in front of her. In the corner, a group of small girls in party frocks danced with each other. Cat was there, with her hair painstakingly ringleted, bossing the other girls, organising and lining them up. Billy stood in front of the drummer with his hands in his pockets watching his every move. Eddy's gaze wandered from time to time towards the red corner where the prisoners sat. People came by in ones and twos to ask her about the war, where she had been, what she had seen. Had she seen their son, their nephew? No one asked her to dance. Max trotted by, each time with a different woman in his grasp. He loved to dance and never missed a set.

Gretel was in the prisoners' corner speaking to Giuseppe. She had a tendency to exhibitionism. He smiled and nodded. Eddy watched with irritation. It would draw attention to him. Make him look like some sort of Lothario. There were always rumours about the prisoners. The word was that the Latin in them made them hot-blooded and irresistible. Everyone knew that it was strictly against the law to have romantic dealings with prisoners, but even women who fraternised without romantic intentions were considered cheap, and the prisoner branded a troublemaker. Rumours about poor old Alf McClusky bounced and rebounded through every conversation. His isolated farm was twenty miles north of Grey Tamma Farm. People said that they had a *ménage à trois* operating there. He was in his fifties and his wife in her thirties. They had no children. They had taken only one prisoner to work for them because they could not afford more. The story went that a liaison had grown up between wife and prisoner. When Alf wanted to send the prisoner away she threatened to leave. So he moved out to the spare room while his wife and the prisoner shared the marital bed. It was an unsuitable marriage from the beginning and now it had turned into hell for him. In general, the gossips were contemptuous of Alf for putting up with such humiliation, but there were those who pitied him.

Gretel was trouble. She was laying Joe open to the same sort of speculation. She would never think of someone else's comfort. She was spoilt and selfish, not a bit like Hal, and she was wearing Eddy's blue crepe de chine, cut off at the knees. One of those colours that stays with you. It had grey in it but it had light as well, like a winter ocean. She looked lovely. Just when Eddy was beginning to feel quite uncomfortable Yvonne said, 'What is that child doing now?' and she leapt from her seat and grabbed Max by the sleeve as he was about to disappear out the door again. The music struck up and he went to Gretel and took her by the elbow and led her to the floor. Giuseppe watched expressionless, hands in pockets. The way Gretel pursued Max was transparent, but Eddy figured that it was better to watch them dance than for her to make a fool of Giuseppe. He was safe now, in spite of the smile he had given her.

When Yvonne resumed her seat, Maisy Spry leaned across Eddy to Yvonne and shouted over the music, 'What was your girl wanting with those dagos? I wouldn't trust them.'

'No,' said her friend, 'they stick together.'

Maisy then turned to Eddy and said, 'That's that Joe Lazarus. One of yours, isn't he? Been giving you any bother?'

'They're not criminals, they're soldiers.'

Eddy fled outside to stand in the dark and cool off. This stupid dance. Stupid because it brought her up against people who caused her anguish. She wanted to think properly of Maisy. She wanted to love her humanity. All she could do was dislike or pity her. To her, Maisy breathed in sweet air and let it out putrid. Eddy felt that if people took the trouble to get to know others they could not feel superiority, and now here she was feeling superior to Maisy and she did not want to get to know her better. She had no interest in her. She felt disappointed to be of the same sex.

Behind her the hall reverberated with music and the rhythmic shuffle and thump of footsteps, alight, alive in its brown creosoted skin, buzzing delirious like the inside of her head in the throes of malarial fever. And all these signs of life were unwanted by her. They were the wrong signs. This was her home. These were her people, but they did not feel connected to her any more than she did to them. She stood in the shadows near the door and longed for silence. Unlike the farmers who lived and worked in silence all the time, she had worked in noise and bustle, shelling and screaming Stukas.

At eleven, the band left their instruments. The saxophone was placed with consideration on a chair of its own and the drums were turned over to a pack of jostling bare-kneed boys. Children of all ages ran on to the dance floor and began to slide up and down, racing from one end to the other, little girls holding hands and screaming, boys elbowing and shoving. The men had brought beer to drink in conspiratorial groups around the boots of cars. It was illegal to drink in the hall or in any public place, but flouting the law was acceptable providing it was done by starlight. While the women, children and prisoners ate the food displayed on a trestle table near the band, the men disappeared out into the dark to their cars and trucks and came back smelling of beer. For the next dance, the women would put up with partners who were benevolent and patronising and a little or a lot out of step.

Eddy stayed outside watching the men drink. She wanted to go over and join them. She wanted to put a foot on the fender of a car like they did and lift a bottle to her lips and to talk about ploughs and football and swap disaster stories and laugh about sexual escapades in the city. And she wanted to do all this while still wearing a pink dress and lipstick. She saw them there and felt alone. If she walked over to them their conversation would stop. They would be embarrassed for her, even hostile. No one would offer her a drink. She had never seen a woman drinking with the men outside. These men had not been to war, not lately anyway. They did not know that women near the front were in great demand for conversation and that their opinions were listened to with interest.

Here, women spoke to other women, not to men, and their talk was called gossip. Eddy had no talents in that area and wanted none. Early in life she had learnt to despise gossip in order not to be despised by men. But that reason had faded and now she saw only the restrictions of a conversation where judgements and disapproval were put on every topic, ahead of anything that might be useful information, or a new idea. Maybe the men had just as many uncharitable thoughts as the women, but they didn't speak them. She had a shadowy understanding of the meaning of gossip and why it was a female domain. She knew that it was about collecting knowledge, the having of which gave the collector authority. She knew it was the only place where men did not go and where women ruled. She rejected it as a desirable place to go. She was too young to believe that this had to be so, that there wasn't a more useful way to have a say. A man walked between her and the cars through the strips of light escaping from the hall windows. She knew the walk and the coloured uniform. He saw her and stopped. He stood in a strip of light, looking at her and hesitated. Perhaps he also wanted someone to talk to. He moved to approach. She wanted him to stand beside her and talk to her. She saw one of the drinkers beyond turn to look. She looked down at her feet and went quickly up the steps into the hall.

If Giuseppe was growing tired of being a prisoner, this evening was designed to make him even more so. He walked about in the dark for a while and then sat on the step where he had seen Eddy standing earlier. Back in the hall, Eddy noticed he did not rejoin the group of prisoners in the corner. She thought about his loneliness out there in the night. He would be waiting at the truck when it came time to go home. He never gave them any trouble. Guilt for the insensitivity of her earlier remark made her think for the first time about his situation. She had always hated the way everyone sat around the edges of the hall and the way the men rushed across the floor to find a partner when the dance was announced, but now with the prisoners stuck along the end together in their strange fancy dress, it was barbaric. She had not felt anything much for them until now. Wasn't her friend in prison somewhere in Malaya? Why should she feel for these men whose lives were so easy in comparison? But tonight she thought of the years that had separated them from their wives and children. She watched them talking and laughing together, and hoped that Hal and Jimmy still had enough spirit to laugh with their fellow prisoners.

When the last set was announced someone asked her to dance. Herbie Cann. Middle-aged, thin, badly shaven, no tie, his plump wife never danced. She spent her time in the kitchen. Eddy refused him and had to watch the look on his face turn to disappointment and shame, and was sorry but could not bear to think of herself smiling into the face of this man who seemed to have lost another tooth every time she saw him. The thought did flicker through her mind that the shame was only hers.

After midnight, they bumped and crashed home in the badly sprung truck over ruts and potholes. Eddy, between the two men, was clutching the empty plate and wishing there were some way to lift the spirits of the silent prisoner. She was mortified for him.

Max began to talk. 'Well, what did you make of your first Australian dance, Joe?'

'The men and women are separate. They dance but they do not talk.'

'You don't go to a dance to talk, you go to dance.'

'Many of the men did not dance. They stood at their cars with their beer.'

'Yeah, I'm afraid you're wise to us. We're a nation of social cripples.'

Giuseppe laughed and said, 'Only the men, not the women.'

'The women let us get away with it. So they're to blame.'

'Women are always to blame,' Giuseppe said and both men laughed. Eddy could sense them colluding to tease her.

'Did Gretel ask you to dance?' Eddy asked as though she hadn't heard a thing they had said.

'She asked me about Enzo. When he would be home.'

'I'm going to get him on Monday. You can come if you like,' said Max.

'It is good that you bring him back, even though he cannot work.'

'He didn't want to go back to the camp, and it's pretty quiet around here just now. By the time things get going again he'll be back on his feet.'

There was a pause in the conversation and then Max asked, 'Why didn't you dance with Herbie, Eddy?'

'I couldn't.'

'Why not.'

'I don't foxtrot,' and, she thought, I don't dance with men who don't clean their teeth.

'You used to, you knew all the dances.'

'Well, I've forgotten,' she lied.

In the morning she woke early and headed down the path through the tall yellow grass to the cow bails to help with the milking. She found Giuseppe already at work. The iron roof was starting to radiate heat into the shed. He did not look up to greet her. She took an empty bucket and a stool and sat down beside one of the waiting cows. The only sounds were of the milk's neat stream swiping through the froth of his half-full bucket and the zing-zing as it hit the sides of her empty one and the cows' slow chewing of the hay. In half an hour they had filled four buckets. They let the cows into the paddock. There was no market for butter on a Sunday, so they poured it straight into the trough of the grateful pigs. One they took to the kitchen to be scalded and used for cooking and clotted cream.

On the hob of the stove half a pot of porridge stood coagulating around a wooden spoon. Max had already gone out to shift sheep. No one ate porridge in summer except Max. Eddy picked up the pot and sniffed the contents.

'Don't suppose you want any of this horrible glue.'

'It tastes very bad. It is bad on the tongue. Slimy.'

'What would you like?'

'Coffee, fresh bread, jam.'

'How about tea, toast, and help me pick some apricots so I can make some jam for another day.'

She handed him an empty bucket and compliant, without words, he disappeared into the garden to do her bidding. When she had made the breakfast she went to find him. He had filled the bucket and was sitting on the edge of the verandah looking up into the trees.

'What are you doing?'

'Watching the birds eat the fruit.'

'Twenty-eights. They'll eat everything in the garden if you let them.'

She crossed the verandah and went through the casement doors into Max's room and came back with his .22

rifle. She filled the breech and handed it to him. 'You'd have to be a better shot than me.'

He looked at her surprised, but she would not meet his gaze. He hesitated a second, but took the gun and walked slowly to the middle of the lawn and, hidden by the lower branches of the cape lilac, put the sights to his eye. The shot dislodged a bird from a high branch. It thudded in a heavy lump at his feet.

'Now it is twenty-seven,' he said grimly.

She wasn't enjoying this. She had been shooting birds as pests since she was twelve years old, and rabbits and foxes and kangaroos and emus. Only the rabbits were used for food, the rest were left for the crows. It was all part of being able to survive on the land and make it productive. For the first time she thought about the killing, about what it was they were actually doing. It was just like war, indiscriminate killing. It made her sick. The green tree shadows on the lawn were darkening and moving as the sun rose higher. In the deep shade, shadows played about the way they had always done when she was young. She was being crowded and buffeted. There was hardly enough room for the two of them to stand under the tree. She felt bitterly sorry for killing the bird.

He stood quite still for a while. Then he turned to her. 'We won't shoot them,' he said softly.

'I know,' she said, 'I mean, no.'

'You are not so hard-hearted.' The warmth was coming back into his voice, the energy into his face.

She could feel herself turning red. Why would he describe her as hard-hearted? She was compassionate. 'No,' she said shaking her head. 'No.'

Another parrot landed on the fence. Green with yellow collar and stomach, its head and wing tips singed black. An identical bird came to rest beside it and they began to nod and chirrup together. They flew as if in agreement to the apricot tree and worked their way around it with measured sidesteps and turns, swinging between thin branches to get to the fruit. Balancing on one foot, the birds picked the fruit with the other foot and brought it up to their beaks and bit off pieces and tongued them around their mouths and swallowed before taking another bite.

'They are beautiful.'

'They eat our fruit.'

'They are hungry.'

'I know,' she said again.

He put his hand in his pocket and took out the other bullets and poured them into her hand. He smiled. She could see that his spirits had lifted.

'You are not altogether hard-hearted yourself,' she said.

'Whatever of this fruit would have been ours, today is theirs,' he said.

And whatever they had killed and hurt and wounded in the past, was to stay in the past. To show that they could kill, meant that they could turn the gun on each other.

'You are not a good gaoler to give your prisoner a gun,' he said, handing it back to her.

She had given him the gun on the spur of the moment and if there had been a risk, she felt it worth taking to salve the insult she had dealt him by the side of the road before the dance. It was a chance to apologise.

'I don't want to be a good gaoler. I don't want to be any kind of gaoler. I wish the war would end and you could go home and Hal would come home. I shouldn't have said that last night. I meant it to be a joke.'

'It was a joke.'

'It was a rotten joke.'

'Yes.' He turned and smiled at her. 'It was a rotten joke, but a joke all the same.'

'You are alarmingly honest.'

'When it suits me,' he said, and she laughed.

When they turned back to the house he said, 'You did not dance last night.'

'No one asked me.'

'You were the most beautiful girl.'

'Not much competition.'

'Gretel is pretty.'

'So she is, and she dresses well too. Wonder where she gets her clothes.'

'Not from Paris, I think.'

'I wouldn't be so sure about that.'

'You don't like Gretel.'

'Well, I do actually, I've known her all her life. But she has a few things to learn. She's interesting, and full of ideas, but she's vain and selfish.' Her words echoing in her ears sounded hard and critical and indiscreet.

He was not thinking about her words. 'Did you want to dance?'

She stopped, taken aback, deciding whether to answer. She didn't have to answer a question he shouldn't have asked. 'I don't know.'

'Do you like dancing?'

'Look, I realise it's because your first language isn't English, but you shouldn't be asking me such probing questions.'

'Because I am a prisoner.'

'Because you don't know me that well.'

'It is the same in my language.'

'Well then, you know what I mean.'

'You think it too familiar for me to ask if you like dancing?'

'Yes I do. Anyway, I had no opportunity. Let's change the subject.' She disliked his curiosity more because she should than because she did. He knew her well enough to know that if she had been determined to dance, then she would have danced.

'I think they don't ask you because they know you wait for this Hal.'

'This Hal, as you call him, is not my boyfriend. He is my good friend.'

He gave her a look of disbelief, at which she knew she should be annoyed but at which she felt flattered. Flattered that he might be having trouble imagining a man who was cool-blooded enough to be just a friend to her. He was still asking questions. She knew he could sense that she didn't really object.

Back in the kitchen eating breakfast he asked, 'Will you come back here to live after the war?'

'I shouldn't think so.'

'It is your home.'

'There's no life for me here.'

'You are a good farmer.'

'I'm a nurse. Anyway, Max lets me work in the paddock because there is no one else and because I used to as a child. But I'm not a child now. After the war, everything will go back the way it was. Men in the paddock, women in the kitchen.'

'So you will live in the city.'

'I expect so, though I don't like the stupidity of the city. The self-importance, the laziness, the greed, but I expect I'll live there. I enjoy my job.'

'You find more stupidity in the city than the country?'

'Infinitely more. City folk are smug and parochial.'

'You are hard on them.'

'Doesn't matter what I think. I'll need to be in the city if I want interesting work.'

'Yes?' He smiled at her. He was a good listener.

'In Egypt I worked with a plastic surgeon. A clever man. At first nobody wanted him there. No one could figure out why on earth they'd send someone like that to a war zone. They gave him a theatre just to humour him. But after two months they could see what he did was so much better for fast recovery. He changed everything. It was exciting work.'

'You help people. Like your mother.'

'I get paid. She does it free.' She was pleased to see him animated again and to know that she had not dented his pride permanently. 'Tell me about your home,' she said.

'Do you know me well enough to ask such questions?'

'Not really.'

They both laughed.

'What do you want to know? It has not been my home for a long time. It has walls of stone and a roof of stone. It is cold. It is often full of smoke because it has no chimney.'

'Not the house. The family, the life.'

'But the smoke is important. It fills the house and leaves no room for words. And so it is a house of silence. The cold stone walls paralyse the throat. All the energy is kept for toil.'

'Was it always like that?'

'As long as I can remember. After ten years of age, I lived with my grandparents in the town, in the valley, to go to school. They were different. My grandmother came down the mountain to marry my grandfather, and my mother went up to marry my father. My grandmother used to say, "Even a handsome man grows ugly if he lives in poverty." It is only since I became an adult that I realise she had been talking about my father. She knew what her daughter's life would be, she had seen her own mother live it.'

'And so you stayed away from your parents' house.'

'Yes.' He put his elbows on the table and held his head in his hands, sliding his fingers into his hair. 'It will be very bad there, now that the Germans occupy. The communists come in small bands for help from the farmers. If the farmers help them, the fascists come and kill them. If they do not help the fascists they will be killed, if they do then the communists will kill them. I cannot bear to think about it.'

'Your grandparents will help them.'

'My father is too proud. Anyway, there is nothing they can do.'

She looked at his fingers threaded through the brown curls on his head and thought, well done, Eddy, you've made him miserable again.

COMFORT FOOD

Eddy lit a fire under the copper in the laundry. It was Monday and since her mother was away, she would have to do the wash. The prisoners washed their clothes, but clean linen was supplied from the house each week. While the water in the copper was heating she took an armful of clean sheets and towels and headed for the prisoners' hut. Inside, the beds were made and everything arranged to advantage. An alarm clock and a framed photograph of Enzo's family stood at one end of the starched runner her mother had put on the chest of drawers between the beds, on the other end was a neat pile of books with marks at various points. Above Enzo's bed a small wooden crucifix was fixed to the wall. It looked like something he might have carved himself. On the windowsill an arrangement of wheat heads and gumnuts poked out of a handleless cup. She wondered which of the prisoners was responsible for that. Against the wall, half hidden by the wardrobe, were a number of boards that looked to be unframed paintings, roughly wrapped in cloth and tied with string. Vince perhaps, she thought, was a bashful artist.

She stripped Enzo's bed and remade it tight, symmetrical, free of twist or wrinkle. She worked fast from habit. She stripped Giuseppe's bed and was unfolding a clean sheet when the door opened and revealed the prisoner himself. The contrast between the darkness of the hut and the brightness of the day prevented him from seeing her at first. He ran up the three steps and stopped inside the open door. She froze as though he had caught her riffling through his drawers. They stood for a moment without moving. The look on his face was of the greatest surprise. He did not move or take his eyes from her face. She dropped the sheet on the mattress as if it had burnt her fingers.

'I thought you'd gone with Max.'

'Why do you do this?'

'It's wash day. My mother's not here.'

'I will do it.'

He picked up the sheet and spread it over the bed. He went around the edges tucking in first one sheet, then another, and finally the blanket. When he had finished, he stood back and looked at his work.

'Not as good as yours,' he said pointing at Enzo's bed. 'You have made nice corners. Medical corners.'

'Hospital corners,' she said, and then wondered if he had made a joke, if his English was good enough. She gathered the used linen into her arms.

'Let me,' he said taking it from her.

'I can do it.'

'I do not want you to do these things for me.'

'My mother does them every week.'

'It is not the same.'

She knew it wasn't, but didn't know if she wanted him to say it. He helped her fish the boiling linen out of the copper and rinse it. He turned the handle of the wringer while she fed in the sheets. He carried the heavy basket to the line that drooped between two sturdy gums and lifted the wet articles for her to peg. Then he went to the prop and hoisted the laden line high into the air, much higher than she could. The wet items at once caught the breeze and began to flap in long heavy waves. The prop strained the line tight. She wondered if she would be able to get it down.

'This is heavy work,' he said.

'My mother does it on her own every week.'

'Next week I will help her.'

'I don't think Max would like you taking time from work. I'll help her.' A moment passed and then she said, 'Is Vince an artist, a painter?'

'I do not think so.'

'You?'

'Not me.'

'There are paintings in your hut, wrapped up.'

'Filippo. He did them in camp.'

He was speaking slowly, retreating from the conversation. She sensed a reluctance to discuss them. She looked for a way out.

'You could hang them up.'

'I never look at them. I have things to do in the shed,' he said.

'I'm sure you do. Thanks for the help.'

He nodded and stood watching her lean down to pick up the basket. She turned with the basket on her hip thinking he'd gone. They stood for a few seconds.

'What are you doing in the shed?'

'Putting the harvester together.'

'On your own?'

'I have done it before.'

She watched him from the steps of the verandah, walking back to the shed with his head down and hands in his pockets. He was beginning to come around corners and appear out of nowhere, and when he did a sort of cold underlying loneliness in her went away.

Enzo came home pale and in poor spirits. He'd been the object of visits from many POWs from other farms, even some he'd never met before. The hospital food had made him devious. He'd engineered schemes to get rid of the inedible grey stews that looked like plates of boiled mice, defeated grey mashed potato and collapsed cauliflower. His prisoner friends brought him bowls of spaghetti, which he ate under the disapproving gaze of the nurses.

Eddy set up a daybed for him on the verandah of the farmhouse. He spent most of his time carving at a piece of wood that he was making into a jewellery box and the rest writing long letters home and looking at ancient Italian magazines brought to him by the officer from the control centre. He was subdued for the first time, showing signs of depression, not unusual after an operation or an accident. Eddy tried to lift his mood. At breakfast the morning after his return she asked Giuseppe if he could cook.

'A little. When I was a student I cooked for myself.'

'What can you cook?'

'Nothing interesting. Pasta, risotto, polenta, a few other things.'

'Would you cook spaghetti for us? Vince bought some from the canteen.'

Giuseppe couldn't hide his surprise at this sign of consideration for his fellow prisoner. He looked at Max to get an indication of the sincerity of the request.

Max grinned and nodded. 'You can knock off an hour early tonight.'

At sundown Enzo sat at the table and watched. Eddy found pots and implements and set them out on the table.

'Where is the oil for frying?' Giuseppe asked, returning from the pantry with an armful of onions and tomatoes.

'We use mutton fat.'

'You have no oil?'

'What sort of oil?'

'Olive oil.'

'Olive oil. I've got a small bottle in my medical chest for rubbing on rashes.'

He stood looking at her, waiting for her to offer it to him. When she didn't, he said, 'Do you have a rash?'

'No,' she said with a laugh, astonished at such a personal inquiry.

'Then I would like to have some to cook.'

She wondered that he did not just get on and use mutton fat, why he must have every detail correct, when she was going out of her way to be friendly. He should not push, he should appreciate small privileges. He followed her out to the first-aid cabinet hanging on the laundry wall and stood behind her while she opened it.

'This stuff is so difficult to get now in wartime. It's imported.'

'I will buy a bottle for you from the control centre canteen. You will not be without it for long.'

The way he spoke, looking at her with a half smile, made her feel wrong to have resented him the minute before. Why should she object to him using the oil? The bottle had never been opened. It was still full. She had put it there almost a year ago when she first came home. Giuseppe had a lack of formality in his dealings with her now. It was not cheek, it was just that he was comfortable with her. She knew that stage when an acquaintance becomes a friend. One has to make the first move. It had been her. She had made a succession of moves. She had handed him a rifle and bullets. She had let him help her do the washing. She had invited him to cook. Still, it did seem wrong that so many luxuries were available to prisoners from their mobile canteen and not to ordinary Australians. Who was winning this war?

When they sat down to steaming bowls, the two prisoners had smiles on their faces. Max was delighted with the occasion.

'Smells pretty good,' he said. 'What we need is some red wine.'

He sprang to his feet and disappeared into the living room and they could hear him rummaging about opening and closing cupboards. He returned holding aloft an ancient and dusty bottle with no label. After a further rummaging he found a corkscrew. Glasses were poured, and raised. There was a brown rim at the top of the dark liquid, the bouquet was of a musty pile of unwashed clothes. The prisoners took a polite sip and said nothing. Eddy stood up to fetch a jug of water.

'Bit long in the tooth,' Max said in understatement. Enzo looked mystified, and Giuseppe laughed.

'Where on earth did you get it?' asked Eddy.

'I think I was given it for my twenty-first birthday. I thought wine was supposed to last for ever.'

'Different wine, different climate,' said Eddy.

Enzo and Giuseppe conferred for a moment in their own language.

'Enzo wants me to get his bottle of grappa from the hut,' said Giuseppe.

'Grappa? You have wine in the hut?' Eddy was astonished.

'Not wine exactly. Grappa is distilled, like brandy.'

'Where did you get it?'

Giuseppe looked at Enzo and then shrugged and said, 'The prisoners on the Hoadley farm gave it to him. They have a still.'

'Yeah? What happens when the control centre officers do their inspection?' asked Max.

Giuseppe turned to Enzo and spoke in Italian again.

'They keep the still in a shed, a long way from the house. The officers do not know it is there. Would you like to try it?'

'Eat your dinner while it's hot, we'll have some later.'

The prisoners ate with concentration. Eddy could sense their smiles, even if she could not see them. Max cut his spaghetti into two-inch lengths which made him slow to start, but once started he made various comments to Giuseppe like, 'This is all right, you know.' Eddy had eaten spaghetti before, but this tasted better than the meal covered in strong-flavoured cheese she had eaten in a Fremantle café. She was pleased that her plan had worked. In fact, she felt really happy. Even she was capable of feeling the effect of comfort food.

Afterwards, they all sat on the verandah and sipped grappa. They discussed the details of the making of it and where the neighbour's prisoners got the grapes to make it. They became relaxed and Giuseppe was able to hear again the sound of Eddy's laughter.

* * *

At two a.m. Eddy sat up in bed aware of a light moving around the kitchen. She tumbled to her feet snatching up her gown. Giuseppe, in pyjamas, was looking into a drawer trying to see its contents by the light of an oil lamp. He jumped when she spoke.

'What are you doing?'

'Looking for aspirin. Enzo cannot sleep. He has pain.'

'He'll need something stronger than aspirin.' She went to her room and brought back a bottle of pills. 'I'll come down and take his temperature.'

They headed off into the dark in the circle of the lamplight. The air hung about between the trees, still as death, no cricket sounded, nothing broke the shell of silence until the low burn of an aircraft pierced its eastern corner. She stopped and held her breath. A droning aeroplane high in the sky at night, even in this forgotten corner, terrified her. It was the sound of torn flesh and shattered bones. Her teeth began to chatter and her body to shiver. She could not stop the shivering, even though she knew she was in no danger. She clamped her jaw together, but she could not stop shaking.

The prisoner put a hand on her arm. 'Are you all right?' He waited for an answer but none came. 'Are you afraid?'

Eddy could not move or speak. She had these terrifying episodes from time to time on her own in bed at night. It was panic. She could do nothing to stop it.

Giuseppe put his arm around her shoulders. 'There is no danger,' he said, but still she could not speak. After what seemed an hour, but was more likely a minute, the plane took its terrible noise across the sky and away to the west, and the silent dark closed over again. The white moon watched the transit like a cool eye and Eddy stopped shivering.

'I'll take you back to the house.'

'I'm all right.' She hurried on down the path, folding her arms and hunching her shoulders.

Giuseppe entered the hut first and spoke in Italian. '*Ecco la signorina. E' venuta a vedere come stai.*'

Enzo sat up surprised, relieved, to see her. Her hands were still shaking as she felt the skin around his cast for heat. She felt his forehead and took his temperature, his pulse, and sponged his face and shoulders with cool water fetched by Giuseppe. She could see him relax with her ministrations and she too began to relax with the help of his quiet gratitude. A cool hand on the forehead. The laying on of hands.

'Your temperature is only slightly up. If you get worse in the night, send Joe for me. I don't mind coming out.' She gave him two pills and angled the louvres down so that he would get a breeze if there were one, and propped the door open with a chair.

Giuseppe showed her the way back to the house with the lamp. She stopped halfway and said, 'You needn't come the rest of the way, there's plenty of moonlight.'

He put out the lamp and she turned to walk on.

'You are kind to Enzo,' he murmured.

'Just doing what needs doing.'

'You do it well.'

'How would you know that?'

She was disappointed that he wanted to see her as some sort of Florence Nightingale. It was what everyone wanted, especially young men. A ministering angel. She had become a nurse because it was the best paid of a very narrow set of options. She had no taste for teaching and secretarial work was deadening. She was practical and efficient and it called for that. If people wanted to make her into something else, it was childish, like believing in fairies at the bottom of the garden. Fine for the under-fives, otherwise inclined to put undue pressure on people like her, who were just going about their business. You rarely heard doctors talked about in this way. They could be good or bad in their private lives without it tainting their medical practice.

Rebuked, but not discouraged, he changed tack. 'Where were you in the bombing?'

'The Middle East. They weren't actually aiming at us. But you never knew for sure. In New Guinea they moved us away from it pretty fast, but by the end I started to get a bit rattled, that's all.'

She began to feel embarrassed that she had put on such a show for him. In the course of one minute he had made her feel uncomfortable twice. She wished for a better conversation, but seemed to be at a loss as to how to make it so.

'You are brave,' he said.

'I think we both know I'm exactly the opposite.'

'Because you are afraid does not mean that you are not brave.'

'If you say so.'

She stood in the night waiting for the conversation to continue. He did not pick up the cue. What had been said was all at odds. The silence between them now was quite the opposite. It was a silence of accord. She could have stood there like that for a long time, but it began to occur to her that he might think she meant to encourage his attentions.

'Good night,' she said and turned to go.

'I will come with you to the house and then go on for a walk.'

'In the dark? You'll break your neck.'

'There is moon. Would you like to come?'

'It's late, we need sleep.'

'I will not sleep.'

'Why on earth not?'

With the return of conversation came the discord again. She would not walk with him. She thought about going into the house and lying in her dark bedroom. It seemed bleak.

'It would be the first time I'd been out walking in my pyjamas with a gentleman.'

'You think I am a gentleman?'

'You think I'd be standing out here like this if I didn't?'

'No,' he said, and they walked towards the house. He was subdued. 'We could take the road, not so many things to fall over.'

'And if someone drives past we'll have to hide in the bushes, or cause a great scandal.'

'We should not waste a scandal on a walk.'

'Scandal is not something you can waste. It doesn't have a use,' she said.

'Scandal is just a word. The more it is spoken the less it means.'

'People find meanings. They have them hanging around, waiting for a place to put them.'

'But there are no people here, only you and I.'

'Around here, as if by magic, everyone knows everything and puts the worst possible slant on it. You come from a small village, you should know how it works.'

'I never think about such things.'

'I have to think of Max and my mother. Besides, it wouldn't be fair.'

'To you?'

'To you.'

'You think so?' He sounded amused.

At the house, she thought he might kiss her but he just opened the gate for her. She walked up the path and when she turned on the step to say good night he was gone. The moonshadows of the trees had taken him. Then she couldn't sleep.

When she first came home and saw the two prisoners, she had hated their intrusion and even though she had never spoken the words, she too thought of them as dagos and wops. Hated their diffident effort to fit in to the farm and the family, especially Joe. Vince had a light-hearted demeanour. It was impossible to hate him. But Joe's intelligent gaze impinged. It threatened to change whatever it rested on. He was assessing the farm, measuring their life — and how dare he — and the air was heavy because of it, and if they didn't take care their tiny cosmos would be diminished.

Her father, in spite of himself, had introduced a culture of respect for the animals that provided his wealth. Successful husbandry, and the effort needed to achieve it, had built a small but entire world. The old man went away and left Max the burden of keeping their home intact. In less than twenty years, that sweated commitment grew and created a place of meaning. The way a town evolves by generations of work and belonging, this small piece of dirt had evolved in one generation into a home, a good place of work and hope.

She had not known the value of it, the fragility, until she saw the prisoner walk through the kitchen to her bedroom with her kit bag the night she returned from New Guinea. Surreal, the foreigner, dressed in a bizarre burgundy army uniform, disappearing through the kitchen door in possession of her things. She had never experienced such trespass. Not even in all the army years, sharing everything. Sleep, ablutions, food, even thought. In war, only fear is private. Much had changed. The look on the faces of the prisoners had changed. When she first came home and saw those enemy faces they were passive, wary, but now they were part of the living and the working here, adding to it, even moulding it. They exchanged with their surroundings a quiet energy of inclusion.

Her initial hostility was because she saw them as a threat, an enemy intrusion. Then it was herself that she was fighting against. But she could see that Joe was no threat. There was no sharpness in him, in his body, his face, his thoughts. He would not make the first move, she was sure of that. She had called him a gentleman. He seemed to have mastered the art of being a person very well indeed, but he hadn't drawn her in yet. She could feel a pull and she could resist.

It was time for a strategic retreat to the battlezone. The war in the Pacific was threatening to last for ever. There were plenty of other nurses who could do her job. Max needed her more than they did, but the presence of the prisoner here made enemy lines there look like a wise option. She would leave after harvest.

LETTER FROM LOMBARDIA

His sister's letter says:

Dearest Pino,

I do not know how to write this letter it is so terrible, or if you will ever get it. But I must try to tell you our dreadful news. Last Thursday night we were in the kitchen having supper. It was snowing again and very cold. Papa was not happy as the weather has been harsh this year. The door crashed open and six men crowded in. They were all wet and cold and they stood around the fire. They had guns. We had seen two of them before many times and given them food. They were partisans living in the mountains. We gave them what we had to eat and after a while they left. It is so terrifying to have them in the house because if you get caught by the military. These men were caught and tortured and gave our name. The fascists came and took Papa away very early in the morning before light. We have not seen him. We don't know where they took him. There are rumours. Some even say he was shot with the others. We have come down from the village and stay here with Grandma. Grandpa is very ill and cannot get out of bed. I wish you could be with us. We are so afraid for Papa and for ourselves. Gianni is still missing, I don't know what has happened to him. It is so cold this year. It would be terrible for him in Russia. I hope you are all right. I pray for you. Bless you.

With all our love,
Rosa and Mama

'Where's Joe?'

Mrs Nash is putting meat, bread and cheese on the table as he comes through the door. He takes his place.

'I am here.'

'Joe, you all right? You look as though you've seen a ghost.'

He lifts the food to his mouth, but cannot open it. His jaw has clamped together.

'You had a letter from home, didn't you? Not bad news, I hope?'

He can't sit there and be questioned and make answers as though he were having a normal lunch. He stands up. 'I'm sorry. Please excuse me.'

He goes back to the hut. It is small and airless. He walks out and keeps walking until he finds his way to the rock again. It is the only place to go, but this time he doesn't sit. He keeps walking. It has nothing to say to him, no comfort. He is beyond grief. He has had so little of his father in his life, and now he is gone for ever. His father sent him to the town to live with his grandparents and then to the city for university. He was not a happy man. Did he love Giuseppe's mother? Perhaps Giuseppe was taught by him not to understand her. He feels no hope for him. He is dead. The fascists do not hold partisan collaborators. They get rid of them. They would like to wipe them all out. Any small suspicion is enough. What has happened to his mother and sister? Have they been taken away too?

He has never been of use to them. He has lived his life separately. His father wanted this. He wanted his clever son to escape. He didn't want to send him to Australia to work or every winter into the bigger towns and cities to find itinerant work mending pots, shoes, menial winter chores. He wanted him to find a better way to live in Italy. And he has ended up in Australia after all. His father was taken so long ago, ten months. What has happened to Rosa and Mama? What has happened to Nonno? Why could he not get out of bed? Giuseppe has no hope of seeing his father again.

He has come to the end of a track and must go back the way he came. The afternoon has slipped away. He returns to the rock and climbs it in the fading light and sits on a ridge and watches the sun set. Clouds lie strewn like red fleeces across the horizon. Below the rock, yellow stalks of harvested crop pick up the light like waves. They transform into a smooth peach reflection of the sky. The rock around him now has no light. He is suspended above his surroundings, disembodied, looking at a changing screen of light. The sun that he sees off here is the sun his mother and sister will greet when they awaken. It should make him feel connected, but it does not. It tells him that nature is impersonal. The sun provides everything, but sometimes that is nothing. Thoughts and feelings are not important to the way the world works. And they are not important to the way the human race works. Riding over the wishes of others is the way of ambition. The only way to power is a road called subjugation. The gods of power and dominion are gluttonous monsters and there is no limit to the number of lives that must be thrown into their jaws to satisfy their greed. The sun has gone to the next country, Africa, and to his country for a new day. But his father will not see it. He will see only darkness.

And now it is dark here for Giuseppe also. The moon is not yet up. He must rely on his memory to find his way back to the hut where he washes and changes his clothes.

Enzo is quiet, but finally says, 'What has happened to your family?'

'My father has been killed by the fascists.'

Enzo does not try to comfort him. He sits on the bed and shakes his head. He no longer needs his crutches, but he still uses a stick to walk. He stands up and presses Giuseppe's shoulder.

'*Andiamo a cena*?'

Giuseppe shakes his head and Enzo limps away towards the house. He sits on his bed. He can't think of anything he wants to do. To stand is an effort. To lie down is too much comfort. After ten minutes there is a knock at the door. It is Max. He comes in and sits on Enzo's bed. He does not speak straight away.

'Vince told us about your father. I'm very sorry, Joe.'

'Thank you.'

There is more silence.

'Your father was a farmer, wasn't he?' Giuseppe answers him and then they drop back into silence.

'You know, there are some farmers out the back of the Cross who come from your area. I think they do. I'm going up to collect some spare parts tomorrow, you could come with me and we'll call in on them. Polifrone. Your families might know each other.'

There are a great many people in Giuseppe's home area with that name. There are not many surnames left in that valley.

'Do you want to come? I'll get on the blower and organise it tonight if you do.'

'Thank you, I would like that.'

Max sits with him a while longer. He knows what to say. 'Were you close to your father?'

'Not after I was ten years old. And I have not seen him for six years. I had not been home for two years before the war broke out.'

'That's no good.'

'Not really. My father was always glad to see me and eager for me to be away again. He didn't want his son to live the same life he lived.'

'He was proud of you.'

'He liked the respect he got because I have a university education. It wasn't as important for him as for my mother.'

Another knock at the door brings Eddy. The beautiful Eddy. She carries a large metal tray with his dinner on it. She looks different. Her hair is loose and she wears lipstick. She brings a faint scent of lemon into the hut. Max gets up and puts his hand on Giuseppe's shoulder.

'All right, I'll let you know at breakfast. Now tuck into that tea. You'll feel better.'

Eddy puts the tray on the chest of drawers. 'Nearly broke my neck a hundred times. Couldn't manage a lamp and a tray. Had to just feel my way.' She lifts the tea towel off the tray. There is a small flask of Australian whisky beside the plate. 'Medicinal purposes only, of course. I found it in the first-aid cabinet. No one will miss it. I think Mum's forgotten it. Probably been there since Dad was here.'

She doesn't have a father any more than he does. But she doesn't have to imagine him dying in terror, being tortured and shot. She takes the bottle from him and pours the golden liquor into a teacup. 'Drink up.'

He takes a mouthful and wonders why she thinks he must drink whisky because he knows that his father has been murdered.

'I couldn't think what else to bring,' she says, reading his thoughts. He offers her the cup and she takes a gulp and fills it again and hands it back. 'This is good,' she says and takes the cup from him and swallows another mouthful. 'It usually tastes like cough mixture, but this isn't too bad.' She picks up the bottle to read the label. 'I didn't know we made whisky in Australia.'

'It is not like Scotch whisky,' he says.

'That's probably why I like it.'

He can't help smiling at this. The whisky they're drinking tastes very bad. This time she doesn't read his thoughts and smiles back. She also puts a hand on his shoulder. The third time this evening he has received that sympathetic gesture. But she touches his hair. He leans his head against her.

'Are you like your father?' she asks.

'He is not as tall, but he is much tougher.'

'Was he a good father?'

'Very good. Hard but kind. He was a friend to me.'

'What was his name?'

'Claudio. Claudio Lazaro. The name of his grandfather.'

'Do you have your grandfather's name?'

'No. For me he broke with tradition. He wanted me to change the pattern.'

'Claudio sounds like sky and wind and rain. Much better than Claude. Claude is so plodding. It's unusual for a man like your father to want his son to go away and find another life.'

'Like my father. You mean a peasant?'

'If you like.'

'He used to say, "*Chigliöga i ghèi ia mai cagà gnàa is àsan*," donkeys don't shit money.'

'Strong words.'

'Strong man.'

'Is that why he died?'

'Of course. It is people like him who keep the Resistance alive.'

'You can be proud.'

'What use is that when he is dead?'

'None to him, but everything to you. He is a true martyr, a mystic, he has given his blood.'

'Do you believe that really? You would rather your father was a dead hero?' He is fearful she will say something that shocks him, that he might have to finally admit that she is cold and hard.

'Half of me does and that half feels it very strongly, but that is all selfish because as soon as he dies he will be a better person. The dead earn respect from the living. The other half still hopes he'll turn up and put my mother's life to rights.'

He had not counted on her honesty. He holds her hand in both of his.

'She might be happier without him. My mother will be,' he says, wanting to match her honesty and wondering whether he is being honest or wrong.

She is silent for a moment. Perhaps he has shocked her.

'Was your home full of argument?'

'No. My father kept an angry silence with my mother. I used to think it was my fault, or hers, that we had done something wrong. I know now he was being strangled by the deadening work on the mountain.'

'You blame yourself?'

'Not now, of course, and I don't blame him. He used to escape from us on cold nights. He would lie under the house in the hay with the cows for warmth and smoke with his friends whose wives also lived in silence.'

'He didn't talk to you either?'

'A little, but not about my mother, never. And then I went away.'

'Has Max told you his idea?' she asks.

'Yes.'

'What do you think?'

'I will go with him.'

She goes to the door and stops. She touches the corner of one of Filippo's paintings sticking out from behind the cupboard.

'Where is your friend?'

'Filippo? Under the soil at Myrtleford.'

She looks away, afraid of his answer, not wanting to leave at such a bad moment. 'Oh,' she says. She is unworded.

He has never seen her like this. He takes pity on her.

'He took his own life.'

'Oh,' she says again, but this time it sounds like a sigh.

'It was his to take.'

'Yes.'

Because she says nothing else, he is drawn to her more strongly than he has ever been. She moves back to the bed and sits beside him.

'Try to eat. You missed lunch,' she says. 'I must go, they'll be wondering which rabbit hole I've fallen into.'

'Thank you for the whisky.'

'It was terrible, wasn't it?'

'No.'

'You lie to save my feelings.' She smiles and stands up.

'A little perhaps.'

'Good.' She leans down and kisses him.

It is the kiss he has been thinking about, but it is not what he expected. It is gentle, and loving. He knows that sympathy is often mistaken for love. Whatever it is, it will do very well for now. His thoughts of her have probably been more of lust than love. Lust is safer, but he doesn't have enough room in his brain to think about that now. They don't hear Enzo's footsteps on the gravel until he is at the door of the hut. He opens the door and Eddy moves past him and out with a quick, 'Good night, Vince.'

'*Buona sera, signorina*,' he says and watches her go. He looks at Giuseppe, questioning, and Giuseppe looks at his tray of food and prepares to eat. Enzo says nothing, but his silence is loaded.

They potter along the road in the old truck. The corrugations are getting worse as the summer goes on and farmers cart their wheat to the railway line. It is thirty-five miles to Southern Cross. It is like a set from a western. Every building, person and car is covered in a layer of red-orange dust. A complementary colour for Giuseppe's faded magenta uniform. It could have been chosen for this place. Streets are wide enough for a bullock train to turn around. Cars and trucks park in the middle and traffic goes either side. There are no trees in the streets. Every shop has a wide verandah to shade it from the sun which seems hotter here than at the farm. There is a gold mine at the entrance to the town and the rig stands high in the air on the only hill. On the side of the hill are spindly trees and hundreds of small red slag heaps glinting with pieces of white quartz left over from the goldrush at the end of the last century. As soon as the engine of the truck is quiet they can hear the battery from the mine stamping the ore. On the other side of town a salt lake shaped like a bow lies in a depression surrounded by saltbush and salt-tolerant gums. The edges are crusted into permanent ripples of salt. It is dry at this time of year, white and still, like a frozen lake.

After Max has finished at the machinery shop, they clatter across the dry lake over a loose-boarded bridge and head south. A group of shanties crouch among the trees and scrub. Aboriginal people sit beside them on the ground. These are not native bark huts. They are made from bags and flattened kerosene tins.

'Do the black people have to live here?' Giuseppe asks.

'No,' Max answers.

'Why don't they live in the town?'

'They can't live in the town. Can't afford to.'

'They have no work?'

'Some of them do, but they don't get wages, just keep.'

Giuseppe falls back into silence. He is thinking that there is something worse than being a prisoner of war.

Ten miles brings a driveway and half a mile along this, a house. It is a small house made of unpainted asbestos with the front fence so close that it allows for no garden, only a row of cacti in pots. They drive along scattering fowls, turkeys and geese around to the back and there before them is an enormous vegetable plot. Rows of fat, ripe tomatoes weigh down their staked vines. Melons loll about the ground and beans hang on every fence. Dusty red grapes drip bulbous and juice-heavy from frames. Here is a fine show of fertility and abundance that Giuseppe has not seen since he was last in his home valley.

Three dogs bark and run mad around the truck. Another is tied under a bush next to its kennel made from a large drum. It leaps at them snarling as they get out of the vehicle and is pulled back with a snap when it reaches the end of its chain. The house sits alone without the softness or protection of trees. The heat of the day and the lack of shade make it harsh in spite of the garden. Signora Polifrone pushes open a flywire door and stands on the back verandah wiping her hands on her apron. She is in her fifties and a little solid around the waist. She wears earrings and high-heeled shoes. A sign that they are expected. She greets Max in English and he introduces Giuseppe.

'This is Joe Lazarus,' he says, 'Joe, Mrs Polifrone.' He pronounces Polifrone without the last 'e' to rhyme with telephone.

She reaches out to shake Giuseppe's hand and immediately begins to speak in Italian, asking who his parents are, where they live and what his father does. She speaks the *lingua volgare*, the dialect he knows, from a village near his own. She invites them into the house. Giuseppe feels disappointed that her husband is not there, but when they are inside the kitchen he sees that she has set six places for afternoon tea. She gives them a cup of cool water from the waterbag hanging on the verandah and asks them to sit down. He admires her garden and they make awkward conversation about fruit and vegetables in English to include Max. She explains that they put in two dams to water this garden.

She has made a cake and cut it into wedges. She puts it in the middle of the table with *savoiardi* biscuits which

Giuseppe has not seen since he left Italy. She offers them coffee. Giuseppe accepts, but Max hesitates.

'You have real coffee?' he asks.

'Where would I get real coffee?' she laughs.

Max asks her where Bruno is.

'Clearing, but he will be here soon.'

A long half hour later the men arrive. They are clearly not used to such niceties as afternoon tea in the middle of a working day. They wash their hands at a tap in the garden, using a piece of grey soap that rests on a mallee root, and take off their boots to enter the kitchen. Bruno does not know Giuseppe's family. Giuseppe does not know his. His sons were born here and have Australian names. They do not speak Italian except to their parents.

'We came here in 1921. There was nothing here. We had to make everything,' Bruno says. He asks about Giuseppe's family. Giuseppe hesitates.

'He got a letter yesterday,' says Max. 'His father's been taken by the fascists for giving food to partisans. It doesn't look good.'

Signora Polifrone stops eating and puts down her cake, unable to find anything to say. Bruno and his sons go on eating and drinking in embarrassed silence. Finally Bruno shakes his head and says, '*Brutti porci.*'

After another half hour of trying to find conversation, Max gets up to leave. Everyone is relieved. As Max turns the truck around the Polifrone men are already speeding up the track to their work. The visit has not been a success. Max has gone out of his way to arrange this meeting to make Giuseppe feel better. Giuseppe was not a good visitor with the weight of his father's death on his shoulders. They are kind people trying to be good to him, but they had nothing in common, aside from being born in the shadow of the same mountain. Compared with his parents, they live a more prosperous and probably a happier life, but he sees that it has been a hard life here too. Hard for the women. They live with heat and isolation. The men seem more hopeful of success and prosperity.

As they drive towards Grey Tamma Farm the vegetation changes. The stunted sand-plain bushes give way to taller, more luxuriant trees. The colour of the earth changes twice from bright red to pale then to dark red. It is beginning to feel familiar to Giuseppe, to feel like home. He is not yet bereft of everything he likes.

Tonight the milking cows are restless. The signora says that only when cows are happy will they let down all their milk. It must be so or perhaps he has lost his touch, but instead of four buckets he gets three. He takes them to the cellar. Eddy says nothing about the empty bucket. She asks him to stay and help. He takes over the separating while she fusses about with the butter churn. She is offering her company in consolation. She stops work and turns to him.

'What can I do?' she asks.

'Nothing. The grief for my father goes far back. I can't remember where it starts. I have all my life lost him. To his own miseries, to his ambition for me, to his lack of love for my mother, to his work on the mountain. I suppose I thought that one day I would go back to him and we would be friends.'

'I'm not sure,' she says. 'It's a trick we play on ourselves when they're no longer with us. Blaming ourselves for what they couldn't give and now will never be able to give. We always want so much of our parents. It's unreasonable. Our fathers gave us enough, but it'll probably take us the rest of our lives to realise it.'

'All I really wanted, I suppose, was for him to love my mother.'

Eddy looks up sharply when he says this and then down again at her work. She knows what he means.

He watches her turning the handle of the butter churn and envies her independent spirit. Being a prisoner strips you of that. He takes the skimmed milk to his friends, the grateful pigs. They run in and out swapping places. A few tears slip down his cheeks and onto the splintered rail of their pen. He likes these pigs, but he will not save them from the knife. The only thing he knows with certainty is that in the future everyone will suffer loss. War punches its random fist into everyone's future, destroying and maiming. Peace takes away quietly but just as surely.

After dinner, Max asks Giuseppe to play chess with him. Giuseppe is exhausted, but he feels obliged to accept this consolation. They play a long and evenly matched game. He suspects Max lets him win. Victor Silvester plays bright Noel Coward songs on the wireless in the corner. Enzo and the signora talk about the garden. The signora offers Giuseppe hot milk, to make him sleep. He refuses and leaves for the hut. Someone turns off the wireless and the room falls silent. They have been making diversions for him. When Enzo comes to the hut he brings a small packet. Inside are two tablets and on a scrap of paper in a wild sloping scrawl: '*Take these if you can't sleep. Eddy.*'

MacGILLACUDDY'S

They began to talk at table about her return to New Guinea. She grew quiet and determined and snapped at her mother and brother, sneered at Giuseppe and ignored Enzo.

'Of course I'm well enough. I certainly won't be working any harder there than I do here.'

In an attempt to remove the personal, Giuseppe asked a question about transport.

'Yes, it is a long way to New Guinea. How I get there is not something I should discuss with you.'

It was not his business. His business was to work the land like a dumb beast. Like the obliging old hack he rode to round up sheep. It was time for shearing sheep. The weather had stayed dry. Two men had come with a noisy diesel motor that drove mechanical shears. They worked hard. Giuseppe and Enzo admired the athletic ability of these men. Enzo worked in the shed yarding sheep, gathering and skirting fleeces, pressing wool into bales with Max who classed the wool. Giuseppe was not sorry to be away from the shed and the shearers who assumed that Italian prisoners did not speak English and so insulted them, even to their faces.

They arrived at first light to set up their machine. They wore navy trousers and flannel singlets. Shearers' traditional dress. They were both aged between thirty and forty. The war had taken all the younger men. Tiny was probably already forty. Shearing is a hard business for a forty-year-old back. Tiny owned the plant. He was bellied and bearded and almost six feet two inches in his greasy soft shearer's boots made from a piece of thick jute from the top of a wool bale. He was no longer a gun shearer, but he could still get through a hundred a day. When he saw Enzo in his magenta uniform, he muttered, 'Not another bloody dago.'

The first fleece the Italian picked up fell apart, half of it trailing behind as he walked towards the table. Max had shown him how to hold and throw a fleece so that it spread out wide across the table. His first throw ended with half of it on the floor. The shearer dragged another sheep across the floor and called out to him, 'Hey dago, you dropped your dags,' and snorted into his beard. The younger smaller man was aggravated at the sight of an Italian prisoner in the shed. His name was Chook. Red hair, red skin and seeing red. He had snakes, eagles and dragons tattooed on his arms. Perhaps he was once a seaman. He could shear thirty or forty a day more than his boss. At the nine-thirty smoko the deafening blitz of the engine ceased for half an hour. The bleating of the sheep and scuffle of their feet as they pushed each other into the corners of their pens took over the shed. Enzo's ears throbbed in time to the sound imprint of the now silent machine.

Chook wandered over to the bale where Enzo sat and said, 'Hey, fascist.' He picked up the blacking brush used to paint the stencil on the bales. 'Want a nice Hitler moustache? He's a friend of yours, isn't he?' He began to dance about, jabbing with the brush at the prisoner's face.

At that moment, Max ran up the steps from the yards where he'd been branding shorn sheep with the long-handled branding iron, dripping red paint on the boards. He walked over and stood beside Chook, holding the branding iron at shoulder level. The shearer put down the blacking brush and retreated to his side of the shed, clearing his throat and spitting into one of the dag heaps, where they threw the dirty wool. He sat down on a pile of bags to roll a cigarette and chuckled. 'No sense of humour, dagos.'

Tiny stood up and went away to oil his cutters. Enzo was more astonished than offended, but he was ready for anything after that. So when Chook walked to the pen to get another sheep and dragged his foot through the fleece spreading it across the floor, making it impossible to throw in one piece, he knew it was not an accident.

The shearers pitched a tent beside the prisoners' hut that was normally theirs for the week. They had to share the wash house. By the time Giuseppe arrived on the first evening, the bath heater had gone out and the water was cold. He had to take a cold shower.

'Why didn't you keep the bath heater going?' he asked Enzo.

'I did. The shearers came after. They are animals. Pigs.'

After a dinner where talk was all but drowned out by the noises of eating, the shearers went back to their camp and Max attempted to explain their behaviour.

'It's not personal. It's a union thing. Up north they've been using prisoners to do the shearing. The pay is less. The shearers are just looking after their jobs.'

His mother was not pleased. 'It's a shame. There's no excuse for rudeness, whatever the issue.'

Max laughed and leaned back in his chair.

'Rudeness doesn't come into it. It's the least of our worries.'

'What do you mean?'

'Some of the shearers up north have been fighting with the prisoners and wrecking their huts.'

'I don't believe it,' she said.

'These blokes are pussy cats compared with those. They're locals, they're not about to foul their own nest.'

'Well, I won't stand for it.'

Max laughed at his mother's view of a world that she was immersed in but unable to influence.

'It's all right, Mum, Vince can handle it if anyone can.'

'I know shearers are rough, but they don't have to be criminals.'

'They're not criminals. I've had my run-ins with them, but on the whole they're hard-working and honest. Most of us couldn't last half a day doing what they do. They earn twice, three times every penny they make.'

At the end of the second day when the shearers had washed their combs and cutters and hooked them up to dry, they stood painfully stretching their backs and watching Enzo sweep the greasy floor. Then out of the blue they offered to share their bottle of beer with him.

That night during tea Eddy spoke through the scraping of knives on plates. 'Max says you're an excellent shed hand, Vince. He says you learnt to throw a fleece in one minute.'

'Is no *difficile*.'

'It's not so easy either. Been trying to teach me for twenty years. I'm useless. He won't let me near a fleece.'

Enzo grinned. The shearers went on shovelling food and scraping their feet on the lino. Tiny lifted his head just far enough to say, 'Wouldn't need a lot of shearing in spaghetti-land, eh?'

A sort of truce was at work. The evening of the third day, the shearers invited both Enzo and Giuseppe to share their beer while they sharpened their cutters on the mechanical grinder attached to the thundering engine. In return, they gave the shearers some packets of tailor-made cigarettes from their supply.

'No wonder you're so cack-handed at roll-your-owns.' Tiny spoke with a mashed smoke hanging from his bottom lip.

Enzo didn't follow. Giuseppe translated for him. Enzo told him they'd offered him their makings during the smoko and he'd spilt them all over the floor.

Before they left, Enzo presented each of them with a large pumpkin from his vegetable patch. They were happy to accept, but were puzzled to see Enzo laughing so much. As they drove away the signora said, 'That was nice of you, Vince, though I know you won't miss the odd pumpkin. You don't really care for them, do you?'

'Si signora, but is good food for pigs,' and he laughed all the way back to his hut.

Giuseppe spends the shearing marshalling sheep in and out. Bringing them in heavy with wool and out again stripped bare. With their change of clothing their personalities change. He brings in substantial members of the livestock community. He takes away belittled meat on legs with confused yellow eyes. He tries to like the bare bony backs as well as the soft rounded ones, but he cannot. This is how he looks in his magenta prisoner's uniform — bare, insubstantial, less than a man. He has been shorn of himself.

He takes them to paddocks where there is timber standing. It is now autumn and they need protection at night.

The last day of shearing is Friday. The shearers leave at midday. Eddy has said that she will be leaving after shearing. She has not said whether it will be a day, a week or a month after. A strong autumn sun is flashing itself about late in the afternoon. The horse and Giuseppe both need rest after returning the last flock of sheep to their paddock. He stops at a dam that nestles into the edge of uncleared salmon gum country and waters the horse and ties it in the shade. Then he strips and wades into the icy opaque water and swims about to wash away the lanolin dust and fatigue. It's not until he climbs the bank that he sees the horse has gone, a mare, impatient to be home as the hour for her food draws near, with no respect for reins looped over thin branches. He sits on the bank drying his skin in the last of the sun. When he hears the motorbike approach he stands up to put on his clothes. Enzo has seen the horse galloping home and has come to find him.

'Bit icy in, I should think, this time of year.' It is not Enzo.

'The lakes of my home are never warm.'

'You haven't broken your neck?'

Eddy is standing on the bank looking down at him while he fumbles with the buttons of his trousers. She has been hostile for so long that he has learnt to expect it. He is surprised to observe that she might be pleased that he didn't break his neck.

'Max and Vince have taken the wool to the train,' she says.

'I am fortunate then. It would have been a long walk.'

'No.' She is looking down at her boots. 'You're not fortunate.' She seems to be talking to herself. 'I'm fortunate.'

'Why, because you did not lose your horse?'

A quick smile flashes across her face. 'No, because I'm at home with my family, in my own country which has a prime minister I admire.'

'But you are leaving. Going back to the jungle, to the killing. That is not fortunate.'

'It's all right . . . if you believe it's vital for the country. There are worse things.'

'But you are so afraid of the bombing.'

'What's that got to do with it?' She stares down at him. It disappoints him to see hostility creeping back across her face.

'If you want to go . . . then . . .' He shrugs, finishes lacing his boots and stands to put on his shirt.

'We should have given you civvy clothes, something other than purple prisoner's clothes. Awful. I wish we had . . . months ago.'

'Months ago you didn't like us very much.'

'True. And I'm beginning to hate you again, now that I feel like this because I'm going away.'

It takes him a minute to understand.

'I'm going on Sunday. I just wanted to say . . .' Her words fade as though she has forgotten what she wanted to say. Whatever she says will make her leaving worse. Kind words will be cruel for encouraging false hope. Hard words will be cold memories after she is gone.

'Say nothing.'

'I hadn't intended to but . . .'

He hangs his shirt over one shoulder and moves up the bank. Eddy absently tucks her faded red and white striped shirt into her trousers even though it is not hanging out. She is no longer thin. She is strong and tanned. She nods towards the broken branch.

'You tie up MacGillacuddy's while you swam?'

'Yes. A mistake, I think.'

'At this time of day. She's a greedy girl, likes her feed.'

'I know.'

'But . . . you thought you'd take the risk. I wouldn't have thought you were a risk-taker, Joe.'

'I thought she would be loyal. She knows me. I had trust in her.' He is beginning to feel like the mouse the cat plays with before it kills.

'You don't trust me,' she says.

Perhaps it is true. He hadn't thought about it until now. He tries not to let her read his face.

'Can't blame you. I don't know how to lead into this so I'll just say it straight out.' For some moments she says nothing at all. Then, 'I'm sorry,' she says, 'I apologise.'

'For what?' He laughs, surprised.

'You don't need to ask that. You've put up with a lot.'

He had grown used to her anger. It was a way of keeping them apart and they had to stay apart. He liked her for it. She believed in things and was uncompromising. Now that she had changed, would he dislike her for weakness and inconsistency? Unlikely. He can't help smiling. He likes irony even when he is the victim of it.

'I want no apology,' he says.

'We'll probably never meet again so I want you to understand.' She finishes speaking and waits, looking at the ground.

'I don't mind that you are angry. You are honest.'

'But that's the whole point, I haven't been honest with you. I wanted you to think I disliked you. It was stupid. It wasn't true.'

There is silence between them now. To say these things to him changes everything. Her honesty calls him out.

'Before you came back from New Guinea I was content, grateful to be here and not locked in the camp. But after you leave I will be lonely.'

Silence.

'We should go back to the house,' she murmurs.

'Do you think I would harm you?'

'I think you're too bloody nice to me,' she growls. 'You're a prisoner for God's sake, can't you even pretend to behave like one?'

She is making a noise but she is not angry. He starts to laugh, shaking his head at her nonsense. She laughs grudgingly. She knows it's nonsense. She slides sideways in her boots down to the water's edge and picks up a handful of stones and skims them hard one at a time across the water like a boy. He watches with his hands in his pockets. She picks up another handful of stones and offers them to him. He shakes his head.

' No one taught you to do this?'

'No.'

He slides down the bank and stands beside her. He picks up a flat stone and skims it across the water. It touches three times and reaches the opposite bank.

'You said you couldn't do it.'

'I said no one taught me. I grew up near a lake. We are born knowing how to skim stones.'

'If Max saw us here now, he would send you away,' she says, handing him another stone. 'You'd be given detention and I'd be court-martialled and ridiculed by my friends.'

'For talking to me? That is a little extreme.'

'Exactly. And that's why we must be . . .'

'Be what?' He presses his question. He detects more of her nonsense about to emerge. 'What must we be?'

'Friends. We should be friends.'

She offers her hand for him to shake. He takes it in both of his and raises it to his mouth, turns it over and kisses the palm. She pulls it away slowly. The orange light of evening has lit up her neck and arms. He watches her twist her hair into a knot and fasten it at the crown of her head with a twig. She does it unconsciously in a nervous gesture.

'Bloody hell,' she says, raising her hands in the air, 'right now I don't care who finds us here.'

'Who will find us? It is too far to walk. We can hear the truck coming for miles.'

She takes a deep breath, looks about restlessly and then back at his shoulders. 'You're so brown.'

She looks so miserable. He reaches out to touch her cheek. She turns her head and brushes his wrist with her lips. She leans her face on his shoulder. He can feel her breasts under her shirt, against his skin, the smell of her hair, her cool skin. He puts his lips against her throat.

'Do you want to make love to me?' she astonishes him by asking.

'You know the answer to that,' he says, trying to sound calm.

She lets some time go by before she asks, 'Why don't you ask me if I want to make love to you? Is it because you already know the answer?'

'No.'

'Why don't you ask?'

'I would not speak of such things to a signorina.'

'But you would do it.'

Silence.

'And she wouldn't speak of such things to you?' She continues with her goading.

'No.'

'You think I am crude?'

'I think you are Australian.'

'Australian women don't speak of such things either.'

'But they do them,' he says and they laugh.

'If we don't talk about it, how can I tell you why we should not?' she asks, and goes on to make a convoluted argument without a premise and that is how it starts. And then her kiss keeps it going and the rest is an awkward struggle with buttons and the making of a bed with their discarded clothes and the sighs and noises that are held back in a first encounter. It is too rushed and intense and new to be really successful, but they get through it and they laugh. It is funny. They are excited. They swim about in the dam to calm down, and then it isn't funny any more, because this is goodbye. The beginning and the end all at once are a lot of things happening.

They lie on their clothes in the grass for how long? For a while, for moments of deliberate disregard for the future. He feels her skin on his skin and traces with his hand the sculptured curve of her stomach. Their bodies press tight so that no air or light will separate them. In the last of the slanting sun, before the air thins with cold, he sees their skin shining in patches of brown and cream. She would stay here listening to the shy birds that never come near the farmyard, bells and chimes, sounds that escape from a mysterious treetop world. He is the first to move. He finds her clothes and puts them on her, sliding the cloth over her legs and arms, putting buttons into loops and holes.

'You wear man's clothes.'

'Men's clothes,' she corrects. 'I do men's work.'

'At home, work in the field is done by women as much as men and they wear skirts.'

'Why?'

'Custom, femininity.'

'What use is that when you're working on a farm? What is it?'

'Femininity? It is you.'

'Even in men's clothes?'

'Especially so.'

She smiles and shakes her head. 'You poor desperado,' she says.

'I admit it. But you knew I loved you for a long time,' he says.

'I thought maybe.'

'And you despised me for it.'

She is silent for a while, then she says, 'I thought it was lust.'

He laughs, she is as honest as he would wish her to be. 'It was,' he says.

'Is,' she says.

'Not is for me. Maybe for you.'

'Not is for me either,' she says and he thinks he has never heard a better phrase.

He straightens her clothes and brushes away the dust and grass seeds. She has become for him delicate and precious. They tie each other's shoelaces like children. Her leaving stands beside them like an executioner.

Perhaps she is looking for a lighter moment when she says, 'We must not forget to thank MacGillacuddy's.'

'Why does the poor creature have such a name?'

'Ah well. I can tell you that.'

He pulls her to him and she sits armchair-style between his legs.

'My father bred her. She was born the same year as me. So she is very old. He sold her to a miner from Menzies. A lot of men had their own small diggings. His name was MacGillacuddy. He bought her at auction in Perth and said he'd send for her when he was settled back at his diggings. But he never did. My father waited and after two years made inquiries and found that he'd been killed when his shaft fell in. He was an Irishman and no one knew where his family lived or if he had a family. If he did, they never knew that they had a horse to inherit. My father expected that one day his heirs would turn up and claim what was rightfully theirs, so he never sold her. We've never called her anything but MacGillacuddy's mare. She's the best little mare we've ever had. Other good horses were always sold as soon as they were trained and going well.'

'She is like me.'

'A little hairier, I think.'

'She lives and works here by accident. She is a victim of fate.'

'Perhaps, but she is loved.'

On the way back to the farmhouse she rides pillion, arms tight about his waist, cheek pressed against his shoulder. He parks the bike in the darkened shed. They stand kissing.

'This is dangerous,' he says.

'I hope that's not its only attraction.'

'I do not take unnecessary risks.'

'I'm necessary?'

'After the war I will show you how much.'

'Don't talk about that.'

Her words shove him into the present and reality. They leave the shed separately, him to the hut in a mist of having and losing which rolls across his chest and thighs. Enzo is there, cleaning up for dinner.

'You're a crazy man, Giuseppe.' He is shaking his head. 'You will get six months in the camp prison.'

Giuseppe is not used to being spoken to by Enzo in this way. Giuseppe is younger but senior in rank and, although they are friends, Enzo always defers to him.

He tries not to sound apologetic. 'She is leaving.'

'Good.' He shakes his head again and goes out to the wash house.

At dinner she is brusque as usual but distracted and does not look anyone in the eye, except Giuseppe from behind her mother's chair as she pours tea.

The signora hands him a steaming cup. 'Joe?'

He tears away his gaze and says automatically, '*Grazie, Signora.*'

She responds, '*Prego.*' Everyone laughs. The signora is learning her Italian well.

He looks back at Eddy. She has turned away and is stacking plates into the sink.

'What was MacGillacuddy's doing in the yard saddled up, Joe?' Max asks.

'She escaped from me at the dam in the top paddock.'

'How do you mean? She didn't throw you?'

'No. I tied her to a tree and she ran away.'

'What did you do that for?'

'I wanted to swim.'

'Swim?' Max looks nonplussed. He never swims in the dams. He doesn't like to think about what might be in there besides water. 'Did you walk back?'

'I went up with the bike when I saw her come back.' Eddy does not turn around from the washing up.

'What time did she run away? It was after dark when I heard the bike come in.'

Max senses something unusual, but it is clear that he does not know what. Eddy does what she can to sound cool.

'It took me a while to find Joe. I didn't know where he had gone.'

'Surely he was on the track walking back?'

She lets that one go and the questions stop, but he is not satisfied. He is a good farmer because he is observant. He never misses a clue — where sheep are, what disease is killing them, what bugs are eating the crop. He is observing and thinking and solving problems when others are just musing about the weather or the next twenty-gallon party.

If he had been able to say goodbye to Eddy before she left, what would they have said?

He: 'After the war . . .'

She: 'Don't talk about that.'

Even that would have been better than a shake of Enzo's hand, and then his, before her mother and brother drove her to the train. He watches the model T slip along the road, the long afternoon shadows flickering rhythms against the shining black car, smoke spurting from the gas producer. He has been nothing but predictable. She is lively and enigmatic and he is woman-starved. Under those circumstances everything has happened the way nature expects. He knew she would go. Now she has gone. He still objects. He is beginning to hate himself. He stands for some time under the trees beside the gate, looking at the road as though he has forgotten how to walk.

Back at the hut, Enzo puts his hand on Giuseppe's shoulder. '*C'è la guerra*.' It's the war, an obvious statement, but a comfort because it is meant as such. His brain might have seized but his arms still work. It is his day off, but it seems like a good idea to cut wood for the fire. After two hours, there is a tall stack for the signora's stove and a prisoner with smarting palms and aching back muscles.

At dinner the signora is upset, eyes red, voice shaky. After the meal she says, 'Play a couple of your pieces for us, Joe. It's so quiet now.'

He has not played for many months. It does not sound good. What it sounds like is how he feels. The signora pats him on the shoulder and goes to bed before he is halfway through one piece. He closes the piano and walks out into the night. It is growing cold. Max has said it could frost tonight. An early start to winter.

Later, Enzo comes from the house with two blankets. 'From signorina Eddy's bed. La signora says is too cold tonight.' He tucks the blanket around his bed.

Giuseppe puts his face into her blanket and smells the lavender. Enzo makes an effort not to notice.

CORRESPONDENCE

After two weeks, a letter came for the signora and Max from Eddy. There was not much she could tell them except that she had not gone to New Guinea and was working at a hospital in Australia. She described plastic-surgery cases. The signora said she must be in Brisbane, Melbourne or Sydney, which is where plastic surgery is performed. She had seen articles in the paper about the clever British-trained surgeons reconstructing the faces of the war-injured. The postmark was Victoria so Melbourne was settled upon. The voice of the letter sounded different from the one Giuseppe knew. Her words were soft, infused with pity. He itched to snatch it away and read it all.

Some days later the officer from the control centre brought him a letter. Typewritten, from Victoria. It caused much interest.

Max was completely mystified, ready to be suspicious. 'Who's writing to you from Victoria, Joe? You've been here for two years and never had a letter from inside this country.'

There was only one person in Australia who would write him a letter. He thought of a lie. 'My grandmother's sister settled in Victoria. She must have discovered I am a prisoner.'

The signora was alert. 'And you haven't contacted her? Joe, that's terrible.'

'I am not a good writer. I prefer to read.'

'Well, people who don't write letters don't get letters as a rule, unless they are bills.'

She turned her head sideways to read the envelope he held in his hand. He wanted to put it in his pocket, get it well out of sight, but was afraid of any show of secrecy that might alert them to the possibility of deceit. She was not ready to leave the subject alone.

'You don't often see a typewritten letter unless it's business.'

'My cousin, her granddaughter, is a secretary,' he said and they discussed at length a fiction that he was trying not to make so complicated that it would be difficult for him to remember if challenged on it later.

'They are not interned, I hope?'

'I don't know. I mean no, I don't think so.'

'Well, you must make sure you reply. Your mother must be happy knowing you have people in Australia.'

If any of the story were true, his mother would not be happy, she had no happiness in her. With relief, he sees the signora turn back to her tasks. The prisoners did not help in the kitchen after lunch. Giuseppe walked to the hut in measured paces trying not to show haste or any sign that he was eager to read the letter. Enzo was already there, sitting on the bed.

'You play a dangerous game. The signora does not know because she does not want to, not because she cannot figure it out.' He made a growl of exasperation and shook his head. 'Here you can have a comfortable war with kind people. You seem to want to be locked up in a cage. Do you think you are a chimpanzee?'

Normally this from the good-natured Enzo would make him smile, but today it irritated.

'It's not your worry.'

'To a senior officer, I would not speak. But to a friend I cannot be silent.'

'You go back to work, I'll be there in a minute.'

He walked out across the paddock to his favourite clump of trees and sat on a log.

Joe,

I suppose you read English as well as you speak it. I know this is a risk, but I cannot not write. I'm not the efficient nurse I used to be. I spend so much of the day thinking about you and night too. I've been promoted to acting matron of this hospital for a week while the matron is on leave, which is why I have a typewriter I can use very slowly with two fingers. I can't tell you where I am or how long I'll be here. I'm not near any fighting, nor am I likely to be. No bombs. There was no urgency for me to leave the farm. Plenty of others could have done this job as well or better than me, since my mind is only half on it.

I can say things in this that I could not say to your face. I can say things like: the harder I tried not to like you the more I did. War has a way of doing that. For you, I was the only girl around. Would you choose me if we met in the city? Don't run too many errands to the Fischer place because I'm sure Gretel will be knocking on your door in the middle of the night if you encourage her. She is pretty but a little young for you. It will be impossible for you to reply to this with any safety. Do not take the risk. I'll write one from you. It will go something like this. You would say:

Cara Eddy,

A year ago you were angry and grieving for the loss of your friends to the war and hated the enemy. But I saw you change and if you did not learn to understand the dilemmas faced by the people of our nation, you did learn that an individual is always a case for understanding and friendship. And so I forgive you for not liking me once, and cannot even remember it. (How am I doing?) I miss you and will not speak the words 'after the war' because they are too hard to hear as I will be sent back to my country and far away from you. Please think of me as often as I think of you, which is every minute, and write again soon.

Have I overdone it? What would you have said that I left out? What would you have left out that I said? Here is my answer to your letter. I have known you a little longer by now and feel confident with a little more familiarity, so I say:

Dearest dearest Joe, (maybe just one dearest is enough, at this stage)

Your letter was exactly what I wanted to hear. Your English is excellent. I knew it would be. I've left some things for you, sheet music and a locket my father gave me. I usually wear it. It was my talisman for a better time to come when I was a child. Look for them under my chest of drawers in the bedroom. No doubt Mother will shift you straight back in there, only this time I'm glad of it.

This is a photo of me sitting on the verandah of the hospital enjoying the sun with my friend and deputy Shirley. We look angelic in our white veils. We are not. The junior nurses don't think so anyway. I have a photo of you riding old MacGillacuddy's. She loves you even though she runs away. I showed it to Shirley and told her your name is Joe and that you are a farmer in the area where I live. It's not a lie. She says you are very handsome. Good praise, but not enough. I wouldn't say very, I'd say extremely.

The night is disappearing and I have reports to write, which I'll do with a pen, it will be faster and the secretary can type them in the morning. Remember, everything you do I can picture, because I know what you do and what time of day it is, so if you should think of me, I'll be thinking of you too. You'd better burn this letter. All my love, every last scrap of it. (I wonder if you understand that phrase.)

Eddy

PS I'm not pleased that you have taken over my thoughts, because how can we meet again? Unless at the end of this war another war breaks out and either I am sent to Europe or you are sent out here again. Otherwise, by the time I have saved enough money to go to Italy we will be past caring.

'Where the hell were you all afternoon?'

Max was not happy at tea. His mother had an explanation.

'Were you upset by your letter, Joe?'

'Ah . . . yes,' he answered truthfully.

'Not bad news I hope, was it?' La signora was curious.

'No, not bad, just . . .'

'You must miss your family.'

He did not want this conversation to continue. He turned to Max. 'I'm sorry, can I do some more work tonight?'

'Yes, you can, there's plenty of machinery to get ready for seeding. We have to be ready for the rain when it comes or we'll miss out.'

Giuseppe did not mind working, it was better than brooding and he was becoming interested in machinery and more useful at fixing it. They walked together from the house to the shed, leaving Enzo to help the signora.

'Who was the letter really from?' Max asked as soon as they were out of earshot of his mother.

'What do you mean?'

'Yeah, well, I can't expect you to tell me, you've got too much to lose if my suspicions are correct.'

Giuseppe did not want to keep weaving a complicated lie to get trapped in later. Besides, he respected Max too much to do that. What to say was difficult. 'What are your suspicions?'

'If I tell you, you'll deny them. So I'll just say this. I should send you back to camp but you're a good worker and my mother seems to like you a great deal, although I doubt that she would if she knew what's been going on.'

'Not much has been going on.'

'More than it should have, I'll guess. Too much anyway. I'd never have known, except for the change that came over you when she left. It took me until the letter arrived this morning to put the two things together. Tonight you were happy for the first time in weeks.'

There was nothing for Giuseppe to say, only to listen.

After a silence Max continued, 'I should blow the whistle. I didn't expect you to be such a deceitful bastard. I thought you were someone a bit different, I don't know. I won't put you in, but don't you try and contact her. And the next letter from Victoria for you I'll open. You've never done anything since you've been here to cause any problems. I suggest we go on like that, all right?'

Giuseppe wanted to say something to make him feel better, to reassure him that he had not turned into a monster, but what could he say? Anything he said would either be a lie or incriminating. He was not going to tell him that he did not care for Eddy, that would not be believed and it was all he had to hang on to. It was not likely that Max would let the secret out. His sister had too much to lose. The whole family would be compromised. He could send him back to the camp on some other excuse. All he needed to say was that he could not afford him any more and he would be gone tomorrow. The prisoner was sorry to have lost a friend. He tried reassurance.

'I'm sorry. I do not take this lightly. You must know that I am serious about this.'

'That makes it worse. If you had any real feeling for her, you'd have kept well clear of her, never even thought about it. I should get rid of you, but I need you for the machinery and I'd find it difficult explaining to my mother why you had to go.'

'I will not cause trouble. Too many people would be injured. People who are important to me too.'

'Yeah, well, don't you let me down. I should've known you'd be trouble, a smart bugger like you.'

'And I am smart enough to know how to avoid trouble. I know this could be very bad for all of us. There will be no more letters.'

'You're dead right there.'

Before bed, the prisoner stood in the cold wash house with the lamp, looking at the photo of Eddy. It was a little bleached by the sunlight, but he could see her lovely face and straight dark hair looped behind her veil. She looked remote, intelligent. She looked like someone he had loved for many months now.

SUNDAY SCHOOL PICNIC

The granite outcrop at the Fischer farm covers three or four acres and rises to a height of thirty or forty feet, not high but the highest point for many miles. It punctuates an unvarying landscape. It is dented, gullied and weathered bare, except for a few gnarled she-oaks clumped on ridges. Pale stripes wind down the sides like icing dripping from a cake. Ditches and protected areas grow moss, soft grasses and patches of pink everlasting daisies in spring. In winter, rain ponds in hollows and tadpoles appear. A special bright softness greens the grasses near the rock. It had become a place of refuge and contemplation for Giuseppe, a favourite place. But it was a favourite place for others too.

Duke, who had been christened Marmaduke, lived in a hut at the base of the rock that he tapped for fresh water. In this lush hide protected from the east wind, deep-green casuarinas enveloped him in dark whispers that remained unheard by him and his absent visitors. In flying cap and leather jacket, riding his motorcycle with its sidecar occupied by his one-eyed kelpie, he was a constant reminder of another war — the war that far from ending all wars, now seemed to have extended itself and become this war. The same enemy. His almost useless ears that had not stood up to his encounters with the Red Baron were another reminder. Whatever horrors of blood and carnage had made him retreat from the world, his wounded presence did not deter Jim Fischer from rushing off to sign up. As soon as Prime Minister Menzies declared that due to the 'persistence' of the Germans in their invasion of Poland we were at war in solidarity with Britain, Jim and Hal Fischer and their father, Karl, rose as one from their comfortable chairs and moved away from the wireless to walk about the room. They stood together near the door for a while and went out to sit on the step to talk in low voices. Left alone, their mother began to worry about how her husband would farm the land without his sons and she remembered her dead brother who lay under the hillside at Lone Pine.

Whatever Duke had done over Europe in a Tiger Moth was sure to have been heroic. To go such a great distance to fight for an ideal, for the greater good, was certainly heroic. To his neighbours, he represented the dead heroes who did not return. He was loved because of what they had done, especially because of their dying. He never spoke of his war. If he had been ground staff or clerical, no one wanted to know. Every day he puttered slowly to the post office and general store. There he collected his mail and newspaper and sometimes an interesting brown paper parcel tied with string. They saw him — the children, the youths, and the old — and they remembered.

Unlike most other places, the district had not lost its sons. It had not waved them goodbye to a great adventure and never seen them again. This area had been settled after the war so its heroes came from near and far. Duke was not the only returned hero from the First World War. At the back of Grey Tamma Farm, there was a couple from

England. The north country. He had been the master of a minesweeper in the Battle of Jutland and had been decorated by the King for bravery and devotion to duty. The future of this raw place was assured of success if it attracted people like that. His presence introduced some importance to the place, even optimism.

Once a year, old Duke's hermetic camp at the rock was violated by the Sunday school picnic. He would churn the ice cream, grinning shyly. For a day he became popular with the children who waited all year for the treat. Sometimes the rector's wife would ask him to present the prizes for the races — running, three-legged, egg and spoon. Not an honour normally bestowed on a man without his own piece of land, but his war hero status created an exception. With awe and fear, the children reached out their small hands for the pencils and religious pictures they won. They knew him well by sight, but never attempted to speak to him. His deafness isolated him and you don't speak to a memorial even if it is alive and hobbling about on bandy legs.

The control centre did not encourage farmers to take prisoners on outings, except to church, but on Sundays they were permitted to walk one mile from the farms at which they worked. This regulation was ignored by prisoner and farmer alike, since farms could be ten miles apart, and since the rule was set up to allow visits between neighbouring POW farm workers, no one enforced it. A Sunday school picnic was considered an ideal opportunity for prisoners to assemble and talk. There was no need for military supervision. Each farmer brought his own prisoners and took them home again afterwards.

Giuseppe and Enzo arrived on the back of the truck with Max and Mrs Nash in the cab. They could see a small mottled group of prisoners standing apart in their magenta uniforms that had faded at different rates. Enzo came in good spirits, eager to meet with his fellow prisoners and swap stories. Giuseppe had not crossed the officer/private divide and was almost ready to give up trying. Children walked about in twos and threes eating toffee apples and staring at this strange collection of aliens. Some of the prisoners called them over and tried in broken English to converse. They handed out sweets the children could no longer get, but which the prisoners were able to buy from the deliveries out of the control centre. These were men who thought of their children left at home, not seen since before the war.

Halfway through the afternoon a stranger appeared and caused everyone to stare. She drove a large American car. Not many were left on the road, with petrol being in such short supply. A tall woman dressed in army uniform, suit jacket buttoned, hat at a jaunty angle, got out and walked towards the crowd. Max, who was marshalling the start of the races, looked up and froze. He handed his bag of numbers to the nearest helper and walked towards her. He wanted to say, 'What are you doing here?' but the look on his face said it for him.

'I was going past,' she said without a smile.

'Where to?'

'Kalgoorlie. My father has just flown in there. He asked me to bring the car. He has a few camps to inspect on the way back to Perth.'

'Your father.' Max could hardly keep the loathing out of his voice.

She ignored it. 'He's a colonel. Gets about a bit. I'm his driver.'

They walked slowly away and stood out of sight around the rock. She was edgy, pulling a leaf from a small tree and crushing it for scent, turning her body to take in the countryside without seeing what she looked at and, above all, not looking at Max.

'Why did you come, Alice?'

'I didn't intend to. I drove past Noonalbin and then turned back to ask where you lived. I'd driven ten miles past. I didn't know if you were here. You might have been at the war.'

'Curiosity.'

She was not surprised to find him a little sour but at least he had not warned her off the place.

'If you like. Curiosity doesn't describe it completely.'

'Did you want to see what you'd missed, or what a lucky escape you'd had?'

She walked away again and he had to follow her. They entered a little copse of bottlebrush along the edge of a soggy run-off. The yelling and cheering of the children for the races was dampered and as they walked diminished to silence.

'Donkey orchids,' she said. Yellow and brown long-eared orchids were peppered around the base of the rock with bachelor buttons and spider orchids. She pointed to an oval hole in the rock about two feet across with smooth edges. 'You'd think that was man-made.'

'It was. It's a gnamma hole. It's got a lid.' He picked up a flat rock lying on the ground beside it and placed it over the hole. 'Keeps the rubbish out and stops evaporation. The natives had these waterholes dotted all around what looks like totally dry country.'

He walked up the gentle slope of the rock and disappeared over the side of a ridge. She followed him into a hollow of moss, carpeted with low bushes of white star daisies.

'Huh,' she said, and he didn't know whether it was a sob until she looked at him, and smiled. Max regretted that his first remarks to her had sounded cynical. He needed to show some mettle, but he didn't want to sound sulky and bitter.

'Drive us back to the homestead. I'll make you some tea.'

He was good at calling people's bluff. If she wanted him to be ashamed of his situation and how much less it was than hers, she had chosen the wrong man. Max was proud of his place. It needed some improvements, but nothing a few thousand pounds wouldn't take care of. It was only money. He saw himself and his family as no different from her father and her family. They were both farmers who owned their land and earned a living from it.

They left the picnickers behind to stare and talk. People knew that Max had once had a smart girlfriend from a grazing property down south, and that it had gone badly. That was all they knew. Letters home full of talk about his girlfriend had suddenly stopped and no more was said on the subject. He was not the sort of man you teased about things like that. The mystery of the break-up, at first the subject of speculation, faded. The war had brought much more interesting gossip.

The Buick lunged and pitched across the paddock. Max sat smelling the rich comfort of leather upholstery and trying to think. He was not calm. He looked at her hand for a ring.

'You never married.'

'Almost, once.'

Silence.

'You have a lot of hay,' she said finally, pointing to a yellow church-like structure beside the horse yards.

He took her around the garden. There were not many as good. Certainly the garden on her father's place was nothing in comparison, but he had not had a wife for fifteen years. A garden was strictly a woman's domain. They stood beside the flowering peach to discuss varieties suited to the climate, then under the grape pergola just budding up for leaf, and between the two fig trees, one good, one bad. In the citrus grove he tore off a navel orange taking some dark foliage with it and gave it to her. She held its cold skin against her face and smelled the sweet tang that echoed the long-faded flower. On the screened porch at the back they sat and drank tea, sipping in a little more ease with each mouthful. Remembering is sometimes physical. The remembered comfort of another's presence. They sat, legs stretched, ankles crossed, drinking the tea from identical cups, mirroring like the potted palms in the opposite corners of the porch.

Finally she said, 'Nice. I knew it would be.'

He supposed she meant the house. She was capable of aiming a remark like that at him. She had that sort of bravura. It was still pretty interesting. Wide-apart eyes and a large mouth opened her to people. Fair hair gave her an innocence that was or wasn't there. He thought it might still be. He didn't know any more.

She leaned slowly out of her seat preparing to go. 'Thanks.'

He got to his feet, disappointed at something he had no expectations about, and moved towards the door. She stopped beside him and touched his sleeve.

'Thanks for not sending me away. When I asked in the village and they told me everyone was at the picnic, I thought it was a perfect opportunity. You could hardly abuse me in front of the whole district.'

He walked quickly across the garden to her car and opened the door for her. She got in, started the engine and wound down the window.

'I want to bring my father. Can we call in on the way back?'

Her father was one of the few people he had no time for. He seemed to have no redeeming features, unless you could call his daughter a redeeming feature. Now that he wasn't involved with her any more it was a matter of indifference to him what her father did or where he went.

'I'm sorry, I shouldn't have asked.' She held the steering wheel with both hands and looked down at her knees.

Max leaned his arm across the black hood of the car. Over the fence, lush green stalks of wheat were ready to flower and make heads. He didn't say, why do you want to bring him here?

'It's all right. Silly idea.' She put the car into gear.

'No. No. You come. Bring him. What time are you leaving Kalgoorlie?'

She waited and then slowly looked up at him. 'Six, something like that.'

'We'll expect you for lunch.'

'Thanks.'

'See you tomorrow then.'

Watching the mountainous black vehicle purr away, it occurred to him to wonder how on earth he had been prevailed on to issue such an invitation. He shrugged and turned back to the house. A few quiet hours to pay some bills. Not so quiet inside his head. He kept rethinking her visit, trying to make sense out of it. Did she really think he'd abuse her?

She turned out of the drive. A flash of late sun struck the windscreen. The six-hour journey ahead would give her time to figure out whether his acceptance of the meeting was absolution or indifference. She wanted to see if he could meet her father with civility. Max was always civil, her father, she knew very well, was not. For the first fifty miles she was not happy. She began to lose her nerve and wonder at her bravado. On dusk, she pulled off the road and walked up a stony ridge to look at the sunset. She sat on a block of granite crusted with lichen. Driven by a powerful thirst, she sliced the thick peel from the orange with a small knife. The syrupy liquid ran onto the ground. The flesh was so soft it fell apart as she removed the skin and so sweet her tongue flinched at first contact. The cold of the evening bit into her shoulders through her woollen jacket. The juice on her hands was freezing on her fingertips. As soon as she had swallowed the last segment her thirst intensified. The juice had run down her wrists to the cuff of her white shirt, staining its edges. She shivered and walked back to the car, wondering if it would start. She could be left in the middle of nowhere to spend the night. She was not afraid, but her father would be worried and would send out a search party and cause a huge fuss.

She tried to wipe the stickiness from her hands with her handkerchief. She had meant to refill her water bottle at the farm. She thought of unscrewing the top of the radiator and dipping her handkerchief in the water. Metallic water, reheated and cooled until it turned into something else.

Not sweet for washing hands. In the end she grasped the steering wheel with the dried juice still on her hands and pressed the ignition button. The motor turned over and she swung onto the road towards a father she blamed and away from a former lover who blamed her. She could smell the sweet complexity of dried juice on her skin and on the leather cover of the steering wheel. Her father would smell it. He noticed things like that.

Her head floated above her shoulders alight with images and sensations. Her body had detached itself from the world, cotton-woolled by the dark. No other cars came her way. The lights of the Buick created the road for itself continuously, out of nothing, closing back to nothing over the rear bumper, flat, straight, becoming more rutted as the miles peeled back. The road was dangerous at sundown. Thousands of kangaroos waited in the darkening bushes to leap at the oncoming headlights, bounding to their destruction with rhythmic ritual. Cars and trucks with their fronts pushed in lined the streets of every town. Sometimes the sacrifice of the animal caused the death of the driver as well, and they went together to the hereafter in a tangle of twisted metal and spinning wheels.

Tonight she did not wish to be part of a ritual of sacrifice. Her head was full of impressions sloshing about like row boats at a jetty or coming and going like ferries at a wharf, in and out, not staying long enough to turn into thoughts. It was that place. A collection of iron-roofed buildings. Max and his big personality, but at that place he was more. What she had long imagined had disappeared and been replaced by real things.

Earlier that day, driving the main road from the city, trees had given way after about five hours to scrub, spiky grey wattle and tea tree, uniformly around ten feet tall, as though they had been trimmed into hedges. The land had become continuously flat, the soil pale and unproductive. Then, quite suddenly, the soil had turned dark red and tall trees had begun again. Undulations had come back into the land and a shallow valley with red-limbed trees went off to the north. It was into this valley that she was directed when she came back to the general store and post office to ask for the Nash farm. Trees hedged the paddocks and reached a canopy across the dirt road. She drove past the house on the way to the rock, but she could see that it was well-situated. A dam nestled to the north of it in a glade of slim-branched trees that stroked the ground with their airy shadows. Pendulous eucalypts that gradually climbed the slope to weave between the European trees of the garden. A cluster of bough sheds stood to the south beneath a clump of taller salmon gums. Beyond them you could see across three paddocks of wheat and grass to where the trees closed in again along the Old York Road.

Max had disappeared from the city and the south and its civilisation to a place no one knew about. A flat, dry place, where towns were eighty miles apart and where no one of consequence lived. But now that she had been there, it was not so much what she saw but what she felt that stayed with her. Unlike a city, filled with thoughts and ambitions boiling together in a potent urban concoction, this place did not rely on people for its soul. It had its own purpose. Some people were rejected and went away, others went there and kept going back until they stayed. She had turned around the car. The place had reached out and pulled her in. Whatever history she and Max had between them was now in a new framework. The place could heal and destroy, like bathing in the sea. She would go back there with her father because she could not drive past. He would be affected by it too. He would know then that he could no longer hold her and that she was capable of finding other worlds.

Right on midday the phone rang in the front hall. Mrs Nash answered it and handed it to Max. It was Alice asking if he would come to the siding and pick her up. She was waiting at the store. His car took a bit of starting, but once it was going it was reliable. He found her inside the store talking to Maisy. He didn't know if he was capable of imagining the hyperbole the postmistress would use to make juicy gossip out of this. It had rained in the night, the air was sweet and the tyres crackled on the damp ground.

'Thanks.' Alice sounded shaky.

'What happened?' he asked, even though he thought he knew.

'My father refused to even think of stopping for lunch with you.'

He wondered why she seemed so surprised.

'I pulled up here for petrol and then refused to get back in.'

This must have delighted Maisy and her customers.

'He called my bluff and drove off shouting that he'd have me court-martialled.'

'Can he?'

'He can, but he won't, and even if he does ...' She drifted out of the conversation into thought, turning her head to watch the crops spinning by.

Max felt a surge of renewed interest in her. This was the Alice of before, but even more so. It didn't impress him that she would defy her father and flout army rules, but it did impress him that she did what she set out to do. A person could go a long way on that quality and you didn't always find it in women, especially when confronted by a bullying man. He turned often to look at her profile as they drove along.

When Max introduced her to his mother and it was clear that Alice had not brought her father to lunch, there was some awkwardness. Mrs Nash stood for a while as though frozen. Max was not sure if it was Alice's statuesque presence or the disappointment at not being able to feed a colonel on steak and kidney pudding. No question about it, it was a man's menu. He knew this would discomfort her. If she'd known it would be only the daughter, she'd have cooked a lighter pie, egg and bacon. He hoped Alice hadn't noticed her behaving as though she sensed a threat.

Alice, though polite to the mother, had thoughts only for the son. There were a lot of things she would tell him if he showed signs of rekindling his interest in her.

Part Three

Martyr

Scourge deep, and quick be done,
Dislodge the marrowed bone:
He did not wince or shake,
Nor did that rack his noble silence break.
Three hundred years ago!
But life still has it so —
Tests for the splendid blood,
And martyrdom for regal hardihood.
Mouth-deep amid the tide,
She strove and saved, and died,
Giving the stranger place,
Though waves climbed upward o'er her shining face.

'E'

SPRUNG

Mrs Nash had been cleaning Eddy's room. 'What a waste of a day,' she said. 'My mother used to call a day like this a day of sighs,' and she turned and beamed at the three men sitting at the table. 'We get them sometimes in the middle of August when it should still be winter. There's no wind. The warm air sighs on the wattle and lifts the scent in the air and holds it up. I'm always pleased I've spent time in the garden in autumn when a day like this comes and you're looking for colour to go with fragrance and it all builds up the promise of spring. The sweet peas went in on St Patrick's Day and they are nearly ready to flower. They are spring in one flower, colour, fragrance, the early ones, not afraid of a late cold snap.'

'Well, there's not much evidence of spring in here, except for the blowies.' Max was the last to sit down for lunch.

The signora's delirium at the warm day astonished Giuseppe, since she had poisoned the air in the kitchen with the odour of poaching salt cod and steaming cauliflower. Flies had darted, crashed and wriggled into the kitchen in pursuit of these delicacies through any secret hole in gauze or warp in window frame and were buzzing in deafening death throes at the window trying to escape. Even for them the smell was too strong.

Four eaters sat at the lunch table consuming what three of the four found to be unappetising. The signora Nash not only adored the flavours on her plate, but found they added to her already happy anticipation of spring.

'I was so lucky to get the last piece of fish. The fish man only comes once a month and I just happened to arrive at the siding when his van was pulling out.'

Fortunate perhaps for the fish man, but not for his victims, his customers. Max was eating large lumps of bread with his fish and washing it down with gulps of tea. Halfway through his meal he went to the wireless in the corner and turned it on. They were all impatient for it to warm up, eager to hear the news.

'This is the news, read by Peter Evans.' They sat up a little in their seats, silent and still. 'Japan has surrendered to the allies. Today Emperor Hirohito of Japan accepted the terms of the Potsdam Agreement. Unconditional surrender. "I cannot bear to see my innocent people suffer any longer," he said.'

They hear the voice of the Australian Prime Minister, Chifley, tell his citizens that the war is over. ' "Let us remember those whose lives were given, that we may enjoy this glorious moment and may look forward to a peace which they have won for us. Let us remember those whose thoughts with proud sorrow turn towards gallant loved ones who will not come back." '

Max had been standing near the wireless. He turned it off and came with the slow steps of thought back to the table. 'Thank God for that. I thought the Yanks might have to go on dropping bombs on them till there was nothing left.'

'Nothing might be just the right amount when it comes to Japs.' The signora had no sympathy for the people in the bombed cities. 'They deserve everything they get. If we let them off easily, they'll re-arm and be down here in a flash. And we'll be in the middle of another war before we know it. Look at Germany. They took no notice of their defeat last time and heaven knows if the Americans will help us again. We know the British won't.'

'You don't have to worry about that, Mum. There's not going to be another war. Now the Americans have got an atom bomb, any future war will be over before it starts.'

'What if the enemy gets one?'

'They'll get one, there's nothing surer.'

'We'll all be wiped out.'

'There's every possibility. For the first time in history, we actually have the wherewithal to annihilate the human race.'

'How dreadful.'

'I wouldn't worry about the Japs, they're finished for a while at least. The thing we have to worry about now is the commos.'

'Commos?'

'Communists, Russians. Stalin, that lot.'

'But they're so far away.'

'Not really, nothing is far away any more.'

'What a pity Mr Curtin wasn't alive to see this day,' she said with regret. 'He was a good man for Australia. He stood up for us, not like Mr Menzies.'

'We haven't heard the end of Menzies yet,' Max said, pushing his plate away and taking his tobacco pouch from his pocket.

'I must telephone Yvonne. She'll have her boys back now. Thank God.'

'If they're still alive.'

Max's last comment brought a lull in the conversation.

Enzo was emotional. He could go home now to the six-year-old son he had never met. Giuseppe was pleased to be going home, but there were things here that he would miss.

'This is a very good day.'

'Yes, Joe, it certainly is,' said the signora. 'You boys can go home now. We'll miss you.'

Enzo stood up and said in his broken English, 'Please excuse,' and left the house to be with his own thoughts. Giuseppe felt a pang of envy that Enzo had so much to go home to.

'Well.' The signora rose from her seat. 'I'm going to leave the dishes until I've finished spring-cleaning. What a good day to begin. Out with the old and in with the new. We can all start again in a better world. I must say I don't know what's got into Eddy, she's put some jewellery and sheet music under her chest of drawers, can't imagine why. Anyway, it's clear she doesn't want them. I'll put them in the jumble at next week's church fete.'

The things that Eddy left for Giuseppe. The locket her father gave her. If he tried to stop the signora from donating them to the stall, he'd give himself and Eddy away, so he said lamely, 'If you know they are hers, you do not need to sell them at the stall.'

Max shot him a glance that said either, 'It is not your concern,' or, 'What are you up to now?'

Giuseppe had not had an opportunity to get into her room and find the things she had left for him. Enzo and he had not been invited back to the house. They were settled in their hut now, and it was possible that distance from the family was preferred by three of the four of them. He walked around the table and held the door open for the signora and casually asked if she needed any furniture shifted.

'Good idea, then I can clean properly behind the wardrobe.'

Max, who had been scowling through his eyebrows, followed them into the bedroom and together they moved things about as his mother cleaned. Eddy's room was deep in the house, cushioned from the world by the dampened quiet of thick mud walls. The absence of sound, the scent of lavender, the cold of the room even on this premature spring day, emphasised the absence of its owner. Occasional whiffs of jasmine drifted through the open casement to be immediately absorbed into the cold air and the fragrance already there. Two large men clomping about her room in work clothes seemed like an intrusion.

The music and locket Eddy had left for Giuseppe were on the dressing table in a basket, with various small jewellery boxes and scarves, pieces of lace and a beret, for the jumble sale no doubt. He had an idea to pocket the necklace without a word, but realised before he committed this folly that the situation had become absurd. It was only a silver chain with an embossed oval locket on the end. Losing it would not be the end of her connection with her father, it would not change her memory of him or his of her. Even so, it had better be saved if possible.

'Joe, you can go, I'll manage here,' Max said.

'Don't be silly, Max, how will you lift the wardrobe on your own?' the signora asked.

'Why do you want to lift the wardrobe?'

'Dust, dust. We are going to need this room if Miss Anderson is coming to stay.'

'Call her Alice, Mum, and she's not going to look behind the wardrobe.'

'Yes, but I like to know it's clean.'

'You don't have to clear Eddy's things out. As soon as the war's over, she'll be back.'

'You think so?' said his mother, as if she was discussing the weather. She sounded remote, as though she'd lost interest in her daughter.

Giuseppe felt put out for Eddy. He thought of the night on the way to the dance when she'd become angry and shouted at Max that her mother never considered her. He had laughed at her, but she may have been somewhere near the mark.

Max and Giuseppe stood at each end of the wardrobe. 'We'll lift it straight forward,' Max said. 'Awkward bloody thing. One, two, three, lift.'

They could shift it only two or three inches. Giuseppe moved around to the front of the monstrous piece of furniture and knelt down to remove the drawer that ran the length of the base. A whiff of naphthalene rose into the air as he pulled it out onto the floor. Here was part of her story preserved in knitted clothing. As it slid away from the frame he caught sight of something white on the floor behind the drawer. As soon as he placed his hand over it he knew what it was. He held up the handkerchief parcel to Max.

'A gift from Carlo, I think.'

Max snatched the parcel and moved quickly onto the verandah. Giuseppe and Mrs Nash followed and watched his thick fingertips open out the fabric on the palm of his hand like a child unwrapping a cache of sweets. He shook his head in disbelief at the two sticks of gelignite. Mrs Nash clapped her hands to her cheeks and whimpered, 'Eddy could have been blown to smithereens.'

Giuseppe was relieved to see the explosives after all this time. He had sometimes wondered whether they had all been too hasty in blaming Carlo for their disappearance. His prickly personality had made him an obvious scapegoat.

The telephone rang in the hall outside Eddy's room. Mrs Nash answered it. She spoke in an excited clatter of words and then came back onto the verandah. 'There's a Victory Day dance tonight. You can come too, Joe, you and Vince.'

She had been quickly distracted from the horror of her daughter's detonation. A victory dance did not sound like the sort of occasion at which a prisoner of war would be welcome. Giuseppe judged that no one would be pleased to see them.

'Thank you,' he said quietly. Later he would make an excuse. Enzo would not want to go.

Walking along the path to the shed through green, knee-high wild oats and yellow-faced, black-eyed cape weed, they could hear Enzo attempting to straighten a ploughshare, the blows of his hammer clanging against the metal. Max was not pleased. Giuseppe guessed that it was he as well as Carlo who caused him this displeasure. Giuseppe had joined a select group. No doubt Max felt the betrayal of Giuseppe being in his sister's room in what Mrs Nash thought was all innocence, but which Max knew was not. Max didn't want to conspire with the Itie prisoner against his mother, but to do anything else would have caused repercussions. Finally he said, 'What did you think you were playing at?'

Giuseppe thought for a moment and decided to be honest, since every other option would have been worse. He was in danger of looking like a pervert who wanted to creep around a woman's room. He explained that in her letter Eddy had written that she had left some things for him under the chest of drawers, as she thought Enzo and he would be going back into her room.

'My mother wanted you back in there, but I wouldn't hear of it. I don't want you in her room. The best thing that could happen is for that stuff to go to the church fete.'

'I do not think so.'

'I'm not asking your opinion.'

'Perhaps, but I have something to say.'

Max stopped short of the shed so that Enzo would not be within hearing distance. He turned to Giuseppe and with hands on hips said, 'Well?'

'I make no claim on the things she left for me, but I ask you to save the necklace. It was a present from your father. Don't let your mother give it away.'

Max grunted and puffed air through his nose and nodded as if to say, 'I might have guessed,' and turned to walk into the shed.

Giuseppe spoke quickly to prevent him. 'Will you report the gelignite theft? We know that Carlo did steal it now.'

Max paused and half turned to the prisoner. 'The war's over. You blokes'll be on your way home any day,' and he disappeared into the shadows of the toolshed.

Giuseppe imagined he heard relief in this statement. Eventually, in spite of their hard work and companionship, the Italian prisoners had become a nuisance. Giuseppe felt discouraged. It was all such a waste. The war, pervasive to the most obscure place, had become personal. Max wanted to judge how personal. A friendship between two men was acceptable to him, but an attachment between a man and woman overstepped every boundary. Giuseppe was not without sympathy for Max's point of view. The only hitch was that it applied to him and to Eddy.

That the necklace had sentiment attached to it was the reason she wanted Giuseppe to have it. He was unkind enough to wonder whether her mother was aware of Eddy's attachment to it, and whether she was eager to get rid of it because it came from Eddy's father. He wondered what it was that made this good and generous woman give the things of her children away when they left. He remembered the emotional disbelief of the young woman who found her wardrobe empty when she returned from military service. He had thought then that the mild patience of the mother in the face of the hysteria of her daughter made the younger woman look to be the one at fault, but was beginning to suspect that this might not be the case. Eddy, like her brother, was uncompromising, but usually right in matters of honour and honesty.

Max sent him to the eastern boundary of the farm for the rest of the afternoon to fix the fence. He piled posts, wire and tools on the back of the truck and drove away feeling like a schoolboy ordered to sit in the corner and face the wall.

For dinner the first night of Alice's stay, the prisoners found themselves eating alone in the kitchen. The others were to eat later in the dining room. Instead of her usual evening clothes, the signora had on what she might have worn to church, but she had tied her apron over the top. Max had shown Alice around the farm. She had spoken to the prisoners, asking them what they were doing and where they came from. She was as tall as Max with blonde hair and icy translucent skin. After a few days, she made friends with Giuseppe when she discovered he liked to play chess. The family had gone back to eating the evening meal with the prisoners and the signora invited them in to sit with them after dinner, and asked Giuseppe to play the piano.

Alice showed no particular interest in music. She wandered around the room, warming herself at the fire and taking books off shelves to look at their covers, or looking at pictures in their frames. She picked up a photo of Eddy in her military uniform with her hat at a stylish angle over her right eye and said to Max, 'She's like you, only dark.'

'She's nothing like me,' he replied from behind his newspaper.

'Who uses the chess set?' she asked.

'I do.'

'Who else?'

'No one.'

'You play against yourself? I bet I know who wins.'

'Joe plays,' he said reluctantly.

'Let's play,' she said, opening the box and setting out the pieces on the board.

'I'd like to but I've got to write some letters.'

'Just one game.'

The signora had been looking sternly at her needles while she knitted at the speed of light. Giuseppe had witnessed a conversation between the mother and son in which he explained that the troops no longer needed woollen jumpers as they were now in the tropics. But she had replied that she was knitting for the Russians.

'We'd better let him do his office work, dear. Joe will play with you,' she said.

This was not a good suggestion. Max, already out of

sorts since the bedroom incident, would not want Giuseppe taking his place on the other side of the chessboard from his girlfriend. Alice, as though she hadn't heard any of what the older woman said, sidled up to Max and peered over the top of his newspaper.

'Just one game, I'm not much good, it won't take long.'

Max stood up, folded his paper and put it on the table. 'Maybe later.' He gave her a slow half smile.

On a winter's night he usually brought his papers in to work at the dining table as his office had no heating, being a thinly clad addition to the side verandah. A gust of freezing air pierced the room as he opened the door and before he went he turned and said, 'If you play with Joe, watch out, he cheats.'

It soon became clear to Giuseppe that she had not been honest about her ability. She was not a bad player at all.

After some minutes she said, 'How do you cheat? I'd love to know how to cheat at chess.'

'I do not cheat, but if you are so eager I'll think of something.'

By ten o'clock Giuseppe was ready to go to bed. Enzo had gone an hour before, followed soon after by the signora who said good night after primping and tidying the room. Max came back from his office.

'You still here?' he said eyeing Giuseppe with hostility.

The prisoner stood up. 'Perhaps we should pack up.'

'We can't do that,' Alice said, turning to Max. 'He can't be much of a cheat. I'm winning. We must finish the game tomorrow night.'

Giuseppe left them standing in the middle of the living room together. She was an engaging woman. A good match for Max. He regretted being the object of his dislike.

He began to notice that Alice was not finding her visit easy. At first, she would jump up from the table to help with the serving, cooking or clearing up. None of her offers of assistance were accepted. After a while she kept to her seat. On days when she was not with Max she would wander about the farmyard idly enjoying the sun or watching Enzo or Giuseppe at their chores. She never seemed to stay at the house.

On Sunday, the prisoner took his customary walk to the rock and stumbled upon her dozing in a sunny recess.

'You have walked far,' he said.

'Not so far, is it? I kept asking Max, but he just never got around to bringing me here, so I came myself.'

'No one comes here, except once a year for the Sunday school picnic.'

'Ah yes, the Sunday school picnic.'

'And old Duke lives on the other side. But he never bothers anyone.'

'A hermit?'

'I am sure he would like to be, but he cannot succeed in it. Not quite.'

'Poor man.'

'He is happy.'

'To want to be a hermit and to fail. That's dreadful. There are so many things to fail at in life, but to fail at being a failure. Tragic.'

He laughed and nodded. 'You are a little wicked, I think.'

'Mrs Nash thinks I am. Actually, I'm dutiful and conventional. But I'm always rubbing her up the wrong way.'

'Rubbing?'

'Not literally. It means annoying someone, like stroking a cat against the lie of the fur.'

'That's very good.'

'English is, sometimes. How do you come to speak it so well?'

'I learnt at school and university. Languages are not so hard for me. And at university I had an English friend. The English make colonies all over Italy.'

'And tell me, why is it that Mrs Nash likes you such a lot and Max doesn't seem to like you at all?'

'I could ask you the same question only turned around the other way.'

'Yes, you could. And I would answer that Max likes me because I like him and I'm here, and I don't know why Mrs Nash doesn't. What would you answer?'

'I would answer that I don't know why in both cases.'

'And I would say that you are not telling the truth, because I know Max and he doesn't dislike anyone unless they have done something he disapproves of and then he is not easily moved to forgiveness. So, what have you done?' She had him in a corner.

He laughed and said, 'You are very clever, but perhaps not always right.'

'And you are evasive.'

He let that go and they lapsed into silence. He moved to walk on and she said, 'Must you go? I'd be glad of some company. Wouldn't you like to sit in the sun for a while?'

'I don't think Max . . . I was going for a walk.'

'You've just been for one. Have you been here before?'

'Many times.'

'And you're tired of it.'

'Not at all.'

'Have you seen the gnamma hole?'

'The nam pole?'

'Gnamma hole. Come with me.' She climbed up and over the top of the rock and through the gullies that had been full of white star daisies the first time she'd seen them until low on the edge of the rock she squatted and slid the rock lid away from the hole. 'It still has water in it. It's deep, at least ten feet, like a tank. I've put a stick down, but can't find one long enough to reach the bottom. It was made by natives.'

'You are observant. I have been coming here for two years and I did not find that.'

'Max showed me, the day of the picnic. I love to think of the Aborigines squatting here, dipping water out of the hole. The women and children. I wonder how long since they did. I found an even larger one around the other side, but the lid is gone and it's full of dirt and leaves.'

They sat above the hole in a moss hollow. The sun shafted its rays through his skin until he felt warm to his bones. This place had taken on a completely different character with her in it. Alone here, his thoughts drift out and away, across the granite like fog, seeping into crevices and lying on ponds, resting, re-forming, becoming part of his beliefs, or floating away, for ever lost. Today these thoughts stayed inside his head. He didn't mind. When Enzo went visiting, and now that Eddy had gone away, Sunday was a lonely day.

'You don't go to mass?'

'No.'

'I thought all Italians went to mass.'

'When the men are home they go with their wives. Here we are free to choose.'

'You have a wife?'

'Not me, Enzo does.'

'So, no one makes you go to church at home either?'

'My mother and sister, but I don't live with them.'

'Where do you live?'

'Trieste.'

'And where do they?'

'In the mountains, near Lake Como.'

'I've been there with my father. It's the most beautiful place I've ever seen. You must long for it.'

So many people speak this way of Lombardia, thought Giuseppe, but how many know that its beauty comes at a price. You cannot eat scenery or build houses with it.

'The beauty of a place isn't everything,' he said.

'I think it is.'

'Do you want to marry Max?'

'You ask pointed questions.'

'If so, then you will have to live here.'

'This place is beautiful,' she said, lying back to see more of the sky.

Giuseppe believed this place was not valuable for its beauty so much as its productivity. It offered a better life because there were not more people depending on it than it could sustain. It had an attraction, a feel, but to use the word beauty to describe it, and then the same word in the same breath for his mountains, made him laugh. 'You admire the Italian lakes and you admire this?'

'Why not? They're opposites, but this place has a spirit. I loved the beauty of your lakes and mountains, but when I came here on the day of the picnic I was surprised.'

'Perhaps it was the people not the place.'

'It was the place.'

'What had you expected?'

'I don't know, nothing, just fences and dry grass.'

'Even dry grass was green once.'

'I suppose so, but I thought it was always summer here.'

'Summer is long here, and hot.'

'Even in summer I think I would like it. It's clean, in a dusty sort of way, and tidy in a bare sort of way. And it's so full of sky. The sky fills up everything. It reaches down and fills any empty space, look.' She pointed to a pond near her feet, reflecting the sky perfectly, as though it had reached down to fill a void.

'And when you finally get to the trees they are so inviting, so oasis-like, you just want to dissolve into the shade beneath them. I walked across the paddock to that small lake among the trees and it's teeming with every kind of waterfowl. I disturbed some wild geese and they all rose together and skidded low across the water and flew off in formation. Lovely.'

'They will be gone soon, all of them. And by the beginning of summer that lake will not be there. It will disappear. It is quite shallow.'

'All the better for reflecting the sky. All the more appreciated for not always being there.'

She was determined to be pleased by everything in this place, even the things it did not have. Now that the war was over, Giuseppe's attachment was beginning to change. It was unlikely that he would ever be back again. It was unwise to become attached to things you are never going to have. He should have thought of that when he became obsessed with Eddy. Alice was not like Eddy. Alice was serene and knowing, where Eddy was sharp and witty. Eddy was all-encompassing. Whatever she was thinking or doing was bound to be something he had not thought of. She would follow an idea as far as she could, to where it disintegrated or took up a new form. Every shadow was darker, every shaft of sun lighter. With her, he did not feel any pressure to be what he was not, to conform, to live up to a social formula. All he had to do was be alive, and with her he was a hundred and fifty per cent alive.

Two weeks later he returned in the evening from fencing on the east boundary to find that the officer from the control centre had been. There were two letters waiting for him. One was a typewritten envelope postmarked Victoria, the other was from Italy. Enzo had bought cigarettes and soap, and writing paper for him. They sat on their beds waiting for the dinner bell to sound. He turned the letters over in his hands. He would read them later, when he had enough time to properly digest them. He was not eager to open them. Their contents could be anything. He had reason to dread.

Enzo interrupted his thoughts. 'That will cause trouble,' he said, pointing to the one from Victoria.

'Not if they don't know about it.'

'The signora knows, she brought it here.'

'Two letters for you today, Joe. Another one from your Victorian aunt?'

Max stopped eating and put down his knife and fork.

'Pity you can't see her before you go home. It may be your only chance.'

Max got up and left the room. After five minutes he came back to the door and said, 'Joe, could you come out here for a minute? There's something I want you to help me sort out.'

The prisoner stood up and started to clear the table.

The signora said, 'You go, Joe, Max is probably waiting.'

Enzo stood up and took the plates from him, giving him a look that might have said 'I told you so,' if it hadn't said 'you fool!'

Alice looked at the faces of the three in the room, trying to work out what was going on and then, coming to no conclusion, began to help clear the table. As he left the kitchen Giuseppe heard the signora say, 'Now my dear, I'll do this, and Vince is here to help. You go and sit by the fire.' Poor Alice, it seemed that the signora could not bear to have her in the same room.

He stepped out into the moonlit night. The air was crisp in spite of the warm day. He could see by the red glow from a cigarette where Max was standing, beside the post and rail fence near the old bough shed. As he approached, he saw him throw down his cigarette and step on it. He then succeeded in surprising him, although when he thought about it afterwards he should have predicted it. He squared up to the prisoner and threw a big swinging right-arm punch that connected with the left side of his jaw and mouth and knocked him sideways where he crumpled into the dirt. He did not pick himself up straight away, more out of shock than physical injury. When he finally scrambled to his feet Max had turned his back and was leaning over the fence clearly feeling confident that Giuseppe did not intend to return the blow. The prisoner could see him holding his knuckles and hoped they were bleeding and stinging like his lip. He hoped that when his teeth had gone through his lip they had gone through Max's fist as well. He could taste the metallic saltiness of his blood and feel his lip starting to thicken.

'You mightn't think it's very Geneva Convention to whack a POW on the jaw, but I'm sure you know why I did it.'

Giuseppe stood behind him pressing the back of his hand to his lip to stop the bleeding. He fought the urge to take a swing at him and turn it into a brawl. His years as a prisoner had made him more passive than he used to be.

'You did it because your sister wrote me a letter.'

'That's right.'

'The logic I cannot follow.'

A sneer slipped into Giuseppe's voice before he could check it. Max turned quickly and he jumped back.

'I'm not going to hit you again, but I don't like the tone in your voice. You can pack your bags. I'll ring the control centre tomorrow and if they don't come and get you I'll take you to them. I warned you I'd have none of this. I believed you when you promised to put an end to it.'

Giuseppe tried to sound calm and respectful. 'You should have told her of our agreement. She did not know of my promise. She does not know that you found out about us. You have taken this out of proportion. Nothing happened between us until she was about to leave, and now she is not here, nothing can happen.'

'What does she say in the letter?'

'I don't know. I have not read it yet.'

'You don't expect me to believe that?'

'Nevertheless, it is true.'

'Well, you can give me the letter.'

Giuseppe was silent. He was not going to betray Eddy by letting anyone else read a letter she had meant for him, not even her brother, or especially not her brother. Max read his silence accurately.

'You're a snake in the grass. I was an idiot to trust you.'

'Neither of those things are true. I did not write to Eddy. I kept my word, although I see it has done me no good. We will be sent home soon. Could I not stay and help with haymaking and harvest until it is time for us to leave?'

Max started to walk back to the house and as he went he said, 'Yes you could, except for one thing. I can't stand to look at your deceitful bloody face.'

These words from Max hit harder than the punch. They had been friends, in an unequal sort of way, and now he was bitterly disliked. Of late, he had been giving Giuseppe the worst jobs as far away from him as possible. He had been looking for a reason to get rid of him. Giuseppe was beginning to feel angry with Max. There was no future here for him. He was to go back behind barbed wire. It was better to go. Perhaps he could be sent to another farm. He was confident the reason for his dismissal would never be told.

He sat on the bed in the hut holding the unopened letter. He no longer feared losing Max's trust by reading it, but its appearance had made him unwelcome at this place for ever. He dreaded going back to the camp. He hoped that his stay would be short before he was repatriated. He hoped Max would find another prisoner to replace him, so that Enzo would not be lonely.

'You have been fighting,' Enzo said.

'Yes.' Giuseppe was not going to tell him that it was one-sided. He did not want him to lose respect for Max and lose his place here too.

'I will miss you.'

'Thanks.'

They were unlikely to meet again. Such a warm-hearted man.

Dear Joe,

I have just hated not getting a letter from you. I know I told you not to risk writing, but I wish you had not heeded my request. Anyway, I have news. I wanted you to know first, and in a couple of days I'll write to Mum and Max and tell them.

I am coming back to WA to work in the repatriation hospital in Perth. They are to set up a plastic-surgery unit there as well. It is a promotion as I'll be sister in charge, whereas I am only second in charge here. In the army you only ever hear about these sorts of things when everything is all set to go, so I'll be leaving here at the end of the week. I'll catch the train home the first leave I get which will probably be about two weeks after I start. So, instead of never seeing you again I'll see you again, very soon, if they haven't sent you back to Italy by then.

I'm not going to spend a lot of time and ink telling you things I can tell you in person when I see you. When I see you. That sounds good. I can't believe the war is finally over. I thought it might go on for a hundred years. I can't believe we will see each other again. I thought it would be a million years before we did. I hope that you will be as pleased as I am and if you are looking forward to seeing me half as much as I am you, then it will be a very great deal indeed.

With all my love,
Eddy

He was not pleased. He was devastated. For this letter he had lost his job. He had lost the opportunity to see her again. If he is in camp, he will not be allowed to see her. If she had not written to tell him she was coming, he could have seen her. He used to think he liked irony, but he found he didn't. Only God enjoys irony. He didn't know what to do with the anger that was mounting in him. He wanted to go to the house and tell them everything. He had nothing to lose. If it were not for Eddy's reputation, he would announce it to the world.

Without enthusiasm he opened the second letter. It was from his sister. She had information about their father. He had been shot with the partisans that he had helped. She was trying to find out what they had done with his body.

EVERLASTINGS

'Why do you want to marry me?'

'That's a funny question.'

'I'm not trying to be funny. I really don't know why you want to marry me. You'd never have contacted me if I hadn't crashed the Sunday school picnic.'

'It was you who sent me away. Your father chased me off with his gun, like I was some sort of poacher.'

'I was young. He said you didn't care about me.'

'I did care about you, I still do and I want to marry you.'

'But why? You don't spend time with me. I have to play chess with Joe and explore the rock with Joe. Why aren't you jealous of him?'

'Jealous? Not of him.'

'You don't like him.'

Max was silent. They were walking up the slow rise behind the house with evening sun splashing an orange wash across drifts of pink everlastings. He had agreed to her request for him to show her the wildflowers, but he was clearly humouring her.

'You've seen everlastings before.'

'Not like this. This is vast. Goes on for miles.'

'And shows me where the sand plain starts and finishes. I have to admit that I've got plenty of poor land when I see this.'

'Doesn't look poor to me, looks like heaven.'

They walked on in fading light and musk air.

'Where's Joe?' she asked. 'He wasn't at lunch.'

'The control centre officer took him this morning, back to camp.'

'That was sudden.'

Max was not looking forward to telling Alice that he had a sister who was weak and wilful. He wanted to offer her a better family to marry into.

'What happened last night, after dinner?'

'I had to send him away.'

They walked on past the flowers into the scrub where a few kangaroos were coming out for some evening grazing. They turned their heads without fear to look at the two walkers and loped away to find sweeter grass.

'It's none of my business?'

He wanted to tell her, but the thought of exposing Eddy was stopping him.

'No, I just find it hard, don't know where to start.'

'Start at the end. What happened last night?'

'We had it out, I sent him packing.'

'I know that, but why?'

'This is the hard part for me. I suppose everyone is going to know eventually.'

She waited while he collected his thoughts. 'You don't think I would betray your confidence?'

'Not at all. It's just that this is juicy gossip and we all know that there's no containing that.'

'Juicy gossip? He doesn't seem the type.'

'Exactly. I've been completely fooled about him. It turns out he and Eddy are having some sort of liaison.'

'And . . .?'

'And nothing, that's it.'

'You sacked him for that?'

'Of course.'

'I don't believe it.'

'He's a prisoner of war, Al, an enemy alien.'

'Is that all you've got against him?'

'He's a working man.'

'And Italian? Is that worrying you?'

'Probably.'

'So you think he's her social inferior. You don't like him because he's from a Mediterranean country of inferior people?'

'Al, it's not that simple. Eddy and . . .'

'Even though he is better educated than any of us and has better manners?'

'Manners are nothing if the man underneath lacks character.'

They had stopped over the brow of the rise. The shadows were long. It was cool now. She had turned to face him. He was astonished to feel her hostility. He hadn't expected her to take Joe's side. He couldn't see that Joe had a leg to stand on. She went on building her argument.

'He lacks character? Have you ever had a good conversation with the man?'

'He lived here for over two years.'

'What did you talk about? Marking lambs and fencing paddocks? I talked to him. I had to. There was no one else. You are too busy and your mother doesn't want to look at me, let alone talk to me. And after a while I began to realise that he was the first man I've ever had a real conversation with. The first man who seemed to enjoy my company and value my opinions. He didn't get up and have an important job to do if I happened to introduce a topic that interested me. Is that what you call lacking in character? If your sister has managed to foster a serious attachment in a man like that, she has my admiration.'

By this time Alice had become quite heated. Max could see tears in her eyes. That pansy bastard, creating problems between Alice and him as well as ruining his sister's life. That Alice would compare him with such a poor excuse for a man and find him wanting. He turned around and started back to the house, too angry to say anything. He felt betrayed by Alice. He would never have thought that she would like a pathetic European dandy in preference to a good down-to-earth Aussie. What was the matter with women? They wanted men to kill other men to save the country and starve in concentration camps and work clearing land like draught horses and down mines until they died from dust on the lungs and then talk about flower-arranging and hair-dos. No wonder he'd never found anyone he wanted to marry until he'd met Alice and even Alice was turning out no better than any of the others. He accelerated his pace and lengthened his stride. Alice tried to match him and then fell back. He walked ahead for a while and then decided he would wait for her. He might be an ignorant insensitive bloke, but he wasn't a cad. He wouldn't take a girl for a walk and leave her in the middle of the bush.

At the table Mrs Nash chatted on, asking Enzo about Giuseppe, why he had to go back to the Northam camp to attend the hospital when there was a perfectly good one seventy miles from here. Asking Enzo if he'd heard from his wife, fussing about his son, praising his patience. Enzo endured it all and Max was grateful that he kept up the charade. His mother would find out one day, but hopefully by then the whole thing would have blown over. He believed that Eddy was just suffering from a bit of wartime madness and Joe, like most men, was not going to pass up a good thing when it was offering. Time would solve it. Eddy would come to her senses after she hadn't seen him for a while, and it would all just fade into the past. Meanwhile the idea was to keep a lid on it, not let it get onto the gossip circuit.

Alice didn't offer to wash dishes. Max noticed that she hardly spoke at dinner. She left the kitchen early and when he looked for her in the living room she wasn't there. He went to her bedroom, Eddy's room, and knocked. She was sitting in the dark on her bed holding her knees. He sat down beside her and they held each other. Max was unhappy to see her low, but wild with delight to think that she might be upset because they had argued.

He said, 'Alice, I'm interested in your ideas.'

'It's all right,' she sniffed. 'You are you. I like that.'

'You understand why I sacked Joe?'

'Not really.'

'Is that what you're crying about?'

'Not really.'

'What else have I done?'

'Not just you, me too. I have things to tell you, and when I finish you're not going to want to marry me.'

Max didn't believe this. She was a bit silly when it came to men with smooth manners, but that was no different from any other woman he'd ever met. He reckoned he could live with that. What could she say that would make him change his mind about marrying her?

They sat in the bedroom and talked until grey light seeped between the branches of the cape lilacs outside the casement doors. Then they slipped down into her bed and slept in each other's arms, holding tight together because of the narrow bed and because of the things she had told him. Rather than not wanting to marry her, he was never going to let her out of his sight again. She had put up with the shame and terror of pregnancy at the age of eighteen. Of having an illegal abortion turn to septicaemia, of touch-and-go weeks in hospital under the disapproving eyes of the doctors and nurses, of begging forgiveness from an overbearing father who now really had something to bargain with. This long night tore out his gut. His own faults grew uglier as the hours passed. He blamed himself for going off like some cowboy out of the wild west to make money without letting her know where he was. He was so burdened by the need for money. With the responsibility of his mother and sister and the farm. He could have no claim on Alice without something of security to offer her, let alone wealth. Anyone else would have learnt to hate him by now. He was glad he'd confined his resentment to her father and never allowed himself to grow bitter towards her.

'We'll get married.'

'Children, Max.'

'So what?'

'You'll want them later.'

'So long as we can get some from somewhere, I don't care whose they are. Children are children. I like them all.'

'What about your mother? She's not delighted with me.'

'She'll have to get delighted. What can she possibly have against you?'

'She doesn't want to share you.'

'She's got no choice. Same as your father. It's going to happen. He'll get used to it. You'd better get on the phone when the exchange opens and tell him.'

'Oh dear.'

'Want me to tell him?'

'No. Yes. I tell you what, why don't you ask him? He'd like that.'

'Bit old-fashioned, isn't it?'

'Yes. Perfect for him.'

'It gives him the option of saying no.'

'I'm sure you'll handle that.'

And so Max had to lay down the law to his mother and Alice's father in the course of one short hour. It didn't bother him unduly that neither parent was overjoyed by the match. He'd have preferred more enthusiasm, but that was a side issue.

ARROWS OF DESIRE

If you are Edith Nash, this day threatened never to arrive. Sharp early September day. Breezes chasing pale clouds, collecting them, dispersing and reforming them into great tumbling piles, sometimes obscuring the sun, other times keeping to themselves in another part of the sky, making momentary winters between long stretches of summer. This day the train travels more slowly than on other days. The hands of the clock drag with sullen weight. New thoughts are strangled before they are born. Old thoughts repeat their transit across your mind and spin tiny circles. And when the train brings you to your destination, making its stop in heaving belches and slow squeals, you have nodded into unconsciousness and are stupefied when shaken awake by another passenger.

You tumble onto the platform in the dark without dignity or confidence that you have your possessions, relieved that you have not overshot your destination. You sit beside your brother as he drives too fast over potholes to the chagrin of the ancient car that rattles like a bucket of bolts. You are happy to see Max again, but you don't feel that he returns your enthusiasm. The house is dark. You stand in the kitchen and listen to the asthmatic ticking of the wall clock. Max asks if you want anything. You want only to drink some cool water and fall into your familiar bed, exhausted.

In the morning, early, while roosters still crow, and crow again to top each other, and magpies are broaching the first topics of their day, Eddy will light the fire and make the breakfast. She will stir porridge until it thickens, fry eggs until they set and curl brown at the edges, and toast bread until it fills the house with its comforting aroma. Giuseppe, her object, will be milking the cows. Steam will blow from the animals' nostrils, buckets warm gradually between his ankles as they fill with milk. She will not go to the milking shed for fear of arousing suspicion. She will wait until he brings the milk to the cellar.

Her mother has left a row of bottles draining on the sink under a cloth. She lifts the cloth and discovers that the bottles are for a baby. There is a rubber teat next to each one. She goes to her mother's door and knocks softly. No answer. She opens the door and walks in. Her mother has the curtains pulled. She is asleep. There is just enough light to see that on the other side of the bed there is a cradle and in it a sleeping baby. The intruder backs out of the room.

From the kitchen window she watches Max and Vince carry the milk in shiny buckets back through the sparse trees which separate shafts of pale dawn light. Giuseppe usually does this on his own. She goes down the steps into the cool cellar where her nostrils fill with the damp hidden smell of earth and boxes of oranges and quinces.

Max says, 'Vince will do this, I'd be glad of a hand with the cooking.'

Enzo greets her with a smile. She is happy to see him.

'*Come sta, Enzo*?' she asks and waits to see his surprise. He smiles at her, polite, not surprised, as though she had always addressed him in his own language.

With Max she climbs the cellar steps into the crisp morning. 'Who is the baby?' she asks.

'That's Jenny. Mum brought her back on the weekend. Grace is having a few problems.'

The baby is a surprise and she should show more curiosity, but the only question in her head is why Giuseppe did not bring the milk. She sets about the tasks of breakfast, fighting a notion that something has happened and that Max knows about it.

She goes out to the verandah and rings the cowbell loud and long for breakfast, forgetting about her mother and the sleeping baby. Max calls out from the kitchen, 'Hey, keep it down. Mum's been up half the night.'

'Sorry,' she says, not really sorry, and not a little panicky. The smell of the food she is cooking is making her feel sick. She sets places for five and puts bacon and eggs on the table. Only three sit down to eat. She clears her throat and with a flickering smile asks, 'Where's Joe?'

Enzo puts down his knife and fork, looks at Max and waits for him to speak. Max does not look up. He continues blotting egg yolk with toast.

'He's gone.'

She waits. Her hands begin to tingle. They know. They all know, she thinks.

'Back to camp.' Max's explanation is reluctant. He sounds bored.

'He hates camp.'

'Long story. Tell you later.'

'Tell me now.'

Max looks at Enzo, who gets up and drinks the last of his tea on his feet and heads out the door with an inaudible '*scusi.*'

Eddy turns to her brother with a look that could burn paint off a fence. 'Well?'

'I gave him the sack.'

'Why?'

'I think you know.'

'Do I?'

'Yeah. You're ... how can I put it ... having an affair with him. A bloody ding and a prisoner.'

'Did he tell you that?'

'He didn't deny it. Anyway, I guessed when your letter came. And when the second one came I'd had enough. Sent him packing. He's too snide to work for me. He's a worm.'

Eddy stands up and pushes her chair back from the table with her legs. It makes a strident screech across the lino. Her throat has tightened, forcing back the words she would like to shout at him. This man, this brother, thinks he must play father and gaoler. Joe might be a POW, but to Max he's an employee and nothing more. He thinks that she will apologise and everything will be fine. Too late for that. She sees signs in Max of arrogance, a new look for him. It is no wonder men have a bad reputation for high-handed bullying. Even in the nicest of them it is there, just under the surface, waiting for an opportunity. How disappointing. He had always promised more. Their usual give and take enjoyment in each other had been based on the possibilities of not being locked into the conventional.

'All right.' She measures her words with cool deliberation. 'You can sack who you like. But you can't tell me what to do. I won't stay here and embarrass you. I'll catch the train this morning.'

She goes to the telephone in the front hall and makes a reservation with the stationmaster. When she gets back to the kitchen her mother is sitting at the table in her dressing gown with the baby in her arms. She gives her to Eddy to hold while she gets her bottle ready. She opens a tin of Carnation milk and pours it carefully into a pot and sets it on the stove to boil.

'Well,' says her mother, 'there've been a few changes around here since you went away.'

'So I see.'

'Poor little mite. Poor Gracie. Those children are far too close together. She just couldn't stop crying. The doctor had to put her into the psychiatric ward.'

Eddy watches her mother and tries to summon polite curiosity, and to think kindly about Grace. 'Where are the other children?'

'Clive's mother, but she's too old for fussing with this little one. Fits in here just fine, doesn't she, Max?'

Max, hands in pockets, stares at the baby in Eddy's arms.

Mrs Nash is jaunty in spite of her disturbed night. 'How long are you staying, dear?'

'I'm going back today, on the train.'

'Whatever for? You've only just got here.'

Eddy looks at Max with sudden realisation and says, 'She doesn't know.'

Mrs Nash is at the black polished stove watching the milk. 'Know what?'

'Why Max sent Joe away.'

'He was sick and had to be near the hospital in Northam. And he wasn't getting on with Vince. They were fighting.'

'No. Max sent him away because he found out I'd been writing to him.'

Mrs Nash turns her back on the warming milk and stares at her daughter. 'Is that true? Why were you writing to him?'

'Because I love him, Mum.'

Mother shoots daughter a look of horror like forked lightning. Eddy is shocked. The electricity transmits to the baby and she begins to cry. Mrs Nash leaps across the room to snatch the innocent baby away from the corrupt young woman. The milk expands, rises to the top of the pot and over onto the stove, turns to caramel, then charcoal and fills the kitchen with a pungent ether. Max takes the baby from his mother and rubs its back over his shoulder until it stops crying. Eddy cannot bear to watch this pantomime. A baby isn't going to upset anyone. She is excluded. She has made herself a stranger. For an instant Eddy feels the violence of this as if she has been thrown out on the road with her belongings. But she has to concede that this has not been her home for many years. Her mother's advice has not been important and her affection not relied on. Her mother gives the bottle to Max, he tests the temperature by shaking a few round white drops on the inside of his wrist like some sort of expert. Eddy feels as though she has intruded on something private. She goes to pack her things. Her mother follows her.

'Why are you leaving?'

'I'm going to find Joe.'

'You're not going on with this nonsense. It's not serious for him, you know. What would he want with an Australian girl? He'll go home and forget all about you. He's an attractive man. He won't find it hard to get a girlfriend. He's been a prisoner for four years. You were the only girl he had to try his charms on. I thought you had more sense. Was this going on behind my back all the time you were here?'

'Not really.'

'Not really? What does that mean?'

'It doesn't matter, Mum. It doesn't concern you.'

'It concerns us. The whole community will be sniggering and you'll be the butt of every ribald joke at the pub. You didn't think of that. You're a headstrong, selfish girl.'

'I'm not a girl.'

'You might as well be. You behave like one. Allowing a man to use you like this.'

'He's not using me. I'm using him.'

Eddy flings the last of her things into the case and walks past her mother to the kitchen. 'Max, if you wouldn't mind, I'd like a ride to the station in a minute.' She lets the kitchen door slam and walks off in the direction of the hut.

Vince is sitting outside the door smoking in the sun. His once magenta uniform is unbuttoned halfway to the waist. It has faded to a dowdy pink with repeated boiling in the copper. He stands up as she approaches and buttons his shirt. She sits on the step and indicates to him to sit down.

'Vince, I'm sure you know why Joe was sent away.' He turns his head and looks away from her. 'All I want to know is why you and he were fighting.'

'We no fighting.'

'My mother thinks you were.'

His silence tells her he is not saying everything.

'Why did she say that, Vince? I couldn't believe he would fight with you. He didn't, did he? Who was he fighting with?'

Vince, showing signs of discomfort, stands up and turns to go into his hut.

'Vince, you can't just walk away. Tell me.'

'Please, you ask Max.'

On the way to the station, Eddy looks out at a place that has a purpose in which she has no part. A warming sun is ripening it all like a peach. Trees are shooting up tiny, curled, red leaves. Wheat is yellowing out of its green youth. A few tawny finishing blooms are left on the wattles along the road, and the sky is leaking blue liquor into every space. The air, no longer crisp, is still clean and sweet and the earth almost hums with promise.

Max says, 'You're not going to keep this thing going, are you? You know it's against wartime regulations. You're effectively breaking the law.'

'I would be if it was still wartime. We've done so many things in these last six years, we won't be going back to the way it was.'

'Whichever way you argue it, you're still making a fool of yourself.'

'I can put up with that. It's not your business, Max. It's really not.'

'Don't be naive. It is my business. You've done this to all of us.'

'You think more of the opinion of others than you do of me.'

'Getting involved with a ding prisoner doesn't show a lot of regard for us.'

'It only shows that I'm capable of understanding someone from another culture, an enemy even. That I can see through all that to the man.'

'You're not the first, you know. It has happened before. It's called sexual attraction. Anyway, if you'd wanted to understand someone from another culture, there are plenty of ding farmers around here you barely say hello to.'

'You're being so bloody about this. You fought with Giuseppe. Like a couple of kids. I hope he gave you a hiding.'

'He didn't. I hit him.'

'He didn't fight back?'

Max doesn't answer. She hopes he is feeling remorse for being so pugnacious.

At the station she jumps out and grabs her case before he can offer help. She'd like to put her chin in the air and stalk away without saying goodbye. Instead she leans down to his open window and says, 'I didn't do this to make you unhappy. You're making it worse than it is. I knew it was a stupid situation to be getting into. We both did. But in the end we couldn't see the point of being martyrs. We're not doing anything wrong. The problem's in everyone's head. It's not real.'

'Yeah. Well. When your head clears and you come to your senses I'll be here. All right?'

'Great,' she says.

Max leaves the car running, gets out and strides over to the stationmaster's office and goes inside. He comes out five minutes later and drives away without looking at her.

OTHER PEOPLE'S ROOMS

The train was late. She waited two hours. People from around about came by to pick up goods. She made conversation about peace and the season, wool prices and rationing, while thinking about her confrontation with her mother. Giuseppe had made no move until she sanctioned it. Nothing would have developed if she hadn't set it going. She'd acted recklessly to fall out with Max and get Giuseppe sent back to camp. Her mother was wrong. He was not using her. She would never allow a man to use her. She had been used in a professional sense by doctors letting her take responsibility that should have been theirs. But she and Giuseppe had caused each other a deal of grief and would go on doing so for some time to come. That was on the cards when we became involved, she thought. Knowing in advance is always easier than suffering the actual blows when they come. Right now she was amazed at her mother's and brother's self-righteousness and concern for the good opinion of the neighbourhood.

Her mother was disapproving, insulting even, to Eddy while giving her support and indulgence to cousin Grace. Grace, who'd been seen at a club and again at the races with an American officer while her husband fought it out with the mosquitoes and the Japanese. The baby had been born a year after his last home leave. She was having a breakdown now because the American had gone home to his wife and left her with guilt and sorrow in the form of a baby girl. No one mentioned that. She would not mention it either. She could not see that it was any of her business. In fact, she hoped that Clive would come home and forgive his wife and put the family back together again. What else could anyone hope for?

Four miles away, a conversation that Eddy knew nothing about was going something like this.

'Max, what do you think about this thing with Eddy and Joe? How long have you known?'

'Not long.'

'You didn't tell me.'

'I thought it would blow over.'

'Yes, well, it will of course. He wouldn't have serious intentions. He's still a man however nice he is.'

'You mean, we're all out for what we can get and damn the consequences.'

'Not you, dear, I don't mean you.'

'It doesn't matter, except I think you've got the wrong end of the stick. He's not doing the exploiting. He's just the bunny.'

'What do you mean?'

'I mean, Eddy started this, and when she's had enough fun and games, part of which I gather is stirring us, then she'll end it. Poor Joe, stupid bugger.'

'Don't be silly. I've never heard of anything like it.'

'There's a lot of things you've never heard of, Mother.'

The train finally came and then stopped for shunting at almost every siding. She picked up a copy of *The*

Countryman left by a previous passenger and read the headlines: UNIONS END POW FARMHANDS. The story beneath described negotiations broken down between the Farmers' Union and Australian Workers' Union. With demobilisation, POW workers were to be returned to camp, even if the farmer was left with no labour to make hay and take off crops. There was to be no more POW labour. There were no ships available to return prisoners to their countries, so they would have a long wait in camp. Enzo would have to go back to camp now too, and Max would be back to the dreadful situation of having no one to help him. Eddy's letter to Giuseppe has not caused him to be locked up again. They must all return to camp. But she worried that Max would be in difficulty unless he could find someone to help him. The sight of him feeding the baby with the bottle. Not seated as a woman would be, but standing cradling the child with muscular arms and gently tilting the bottle so the milk ran down and the baby swallowed no air. He'd have made a good nurse. He was as caring as she. On the other hand, if she'd had a chance, she'd have run a pretty fast two-twenty. They had the same talents. She'd have made a good farmer. The long trip gave her time to think, and at Northam she snatched up her case and jumped off the train as it got up steam to move out along the track.

She asked the stationmaster about the camp and he gave directions. It was out of town. She carried her suitcase along the street and booked into the Railway Hotel. She climbed the stair to a room that would not have been so small if it were not so high-ceilinged and musty. A green candlewick bedspread had faded to a nauseous yellow and the ornament for the room was a chipped glass ashtray in the middle of a circular doily on a dressing table. Saturday evening patrons were drinking in the bar and at the back in the beer garden overlooked by her small window. A wireless was turned up to high volume and at half-hour intervals a horse race was called in seamless unintelligible jargon. It reminded her of the muezzins' calls to prayer from the minarets of Palestine mosques. She thought back to then, before the war was underway in earnest, when it was still in the far fjords of Norway, before it seemed like it would never stop. When people were excited to be taking part in a world event. To have crawled and brawled their ways out of the sidelines and be scrumming down centre field. Before dying and bleeding, killing and wounding had shocked them into knowing that to join a fight meant risking, not winning. Before humiliation in Greece, in Singapore, Malaya, the Dutch East Indies. Before misfortune and mismanagement had battered aching muscles and bruised flesh into the submission of captivity or oblivion. Before she had anything to lose. She listened to the sounds of the sunny Saturday afternoon gone sour like the smell of stale beer in the shadowy bar, the clink of glass syncopating with a shout, a door slam, a race call, and felt utterly abandoned by her friends and family. She rejected the idea that she had abandoned them.

She tried to see herself in the mirror, but it was on a pivot and would only balance in a position that reflected her stomach, thighs and legs. When she changed her clothes she saw the smooth white skin of her rounded buttocks through the flecks and dust that matted the sheen of the glass. She'd opened the door to this room thinking she was different from the guests that had come before her. But she saw only the lower half of her body and knew she was the same and she felt humiliated and she felt relieved, free to do what she wanted and if necessary suffer mortification doing it. What constraints were on her? If she was just like everyone else, no one would notice what she did. She was anonymous.

Four other guests in the dining room sitting together at one table turned and examined her. She nodded to them, they did not return the greeting. She ate alone without noticing what. Probably roast beef and Yorkshire pudding, going by the doughy mass skulking under the pale gravy. After a long bath, she wrote a letter to Giuseppe and climbed into bed and, for want of other material, read herself to sleep from the Bible on the bedside table. She started at the beginning when the word was God and could see that things went bad fairly soon after that. By page three, Cain had done for Abel and things weren't looking good, so she flicked to the end where there has been something of a turnaround. Jerusalem is coming down out of heaven. Its walls are jewels and its gates pearls, its length the same as its breadth and height, transparent as glass. The river of the water of life flows from the throne of God and on either side of it the tree of life with twelve fruits and no sun or lamps, just light from God and the blessed washers of robes and outside the walls the dogs and sorcerers and fornicators . . .

After breakfast she set out to walk four miles to the POW camp. The town was Sunday quiet, church doors not yet unbolted. The commandant was not there. Major O'Neil, his adjutant, a round-faced man of fifty-five with bushy brows, offered her a seat and a glass of water and promised to deliver her letter.

She walked back through the town where the people were now inside the churches. They came on foot and by car and truck and some rode in from farms on horses or on the back of carts. In the main street, the Church of England was issuing a chorus of tentative voices and moaning organ. A snatch of hymn reached out through a half-open door: '... was the holy Lamb of God on England's pleasant pastures seen ...?'

She walked beneath deserted shop awnings the same colour fawn as the ground. She looked away from the faded advertisements in the windows. A group of Aboriginal women walked past, their children running and circling about, not a shoe between them. They walked at a pace from another era, just fast enough to make steerage. They made no eye contact with her. She wondered where they were going, what they would do to fill the hours when they got there.

In her room she had her own hours to fill before she caught the four o'clock train in order to be at work in the morning. She waited a forlorn wait. She didn't dare hope that he would come, but perhaps a phone call or someone with a letter. At nine minutes to four she set out on the ten-minute walk to the station. In the unlikely event that the train was on time, she would miss it. She bought her ticket and stood staring at the track, fighting dejection, trying to think of another plan. He was in this town and she would keep coming back until they let her see him.

She boarded the train and found a seat on the side from which she would be able to see the prison camp. Other passengers would stare into the compound with indifference or hostility. She would try to make out a familiar figure or walk. The compartment was already full, full of orange light. Late-afternoon sun had pushed its way in there before her. She lifted her small case onto the rack above the seat noticing its weight for the first time. She sat on the cracked green leather and watched the dancing dust motes. She looked outside through heavy eyes without the strength to focus and when at last she did he was running along the platform peering into carriages. She stumbled past passengers boarding with luggage. He had moved past her carriage.

'Joe!' She did not dare use his Italian name.

He turned. He was sporting a bizarre prosperous grazier look. Someone with a sense of humour had given him civilian clothes. Tweed jacket, moleskins, elastic-sided boots. She didn't know what to do. He took her elbow, turning her around.

'Where is your luggage?'

He followed her onto the train and sat beside her.

The train crawled away from the station and began to get up speed. They were not alone in the carriage. A well-dressed, stiff-backed couple in their seventies sat across from them and nodded a polite greeting. Eddy wished they would read a paper or a book but they did not. They didn't seem interested in the scenery and it was spectacular: near hills of purple Paterson's curse and gold cape weed, far hills gone blue with distance, and a big ruby sun was waiting to plunge behind them. Giuseppe looked out of the window and Eddy looked past him out of the same window and from the corner of her eye could see the side of his face, his jaw and cheekbone, his warm skin, the lashes of his eyes. He did not turn and look at her. A few questions came to mind that she had not asked herself before. What if he did not return her interest? What if he had had his fling and it was over? What if she were making a total fool of herself? He had not written to her. She had heard nothing of him since she had left the farm.

She stopped looking at the scenery and looked only at him. A minute passed. He looked down at the floor and back outside. Another minute, then in a broken movement he turned and looked at her. It was all there, anxiety, excitement, confusion, a long list of things. The last time she had seen that face she'd been thinking she would never see it again. An enormous sob escaped her mouth. He put his arms around her and held her head to his shoulder while she silently howled into his tweed jacket. The grey-haired man and woman sitting opposite looked out the window.

There was no corridor. Each dog box opened directly onto the platform. This made it difficult for the tickets to be collected and Giuseppe was not asked for one. To Eddy, this was a sign that the obstacles to their future were clearing away. Their travelling companions left them at Clackline and they were alone.

'You are beautiful, more than I remember,' said Giuseppe.

'I don't like the sound of that. I hope my charms hadn't started to fade in my absence. You're supposed to exaggerate my good points and if I don't have any then you've got to make them up.' She had recovered fast, her emotional outburst forgotten.

'As soon as I see you again you make me laugh. This is serious,' he said.

She stopped laughing and held his face between her hands.

'No. It's not serious. When you are here nothing is. Everything floats. You can do that.'

'You weep when it is not serious? What do you do for serious?'

'You don't miss a thing, do you?'

At Sawyers Valley, four dusty boys got in and sat swapping gum and comics, digging ribs with elbows and whispering behind grimy hands. The lovers sat in silence, looking out the window, but they were giving off a few electrical impulses that awakened the childish prurience of the boys. Giuseppe and Eddy got off one stop before the terminus where it would be easier to find a cheap room. There was no train back to camp until the next day. The train pulled out and they saw that the grey-haired couple had not left the train but were in the carriage behind theirs.

The room was Calvinist-bare and clean. Mrs Bevitt, widow and landlady, did not interrogate them when they introduced themselves as Mr and Mrs Garibaldi. Situated near the station, she was likely to have had a lot of improbable 'Mr and Mrs' present themselves for accommodation over the last six years. She gave them stew. Stewed mutton, stewed vegetables and stewed apples, plain and tasteless and no lure to gluttony.

They ate. At this time of night everyone eats, but Mrs Bevitt's house guests had no appetite for food. They sat for an endless fifteen minutes pretending to listen to the Sunday service on the radio and read the paper and then excused themselves. Their spartan room was small and they had no reason to assume that the walls were not thin. Hymns from the radio console droned at the widow measuring threads for her fancy work, and through the wall at them standing together at the foot of the bed, his lips tracking the line of her jaw. They laughed on their breath about making love to the sound of hymns. She asked if their physical thoughts wouldn't scramble the old woman's spiritual thoughts on the airwaves. He answered that his thoughts were spiritual, and that she should not speak for him. And they agreed, foreheads together, fingers unbuttoning, that Mrs Bevitt knew they were hiding in her house, that she conspired with them against the world and that she could not see the wrong. Her cool white sheets caressed their backs and legs and twisted around them. The springs of her bed pushed up to hold their weight. Her kapok pillow made a nest for temple and cheek.

At five to eleven, Eddy had to catch the last suburban train back to the nurses' quarters. The radio in the lounge room had gone quiet. There was no sound in the house. Away in the streets a dog was barking. Eddy lay on top of Giuseppe, listening to his heart. He held her to him with both arms tight around her back.

'Perhaps this is the happiest we will ever be,' he said, his lips in her hair.

She pulled away stung, and then straight away began to see the truth of his words. There were obstacles ahead. Even their next meeting would take subterfuge. Was he unwilling to take the risks, to make the effort?

They walked through streets of small houses, weatherboarded, iron-roofed. Gardens trimmed low behind knee-high front fences. House-shaped timber letterboxes with pitched roofs. Few cars were in evidence and even fewer streetlights.

'This place gives me the creeps,' Eddy said.

'These are all Mrs Bevitts,' he said, putting his arm around her shoulders. 'Clean, honest, tidy. They have worked hard to buy these houses and make these gardens.'

'All that work for so little result.'

'Not little. You are spoilt because you have been raised in such a house and so much land. You have a larger vision. These people have come from less.'

'But these people have lived easier lives.'

'With fewer opportunities.'

'More, many more. They've had all the education and entertainment the city has to offer and done less with it. Chosen the easy way.'

'It will not be easy for you to spend your life in the city and you have left the farm on bad terms.'

'Depends what I do and who I'm with. It's people I look for, not places.'

'That is how it should be.'

'But?'

'I'm not sure.'

'Neither am I,' she said, and thought, not in our case. There was an edge to her thoughts making its way into her voice. 'Do you never fear anything?' she asked before stepping onto the train. She looked at him looking through the window at her as she waited for the train to take her away. Interesting unsmiling face. Always so cool-headed. He must have some fears.

He moved closer to the window and made a sign for her to let it down. 'What I fear,' he said, and she waited with dread, 'is Mrs Bevitt's breakfast.'

She broke into a grin and reached through the window and he grasped her hand and kissed it. She took it back and looked around to see if anyone had noticed and sat in the empty carriage and watched the station lights disappear.

What were they going to do with each other? He must stay here. She knew others were petitioning the government to be allowed to stay. There were letters in the newspaper about it every day.

PAIN AND PITY

Matron spoke on a husky monotone. She might have been lecturing a roomful of inattentive students. She could change neither her voice nor her manner to suit an occasion. The occasion must come to her.

'There's a Burma railway case asking for you. A Corporal Fischer. In the chest ward. Not in good shape. Double pneumonia, pleurisy and suspected heart problems from beri-beri, all the other bits and pieces, ulcers, the lot. If there weren't so many in the same condition he'd be on the danger list. You might get a shock. Is he a close friend?'

'Yes.'

'Boyfriend?'

'No, like a brother.'

'In cases like this, better not to get too attached. It could be touch and go yet. I expect you to use good sense, Sister,' she megaphoned.

Eddy walked without haste along the gravel path to her room to fetch a cape. She shivered. A swift sea breeze was raising goosebumps on her arms. She was afraid to see him. She'd never given up believing he was alive. After three years of imagining this moment, it was upon her. Already it wasn't anything like she had imagined and she hadn't set eyes on him yet. Her gleaming gratitude at getting what she had wanted for so long — his safe return — was alloyed with some baser metal. There were things she didn't want him to know.

The almost moustachioed Sister Scadden, flapping about the ward in her white muslin veil like an androgynous angel of mercy, showed her to his bed. He was sleeping. Eddy pulled up a chair and held his hand. She was not expecting to be shocked by what she saw. She had seen the horrors of war and she had felt them too. Day after day over a period of two years, she had been part of the carnage. Without choice, part of the cause. When ambulances from clearing stations arrived with stretchers full of torn flesh and shattered bone, she had instructed orderlies which ones would go straight to surgery and which would wait. She had seen them die while they waited. The official line was to operate first on the soldier with greatest chance of successful recovery so that he could be sent back into the field. But she chose between those who would die if they did not receive immediate surgery and those who might die even if they did. She had to intersperse them with the ones who would be able to recover and go back on active service so as not to anger the surgeons. If this was playing God, no wonder religion had lost its appeal for her.

He opened his eyes and looked at her for twenty seconds before he comprehended what he saw. Others from the Burma railway had put on a stone in weight on their way home on the ship. Hal had not responded so well. His eyes were deep in bony sockets above sunken cheeks. His patchy hair, two shades darker, was no more than an inch long all over. The skin on his face, red and raw, was newly shaven. Someone had been looking after him. The rest of him was brown and shrivelled like an old almond. He tried to sit up and was pulled back down by the pain between his ribs. Her tears erupted before she could check them. He squeezed her hand and waited for her to regain control. She had not meant to show weakness.

She thought of things to say and dismissed them as trivial. She thought of other things to say and dismissed them as weighty. He didn't seem to have the same need to speak. He watched her and smiled and finally lifted her hand and kissed it. 'Come here.' He was barely audible.

She climbed carefully onto the bed and curled up with him, her arms around his bony shoulders, and stayed there until she began to feel stiff. Nurses pattered back and forth across the polished floor. No one disturbed them.

'This is what kept me going, imagining this.'

'I knew you weren't dead, Hal.'

'Sometimes even I thought I'd died and gone to hell.'

'I prayed constantly for you.'

'My atheist friend. To whom did you pray?'

'I don't know. To you, I think.'

'Does that make me God?'

'It makes you Hal.'

'Enigmatic girl. Nothing has changed.'

'Everything has.'

'Not you.'

'Especially me.'

Finally she had to leave him to his medical procedures.

She sat alone until it was time to sleep, then showered and took into bed with her a confusion of agonies. He was not out of the woods yet, but there was every reason to hope. After all, this was nothing compared with the dysentery, malaria, ulcers, and only the very devil in hell knew what else he had suffered. She thought about the men who had survived and the tens of thousands who had not. How will the rest of the people in this country respond? Everyone must feel for these good men, led into a trap by their betters and left to perish or miraculously survive.

His shrunken face and eyes shining with the pinch of starvation kept flashing between her thoughts. She had seen a face like that before, many times, but could not think where. She feared the man was changed. She rested her hot cheek against the cool sheet and thought of his face as it used to be, so different, not intense, kind, intelligent. No one could be the same after such experiences. Friends could never be as close when they had not shared them. Her affair with Giuseppe was like a betrayal, and to think that was to be disloyal to Giuseppe.

She rose before dawn and dressed with half an hour to spare so that she could see Hal on her way to work. In the silent ward, no lights shone. The day had not begun. His bed was empty, neatly made, no sign that he had ever been in it. Panic rose from her stomach to tighten her lungs. He had died in the night. He had seen her and then given up the fight. She stood staring, hardly thinking. Cowering in the corner of her mind there was something, a tiny thread, a whiff of terrible guilt or something worse, like relief. The lights came on and with them the sound of soft voices and the rhythmic squeak of a trolley. They had to ask her to move so that they could get him into the bed. Orderlies, nurse and doctor went on to other tasks in other parts of the hospital and she was alone with him.

She stood and watched him sleep off the sedative. He was nothing like the old Hal, not to look at. The doctor, at first irritated by her presence and her questions, had finally told her he'd had to drain Hal's lungs. A painful procedure done while the patient is conscious. How much pain he'd suffered these last three years. She was always outside of pain looking in. She had observed that pain, suffered stoically, gave the sufferer grace. Was it because the Christian God suffered so much pain or was it the same for every culture and faith? No one wants to suffer pain but those who do, who have some mysterious strength of character and a high pain threshold, can make a virtue of it. Suffering will either bow you down or it will raise you up. What had it done to Hal? Someone with Hal's forbearance would be raised. What would it do to her? She had not been tested. She did not want to be tested.

In the staff dining room she sat in front of cooling toast, taking sips of strong stewed tea. She drank three cups. She had extreme thirst. She recognised that symptom. It was shock. Caused by what? Fear? Guilt? She wanted his forgiveness. She needed absolution.

In the evening, she could not wait for him to open the subject. 'How do you see us, Hal? We've been comfortable and you've suffered.'

'As a beautiful apparition, come to life.' He had little breath in his lungs to make a voice. He sounded wise or priestly or both.

'No, seriously.'

'It's just war. Bad old war.'

'We owe you all so much.'

'What about the dead?'

'We owe them more.'

'You gave up plenty.'

'What? Some petrol and new clothes. How can that compare?'

'You were in New Guinea and Greece.'

And then he was tired and needed to sleep. But next evening she returned to the subject. He didn't show enthusiasm for it but was willing to humour her.

'What did you think, Hal, up there in the jungle?'

'We were surviving, not thinking. Thought was a luxury.'

'What kept you going?'

'Remembering you lot down here. And believe it or not, poetry sometimes. When things got really rough, it helped if you could remember some lines. The familiar words, the beauty of the words and ideas, and the effort of recalling them.'

'What? What could you recall?'

'Just the old favourites from school. Fragments, bits of Milton: "When I consider how my light is spent" et cetera. Wordsworth: "It is a beauteous evening, calm and free/The holy time . . ." Byron: "She walks in beauty, like the night . . ." My repertoire was small. Some men knew sonnet after Shakespeare sonnet and great lumps of Keats. Kipling was a great favourite. We never tired of hearing them.'

'I can't believe it.'

'It's not so strange. Anything that could take our minds off our problems for even a minute.'

'Must have hated us.'

'I hated the Nips and, almost more, I hated the weak in our lot who wanted more than their share and leaned on others who had barely enough strength for themselves. But hating took energy I didn't have, so after a while I taught myself not to care, that nothing mattered. I stopped looking for meaning, for reasons. The meaning of pain is just pain. Life too, it means what it is, if it is. And in the end, the men who were brave and selfless in the face of everything kept me going. In the end, it wasn't hate but love for those who were strong that gave me life.'

'After that, what can we offer? You'll end up despising us.'

'Never. Not after that letter of yours.'

'I wrote hundreds.'

'I got one. When we got back to Changi and the Red Cross came in.'

'What about all your mother's letters?'

'I only got this one.'

He put his bony hand under his pillow and pulled out a dirty piece of blue paper and handed it to her. She unfolded it and looked at the untidy scrawl that she had long hoped would one day turn into something better. She feared that the awkwardness of her hand took away the weight of her message. Her mother told her she wrote like a schoolboy. She hardly remembered writing it. It was one of so many she'd reeled off to convince herself that he was still alive, but by this time it had become torture, finding something meaningful to fit into the regulation twenty-five words.

Dear Hal,

Noonalbin was all out for twenty-nine last Sunday. It is so shaming. You are still our only opening batsman.

Love,
Eddy

She folded it and he reached out to take it back, his eyes swimming.

'Letters don't come any better than that,' he said.

She started to feel a little damp around the eyes too and shook her head and grinned.

'Hope you don't mind,' he said, 'I showed it to Richards. In my unit. Loves cricket. He didn't get a letter. He said it was the best letter he'd ever read.'

This made her laugh which mixed with the crying and made them both feel better.

'Is he in hospital?'

'Died. An hour before we berthed in Fremantle.'

Half a minute went by before she spoke in a voice so low it was hardly more than a thought.

'When you see what you've been fighting for I hope it'll have been worthwhile. What is there here?'

'Better nothing than oppression and dereliction and no respect for humanity. Our lack of anything, culture I suppose you mean, is what I fantasised about. Everyone did. It got to the point where recalling it was painful. The bark of a dog chasing the postie's bike, the smell of mown lawn on a summer's day, the clip-clop of the milk cart, the bread van. The cry of the crows flying over as you stand in the outfield waiting for the bowler to bowl a ball that'll turn into a catch. We'd have given everything for that.'

'You almost did.'

'Yeah.'

'It's not meaningless and trivial?'

'Trivial, of course, but not meaningless.'

'You think it was worth all that suffering and dying?'

'I'm glad it's still here, that's all.'

She couldn't help hoping, in spite of what Hal said, that the sacrifices made by Australian soldiers dead and imprisoned could mean something more than a safeguard for suburban Australia. She had the traditional country person's suspicion of the city person, whose work, however boring or irksome, was soft compared with that of the farmer. Anyone who didn't love the land and wasn't grateful for what it gave was beyond her understanding. Knowledge of what had happened to Hal and those like him at the hands of the Japanese should change the people who had stayed at home. It could be a lesson in barbarity and depravity. When someone went to do his neighbour down, he would only need to think of the saints who survived the Burma railway and the saints who didn't survive and he would mend his ways.

That's where she'd seen a face like Hal's, that first night in the hospital. In church, on the cross. A Christ face. Christ had suffered nothing in comparison and from it started a whole religion. With forty days and nights compare three and a half years. With a short trip up the Via Dolorosa — she had seen how short it was — compare forced marches through the jungles of Burma. The jeers of the good citizens of Jerusalem baying for blood, the shrieks of the baboons insulted at the intrusion, and the frenzied screams of the brutal officers of Nippon.

Had the sufferings of these ordinary men turned them into saints? She had a strong notion of saintliness and did not need to connect it to a godhead. If privations had not made them more saintly, they had made them more human. What then of men like Hal who were already as human as they could get? Such great suffering must mean something. It cannot be meaningless. If it is, that would be the greatest profanity of all, and she clenched this idea like a fist.

She kissed his scaly Christ forehead and stepped out into the gleaming corridor. He called her back.

'It's not any of that suburban stuff that we love and hate. It's people. To have you all back again, the people I love. Do you see?'

'Yes, I see.'

A smile flickered crossed his Christ mouth and in it she read the things he had suffered and she felt tears pricking again and went away thinking, 'We are going to disappoint him.'

FUTURE TENSE

At the Northam POW camp Giuseppe had made friends with Jack O'Neil, the adjutant to the commandant. Being one of few commissioned officers among the prisoners meant that Giuseppe had more to do with the guards than in previous camps. They would ask him into their hut for a cup of tea or a hand of cards. His own men regarded him as something of a freak for wanting to play cribbage with the guards instead of briscola with them. Jack had found some clothes for him, old things belonging to his recently deceased brother who'd run a few cattle on the south coast. Well into his fifties, Jack didn't feel enmity towards Italians. His war had been the Great War, Gallipoli, the Somme. Italy was an ally then. Besides, Jack's son-in-law had been interned for the first three years of the war on suspicion of being a fascist. He was no fascist, but someone, another Italian immigrant with a score to settle, had reported him and then the game was up. Everybody acknowledged the good Mussolini had done for Italy, the hope and self-respect he'd given people, but it wasn't smart to say so in Fremantle after the war began. It was not for the authorities to prove him guilty, but for the accused to prove himself innocent, an impossible task.

Jack lived in Fremantle and was a sailor and a fisherman on his days off. Sailing was always something Giuseppe could talk about. When he finally saw the conditions offshore from Fremantle he realised that Jack was a more intrepid sailor than he had led him to believe. The swell was not a problem so much as the chop and the westerlies that whipped up in the afternoon. Jack, as grandfather, had been the man around the house for his daughter and her children while his son-in-law was interned. He had replanted the flower garden into a vegetable garden and was proud of the result. He liked that Giuseppe had grown up on a farm more the size of a market garden. He was not much interested in the farm in the wheatbelt where the Italian had just spent two and a half years. Like most of the Perth population, Jack thought of the wheatbelt as a flat, far non-place where nothing happened. A hostile place unfit for habitation. If Jack knew why Giuseppe had suddenly found himself back in camp he didn't say so. After Giuseppe learnt to trust Jack he told him about it, rather than leave him to make what he could of the rumours. Jack reacted as though he was hearing it for the first time. He quizzed Giuseppe for a while until he had replaced the embarrassing and fantastic exaggerations with facts and then never mentioned it again. When he handed Eddy's letter over he said complimentary things about her that made Giuseppe feel good. Jack was a good friend. They liked to sit together in the sun smoking, and the younger one was willing to take advice when it was offered, which it was quite liberally.

Rumours about Giuseppe and the sister of his farm employer had seeped into the camp like a foul-smelling gas. He did not suspect Enzo. The news had spread around the Noonalbin district and the prisoners from neighbouring farms had brought it back to the camp. It was ideal for Carlo who was there to greet him when he returned, looking for an opportunity for revenge. He had done his twenty-eight days confined on bread and water at Marinup camp and been sent out to another farm. Now he was back here in the fascist compound whose inmates were forbidden to mix with the other three compounds, but there were no fences and every time he saw Giuseppe he would slouch over to him and deliver an insult about Eddy. He had worn down the patience of most of the other prisoners months before, so he didn't have a large following, but he could make Giuseppe uncomfortable enough. There was nothing to be done but to make sure that he never showed a flicker of reaction, no weak seams, and hope in time he would find there was no sport in it. There was a lot of boasting among the prisoners of conquests of Australian women, fantasy much of it.

Carlo was waiting for him at midnight when he returned from one of his weekends with Eddy. He had been lurking in the shadows and suddenly materialised.

'The commandant will be pleased to know about your excursions,' he said.

'He won't know unless you tell him.'

'Then he will know.'

'If this is revenge, I'd be careful,' said Giuseppe. 'We found the explosives you stole. You will be in detention so fast you won't know what happened. Max will see to it.'

'I hear Max is no friend of yours. Why would he do something to help you?'

'It will have nothing to do with me once the commandant knows about it.'

Giuseppe swung his bag over his shoulder and walked away. He had no more trouble with Carlo.

Northam POW camp was not difficult to slip away from. So long as Giuseppe told Jack where he was going, he would cover for him. When he could, Giuseppe caught the train to the city and met Eddy. They stayed by the sea and swam and made love in a Fremantle boarding house where the ancient landlady wore her false teeth between the hours of nine and five. After business hours she resorted to the informality of gums. This establishment was near a strip of shops not far from Fisherman's Harbour in which lurked a dreaded fish and chip shop that Giuseppe refused to walk past.

Fremantle was shabby, but there was activity on the streets. The American navy had monopolised the meagre amenities of the town for the last three years. If it hadn't been for rationing, the shops might have made millions. The last of the Americans were leaving now, turning the town over to its own people again and the harbour to its own boats. There was little risk that Giuseppe and Eddy would be seen by someone she knew. None of her acquaintance had business in Fremantle. To them it was a netherworld of factory workers and immigrants. Giuseppe could walk into almost any café and order a meal in Italian. They could watch the crowded God-sent ships coming into the port, unloading troops with little fanfare as they were ex-prisoners of war. They could watch the catch coming into the fishing harbour in the morning.

'You are thinking about your Hal.'

'He's not my Hal.'

'He is very sick?'

'He'll recover. Well, just about, anyway.'

They were standing on the end of North Mole breakwater on brutal chunks of grey granite, some as large as a car. The lighthouse at the end had stood patiently waiting for the war to finish, the signs of war lined up behind it along the harbour side of the mole throughout the six years. Submarines with their dwarfing mother ships and camouflaged warships from the Royal navy, the Royal Netherlands navy, as well as the United States and Australian navies. There were only the stragglers left, tucked in behind the man-made curb to the breakers, waiting for their orders for home.

Giuseppe had bought crusty Italian bread which they ate in the park with baked ricotta. It tasted dry and flavourless. They stayed out late seeing a film, walking back the long way, past tiny terraced houses with doors opening straight onto the street from which no light shone, no sound came. And along streets alive with soldiers on their way back to the eastern states, hanging around at the doors of illegal brothels, stumbling about, singing and crying in each other's arms, vomiting into the gutter and swearing at themselves. Men who had spent a stupid peevish war waiting in the northwest of Australia. The lucky ones, waiting for an invasion no one wanted except them. Relieved it had not come, ashamed it had not come. Ashamed of a war of boredom and safety when they could have easily been the ones sent to the jungle. Just the luck of the draw.

Finally, Giuseppe said, 'I think you should tell me what has happened.'

'Nothing. Nothing has happened.'

'Your friend has come home and now you are silent and cold. Do you love him?' And that was how the argument started.

'Romantic love has nothing to do with it.' And like every such argument hurtful things were said by her: 'Don't speak about something you can never hope to understand.'

And by him: 'True. How would I ever understand what it is like to go to war and be captured after one short battle and spend the rest of the time like a dog with a collar and chain?'

'You have nothing to complain about.'

'Except humiliation and lost self-respect and the anguish of knowing my family is in danger and my country in ruins.'

'Have you any idea what was done to those men in Burma?'

'I have read it in the paper. I know they would not print the worst things. But I can imagine.'

'No you can't. None of us can.'

'If I could, what difference would it make to us?'

'Not to us, to them, the ones who suffered.'

'What difference to them?'

He tried to point out that what they did or said now would not change anything. She would not accept this. She felt a responsibility and a guilt. He recognised something from his childhood, something of his mother, and he became angry.

'Live your own life. You cannot live for your Hal. What we do makes no difference to him. He must find his own life. Everyone must.'

'And we must help him.'

'How do you propose to do that?'

'Somehow.'

'Do you think he wants pity?'

'Pity? It's not pity.'

'What is it?'

'Responsibility. Taking the blame. Sharing the pain.'

'You have not caused it or suffered it. Your guilt is not real.'

'It's real,' she said and sat up and started pulling on her stockings and fixing them to her suspender belt as though they had transgressed and should be pulled into line. When she was dressed, she took up her bag and went out slamming the door. He followed her to the bus stop, where the buses had already stopped running. He put his arm around her and they stumbled over the lumpy dew-wet grass and the uneven footpath and back to the room. They lay together in their clothes.

'What is the matter?' he asked, their faces on the same pillow nearly touching.

'What does this — what do we — have to do with real life, with other people?' she asked. 'The two of us, together, are separate from everything. It's just a fantasy that works in secret, and when it is no longer secret and we are found out, it'll disappear. It's too intense.'

'I know,' he said, 'I know.'

Finally they fell asleep. When he woke she was watching him from the chair.

'I can't live separately from what goes on around me. I can't pretend,' she said.

He shook his head. He knew she was still talking about Hal and he knew that the difficulty of their situation was making her angry with him. He was making life too difficult for her.

'You should not think that suffering makes people into saints.'

* * *

On a bright November Sunday they sat on the beach watching the white tips on the deep blue waves whipped up by the breeze and the afternoon sun making tiny mirror faces across the water. The bushes in the dunes still had that soft flat vanilla smell that they got in winter and spring from their almost invisible flowers. Giuseppe stood up as though he had just had an idea and walked away a few paces towards the sea.

'I have had a letter from my mother,' he said with his back to her.

The words washed away under the slosh and gurgle of the Indian Ocean. The warm sand gave off a clean smell, a good smell Eddy remembered from fun-at-the-beach days in childhood. He wanted to discuss the future and she dreaded it.

Before the war, the future was a happy place, flying in and out of the present, pointing to adventures, friendships, new places. The future now stumbled along lost in a fog. During the war the future disappeared. Everyone said 'after the war', but it was just dreams to pass the time. While the war was on, whole life decisions were taken away. People sketched a life around a bigger picture. Now that the big picture had faded, the sketches were expanding into the frame and becoming the picture and they had not been designed for that.

'Is your mother well?'

'My mother is not well, but she does not tell me what is wrong. My grandfather is dying, perhaps he is already dead. My family is only widows. I should be there. I have never wanted anything so much.' His frustration made him sound angry.

You'll be gone soon enough, she thought, and probably for ever.

'Italy is broken. I would not ask you to live there.'

He picked up his shirt and shook out his towel. He might as well have slapped her in the face with it. He made her sound like a burden. He had rejected her before she had even offered herself, before she had decided whether she wanted to offer. Trying to sound casual she said, 'Where are you going?'

He walked up the dunes to the road without answering.

'Giuseppe!' she called, though she knew he couldn't hear.

She lay for an unhappy half hour while the sun burnt her skin, waiting for her thoughts to move forward. But they stayed in the present or went to the past. What kind of place the future would be she was afraid to imagine. What could she offer him? It was terrifying to think of how spectacularly she might fail at any sort of domestic life. She had been used to making decisions, some of them life and death. Her friends were eager to leave the army and their jobs to serve as wife and mother in love, honour and obedience. Led to it by a sense of destiny, they were confident about a future they seemed to be able to see clearly. She wondered how far they could see. Could they see into old age and death?

She could see each tiny grain of sand with its glass faces, separate, integral and nothing without all the other grains. Up close many-coloured, at a distance all white. She trickled them from her fist in a thin line like an hourglass. Symbol of time passing and yet the most timeless of substances, hardly affected by it. She, on the other hand, would be dust soon enough. And Hal, so nearly dead for so long. Death had hovered about them in the jungle, taking a random swipe whenever it saw a chance. He had cheated death while being jostled by it shoulder to bony shoulder, watching its works, watching the wretched Australian soldier whose daily job it was to mound the bodies onto a bonfire lose his sanity. What of Hal after all this? If he was her friend wouldn't he want her to be happy? After his three years in a hell of brutal slavery, it felt like treachery to tell him that she loved an enemy prisoner. But it was a done thing. She had loved Giuseppe for more than a year.

She wondered at his leaving her on the beach. Giuseppe never behaved badly. That was her role. Her company was no consolation to him. She did not think her charms alone made up for his whole family, but she expected some sort of loyalty from him. She had gone out on a limb for him. Or perhaps for herself more than for him. She felt more loyalty to the returning Burma railway prisoners than she did to him. She saw that he felt more loyalty to those who suffered in his own country's ruin than he did to her. By loving him, she had taken him over and could now treat him with the same disregard as she treated herself. And so could he.

She ran back across the grassy sandhills to the boarding house. He was not there. His bag had gone. He had tidied the room. They had made love on the bed as soon as they'd arrived and he had straightened it before he left. Her heart was thumping either from the run across the sandhills or from panic at the sight of the made bed sagging in the corner of the room under its lace coverlet. The landlady, still relatively intelligible with her teeth in place, said he'd paid for the night and left. With his meagre savings. She packed and left too. Peeling paint and sagging beds were part of the charm until he was not there and then it was instantly derelict. Afternoon sun glared through west-facing windows, spotlighting the flowered china basin on the wash stand, bleached away any last shadows of comfort from the place.

No letter came from Giuseppe. After two weeks she caught the train to Northam. At the station, she experienced a small panic attack. Her hands and feet began to feel detached from her body. The only sensation she had left was an aching head. Chasing up to the country after Giuseppe when he knew where to find her was actively disposing of her last vestige of dignity. There was too much dignity around anyway. She could not make herself care for it. A lot of people were going to Northam that night. Army people. She was tired of armies, wars, uniforms. She was tired altogether. She drifted into the sort of stupor you do when you are miserable on a train and, for the first time in her life, thought about marriage and related the thought to herself. She must be desperate. At last, she presented herself at the door of the commandant's hut and was admitted. She stood on the dry boards in front of his desk smoothing her skirt that had twisted while she walked and patting down the collar of her damp-with-perspiration shirt. There was nothing to be done about her hair. She hoped she didn't look as wild as she felt.

Giuseppe, back in prison magenta, walked in with a kind of thoughtful resignation that she remembered in him at the farm. She supposed he had buttoned his cuffs in deference to being summoned to the commandant. He looked formal. The sight of him was painful to her. She stared at his wrists. Just the right skin colour, size, shape, amount of flesh covering the bone.

'Now, Lieutenant Lazaro, it seems you have a visitor. This is not to be encouraged. I would ask you not to tell your fellow prisoners about this. All right, young lady, you have five minutes.'

The commandant sat down at his desk to read the letter she had brought for Giuseppe. She was obliged to say everything in front of him. Standing awkwardly beside his desk she faced Giuseppe. He looked at her kindly. That was his way. Then he gave a quiet laugh. She could have struck him.

'What are you laughing at?'

'Your hat.'

'My hat?' She snatched it off her head and her hair fell out of its pins. She knew she looked wild now. 'Never mind that. Are you well? My mother wants to know.'

'I am not ill.'

There was a pause while she thought of what to say next and how to say it.

'She wants you to know that my sister is getting married.'

He looked at her astonished. 'Who will she marry?'

'He used to work on our farm.'

'What does your brother think of this?'

'It doesn't really concern him.'

'And you, what about you?'

'It is what she wants. She took a while to decide. But she knows it now.'

'What about you?' he repeated.

The commandant looked up sharply at them. Under his scrutiny Eddy became tongue-tied.

'All right, that'll do. Finish up now. Is there anything else your mother wants to say?' The commandant had a penchant for sarcasm usually found in a man of a much slimmer build.

He stood up and ushered her out the door and clapped it shut on her. She stood outside paralysed by humiliation and what she overheard through the hollow-core door deepened it.

'Where does that young lady live?'

'At Hollywood Hospital.'

'She a nurse?'

'Yes.'

'Army?'

'Yes.'

'What's her rank?'

'She is a captain.'

'Is she indeed? And her sister, is she in the army?'

She heard Giuseppe hesitate.

'Didn't think so,' said the commandant. 'You fellows are going to be shipped out of here as soon as there's a vessel available. For heaven's sake don't get into strife, eh? Off you go. Oh, you'd better have your letter.'

The letter, oh God, what had possessed her to expose herself like that. She walked back to the town trying to remember every word she had written, and hoping that he could see the humour and, if nothing else, it would make him laugh.

Dear Joe,

While I was making spaghetti bolognese today I thought of you, even though I used leftover mutton roast. It's not the right way to do it, I know. You wouldn't like it, but to us it tasted good, we don't know any better and at least it wasn't fish and chips. Max asked what you were doing and when you'd be going home, so I thought I'd send you a letter and since I didn't have your address I have asked Eddy to deliver it for me and at the same time see how you are.

We have some news here. Our youngest daughter, you know her, you played the piano with her and put up with her bad temper many times, is getting married to a handsome young man who once worked on this farm. I believe you know him too. You taught him to chop wood and ride a horse. He is now very good at chopping wood, but sometimes loses his horse, but always makes the best of the situation when he does. Eddy knows all about the wedding and she will tell you the details. We are all hoping you can come and will try and arrange a time that will make this possible. We are all meeting at the primary school as soon as we can to discuss plans.

We miss you very much. We know your mother and sister will be happy to have you home, but remember we love you too.

With kind regards,
La signora Nash

She went to the primary school and waited in the shelter shed. After about half an hour five children ran into the schoolyard and began swinging on the monkey bars. After an hour she admitted to herself that he wasn't going to come. The children went home to their teas and she sat there for another hour, stood up. Perhaps he did not understand the letter. Perhaps the commandant hadn't given him the letter after all. Perhaps he had given it to him but Giuseppe hadn't wanted to read it.

She walked through the darkening streets past the houses lighting up to prepare evening meals. She sat on the train feeling completely off balance, in fact quite wonderfully upset. She had no power over herself to remain cool. Her throat was so tight and dry she felt she might choke.

At the nurses' quarters her lively roommate, Dottie, was sitting on the bed sorting and darning army-issue stockings.

'The Old Pan Handler wants to see you. She's been sending for you at half-hourly intervals all afternoon.'

'For heaven's sake. I'm not on duty, what's she want?'

'No idea. To promote you to Colonel in Chief, I suppose.'

'Very funny.'

'Come in, Sister. I've been looking for you for some time.' Matron was hooting in the fog again.

'I went shopping after my shift.'

'Late for shopping, isn't it?' she demanded, puffing out her bosom in a double-arm action like a bird about to take wing.

'I met a friend. We had tea.'

'Very nice.'

The matron stood up in all her grandeur, rather than inviting Eddy to sit, and leaned over her desk using the ends of her fingers for support.

'Now, the charge sister on the chest ward, Sister Scadden, tells me you've been spending a great deal of time there with your friend.' She shuffled through papers on her desk looking for his name. 'Corporal Fischer. He's going to be discharged next week depending on the physiotherapist's report. I want to know what that means to your future plans. You've an important job here and I want plenty of warning if I have to replace you.'

Eddy couldn't hide her surprise. 'Why should it affect me?'

'You're clearly very attached to each other. Sister Scadden thought you'd be making plans.'

'No,' Eddy blurted with more vehemence than she meant. 'We're not making plans.'

'Is that because he hasn't popped the question or is it unlikely to happen?'

'Not just unlikely, I can assure you it never will happen.'

'Good. Sister Scadden's not often right, but she was wrong this time.' Matron beamed with pleasure at her own wit. 'Very good indeed. I don't want to lose you. This is front line work. Work for the future.'

The future was rearing its head again. Eddy had made a life for herself in two utterly different worlds, as separate as Earth and Mars. Nothing stays the same. Planets realign. Asteroids burn up. What could she rely on? Planet Giuseppe was disintegrating while Planet Bandage was threatening to strangle her. At least someone wanted her, but when Giuseppe began to change orbit, nothing about her work seemed particularly attractive. That this should bother her in contradiction to her long-held need to stand alone did not escape her notice. But she couldn't laugh at it. Maybe what had looked like a planet had only been an asteroid. She didn't like the person in her who was so pitiful, so jilted. She preferred the nurse, who knew things, and did things. But she knew she could not be like Matron and live in one world only.

WOGS AND FOOLS

'I've heard it all. Why didn't you tell me?'

Hal was sitting in a cane chair on the hospital verandah. Blue wrens were bobbing about the may bushes in front of him. It was November and it was afternoon. The sun lapped over the edge of the verandah floor and the timber boards gave off a sweet cooked fragrance. The sun had thickened the air to a viscous summer quality, but there was no real heat in it yet. A wide jacaranda shaded the courtyard with its blue canopy and had dropped a matching blue carpet on the bricks and the garden seat beneath. Hal, though thin and looking strange under a mangy thatch of hair and permanently sun-scorched ears, was becoming less frail. No one now expected him to die.

'Tell you what?'

'About the Itie bloke.'

She looked away and made no reply. It hurt to hear Hal speak about him so crudely.

'Mum and Dad, everyone who's been in, they're all full of it. They couldn't believe I didn't know.'

She wanted to say, 'What business is it of theirs?' Instead she said, 'I haven't told anyone, Hal. They found out.'

'It's true then?'

'I don't know what they said to you.'

'That you're making a fool of yourself and your family over a wog POW.'

'Is that what they said? That's nice.'

'It seems … I don't know, unlike you, sort of low, sneaking. Like you know nothing, have been nowhere. Some Mediterranean peasant.' He shook his head in disgust.

'Don't say that. It hurts me to hear it.'

'It hurts me to see you make such a fool of yourself.'

He had never spoken to her like this before. There had never been such a situation before. She was used to the occasional ticking-off, but it was always done with kindness.

'Mum found out from Maisy Spry. People were standing around in groups at the store talking about you. How could you be so stupid?'

'Don't, Hal. I've cried buckets for you. I've longed and prayed for you. Now you are here, don't be angry.'

She took hold of his hand and he pulled it away.

'I'm not angry. I'm dumbfounded you'd throw yourself at some, some opportunist in this way. It's so cheap, so cute. What a war he's had. Whoopee. Being a POW has never been so good. He'll have some stories to tell his mates back home.'

This Hal was new. Hal the bigot. Hal the crude. Hal changed beyond recognition.

'Is that what you think, that I threw myself at him? Why would I do that? He's not the only man who has ever shown a preference for me.'

'A preference. The bloke was a prisoner. He took the nearest available thing. He struck it lucky. All conveniences laid on.'

'I'm surprised you'd want to give it that reading. You know me better than that.'

'I don't think I know you at all.'

She knew he could see in her face that she was thinking the same thing about him.

Out of the corner of her eye she noticed someone, another patient in pyjamas and dressing gown, tottering towards them on crutches. They had been speaking in tight undertones.

Hal looked over her head and said with forced bonhomie, 'Ah Phil, you haven't met Eddy. Eddy, this is Phil Staples.'

She stood up and turned to shake his hand. He took her hand and leaned precipitously forward and kissed her on the cheek.

He looked waggishly at Hal and said, 'You don't mind, do you, mate?' and then to Eddy, 'I've waited a long time to meet you.'

Eddy looked astonished. 'You have?'

'Every day for three years he spoke about you.'

'He did?'

'Yeah, so any announcements you're thinking of making won't come as a surprise to me. How you feeling, buddy? Soon be on your feet again. When you set the date, make it for when I get out of here. I'm not coming to any wedding in my pyjamas.'

The relief they felt when he was gone was obscured by the agony of being alone together. They could not look at each other. Eddy got up and quietly left. She felt weak at the knees. Why had she never thought of the possibility of this? She felt cheated. He didn't love her as a brother. Maybe she had cheated him, expecting to be loved and not wanting to be romantically involved. The war again, the bloody war, everything distorted, nothing real, nothing what it seems. She and Giuseppe were victims of it, she knew that. It was all a mirage. She felt as though she had lost the foundations of her life, mislaid them somewhere.

She saw his mother and Gretel coming down the corridor towards her before they saw her. She thought of diving off into a ward but dismissed the idea. If they had seen her, she would look foolish and guilty. So she walked up to them without a smile. They didn't smile at her. Gretel looked at her and away, and back and away. Yvonne patted her hat and smoothed her gloves and pulled herself up as tall as her dumpy figure would allow and focused her eyes on Eddy's chin.

'Eddy, I didn't expect to see you here.'

'Oh, who did you expect to see?' Eddy said a little too tightly. They can declare a war, but you don't have to march off to it, Eddy reminded herself and added in apology, 'I work here, you know. Hal is on the verandah. He's looking much better. You'll be taking him home soon.' She added a smile to reassure herself but guessed it would later be called brazen.

'When the doctor allows.'

'Of course.'

'Well,' said Yvonne, not as a preface to a statement but as a much too small plug for a gaping hole.

This afternoon, awkwardness seemed to be all the go. The guilt and mortification that Eddy had predicted she would feel when everyone finally found out was not there. The righteous fury of Hal and now the haughty disapproval of Yvonne had chased it away. What she felt now was an invigorating sense of defiance. Her legs felt powerful and muscular, her brain was clear and firing. She liked it. She liked the way her eyes flashed, or she hoped they did. She took in a deep breath, and cool air coursed through her nostrils into her lungs and refreshed like a glass of iced water to a parched tongue.

'Good, well, nice to see you both. Goodbye.'

Her voice sounded strong and musical. She walked on again and as she turned the corner she caught sight of them staring at her with all the hostility they could muster. She suspected that Gretel would not have been hostile if she had not been with her mother. Gretel was not spiteful.

What was she to do with all the spite that people must be looking forward to heaping upon her? Would she have to stay away from Noonalbin for ever? Or would she have to go back as though nothing had happened and 'brazen' it out? What did she want from them anyway, these people of Noonalbin? Approval? Acceptance? Why? She had never really felt part of their world. Part of a world where you washed and cleaned and made sponge cakes as high and light as the laws of physics would allow. And yet, she admired these soft-hearted, hard-toiling people more than many she had met. She had no immediate plans to go back and would not make any until she had succeeded in getting Max to bury the hatchet. How could she do that? She suspected the answer was simple. Stay away from Giuseppe. Go home with her tail between her legs. Apologise. Not an option.

When she thought of Giuseppe, her skin began to sting as though she had been flayed, however that felt. She had skinned her knees often enough as a child, so she imagined it felt like that all over. Painful. He was avoiding her. Perhaps he hadn't understood the reference in her letter to meeting at the school. She had done everything in her power to contact him, short of parachuting into the camp. If he didn't want her any more he must tell her so. Not leave her wondering why all those vows of undying love had only lasted as long as it took to pronounce them. She was beginning to suspect him of coldness. It astonished her. She had been taken in.

She opened the door of her shared room and gagged on the reek of sickly scent. Dottie, out with another beau, had left her authority in the air, occupied it with her sexual confidence. French perfume was only one small part of a collection of trophies she had garnered from the US navy. It had sailed for home, but she still had the loot. Eddy wondered what her Australian men friends thought of her smelling of perfume only an American could have given her. These gifts looked like a transaction. Eddy puzzled at how she had kept hold of her integrity. If people wanted to give her things, did she gratefully accept them without surrendering to an obligation? She had clearly never thought of saying: 'But I can't possibly accept these from you.' On the other hand, Eddy could not imagine her paying for them with sex. She seemed so, not innocent maybe, but good. She had gentle manners and was kind to her grandmother and her sisters. Perhaps she accepted the gifts so as not to give offence and was a better person than Eddy who had snarled at an American soldier in Melbourne when he'd tried to give her a pair of much needed nylon stockings. She had not tried to discover his motives. She had paid him for his presumption in eloquent rudeness.

These were euphoric times for returned soldiers, pleased to be home and in the swing again and inclined to overlook things they did not need to know. All they wanted was for everything to go back the way it had always been as soon as possible. Eddy didn't want this. The war had done much for her, widened her horizons, toughened her, and brought her Giuseppe. She had not yet been sufficiently hurt by him to make her regret ever having met him.

Next day she left the ward at lunchtime and ran back to the quarters as she had every day for the last three weeks, to see if the mail had been delivered. Incoming letters were stuck behind diagonal braiding on a green baize noticeboard. There at last. 'WFX 1290 Sister E F Nash.'

EDGE

Giuseppe kept his mufti clothes in a Mills & Ware biscuit tin behind the ablution block, the most unobserved corner of the camp. A neat pile of discarded things waited there for disposal: splintering fruit boxes, kerosene tins, a broken axe handle and a heap of stones dug out of the vegetable patch by the prisoners. He had procured the tin from the kitchen. It sat in a shallow hole with a small rock on top. On a sun-bleached Saturday in early December, he left the mess hall before breakfast was finished under a pretext of organising the day's events, a duty he had already off-loaded onto an obliging corporal, and went to this cache. He changed his clothes and disappeared into the bush, looping out and around the camp in a wide arc before heading in the direction of the station. Usually on the train to the city and Eddy, his thoughts were of what they would do that night and how they would spend the weekend.

Whatever their plan, it always fell into the same pattern. The first hours were all physical and all pleasures. His body over hers, obliterating the rest of the world, her body on his, nimble, athletic, kissing and coupling until they grew light-headed. It was always Eddy demanding food that broke it up. She would stand naked in front of the lace curtain with the sun washing it opaque from the outside, looking out to the street, talking of toasted sandwiches, and he would stand behind her with his hands about her waist and talk of beer. They would go in search of sustenance and then wander the streets, light-headed this time from the alcohol. They were like old schoolfriends remembering things from the past, from the beginning of the short time they had known each other. Things they needed to revisit now as lovers to recreate a time when they were nothing, or at least very little to each other, return to it and colonise it together as a couple. They would try to outdo each other with tales of their own callow stupidity to make the other laugh. They would lie on the bed talking, their legs entangled as if matching the joining of their minds in the evening with the joining of their bodies all day in order to be absorbed totally in each other. It was only on the second day that they would spare time from making love to go to the beach. Then they played at being an old married couple. He unclasped her necklace and carried the umbrella, she remembered the hats and carried the basket with the drinks.

This time, on the train, his thoughts rushed in and sucked out like a wave heavy with a flotsam of memories and fears. The earnest engine steamed up rises and swept across bridges with one clear purpose, one destination and, inanimate as it was, he envied it. He winced when he thought about the humiliation Eddy had suffered by coming to see him. Having the commandant treat her like a naughty child, read her letter, tip her out of his office like cold leaves from a teapot. She had asked him to meet her and he had not gone. He had sat in anguish, knowing that she would be waiting in the schoolyard. He had been heading off to change his clothes when the commandant had sent for him and spent two hours discussing plans to construct a parade ground with limestone retaining walls. After the meeting he could hardly remember what had been said. He suspected the commandant of creating a diversion in case he had ideas of following the young woman with the dishevelled hair.

The shame of it was that he was relieved to be detained. He did not want Eddy sitting on a cold bench in the schoolyard as darkness closed in around her, neither did he want to go there and talk about marriage. Did she want him to marry her? That is what her crazy letter had surely meant. He couldn't pretend to himself that he had never thought of it. He had fantasised about it for two years. But when it stared him in the face, it was not even for one moment a serious idea. Where had the idea come from? She had never once hinted at it. He'd had the impression that it was the last thing she thought about. She had not allowed him to speak the words 'after the war'. Towards him she'd been enticingly unconventional. It was one of the many miraculous things about her. Thinking of it, he experienced a twinge of desire.

Giuseppe had a tiny room to himself at the end of one hut. During the day he did not go in there. The heat was unbearable. The camp was surrounded by tall eucalypts with dark, rough bark and a habit of languid olive-green leaves tipped with red shoots. The ambience of the camp was entirely different from that of the first camps he'd been in. In Victoria, the camps were a fomentation of jingoism, especially Myrtleford officers' camp. The most ardently fascist of the officers had noted Giuseppe's lack of enthusiasm for Mussolini and had not allowed him, much to his relief, to take part in a birthday pageant for Il

Duce. They had built a huge stage in the prison yard in the shape of the prow of a ship and after dark they had lit flaming torches and enacted a parade with anthems and speeches. To Giuseppe it was a pathetic show of defiance to their Australian captors, who watched with bored amusement. When he consistently refused to give the Roman salute, his senior officers ordered the others to stop speaking to him. About half of them obeyed. In many cases he found it a blessing. When Filippo was no longer around to make him laugh and the officers set up a tribunal to pass judgement on his defiance, it was time to leave.

The prisoners at the Northam camp had been working on farms for more than two years. In most cases they had been treated with respect and often as members of the family. Some had not prospered and had changed farms or been sent back to camp. Most told stories of kindness and acceptance. Some came back to await their return to Italy with notes and coins sewn into the lining of their clothes by the farmer's wife or a new watch presented to them by the farmer. Some had been given parcels of clothing to take back to their families in Italy. Enzo had returned to camp from the Nash farm with a box of clothes for his son knitted by the signora. Max had bought him new boots as a farewell present. He had taken the prisoner into Ernie Spry's store to choose a dusty pair from the selection that hung from the rafters. Enzo was more than pleased. He had a parcel from the signora for Giuseppe, who felt a childlike eagerness as he untied the string around it. Inside was a knitted scarf and a thick pair of socks. He felt a rush of warmth towards her and then disappointment that he would not need them for another six months until the weather cooled or until he was sent home. But in truth he could think of no one in that family without being overcome with emotion and regret.

Many prisoners worried about returning to their country where there was little prospect of work. They wanted to remain in Australia. A few ran away to work for *paesani* who were happy to have them at a reduced wage and to keep their presence quiet. Most were content to go about their waiting lives in docile patience. The number of prisoners still overtly political was diminishing. There remained only a rump of fascist hotheads like Carlo. No one was murdered at this camp for calling Mussolini a gigolo. Giuseppe would not soon forget lifting a dead man out of a pool of blood and carrying him across the parade ground to the commandant's hut. He remembered the sweet metallic smell of blood that had gushed from the victim's expertly punctured carotid artery and darkened the colour of his magenta jacket.

Deep in the frustration of waiting to be repatriated, he felt free with Eddy and at ease with his mind and body enfolded in the pleasures of the flesh, but he could not go on ignoring the future. The war was over. He could see that to keep building their relationship was unfair to Eddy and to himself. His own wish was to stay here with her. But it would not happen. The government would send him home and when he got there he knew he would not be able to leave. He had responsibilities. Three widows to look after. He didn't know if he could get work, and even if he could whether he would be able to earn enough to support four people. He would go back to Trieste where the British and Americans had taken over the reins. There would be more hope of making a living there than in any other part of

Italy, but exactly how much hope he did not know. There would be a great deal of reconstruction needed, but would the money available match the need?

Here, there were plenty of jobs and food and she had her family and friends. How would Eddy learn to live like an Italian woman? Her character was formed on the edge of an unpeopled interior. Her culture, though European, was not weighed down by the constructions of power and tradition. Her life was a salad of air and light. She had learnt about living isolated and spare. She could put her ear to the earth and listen to its steady heart and let her own heart beat its rhythm and her lungs breathe its pale breath. Where in his world could the eggshell of the self be broken open and its contents allowed to mix with the earth? A brusque and knowing earth that watches to see who slinks away from this arena where the sport for the gods is played, where love and earth are the same thing.

She and Max had journeyed there together and been blown about together in the hot east winds and the cold south winds that brought with them the whiff of other spaces. Because of Giuseppe, she was estranged from Max, the touchstone of her life, the human soul at the edge, that stood between her and a desert made habitable by his skill and sweat. He loved the place. It never occurred to him that it was unsuitable for agriculture. He spoke of the 'blackfellas' who had been there before him affectionately, even though he knew little about them. He remained undaunted while knowing that in two or three seasons the unattended land could suck everything back to it as though it had never been cultivated.

Giuseppe had learnt to live there, even though he had come from a lush vertical geography so different from its dry horizontals. He was not the only stranger there. Whoever got a living from it was a stranger, unless they were of the few Aboriginal tribes no longer free to roam its rocks and soil. It was a game played with the elements, a gladiatorial sport. Every year the game began again with the players on the edge of ruin. If Max made a mistake, or if the weather turned dry at the wrong time, or wet at the wrong time, a man from the city on the edge of the sea would drive his sleek car out onto the farm on the edge of the desert and auction the land from under him. Poor deluded folk, was what the city dwellers thought as they turned away their gaze.

And Eddy's life had been part of this fight with the land against the climate. A land that allowed few people to exist on it, but that rewarded those who did with freedom of spirit. The souls of these people did not have to await death to be released, they were free in life to become one with the dust and the air and to listen to the wisdom of the silence. Giuseppe had discovered it for himself. He believed that this is what had brought them together. She saw that he had become part of the space, the light and the air. Only then did she look at him with acceptance. Out there, they let the sky come to them and it was safe to say and to feel things. He would go back there with her right now if he could.

Life was not lived this way in his Italy. A woman did not fight, she submitted. She did not listen to the silence, she spoke to it in prayer. Here and now, meeting on weekends, they could hide in each other from everything that was difficult or disturbing. It could not last. Even though no one seemed to know how long it would be before there were sufficient ships to return the prisoners to their country, they did seem to know that there would not be any available in the near future. He must go back to the bush and find work. He must escape.

Two weeks earlier, he had strolled over to the kitchens as the produce was being delivered. He had made conversation before with this market gardener. They had spoken in Italian. He had learnt a little of his history and his family. He had come to Australia from the Veneto with his parents in the twenties at six years of age and could not remember much about his native country. Giuseppe asked him if he knew of anyone who wanted a worker. The produce merchant said he would ask around.

'What sort of work are you willing to do?'

'Anything except kill animals.'

'I will find something for you.'

A week later he had some news. His friend had a cousin, from Calabria, who had a timber-clearing team in the southeast. He was in the middle of nowhere without an address, but he explained that he was far to the south of Noonalbin, probably two hundred miles. No danger of meeting anyone he knew. If he was willing to accept a modest wage, and if he thought he could bear up under the back-breaking work, it was more than likely this friend's cousin would be pleased to have him. It was worth a try.

'Next week if you are ready, I will take you to the station when I leave here.'

He would soon be back on the very edge, clearing trees to push the cultivation line yet farther east towards the desert.

Giuseppe stared out the window of the train at the withering grass. The sun struck each blade with merciless glare, radiating it out of life, preserving it at just that height and shape to last until it would be replaced by a new green shoot six months from now. Six months from now, would he still be waiting for a ship? Would he be in the middle of the bush working twelve hours a day with saw and axe? Would he be at home with his mother and sister? It was a cheerless fact that not one of these scenarios included Eddy.

FISHERMAN'S HARBOUR

'You didn't bring a bag.'

She was sitting in a mouse brown velveteen armchair by the lace-curtained window of their usual room at the boarding house, reading the same line in the newspaper over and over.

'We must talk,' he said and took her by the elbow.

'I don't like talk that starts this way,' she said. 'Let's go and get something to eat. Talk goes better with food.'

'No. I don't want food.'

'Already we disagree on two things. This isn't good.'

'No,' said Giuseppe. 'Let us go to the sea. I do not want this conversation in this sad little room.'

They sat on the sea wall near the co-op where the fish were sold. There was no breeze and a strong smell of sardines drenched the air.

'From now on, when I smell sardines it will remind me of the day you went away,' she said, showing no signs of hysteria.

'You know.'

'Know? I don't know anything. Every time I breathe, I breathe in more ignorance. Why you wanted me last week and don't want me this week, I don't know. Why I deluded myself that it was love and not just lust, I don't know. The wonder is that this thing ever happened. I should be happy that it did, but I'm not. I can't remember a time when I was strong and independent, when I wasn't lonely. I wish we'd never met.'

To see her like this stung him. He wanted to change it all back. When he took hold of her and rested his cheek on her hair she pulled away to sit on the sea wall. He watched her profile while she watched the sea. The high line of her cheekbone made his lungs hurt. He stroked her cheek. 'This is best. You will be pleased in the end.'

But he would not say what she was in agony for him to say, so she asked him, astonished at her own artlessness.

'If you no longer love me, you should tell me.'

'Of course I do, but we are not children and this is not a game. I have so many people to look after who need me. I have nothing to offer you,' he said.

'You have yourself.'

'But I do not. I am not free. My family have no one else.'

A large fishing boat was hanging up its nets. The small harbour reflecting cloud was as gloomy as the Slough of Despond. She made no angry accusations of betrayal. He must go back to his own country and a life that had nothing to do with this country and her. It would take him a long time to have the money to return, maybe he never would. He would not make promises that he might not be able to keep.

'I did not want you to think the wrong things.'

'Like marriage?'

'We don't live in a vacuum. We live in the world, and the better the world, the more chance we have for a good life. I watched my parents' marriage dry up because there was nothing but work in it. My marriage will be better than that.'

His marriage.

'I cannot stay here, and you would be miserable in my country.'

'How do you know that?' She was feeling pretty miserable here, now.

'You have no idea how people live in my country and how much worse it will be now. I am not heroic, Eddy, not like you.'

'You mean, you're not an impulsive exhibitionist.'

'I mean, it is no accident that we did not win our war.'

'I hate you to say that. You'll say anything to shake me off.'

'What do you want from me that I have any power to give?'

'You could have lied.'

'You are strong enough for the truth. Lies are for the dying. Now, you are free to marry Hal,' he said in a voice that made it sound like he was pounding his fists against a brick wall.

'Don't say any more. So far you've just been a run-of-the-mill war romance, don't make me remember you as a complete bastard.'

Her anger had arrived at last. She knew what to say to cause pain. Whatever run-of-the-mill was, it didn't sound good.

'Is it so impossible?'

'I don't love Hal. I'd never marry a man I didn't love.'

'You have always loved him.'

'Not enough to marry him.'

'I have nothing in Italy except my mother and sister and grandmother. I do not know how they are surviving.'

He waited for her to say she was sorry, that she understood his anxiety, but he was disappointed. 'There is no sign of us going home for a long time. I cannot stay in the camp.'

'Where will you go?'

'There is a gang of clearers, from my country, *paesani*, I will see if I can join them.'

'That's cruel work.'

'It is a good way to stay hidden.'

'You are leaving me.'

He felt he should be the more miserable of the two. She had a healthy country, her family and a home and job and even another man to go to, he had nothing.

'Will you look after these?' he asks.

He opens the padlock on the locker at the station and brings out Filippo's paintings, still wrapped in the same dirty cloth and tied with string. She looks at him in wonder.

'What will I do with them?'

'I don't know. Just look after them. Whatever you think. You will know.'

She stands on the country platform at the station. He kisses her on the cheek because she has turned away her mouth, and disappears into the carriage. And then she is sorry to have been truculent. Truculence is not an emotion. It is like bad breath in a cancer patient, trivial compared with the whole picture. He sits at the window looking out at her. That face. The shape and colour of it. This is the second time she has said goodbye to it for ever, for the rest of her life anyway. She stands there and they look at each other. People walk between them with suitcases interrupting their gaze. A family gathers in front of them to say their goodbyes, blocking her sightline. She turns to go, but there is an arm around her waist. He pulls her round and holds her to him and kisses her. When he returns to the train his seat has been taken. She cannot see him. She turns to go and almost collides with Phil, still on crutches but in uniform and on his way somewhere with a group of people who could be his family. He stares at her. She raises her eyebrows and nods, as if to say, yes, you are seeing right.

'Going home, Phil?'

'Yes, thank God.'

'Good luck.'

'Thanks, same to you.'

Not the same at all. Luck is for other people, she thinks, as she wanders about in search of a quiet place where she can convince herself that the misery she feels is as unreal as the love she has concocted in this madness of war. She pictures Giuseppe sitting in the train as it trundles through forests and over bridges, looking out the window, not able to read or talk to another passenger. She pictures him lonely. She wants him to be as lonely as she is. It is not a kind wish. Why, she asks herself, does she want him to be unhappy if she loves him? Or else she has imagined it all. She has been the nearest convenient object. She feels ashamed. Not of making herself the target of censure and gossip, but of misjudging everything, of thinking he loved her.

She walks with tears washing down her face, through the evening crowds of train-catchers and bus-catchers who, during the last six years, went on just as they had before and who will continue to do so into the future. In wartime, people take no notice of a crying woman near a railway station. People who throughout the war had gone on putting candles on birthday cakes and picnicking at the beach and watching films. People like her who took the opportunity to further their personal lives by falling in love. She could have had four or five husbands if she'd wanted. She'd had at least that many proposals. At the beginning of the war, she'd had no idea how easy it was going to be to have men fall in love with her. She, however, had only fallen once. Fallen. As though she'd had no control, like a victim of an accident. It just came at her and as much as she dodged about to avoid it, it kept coming. Not true. She could have escaped with hardly a scratch. She chose to stay. She doesn't want to try to understand that part, but it won't leave her alone.

She has discovered how difficult it is to have the admiration of an attractive man and remain unaffected by it. If his behaviour had been vulgar or too nice or too compliant, she could have resisted. If he had pulled rank on Enzo, typical behaviour among Italians but loathed among Australians. If he'd not been able to speak the language well, she could easily have resisted. She isn't attracted to strong silent types, which rules out many of the locals. If he had looked different. If he had been stern or surly. By trying to think it out, she makes herself more miserable. Because he was foreign she was able to make up the rules about how she behaved. He seemed to have no expectations. She assumes he had plenty when he was in his own country. He didn't seem to want her to conform, to do what other women did. Because of their unequal situation, when they did finally come together, they had to leave all the usual social rules out of it and just be to each other what they were to themselves. She could never hope to find that again. At this point, a man like that might be expected to make a heroic gesture and marry her. But he was too honest for that. He treated her as though she were a man, an equal. He is not behaving in a guilty fashion, as though he has been exploiting her. She knows he has not. She will not ruin their silent agreement. She will not do anything to force him to marry her. She will not stoop to trapping him.

She had heard countless rumours about prisoners on farms and their sexual exploits with the dairymaid, the bumpkin Audreys, 'country copulants'. She could see it that way, that she had succumbed, become a sexual exploit. Then she blames him and he becomes less in her eyes. It is true, they had indulged in country matters. Copulating in the hay like the rabbits and the chooks. What if she had been as silly, what if her head had been as easily turned as every girl who went down to the quay to welcome the next American warship?

She'd read in the paper that there were seven thousand war brides going to America in the wake of their servicemen husbands. Some cynical observers, men usually, said they were bought women, no better than prostitutes. She is not a war bride, she is more like a casualty, and the worst of it was that the wound was self-inflicted. She could have let it die when she left the farm to go to Melbourne. She had kept it going with her letters. She had caused them to be found out. She hadn't had a civil conversation with Max since.

She feels discarded. War emotions have helped her to make a fool of herself. She feels like rubbish. She still has interesting work to do with plastic-surgery cases and will for quite some years to come, poor devils. Hal has a right to be angry. During the last six years she has not always lived in a way that makes her worthy of his sacrifice. This weighs on her. She has betrayed everyone, especially herself, and Giuseppe has betrayed her. She is ashamed of having thrown her credibility away on a worthless cause. But she is ashamed of the shame, because he has betrayed no one. How will she get over it? How will she bounce into the future? If she starts now, can she remake herself? The task is finding what is left. She feels helium-light. The floating soul, hers, but hard to recognise in this form. Will this empty version of her be enough to win back Hal's approval? Max will take a while to soften, but surely Hal cannot be stubborn for long. He taught her to apologise and to forgive. It will be a test for him. She wants this rapprochement with Hal so much she forgets that her old friend wants much more of her than she can give and much more than Giuseppe ever asked.

She walks the six miles back to the repatriation hospital in the gathering dark, the gloom in the streets and her weightless soul wafting along hand in hand. The paintings become heavy and her shoulders ache. The nurses' quarters are empty, everyone is in the dining room. She stands the paintings, still wrapped, on a chair and sits on the bed and looks at them. She so wanted to see these once. Now she has little curiosity. The paintings, their skill and depictions, no longer have meaning to her. Giuseppe has given her his most precious possession. Not because she wants them, but because he does. She climbs out of her clothes and into her old silk gown. It lifts and billows as she walks along the corridor to the draughty concrete-floored bathroom and runs a bath. She kneels in the steaming water and moans, folding her body down over her thighs. She has never felt so derelict. Other sadness has always been accompanied by anger. This is sorrow. She finds she needs to soak in her sorrow for an hour before she can climb out of the bath and begin the steep ascent towards the rest of her life.

WAR BRIDES

At the wedding, she danced with Herbie Cann. Since his wife was in charge of food it was the least she could do. It was surprising how quickly everyone got used to the idea of this match. They had expected her to marry someone and she married someone else. But it wasn't any of their business. Max gave her away. They'd buried the hatchet well and truly by then. She'd borrowed a white — or was it cream — suit from one of her nurse friends who'd just had a slap-up wedding at the cathedral and the Adelphi Hotel. Max looked down at her flowered boater kindly as they walked together down the aisle created by the wooden benches set out in the old brown hall for the occasion. These would be pushed aside to make room for the reception and the dancing.

The Reverend Albert Cole officiated in his special dearly-beloved voice, altogether out of keeping with the venue and the mood of the bridal party. His daughter Sophie turned up in Eddy's red suit, which made its former owner gape with wonder at the girl's audacity, and Mrs Cole wore a dreadful mauve hat that looked like it had come off a white elephant stall. And Mrs Nash wore something pink and a look of amazement for most of the proceedings. It was a good time of the year for autumn roses, so the bride carried a large pink and orange bunch from her mother's garden, that is, Enzo's garden.

Enzo was allowed out of camp for the weekend. He was quite emotional about it. He seemed happy to be back in the hut again, even if he had to be there on his own. Max shook his hand warmly when he picked him up at the station and told him he wished he could find someone to work for him who was half as good as he was and received a wide grin in thanks for the compliment. Enzo had new photos of his wife and son, a beautiful dark-eyed boy looking at the camera with great concentration because his mother had told him to watch for the mouse. Even neighbours who had never spoken to him in the three years he lived there wished Enzo good luck for a speedy return to his country. It is not difficult to be fond of people who are going away for ever.

The happy couple caught the train at midnight straight from the reception. Max drove them in the car piled with trunks and cases. They would arrive in Adelaide in two days' time. They would get off in Kalgoorlie and wander the streets in the early morning before they had filled with people and cars. They would cross the wide open wilderness of the Nullarbor and lean out the window to watch the stationmaster scurry about while the train sat impatiently, getting up steam at tiny sidings with politicians' names like Deakin and Forrest, and where no tree stood.

Max was astonished when she phoned and told him about getting married. But it was the right thing. He could even congratulate himself that he had brought it about. He had done the unheard of and gone off in the middle of harvest just to sort it out. He had faced Giuseppe and had it out with him. What happened next proved to him that his assessment had been right. The man took off, no one knew where, never to be seen again. It was a good test of his attachment. When it came down to it, he wasn't going to put himself on the line. What had happened between Eddy and Hal, and so quickly, had astonished him. Hal got into the Commonwealth Assistance Scheme and was off to Adelaide, and she was to go with him, as his wife.

Max had a few misgivings when he saw how fast it was all going to happen. Nothing as important as that should be rushed. He wondered how Eddy could be madly in love with one man one minute and with another the next. But madly was the word. The whole thing with the prisoner was pure madness. She had that wild streak. He should have known it would affect her love life sooner or later, since it affected everything else. And he guessed she had really loved Hal all along, so that would account for it. As he walked up the aisle proud of her, for her looks more than anything today, he felt like he was giving her to an old man. Hal looked forty-six not thirty-six.

He had written to Joe and asked him to meet him. The prisoner nominated a nasty-looking smoky Greek café in the middle of Northam which seemed to be one of his haunts. Max suggested they go to the pub. A beer would do them both good. He confronted Giuseppe and asked him what he intended to do about Eddy. He said there was nothing he could do, as he had to go home and look after his mother and sister and grandmother. Max asked him if he was going to take Eddy. He said it would be foolish to do that as Italy was in a state of some dereliction. He said if everything worked, he got a job and settled his family, he would try to bring them out here, or send for Eddy because he loved her. To Max this sounded lame. He was having trouble believing the Italian especially since he had been so deceitful over the letters. Max asked him straight out if he wanted to marry Eddy and he hesitated and that was enough. He stood up and paid for the beers, then he turned to the Italian and said, 'I didn't think so. You bastard. Leave her alone, let her get on with her life. Don't ruin it for her. She could have had ten blokes better than you.'

Max wrote Giuseppe a letter to reiterate his advice and they sent it back with a note to say he'd escaped. Didn't sound like the sort of caper he'd get up to, but anything was possible. A month later Eddy and Hal had announced their engagement and the whole awkward episode was closed.

And from then on everything had gone smoothly. Things had been good since he and Alice had married. Alice had pretty much taken over the looking after of baby Jenny and his mother had been able to get back to her garden and her general do-gooding in the community. The only thing that had given Max pause was when he found Eddy wandering about in the shed sobbing. He went cold. She didn't want to marry Hal. She regretted losing the Italian prisoner. He was tempted to tiptoe away and let things go on as though he had never seen her.

'You're not worrying about losing that smarmy Joe, I hope.'

'No,' she said, but it didn't sound convincing. So he sat her down on a bale of wool and held her hand and asked her to tell him what was bothering her and she did. It took a long time and they were late for dinner, but he stayed with her until she was calm. After dinner, he went to see Hal and they talked well into the night. It wasn't going to be the sort of wedding where everyone was jumping for joy, he could see that, but it had a chance. If anyone could cope, it was Hal.

Max drove Enzo to the station and they stood on the platform and shook hands.

The Italian looked uncomfortable, eventually he said, 'I would like to speak.' Max's heart sank. He had never heard Vince serious like this.

'I want to say that I am sad for the signorina. Giuseppe love her. I think she love him. She will not be happy.'

Max was feeling some consternation. He wondered what had happened to Enzo's manners. He had never behaved in such a blunt, downright impolite fashion when he was working at the farm. He had always been tactful.

'Don't worry about her. Hal is a good man.'

As he said this, Max had an uneasy feeling that it might take more than goodness to make a marriage work, especially one that lacks love. It was called getting married on the rebound and it was happening everywhere at the end of the war. He put Enzo on the train and drove home feeling like he'd had a bucket of dirty water thrown over him. If this all went wrong, he would have to take some of the blame. It was a serious business interfering in the lives of people, even if it was Eddy.

He walked into the kitchen to find Jenny in her high chair rubbing mashed food of a terrible yellow colour through her hair.

Alice turned around from the stove and saw his face and said, 'What's the matter?'

'Look at that mess,' he said, pointing at the baby, and they laughed.

INVISIBLE SCREEN

Once before, Giuseppe had sailed across a Mediterranean Sea that looked small on a map but felt infinite looking out from the middle. Once before, he'd sailed into the Arabian Gulf through the Suez Canal and into the far more infinite Indian Ocean and stood on deck looking out to the endless blue pouring over the horizon and wanted to be a part of it, the neverending, whatever it is. Last time, the year was 1941. His army career had ended after one short battle. He was a prisoner and would remain so for the next five years. On that journey he had travelled in luxury on the *Queen Mary*. Whereas the ship he is on now, in 1949, *Napoli* of the Flotta Laura line, ploughing across the equator, feels every movement of the ocean, *Queen Mary*, elegant, majestic, had shrugged off the swell and the heat.

Queen Mary carried two thousand prisoners and was built to carry eight. *Napoli* is loaded to the gunwales with hope and loss. Men go to make a home for their fiancées who wait to be summoned. Whole families, from the very young to the almost elderly, go to start again at their various stages of life. The hold is crammed with their worldly goods. Refugees and immigrants from seven

European countries. This bobbing cork of a boat brings Giuseppe to the realisation that he is not alone in his quest.

Just as he had on his previous journey to Australia in 1941 he spends much of his time on deck, leaning over the rails looking for flying fish or the fin of a shark. But this time he has another task at hand. He has a letter to compose.

Dear Eddy,

I wonder what will happen to this letter. I wrote so many when I first went back to Italy, even when you did not reply. You have been very angry with me. I hope you are not still so angry that you do not read this letter and not write and tell me you are well and that your life is good.

The passengers aboard this ship are migrants like myself. But unlike myself most of them leave loving families in order to find their fortunes in a new country. Will it be a better life? To relocate is to dislocate. Home is a place where there is no separation between yourself and your surroundings. Where your thoughts swing in the branches of the trees and roll and bump with the wheels of the cars along the street. Where the cat curled in the sun on the fence is as much a part of you as your arm or leg. To give up this for more money in the bank, a better house, better clothes, is that a better life?

At Genova where I embarked and again at Napoli I could hear the wailing of the women who must leave behind their loved ones — parents, sisters, brothers — never to see them again. It sounded like death. They go for the sake of their husbands and children. For themselves they would prefer to remain in the bosom of their family and put up with the privations. I am lucky, because of my education no action is final, no door irreversibly closed.

The swell has increased every day since we crossed the equator. Many people are sick and keep to their cabins. The decks have been deserted these last two days. The ship has no grace in its movements and throws us about without respect for our stomachs. I am a little green but manage to keep upright and occupied. This shipping line gathers wealth from a nation's desperate need for a commodity most other countries have too much of: humanity. They open their arms to us, Mediterranean peoples they reviled only twenty years ago. For me, Australia was a prison and a place where I learnt about freedom. To live without the weight and magnificence of European town and landscape in a loose-tied culture taught me about self-sufficiency and liberation that I had never imagined. I want to have this again. I am not sure it is possible as a free man, because no matter how long I am there, I will always be an alien. I do not go, like most of my fellow passengers, to make a new life. I go because within the tight bonds of my country I had no life. It is better to live as a foreigner than not to live at all.

I leave hardly anyone behind. After our mother died, I took my sister to Trieste to live with me, but she was unhappy in the city and hated her life and mine. At my age, she considered it self-indulgent to wait until I met someone I loved before I married. She had more expedient ideas about marriage. Finally, she packed her case and went to live in the valley with our cousins and grandmother. But Rosa now lives in

Western Australia. She accepted an arranged marriage to a man who left our village twenty years ago. He is fifteen years older. They live in Geraldton. I became angry when she told me. She wanted my blessing. I would not give it. There are other ways to get to Australia without succumbing to that crippling custom, but the war had made her empty — of ideas, of hope, of joy. Her life and her husband were gone. She had nothing to lose. I could not make her see that she had misery to gain. She has to find that out herself. She has written to say she is going to have a baby. She is pleased to know that I am returning to Australia. 'I hope you're not too late,' she says. Of course I'm too late, but as a criminal goes back to the scene of the crime or an accident victim to look at the wreckage, I go back. I think we made a wreckage, you and I. I still have nothing to offer, but I no longer need to support my family. My hope now is that you have not learnt to hate me. My economic and social status will never be as high in your country as it is in Italy, but I live here like a machine, filling my days with activity, going through motions that represent a life without passion, even without enthusiasm.

I had thought that I needed nothing. But I have discovered that there is something after all. I need to make a search. First I need to search for what I am looking for. To do that I must return to the place and, if only I could, to the time as well, where my life began to end. I must return to your thirsty country to see if I have left something of myself there. I hope to find it out, what it is, where it is. I wonder if you believe that, I wonder if it is true.

The months before I left to go back to Italy I lived in a green hell of crashing branches and crushed eucalyptus leaves. The smell of eucalyptus will always remind me of the most isolated and lonely time of my life. I went to work for an Italian clearing contractor in a new farming area. I wanted work that made me too tired to think. I wanted to disappear, to bury myself. If I could earn money at the same time and turn up at Fremantle in time to board the ship, that was all I asked. I could not spend my weeks waiting for brief meetings with you, Eddy. I had to go home and help my family. We had to acknowledge this. You had a strong family and good friends. You had already given up their approval and support. I hope you have become one of them again. I had to pull out before our times together became something to dread. I walked into the dry roasted silence of the forest to quiet my mind.

The men of the timber-clearing team came from Calabria and were suspicious of me every day I worked with them. I did not tell them I was an escaped POW and I did not tell them my real name. Collaborating with escaped prisoners would have compromised their position. After six months, one of the team went to town for the weekly provisions and came back with a Daily News. *He handed me the newspaper and pointed with his dirt-ingrained finger at the headline:* AMNESTY FOR ESCAPED POWS. *It was time to leave the savage silence, the forest echoes of saw and axe, the fracture of the moist trunks, the rush of leaves crashing to ground. I had to return to the noise of the civilised.*

I hope you will read this now and forgive. I am coming to your country to make a life. If I succeed, then I'll have something to offer you. I have given the address of my friend, Jack O'Neil, if you would like to write to me.

With love,

Giuseppe

Giuseppe screws the top back on his pen, folds the closely written pages and tucks them into his briefcase. He packs his bags and goes on deck to look at the ocean. It is ten a.m., 18 January. Six hours from port. The warm air is oily and sweet. His memory is teased by the scent of holiday from days spent at the beach with Eddy. The optimism he has carefully kept in check is bubbling up. If he were that sort of personality he would be excited. Feelings and thoughts and anticipations and hopes combine to make him nervous. He did not eat breakfast this morning. Renzo, his shipboard friend, stands beside him on deck. Renzo comes from his valley. They speak the same dialect. He goes to join his brother in the gold mines at Kalgoorlie. He is twenty years old and showing signs of excitement. He speaks a little louder and faster than usual. As they watch the east waiting to sight land they both shout '*Guarda!*' at the same moment. A family of dolphins are swimming and diving along with the ship only twenty, perhaps thirty metres away. 'A good sign,' shouts Renzo. He jumps up and down, slaps Giuseppe on the back.

Long before they see land, a languid breeze brings the layered scents of burning eucalyptus like votive offerings. The sweet smell of devastation, the smell of summer. It is mid afternoon and the sun is still high in scorching transit across a cloudless sky. Giuseppe's first sight of land is the low, ragged edge of the coastline north of the port of Fremantle that he knows to be the Norfolk pines of Cottesloe from having marched beneath them as a prisoner. Then the tall wheat silo of the Dingo flourmill and the gas storage tanks nearby come into view. A thick pall of grey smoke hangs over the city. The clashing orange roofs and red bricks of the houses baking, absorbing heat, are muted by a veil of smoke and ash. This is architecture from another place, another climate. They had stopped at Port Said and taken on passengers. There the houses were white and cool, reflecting light and heat.

Napoli is overflowing with emotions. Immigrants do not leave their feelings behind when they journey to their new country. A passenger on a ship becomes a willing captive of indolence. When inertia is thrust upon you, it releases you from obligation and you become amoral, like a fish in a bowl, or a parrot in a cage. For a month, they have had nothing to do but lament the loss of their friends and homes and fear the unknown, their destination.

Giuseppe is no exception, his emotions are running high to match the temperature of the day. *Napoli* is escorted around the lighthouse of North Mole by two tugs and a screaming circle of gulls. They tie up at Victoria Quay, the last in a line of ships end to end. It is 99.8 degrees Fahrenheit. He stands on the deck waiting to disembark, listening to the bells of the fire engines in every direction out-clanging each other. It is an uneasy arrival. Renzo has fallen silent. He looks down at the crowd of people standing on the wharf in front of a large grey shed with a two-metre high 'A' painted on it and Giuseppe knows what he is feeling. He has been here before and felt it. He is now a foreigner. An invisible screen is rising before him.

SEA WALL

When Giuseppe is released from the dust and sweat of the customs shed, the air is still thick with smoke but a little cooler and the sun, now a small red ball, is setting over the sea. Jack O'Neil is there to meet him. Jack has a ruddy, smooth complexion and a few strings of grey hair that he drags across a bald pate. They greet each other warmly.

'Good to see you, old fella,' Jack says, shaking Giuseppe's hand and slapping his shoulder.

Giuseppe is not the one who is old. Australians like Italians love to talk in opposites. They walk towards a small green truck. The road lists for the immigrant under his sea legs. Jack throws Giuseppe's bags onto the back among a scattering of wilted lettuce leaves.

They drive to the house where he lives with his daughter, Jean, and son-in-law, Paolo. They have four children, two born before the war and two after. It is an old limestone house overlooking the port. Paolo works all day, every day, and half of every night. Giuseppe goes to the market with him to buy produce for his greengrocery. His shop is not in Fremantle but in a wealthy southern suburb of Perth. He walks with a strut and likes to talk a great deal both in English and Italian. Taxation is his favourite subject and then fishing. He is well-liked by his customers and suppliers. Giuseppe helps him with repairs to his truck using skills taught to him by Max. It is a simple life, hard but good. Jean works every night at the kitchen table keeping the accounts. No one doubts that they will do well. Paolo brushes off his time in internment camp. That, he does not like to speak about. Jean becomes angry and tearful when the subject comes up and he has to comfort her.

Jack does the garden and household repairs. He is the childminder when his daughter helps in the shop. He meets regularly at the Returned Services League with his Anzac mates from the First World War. In this house, occasionally things go wrong and everyone shouts accusations at each other which bounce off the heavy stone walls and rattle in the rafters, but eventually it subsides like an ocean squall and family life goes on in full sail again. At these times, Jack and Giuseppe go for a walk, which takes them to a pub on the wharves frequented by heavy men thickened by muscle and weight. Their navy blue singlets reveal permanently red shoulders burnt and reburnt by the sun.

Jack is Giuseppe's sponsor. At first there was concern that he would not be allowed to come back to this country because of his communist connections. Although his father was a sympathiser, he never belonged to the party. The immigration department had no reason to deny Giuseppe entry. He has read about the activities of Stalin in Russia. Communism no longer attracts him in the way it did when his father talked to him about it. As adjutant to the commandant of his camp, Jack's recommendation would have done much to further his cause.

Fremantle has not changed since the war, except for the number of cars and trucks in the streets. It is a busy port.

Trains loaded with wheat and wool come and go with despatch. The town centre is dominated by a gaol and a hospital built in limestone. Jean and Paolo's second son, Philip, tells Giuseppe he was able to see into the prison from his room in the hospital when he had his tonsils removed. He seems to think this compensated for the pain and suffering. The prison is an ominous reminder of convicts who were forced to work on such building projects less than a century ago. Giuseppe feels sorry for them, whatever their initial crimes. He prefers to walk around the bond stores and warehouses. Wool is the great export. Enormous sheds fill with bales and empty again overnight. It is a good place to come. It feels like the new world is being born here. Fremantle is small and drab, but he forgives it that when he sees the activity in the streets.

Industries are opening up to the south of Fremantle and for an engineer there are opportunities. He goes to interviews every day for two weeks. The people he meets do not understand that he comprehends English well enough to follow whatever they say. They shout words at him so slowly that they become distorted and difficult to understand and straight away begin again, rephrasing sentences in case he has not caught them the first time. It irritates him more now coming here as a free man than it did when he was a prisoner. Then, he expected to be treated badly and wondered at the kindness he received. Now he expects to be treated as anyone else and sees that this will not be the case. In shops, he is passed over at the counter when it is his turn to be served.

It is well into February before he is employed. He gets a job as an engineer's draughtsman from an army friend of Jack's. He takes his friends to an Italian restaurant to celebrate and next day begins the search for a place of his own. There is a shortage of accommodation. Eventually, he finds himself renting two rooms around the corner from the toothless Mrs Caratti. He has to share a kitchen and bathroom. There is a lot to learn in the new job. At night, he studies local government codes.

Some evenings after work he meets Jack at the pub. They have only fifteen minutes to drink their beer before the pubs close at six p.m. A law, Jack tells him, designed to prevent men from getting drunk and to encourage them to go home to dinner with their families. Excessive drinking seems to be one of the characteristics of Australian working men that he had not been exposed to when he worked at the Nash farm as a prisoner.

'It's the Irish in us. And summer. It's a killer, long and bloody hot,' Jack explains.

'I remember,' he says.

Heat haze over wheat paddocks and spirals of smoke on the horizon. Eddy's lemon barley water sipped under the cape lilacs on the lawn to the sound of crows complaining in the gum trees beyond.

'Are you going to contact the Nash family?'

If Jack wants to know something he always asks straight out. It is disarming, difficult not to give a straight answer, but Giuseppe tries to be evasive.

'Perhaps.'

'Why wait? Put it off and you may be too late.'

'Late for what?'

'Well, you didn't need to come back. Educated bloke like you. You're not the typical immigrant. If you ask me I'd say it's a case of *cherchez la femme*.'

'I didn't ask you, Jack.'

'Well, maybe you should've. Does she know you're back? She won't wait for ever. There are single blokes everywhere looking for wives, you know. All those poor wounded soldiers, love to get their hooks into a pretty nurse.'

'Thank you, Jack.'

'Take my advice,' he says and throws his head back to drain his glass. 'Another one?' he asks and heads off to the bar with the empty glasses.

Giuseppe doesn't tell Jack about the letter he has written to Eddy and about the reply he hasn't received. He doesn't tell him that he has heard nothing of her since the day they sat on the sea wall near the fishermen's co-op and they agreed to part, when impossibilities had overpowered him. He had felt no optimism then. It was unlikely he would ever be back. Jack is right. The time has come to look and see what is. To be prepared to draw a line. But it is easier to procrastinate.

At last, he goes to the hospital where she worked. No one has heard from her for three years. He writes her another, shorter letter and sends it to the farm. At least it does not come back unopened. A whole month later, in March, he comes home one evening to find a letter written in a hand he doesn't recognise.

Dear Joe,

It has taken me a while to decide to write to you. I hope I'm doing the right thing. Your letter for Eddy arrived here some weeks ago and I re-addressed it to her. When your second letter came I realised that Eddy had not replied. I took your address from the back of the envelope before I forwarded it.

Eddy lives in Adelaide. She went there with Hal. They are married. He received assistance to study medicine at university after the war. They have a daughter. We do not get much news from them. They are busy and Eddy is still working.

Max and I also have a daughter. I will be bringing her to Perth next week to see the doctor. I will contact you then and we can talk.

Yours sincerely,

Alice Nash

Married. A disease of a word, like a hole in the gut to read. He grew up with his parents' disappointment in it, before his eyes. The word breathes pain. It comes back into his life only to torment him. The vapour wisp of hope he had held for the last three years absorbs into the atmosphere. She had said she would not marry Hal. She was not the type, she said, to marry without love. She must love him. Anything could have happened in such a long time. He had expected it less than he had dreaded it. At least she is alive and well. His hope fades so fast that he can't remember a time when he had any. What now? Nothing. His sister has written him three letters since he arrived asking him to visit her and meet her newborn son. He will take a weekend and go north to Geraldton.

He meets Alice in Perth the following week. She is no different, tall and confident. She stops outside the café to speak to her companion before they part. He is a large, older man, probably her father. She lights up with a big smile when she sees Giuseppe. He remembers her good nature. She is bright and cool in yellow and white. The thick café air is moved around by the languid oscillations of a single fan. He is starting to perspire in his grey suit and tie. He stands and pulls out a heavy timber chair for her. It feels sticky in his hands. There are marks on the linoleum where this chair has been pushed in and out for years. She reaches out and shakes his hand. The place smells of a combination of sweating timber chairs and white bread and butter. There is no smell of coffee or cakes and no sign of them. A bottle of tomato sauce and a jar of mustard stand with pepper, salt and sugar in the middle of each green-painted table. She orders tea from a waitress in a floral dress and felt slippers and when he orders coffee she advises that this would be a mistake, so he too orders tea. A beverage he drank only at the farm. Perhaps she has suggested this less than stylish place in the shabby end of town near the station so she will not be seen by her acquaintances. That doesn't fit with what he knows of her, but there is no other explanation.

She tells him that Max and his mother are well, and that the signora spends a lot of time in Perth with her niece, and she says that she and Max have an adopted daughter, Jenny. She tells him that the signora has recently been to Adelaide to see her granddaughter and came home early. Alice stops talking and concentrates on digging a teaspoon of sugar out of a solid white mass at the bottom of a glass bowl.

'Eddy's life isn't easy, Joe.' She sees him looking down at his cup and says, 'Don't judge her too harshly.'

This surprises him. He does not judge her. He looks up and she leans forward.

'She was so good to us. She persuaded her mother to give Jenny to us. This marriage of hers is a mistake, but she meant it to work. Hal took her on with his eyes open. He's a very forgiving man or he wants to be. But it wasn't the right answer. Who of us knows what marriage is, until we are in one ourselves? And then we still don't know,' she adds and laughs. She stops laughing and looks at him hard. 'What will you do?'

'What can I do?' he says. 'I would not try to break a marriage.'

'What if it's already broken?'

He looks up at her sharply.

'For heaven's sake, Joe. That's why I wanted to meet you. I could never write it in a letter, but I can't sleep. I can't bear it that you don't know the situation. I suggested to Max that he go to Adelaide and bring them back, Eddy and the child. But he says that divorce is dreadful for a woman. He means she'll have very little chance of marrying again. And it's true. For a man it's so different. For a woman there's the stigma.'

Giuseppe looks down at the green table and away. The blood drains from his face. His stomach turns. How can things have come to this for Eddy?

'I'm sorry to upset you, Joe. It's hard for me to do this. Max doesn't know I'm here. I didn't tell him in case he told me not to come. I would have come anyway, to tell you that Hal was terribly altered by the Burma railway. How wouldn't he be? Someone less sensitive might have survived better. I never met the old Hal, but Max tells me he was the best of men, good and clever, everyone loved him. Mrs Nash eventually told us that he was not happy to have her there. He is cold and permanently depressed, when he isn't in a blind rage.'

Giuseppe is clenching his jaw.

'He is not violent?' he asks.

'He isn't a monster. He married her out of his love and her need. He would have known that she was still in love with you. He's a good man.'

'I have heard that said often enough.'

'I didn't come here to comfort you, Joe. I came because I see this turning into a disaster.'

Outside on the footpath she takes his hand and kisses his cheek, once, not twice as they do in Italy. It is an unusual mark of affection in Australia.

'I'd forgotten how nice you are, Joe.'

He'd forgotten how forthright she was. She shows no sign that she thinks of him as a prisoner and employee.

Before she leaves, she hands him an envelope. In it is Eddy's address and telephone number in Adelaide. Mrs H Fischer. She has disappeared. It also contains a photograph of her with her little girl. He takes it to Kodak and has it enlarged. He buys a frame for it and sits it on the table beside his bed. The child's face is familiar to him, he has seen her before, or has always known her. On Eddy's face is the look she used to have when he first met her, intelligent and edgy, without peace. Neither mother nor child is smiling.

He has only been in his job for two months, a job Jack has gone to a lot of trouble to help him get. He would need at least two weeks' leave, or to resign, if he were to travel the twelve hundred miles to Adelaide. What would he do when he got there? Knock on the door and say, I've come to take your wife?

He is back again living the way he lived in Trieste. Going to work and coming home, saving his money for what? To travel to Adelaide? That is what he thinks about. He remembers how he felt when he was returning here on the ship, stupidly, that he was going towards life. He must not forget that life at home is as difficult as it is here, in many ways more so. His is a country staggering to its feet after a thorough flogging. There are no jobs and without jobs there is no hope. It is better for those who can, to go somewhere else. He begins to fantasise about going to Adelaide and taking Eddy and her daughter away from there. It is a fantasy and not a plan.

The fantasies become dreams. At night he longs for sleep and dreads it. He dreams that he is assisting Hal in an operation and the patient turns into Eddy. He wakes feeling that he has collaborated with Hal to harm Eddy. He has never seen Hal. He has seen photos of him. The one he remembers that comes to life was taken in uniform before he left for Singapore in '42. He dreams that they are fighting alongside each other in the same army and then they are fighting against each other. He dreams that he kills Hal and when he wakes he feels happy. Then he remembers the dream and wonders about his criminal subconscious. All three are travelling through the night on a fast train. It stops at a station in the desert. Hal gets off and walks across the line to the opposite platform. An express rushes through obscuring him from view and when it is gone he is gone. Their train continues and when he looks around to claim Eddy she is gone too.

In April a letter arrives from Alice to say that Hal will be moving to Melbourne to finish his degree and that Eddy would be coming home first before joining him there. Every night Giuseppe sits up later, composing the letter that will bring her back to him, but in the cooling dawn he tears up pages of fulsome pleading and is relieved to go out into the day. Ordinary day. Once he despised it as pedestrian, now he wants its bald, unshaded light. He is fading from lack of sleep and his wastepaper basket is overflowing, when a letter arrives from Eddy. He holds the envelope and looks at his name and address written in her chaotic handwriting and laughs aloud. She has crossed out a number and smudged the letters 'WA'. It is a beautiful sight. The letter is short. She says she has read his letters sent on by Alice. He glances at his recent efforts in the wastepaper bin and is delighted to see them still there. She says she will be back in Perth soon and that she would like to meet him. She suggests a time and place. Saturday, three p.m., by the sea wall at the co-op. After she signs her name, she writes, '*There are no saints who are not dead.*'

Clever, sophisticated, naïve, young woman, how long it has taken you to know this, he thinks. He stands inside the door of his flat and reads the letter twice more before he folds it and puts it in his pocket. He hangs up his hat and jacket and brings his briefcase in from the front doorstep and then takes the letter out of his pocket and sits in his armchair to read it again. She signs off without a courtesy, without a greeting.

Depression hits him like a train, then anger and finally dread. The line. He must step across it to where he can no longer fool himself, no longer evade the issue that she may have a life that suits her and have moved on from him. In spite of this, he cannot prevent lost hope from rushing back. He forgets his despair for an hour. He walks to the co-op and sits on the wall in excruciating anticipation. In situations like this some like to say they are killing time. Here on this sea wall time is killing him.

The day arrives and it is Anzac Day. Old soldiers have been marching in the streets to the beat of a dozen different bands. People have gathered at the roadsides in family groups of sometimes three generations, to wave and cheer.

Giuseppe stands in the crowd waiting for the next burst of shouting as a welcome interruption to his jangling thoughts. Noise and fuss from which he is completely aloof envelop him. He can spare not one thought or feeling from the meeting that will take place this afternoon. He waits, suspended from the moment. He tries to stop imagining the meeting. He tries to stop seeing her in his mind. He even tries to stop seeing the sea wall and the harbour. He tries to stop seeing that photo of Hal in his uniform. Was he marching in Adelaide today?

After the parade, people stay in the park to picnic and listen to the band in the rotunda. In another country, a national day to mourn those who had died in wars would be a day of prayer and weeping. Here, it is a day of celebration. He had thought when he first came to this country that it was a place that worships life and not death. But he finds it is not so. Whatever it is of the mystery of martyrdom and national pride that makes this day, in this country and in others, is what has caused his three long years of loneliness. It is fitting that he should meet her again on this day. It is the nature of this country to make bad luck and defeat into a virtue. It started at the very bottom, as a penal colony. It takes strength from being able to remember those depths and from knowing that there is the possibility not just of survival, but of success. They appear to want to hold these darkest memories in their hearts so that they will not be afraid of failure. He also came here in defeat, and then returned in hope. Much as he honours those who have given their lives in war for the protection of their country, he will never choose them over the living.

He goes to the meeting place an hour early. He stands beside the sea wall under a Norfolk pine canopy, on a thick bed of yellowing fronds. Cool air moves through the pines, percussion to accompany the organ in the merry-go-round, playing Viennese waltzes. Petulant waves flick against the sea wall. The sardines have not started running yet. The faint fish odour is not unpleasant, ocean-salt, fresh. The sea pulls his gaze one way and the empty bus stop another. There are no boats and no buses. His mind butterflies about with his stomach. And she arrives, half an hour early. It is like her. He remembers her generosity.

She does not come by bus. She gets out of a car, turns and lifts a small child onto the footpath. The car does not drive away. She wears a blue dress. The sea breeze blows the skirt against her legs and dances her hair about her shoulders. She holds the child by the hand and walks at the slow pace of the child across the park towards him, past people lazing on the grass beside prams, through drifts of discarded sandwich and biscuit wrappers, empty bottles and ice cream cups. Her face comes into focus and replaces the one he has had in his memory for three years. It is a good face. Afternoon sun glints blue in her eyes. She shades them with her hand. She stands in front of him and looks at his face as if searching it for a clue. He can think of nothing to say that would be close in meaning to what he feels. He has never looked at two people who have had this effect on him. In a rush of emotion that contains fierce regret, he begins to hope that she might have come to see him because she needs him. His derelict confidence is reforming. She bends and picks up the child.

'This is Claudia,' she says.

A man is walking across the park towards them. Giuseppe knows that walk. It is Max.

'I just wanted to say hello.'

He puts out his hand and Giuseppe shakes it. They stand and look at each other.

'You look well,' Max says, and then, 'I hope you'll come and see us.'

'Thank you,' says Giuseppe.

They do not smile at each other. There is too much not being said to leave room for a smile. Max walks away, then turns back to look at the three of them standing together.

'Hello,' Giuseppe says to the child.

The child turns away and points at the merry-go-round. 'Mummy, look,' she says and then turns back to stare at Giuseppe.

'Would you like a ride?' he asks. She looks at him hard and nods her head.

'Come on.'

He walks over to the old man with the large leather bag on his hip and buys three tickets. They sit with the child between them inside a white swan while it circles to the *Emperor Waltz*. The slow turn of the merry-go-round creates its own small world. Giuseppe's head begins to spin, the centrifugal force elongating his thoughts, teasing them out in toffee strands. It is a pleasant numbing, but he doesn't want it and he winds his thoughts back in and as they settle they fall into place in a way they have not for years. He looks down at the dark, shiny hair of the child — his child — and at her mother who turns her unsmiling face to watch the parkscape slip by, and he knows what he will do and it is not what he would have supposed himself capable of. At last he has found a battle he wants to fight and win. This is his family. He feels his pulse pounding in his throat, as if for the first time. He reaches his arm behind the child and smoothes Eddy's hair and rests his hand at the nape of her neck moving his fingertips in her hair. She turns her head his way only slightly.

'When did you decide to come back?'

'I did not decide. When I could, I came back.'

'And so you did,' she said, still not looking at him, but with one cryptic phrase she had told him she was angry, that she had no faith in him, that he would have to build it again. Neither spoke for a minute. He was trying to think where to start.

'Why didn't you write to me if you intended to return?'

'You did not write to me after I left.'

'I couldn't. It would have made it harder.'

'If I had written six months ago and you had told me that you were married, I would not have come.'

It was a conversation made sparse by the awkwardness of their situation and the difficulty of talking over the wheezing of the happy organ, louder on the town side of the merry-go-round than on the harbour side.

'If only you'd never gone.'

'I had no choice. My mother, my grandmother.'

'I know.'

'And I had nothing then.'

'What do you have now?'

He has only himself and turmoil and trouble and dislocation and anguish. The emperor waltzes gaily on. The child waves her hands to the music.

'If I had known about the child.'

'What? What would you have done for an unborn child that you could not do for me?'

'You are bitter.'

'I'm not bitter,' she says, her voice rising in pitch.

She turns to him with the sort of intensity he was used to in her. His idealised memory of her vanishes. He expels one sharp note of laughter with the joy of it. She looks at him astonished and he can see that she is remembering him too. She takes the child onto her knee and he puts his arms around them both and squeezes them to him and kisses their cheeks. The child struggles to get free. The music slows and the merry-go-round slows and finally stops. Giuseppe gets down first and offers his hand to help Eddy. She steps down and lifts her child onto the ground beside her and takes her hand. A new lot of young riders push past and run from one long-lashed plaster horse to the next, in order to find the best mount. Giuseppe stops and turns to Eddy.

'Alice did not tell me that Claudia . . . is mine, my child.'

'Alice? Alice is smart.'

Eddy sounds angry, but when Giuseppe looks at her he sees tears, lots of them welling up and running down her cheeks. She wipes them away with the back of her wrist and releases the child's hand and puts her arms around his neck.

'Alice is smart,' she repeats, laughing.

He can feel her tears on his neck. They become aware of the child wrapping herself in her mother's skirt. Giuseppe bends down and picks her up. She twists away from him and he gives her to Eddy. It will not be easy, he knows, but to let them go would be more difficult, even for the child in the end. They walk back across the grass to Max's car.

LOW GROUND

Everyone wants choices. But choices are difficult to make. They are exclusive. They mean turning your back and closing doors. They mean focusing on what you think you want and cutting away whatever does not give it. Giuseppe had made his. In fact, they didn't look like choices to him. He would claim his family. For Eddy, nothing so simple. These were her people. At a point not too distant the consequences of her choices would move into her child's life. Eddy's choices were standing like applicants behind a wrought-iron gate, silent and watchful. They were things of the heart. Her happiness had long depended on Hal's state of mind as well as her association with Giuseppe. Although the one made the other more intense, they were the same thing.

She would be a different person in the eyes of the world if she walked out on Hal and took up with Giuseppe — and she knew that it would make her different in her own eyes as well. Diminished. Four lives would be changed for ever. Three lives had a chance of greater happiness, but Hal's would be thrown into chaos, if not for ever then for the immediate future. She told herself that after a time he would find someone more suitable. As for her, if she could feel other people's judgements shaping her life and making her less, she would drift away from herself. She must hold anchor. It used to be important that Hal should think well of her, but she had given up on that long ago.

Max was the one. She had not lived in his disapproval for long. His dislike of her association with Giuseppe had surprised her. He had been the one person who saw no fault in her, just as she had seen no fault in him. She knew something of his track record with Alice, though not the whole of it. She had pieced together the beginnings of their story and its unfortunate consequence like an archaeologist rebuilding a pot from a couple of shards. She guessed that his role in the affair had not been blameless. But the way she saw it, if she had been Max and faced with the same decisions, it was unlikely that she would have made better ones. If Max wanted to be her friend, she could think of nothing he could do that would make her turn him away. Most people felt the same way about him. This, she reminded herself, was his special talent. Her mother's was a more complicated story.

Her mother would not be happy if she left Hal even though she had seen all the horror of their marriage on her visit to Adelaide. Mrs Nash's friendship with Yvonne Fischer had cooled a little since Hal had been so rude to her. Not that she had discussed it at all. She had mentioned it to no one. She had meant to help, not to interfere. In the past, rudeness had never been his way. Before the war, nothing could provoke him to it, no matter how exasperated he became, and during the Depression life on the farm had become almost impossible. She had asked an innocent question, but the solution to a personal crisis is rarely arrived at so simply. 'What's the matter, Hal?' Her voice was cheerful, piping. Receiving no reply, she had gone on to make a few suggestions. 'What you need is a break. You and Eddy take the weekend and go away, to the beach, or the hills. The ranges will be lovely at this time of year. I'll look after Claudia.'

His answer was unexpected and shocking. 'This house is small and I find visitors very difficult. There's a guesthouse up the road. You can stay there for the rest of your holiday. When you're packed, I'll help you with your luggage.'

She was so aghast at being thrown out of the house that she could hardly take it in. The humiliation. Respect was due to her mother-in-law status and there was the immunity of age. She wasn't very old, but she felt she was owed some small degree of veneration.

Eddy was often impatient and annoyed with her mother, but she never intentionally hurt her feelings. The moment when Hal felt able to discard her mother's feelings was a watershed for her. If she'd had the money, she'd have moved to the guesthouse too. He'd been so rude that she felt somehow the universe would set it right one day. No one can get away with such wrong behaviour. Not even Hal. She didn't need to seek redress. It would just happen. She had applied that idea to the Japanese who had visited such cruelty on their prisoners of war, Hal among them. One day they would all get their comeuppance. The universe would see to it.

She wondered now if she were naïve to think that Giuseppe would never be rude to her mother. She believed he could not intentionally hurt anyone. Even when he left her to go to the bush before he was repatriated, though a brutal separation, she understood why he did it and did not blame him. Well, perhaps she did a little sometimes, but she knew that it was just the warp and weft of fortune, the way things had turned out. Misfortune, having brought them together, had then pulled them apart.

Giuseppe was beginning to see that they would be two different people in a new relationship. It made him nervous. He had enjoyed great freedom as a prisoner. Obligations were on hold. Three years later, the present had finally caught up with the future. Whatever the consequences, he must chase his own desires as far as he could. He had a second chance. He could see that the structure of Eddy's and Hal's marriage had always been weak. It would not take much to bring it down. He worried that the forces of guilt would collapse the new structure that he wanted to build with Eddy and their child.

Eddy left Giuseppe in the park with the old merry-go-round still hooting out defiant waltzes. He'd managed to get Claudia to wave to him as the car pulled out from the curb.

'Bye bye,' she breathed, and closed her fingers over her tiny hand.

At the hotel, Eddy took her upstairs and tucked her into bed. She was sitting watching the child fall asleep when there was a knock at the door. Alice.

'Got a minute?'

Eddy stood up and they tiptoed out leaving the door ajar.

'Max has taken Jenny to find an ice cream.'

Alice left her door ajar too, so that they could hear the child. They settled into armchairs near the window. The room was identical to Eddy's next door, right down to the cot in the corner. They were in the family end of the hotel.

Alice had a pile of parcels at the foot of the bed after yesterday's shopping.

'Do you like these?' She took a pair of brown and white high heels from between tissue paper and held them in front of her knees.

'Yes.' Eddy nodded, distracted. 'Very nice.'

'I've got some sherry somewhere,' said Alice, rummaging among the shopping. She poured an inch into a couple of water glasses on the dresser. 'Cheers,' she said and raised her glass.

Eddy gave a deep sigh and put down her glass. She hated sherry. It was neither fish nor fowl. Then she picked it up and downed the lot in a gulp. She sighed again and shook her head.

'Alice, how is this to be done?'

'Depends on what you want to do.'

'I don't know.'

'You don't know?'

'Well, of course I know, but I don't take it into account because it's not possible.'

'Why did you go and see him then?'

'I couldn't not, once I knew he was here.'

Eddy turned her head, stretching her neck as though it ached and looked out the window where the streetlights were starting to flicker on.

'Say it could be done just the way you want. How would it happen?' asked Alice.

'This is a useless exercise.'

'How do you know? You haven't done it yet. Just tell me how you want it to be.'

'All right. I want Hal to stay in Melbourne. I want him to reply to my letter asking for a divorce in order to marry

Giuseppe and say that he understands, that our marriage wasn't working anyway. I want him to acknowledge that it would be better for us to separate and start again. I want him to say that he will let me divorce him for desertion and give me custody of Claudia uncontested.'

Alice's eyes grew rounder and she bit her lip.

'You see? Never going to happen, not in a million years,' Eddy said and got up to check her sleeping child.

'Now,' said Alice when Eddy returned, 'what will prevent it?'

'He won't give up his family.'

'Does he love you?'

'Hard to tell. He's so angry. Unrecognisable. I've wanted to leave so many times.'

'Would you have left, if Joe hadn't come back?'

'I don't know. Not so soon. Maybe not at all. I can put up with it, but it's Claudia. Such an unhappy home. And now it's me too. I'm exhausted. I don't want to go on making excuses for him. His war was the very worst kind of hell. I thought I'd be able to help. I've been stupid.'

The room went silent again.

Alice went to the dresser to fetch the sherry. 'Well, that's it then,' she said.

'What?'

'What you must do. It's the only way.'

'Where do I start?'

'You already have. You came here instead of going to Melbourne. Now you must set up a life for yourself, not with Giuseppe but on your own. And then you can decide what to do after that. Do one thing at a time. You will have to write to Hal. But you don't need to say anything more than that you've decided you don't want to go to Melbourne with him and that you are going to stay here. Just one thing at a time.'

They sat for a while sipping sherry. Eddy began to think for the first time that it might be possible to leave him. Alice was right. She should not try to do everything at once. She did not want to get into the sort of divorce where there had to be one of them guilty of adultery. Maybe she would have to be guilty of desertion, but that was different.

Eddy and Giuseppe went out for dinner next day and talked until dawn. There was a lot to say. She had never heard him so forceful. He asked her to marry him and when she said she was already married he asked her to get a divorce. She did not give him a straight yes. She warned him that it would take a while. A yes of sorts, but he wanted her to say it.

'This is a bad thing I'm doing to Hal,' he said. 'I never thought I would do this to anyone.'

'We haven't been respectable for a long time. You and I.'

'That is different from doing wrong to someone.'

'It's about getting used to taking the moral low ground,' she'd said, looking sad.

'You are not used to such a place.'

'These last three years have taught me.'

'I am low ground too.'

He had seen himself there for some time, but she knew how to name it. It was a whole new address. She looked at him and, with the lightest of smiles, nodded her head.

'Yes.'

'We are low ground, us.'

They laughed because of the way he said it, not because it was funny. He was struck by her softness. She had a mildness now. What, a maturity? He didn't know.

'Hal,' she said on a sigh and turned her head to the window and the fading light. 'It was wrong. I was wrong. I am to blame. I thought it would make him happy and that at least one of us would have what he wanted. I can't make it right. It's all too late.'

'Take the blame, but then end what is wrong, what does not work.'

'If I didn't believe that, I wouldn't be here.'

And there it was. She had said it and he smiled, laughed, behind his dazed face.

'These last three years,' he said, 'I also have found that I can live in the wrong.'

'For how long?'

'Long.'

They were in a café high in the park above the city and its wide, comfortable river. Lights far below hinted at fairytales.

'You eat fish and chips now?' Eddy asked as their orders arrived.

'I am willing to try.'

'Very brave. They taste better than they smell. Unlike coffee.'

'When have you smelled real coffee?'

'In Palestine. In tiny cups. Black like tar.'

'That is real coffee.'

'Bitter, nasty, great smell.'

'You must have sugar.'

'Wasted on me.'

'Nothing is wasted on you.'

She fished into her handbag and brought out a handkerchief. 'I burst into tears at the drop of a hat these days. If you're going to say things like that, I'll have to buy more handkerchiefs.'

'I haven't even started yet,' he said and offered his own.

They left the restaurant when the waiter had upturned half the chairs in the room onto tables. They walked through the night and their lives, and as the night wore on they made little runs at revising and amending, bringing to account. They walked past illuminated shop windows. Things were starting to reappear that hadn't been seen for ten years. Kitchen gadgets, jackets with fur collars, ballgowns, table lamps and curtain lengths. Important for other people, not for them.

'Did you think of me,' he asked, 'when you were married?'

His question was brutal, but he had to ask. He tucked her arm under his and held her clammy hand. At length she attempted an answer.

'It felt so bad. It had to be wrong,' and she couldn't prevent a groan from escaping.

'If I had known.'

'Don't say that.'

'You think I would have done nothing?'

She made no answer.

'If I had known about the baby and the wedding do you think I'd have stayed clearing trees?'

He waited for her answer but it didn't come. It was too early between them to analyse their roles. Their common ground was scattered with the rags of hurt and blame, needing to be sorted, but not yet. What they needed to do now was to admire shop windows full of washing machines and to eat fish and chips in the park and watch the fantasy of lights shining up at them from below. Tonight he could see no difference between fantasy and reality. But he couldn't tell whether it was all fantasy or all reality. He didn't care.

'Are you strong enough for this?' she asked. 'Do you have the stomach?'

'I can eat fish and chips, I have stomach.'

'This is going to be a lot worse than fish and chips.'

'Is that possible?'

'It'll be poisonous, whatever the outcome.'

They climbed the steps of the hotel. They had walked away a night. A crimson sun below the horizon gold-rimmed a half-dozen or so purple clouds, low in the east. The vast, pale George Hotel had sat here since 1910, the beginning of the reign of George V. It had a whiff of faded grandeur with echoes of tea dances and palm court orchestras, compromised in the thirties by a half-hearted attempt at Art Deco.

'Will you be all right, on your own?' he asked.

'Of course.' She sounded confident, but he knew she was afraid.

He did not know that with heavy legs she climbed the stairs to her room where the light was shining through a half-open door. He did not know that she reached out and pushed it and that the hinges gave a pained squawk. He did not know that Hal had been sitting by the window for three hours or that for Eddy time went into spasm, shuddered and picked up again when he spoke.

'Where in God's name have you been?'

AUTO-DA-FÉ

'There's a bloke downstairs for you, Joe.'

Monday, nine-thirty a.m. Giuseppe has been sitting at his desk for an hour and a half but his mind has been bouncing across the rusty tin roofs he can see from his window. It must be Jack, he thinks. Who else would come here? Giuseppe works with three other draughtsmen on a mezzanine level overlooking the rest of the office. He swivels his chair and there at the top of the stair is his visitor. He knows him straight away. Hal. Like his photos but thinner, older, angrier.

'What do you think you're doing?' Hal demands.

They are standing too close at the top of the stair.

'We cannot talk here.'

Giuseppe tries to move down the stair, but Hal blocks his way.

'Don't you want these people to know that you're sleeping with my wife?'

Giuseppe pushes past him and bounds down the stair and out onto the footpath and looks back through the open door. Hal is at the reception desk with Joss Bentley, a groomed man of sixty-five, a small man who must tilt his head up to speak to him. Joss, a middle-class man of Perth had a great grandfather who landed on its shores from the deck of the *Parmelia* and he wants no show of ill-breeding, no show of emotion. He is a good man, as long as you play the good-manners game. Giuseppe cannot hear what he says, but he sees him gesture, his hands parallel to the floor, as if pushing something down. He sees him go into his office and close its corrugated glass door.

'What do you want?' Giuseppe asks Hal as he steps onto the footpath.

'I want you back in Italy. Go. Go home. Disappear. You're a cowardly adulterous bastard.'

This last phrase is shouted and the women on the street with their string bags bulging with apples and flour catch themselves staring and hurry on their ways. The seventeen-year-old receptionist at Bentley Civil Engineering Proprietary Limited looks up and straight down again at her Remington. Giuseppe moves across the road to an empty football field.

'You have probably lost me my job.'

'You won't be needing it. You're going back where you came from.'

'I am not going back.'

He will not add that he is going to marry Eddy as soon as she can get a divorce. The situation calls for hosing down, not stoking up. Instead he says: 'I am sorry for your situation. I do not mean you harm.' He wants to say that he loves Eddy and will look after her, but he judges that that won't go down well either.

'Not sorry enough to stay away from her.'

'No.'

'I should kill you,' Hal says through clenched teeth, but loud enough for Giuseppe to get the message.

Hal's eyes are bloodshot, his face is blotched and he has a day's growth on his chin. Giuseppe has a flash of fear that Hal could win Eddy back by appealing to her sense of duty.

'Let her go. She wants to go.'

'I am Claudia's father. She loves me. She doesn't know you. You don't care about the child.'

'I care for nothing but Eddy and the child.'

'You think they'll be happy with you? A migrant? A home-wrecker? Do you have anything to offer? Any money, any friends?'

This blow finds its mark. Giuseppe looks down at his feet and kicks at a divot on the field. A crowd of schoolboys descends on the place shouting and kicking balls and tackling each other to the ground. The two men walk out of the field and along the path towards the town centre.

'You think Eddy will be happy when her adultery is dragged into court? That's the only way she'll get a divorce. How do you think it will affect Claudia?'

Giuseppe says nothing for a while and then he says, 'Claudia is named after my father. Did you know that? He was killed by fascists.'

'I won't let her go.'

'It is not for you to decide. It is for Eddy.'

'I won't give up the child. She is mine by law.'

The trump card. Giuseppe has been waiting for this. Hal is triumphant. He stops beside a battered Plymouth and opens the door.

'You can't win, so give up now before you cause a lot of aggravation.'

He gets into the car, slams the door and drives off. It turns the corner and backfires like a lethal weapon.

Giuseppe walks the streets for an hour. Every backyard has a full line of sheets and towels flapping in the breeze, in keeping with the wash-on-Monday rule. Giuseppe eyes these articles with dislike. Why do people stick so rigidly to rules? They should make up a few for themselves. He can see this all going badly now. Hal is formidable. His weapon is the child. He will blackmail Eddy with her. What was the man doing here? He was supposed to be in Melbourne.

The receptionist bends her orange curls and pounds the keys of her typewriter as he walks past and slowly up the stairs to his desk. His colleagues don't look up. He lowers himself into his chair and sees an envelope sitting in the middle of his drawing board. He knows what it is. A formal letter of dismissal saying that the trial period not yet being over, Bentley's has decided to terminate his employment, and advising that it takes effect immediately. It includes his final pay cheque and a polite greeting wishing him well for the future. He places his drawing instruments one at a time into his briefcase. He turns off the lamp over his board and walks down the stairs and out the door without a word to anyone or from anyone. He stops, pauses and walks back inside, past the receptionist and into Bentley's office without knocking. He is on the telephone. Giuseppe waits for him to finish.

'You don't ask for an explanation.'

'I don't want to know. It's not my concern.'

'But you have dismissed me. You have made it your concern.'

'This office works best if everyone is stable and calm and has the same standards. What you do at home is your business, but there's no place for it here.'

'What if his accusations are untrue?'

'Not the point, I'm afraid. I can't afford to have people working for me who attract problems. It's bad business. Thank you for the work you've done over the last couple of months, but we no longer have need of your services.' So saying, he stands, walks around his desk and opens the door. 'Goodbye, Mr Lazaro.'

He has not raised his voice or shown a flicker of emotion, except for a slight distaste for the interview and impatience for it to be over. He will find a replacement easily. Giuseppe has lost this round. Hal now has the upper hand.

Giuseppe pushes through a pair of heavy glass doors with 'George' etched into them and stands in the lobby. A burble of voices and a chink of afternoon-tea china issues from the lounge to his left. At a polished, timber desk he asks for Mrs Hal Fischer. He chokes on the words. The clerk is scowling over his register when Giuseppe senses a change of atmosphere. He turns to find a dozen pairs of eyes on him. They are all there, Eddy's family and Hal's family. Eddy pushes through to get to him. Max gathers them both by the elbow and walks them through the lobby and out the door into the street.

'Stay here, I'll be back,' he says, and disappears back into the hotel. Giuseppe and Eddy stand on the path with the noises of the road bailing them up against the hotel wall.

'Why did you come?'

'To get you.'

'It's too soon. I've only just told them. They're in shock.'

'I'm sorry. I thought we needed to be fast. Hal came to my work. He is threatening to take Claudia.'

'He has taken her.'

'You let him?'

'I couldn't stop him. He thinks we slept together.'

'Claudia is my child.'

'Not by law.'

'We can prove it.'

'No. We can't.'

'She looks like my mother.'

'Your mother?'

'I have photographs.'

'You have photographs.'

Eddy is breathless. She is looking around. She doesn't seem to understand Giuseppe. They tire of waiting on the noisy windswept footpath and go back inside. The lobby is empty. They sit on either side of a circular coffee table miserably waiting for Max while the staff cleans up around them. Giuseppe calm and determined, Eddy agitated, tearful.

'What a mess,' she says.

'We must get advice.'

'I wish we could do without lawyers.'

'Not with Hal like this. We must be willing to take the blame, so that you can divorce him.'

'Take the blame?'

'Adultery.'

'Oh.'

Giuseppe has never heard such dismay in one short syllable. He wonders when she is going to start to fight. Where is the feisty woman of the war years? He does not care about the condemnation of the world. He will always be an outsider, a 'New Australian', and always speak with an accent. He believes that Claudia will understand and appreciate what they have done when she is older. What sort of a father would not fight for his child? He thinks of Eddy yesterday in the blue dress with the child in her arms. A Filippo Lippi Madonna. He is beginning to understand, the adoration, his mother's life. But his Madonna lives. He cannot fear the dead and he cannot love them. He fell in love with her again when she gathered the child into her arms. Serene. There is no other word for it. Now she is slumped in a chair in an old shoe of a hotel in a state of threatening hysteria. By claiming her, he has sliced her in half. It makes him determined to give her back her self and her serenity.

Finally Max arrives. They wait for him to speak. Giuseppe offers to get him a drink. He orders beer. Eventually Eddy asks, 'Where's Hal?'

'I don't know. I've been trying to find out.' There is silence again while they wait for what seems like a millennium. 'You'd better find yourselves a top barrister. And I'd be giving each other a wide berth until all this is over.'

'That could be months, years,' says Eddy. 'I can't bear it.'

'It's no picnic for Hal either, you know. Think about him.'

'I've done nothing but think about him for years,' she says, beginning to sound like the old Eddy. 'I can't do it any more. I can't think about him.'

'You may have to go back to him if he gets custody of Claudia.'

Silence falls on the group like a dump of snow.

'They can't do that.'

'They can. It's the most likely result.'

'Oh God.'

Eddy leaps up and hurries across the lobby and into the lift. Max sits sipping his beer with his usual poker face.

'Hal is not going to bring Claudia back, is he?' says Giuseppe.

'He's within his rights to take his child away from a morally wayward wife and her lover,' says Max. 'I'm sorry, mate. It sounds bad. But that's how the courts'll see it.'

There doesn't seem anything more to say to Max. It is not the moment for small talk. Having expected hostility from him, Giuseppe is puzzled to find sympathy and acceptance. If ever Max were to see him as a traitor, an interloper, surely it would be now.

Giuseppe excuses himself and follows Eddy back to her room. Alone at last, they cannot look at each other. Giuseppe stands at the window looking out and Eddy paces for a while and then stands in the middle of the room.

'I can't stand this. Him taking Claudia. She has been . . . instead of you, you see,' she says. 'She is what made life life and not death. Claudia. She is . . .'

'. . . more precious than me.' He sees by the look on her face that he is right. 'You don't believe he'll bring her back,' he says, moving towards the door.

'Of course not. Where are you going?'

A plum jam sunset spreads across the sky behind them as they speed through a familiar landscape in Max's black Ford, away from the light into the unpromising dark. It was this time of year when Giuseppe first made the journey six years ago on the back of a truck. Then, he had nothing to lose. In the last twenty-four hours he has gained everything to lose. And he seems to be gaining back a friend. 'Take my car,' Max had said. 'He must have gone back to the farm. He doesn't seem to be anywhere in town.'

They turn off to the Fischer homestead at midnight. It has been a horrible drive. They have avoided discussing the central issue. If Hal will not give up the child, Eddy will go back to him.

Hal's car is where they expected it to be, outside the back gate. A light goes on in the house. He comes out onto the verandah.

'Max?'

'It's me, Hal. Giuseppe is here too.'

'What do you want?'

'Are you crazy? You took Claudia without telling me. I've been wild with worry.'

'Did you think I'd harm her?'

'Of course not, but she's never been away from me. Where is she?'

The tiny child appears on the verandah behind Hal and runs down the path with her arms out. Eddy picks her up and she puts her face into her mother's neck and holds on tight.

Giuseppe moves out of the shadows. 'We must talk,' he says, half expecting Hal to punch him.

'And say what? All's fair in love and war? You know that one?'

'Nothing is fair, but we must talk.'

'Eddy knows what I want. I don't need to talk to you.'

'Then talk to me,' says Eddy following him up the steps onto the verandah.

'I won't have him in this house,' Hal says, nodding at Giuseppe.

Eddy walks back along the path to Giuseppe.

'Our house is never locked. Go and find yourself a bed.' When he doesn't move she drops her voice and adds, 'Go. I'll be all right. I'll see you in the morning.'

Giuseppe gets into Max's car fearing he'll never see her again. When he pulls up at Grey Tamma Farm a wave of memories breaks over him. This is where the loneliness that had overtaken him in camp had been absorbed by the warmth of the farmhouse kitchen. Now the kitchen is cold and still except for the movement of the old wall clock. He doesn't reach for the light switch. There was no generator when he was last here. He strikes a match and it burns long enough for him to see a torch on a shelf above the stove. A large tabby jumps off a chair and rubs herself against his legs. He wanders around the house. Things are exactly as they were three years ago. He lies on Eddy's bed and covers himself with a blanket.

At the Fischer farm Eddy takes Claudia back to bed and stays with her until she is asleep. Then she goes to the kitchen where Hal sits drinking tea and smoking. The Fischers have rebuilt their house. It is modern. The kitchen lino is laid in a maddening repetition of red, blue and yellow squares. The benches are marbled in bright red formica. The table matches the benches and has chrome legs to match the red and black vinyl chairs and none of it seems to match the personalities of the owners. Eddy guesses that the younger members of the family are pleased with it.

They sit for a minute. Then they both speak at once.

'Hal,' she says.

'Send him away,' he says.

There is more silence until Hal says, 'You shouldn't have brought him here.'

'You didn't expect to be able to take Claudia like some item on an inventory? You don't own her, Hal.'

'I do actually. I'm her father. She's mine in the eyes of the law.'

'The law doesn't have eyes. If it did it would see you're not her father. And that's the whole problem. I did something really terrible in marrying you. I thought it would be all right. I thought we had a sort of love, a close friendship, and that we would be almost better off than others who are pulled about by strong feelings. I thought it was something we could build into a marriage. A steady civilised thing. I was so completely wrong and I'm sorry.'

'Sorry? You apologise as though you'd trodden on my toe. Sorry is nothing. Whatever your feelings have been, I have always loved you, always wanted you.'

'Why? You are angry with me. You come home at night looking like thunder. You hiss and snarl. Or else you're silent and don't want to see anyone or go anywhere. If you ever smiled . . . I don't ask for laughter.'

'What do you think it's like trying to support three on my scholarship, trying to keep up with brains half my age, trying to prove to everyone that I can do this when I don't believe it myself?'

'I support myself and Claudia. You're depressed. You need to get treatment. The army offered you sessions with a psychiatrist.'

'I tried it in hospital. Waste of time.'

'Well, of course, if you don't cooperate. Did you talk to him, tell him what happened?'

'What good would that have done? I want to forget. No bloody psychiatrist could understand the tiniest portion of what is in the minds of men who were up there. There are no words to tell it. I'd have to invent them and then no one would understand. So what's the point?'

'You could try.'

'I did try. It was almost worse than the real thing. I would have done away with myself.'

'What stopped you?' she asks, in a voice as pale as straw.

'You want to know? I heard about you and the Itie loverboy. It blasted me into life. It made me angry.'

The silence between them is so thick they cannot see through it. They stare at the lino squares in children's primary colours. Carefree colours. The aluminium clock without numbers on its pale face gobbles up their minutes and their life. He is pushing her back three years, where the burden of pity made a mush of her brain. She knows a little more about pity now, that it is not a transitive verb, that it remains a noun and belongs always to the pitier and that Genghis Khan had been right all along. 'Pity is the source of regret.' Where had she read that? In her mother's old book of collected wisdom by an American called Elbert, not Albert, Someone, who read a lot and jotted down his favourite aphorisms. She hadn't believed it then.

She has been so afraid of his anger, like a child of a parent's anger. He was older, smarter and bigger than she was, and he could be terrifying. Perhaps he would go on being angry until he became disgusted with her and no longer wanted her, then he could be persuaded to let her go. He is still a handsome man, plenty of women would give their eye teeth. But then who would want a woman without her eye teeth? Lack of sleep, worry and emotional saturation are having their effect. She is in the greatest crisis of her life and all she can think about is eye teeth.

'You need someone who has not been in Burma with you, to make you happy,' she says.

'What do you mean, in Burma?'

'I've seen a lot of men who were in Burma. There's a pattern. You could only survive if you had a friend there, and if you had someone to go back to, someone to live for here. Is that true?'

'It's obvious.'

'Phil was there and I was your someone to go back to. If I helped to keep you alive I'm glad, but it wasn't me. It was someone you made up, using me as the starting point.'

'I had no need to make you up.'

'After six years we'd changed. If I'd understood that, I'd never have married you. I married you to make you happy and I thought it would make me happy too. A wonderful father for my child. I've been a fool and I'm being punished.'

'How punished? You want to run off with your Latin lover and take our child. Leave me with no one, nothing.'

Eddy presses her throbbing temples with the heels of her hands. Her mouth is dry as gravel. She goes to the sink and splashes her face and sips at a glass of water.

'Do you understand what I said about surviving Burma?' she asks.

Hal opens a cupboard and pulls out a bottle of scotch. He pours a couple of inches into his empty cup and stands with his back against the bench.

'Do you?' she asks.

'Bloody Freudian claptrap.'

'It's got nothing to do with Freud. It's what the men have told me. The patients in my wards.'

'If you think I'm going to let you go off with that ponce of a dago and take my daughter and pity me, "poor old Hal, went crazy in Burma, too bad."'

'That's not how it is.'

Silence.

'I can't go back,' she says. 'If you force me to, I'll take Claudia and disappear.'

'You've got no chance.'

Hal is breathing fiercely. He pours himself another whisky and swallows it down in one gulp. Eddy is afraid of him now. When he looks like this, he is about to fly into a rage. Sometimes she thinks he wants to kill her. There are sounds from the bedroom. Eddy walks quickly past him and along the hallway. She is shaking and feeling ill. The child starts to cry. She cradles the child and they both cry. She and Hal have dragged each other so low. She is to blame. Giuseppe says you can get used to it. You can live with blame. It is always there, but you can live in amongst it. Gradually the child responds to the rocking of her mother's arms and goes to sleep, and soon Eddy is asleep too.

At Grey Tamma Farm Giuseppe is not asleep. He roams the house looking in all the rooms and ends up back in Eddy's room. He opens the wardrobe and there are Filippo's paintings leaning against the back wall of the cupboard, still wrapped and tied with string. He wonders if she ever looked at them. He unties the string. The cloth around them is stiff and dry with age. He lays them on the bed. There are six paintings, all on board. He no longer feels the horror that he first felt when Filippo died. The years have taken the edge from his sorrow. He admires the skill, but remembers the dark pain of the artist. He wraps them and puts them back where he found them. Filippo's works draw him down to the corner of his mind that deals with facts in black and white. He asks himself hard questions that require impossible answers. Will she go back to Hal? She has said nothing negative about Hal. She has not said, though he has given her many opportunities, that she dislikes him. If she goes back to him because of the child, what will he do then? Go back to Italy as Hal wants? She has not told him that she loves him. 'This is Claudia,' she said, and lifted the child onto her hip. He sits waiting politely for her to take leave of her husband and come to him.

In the hour before dawn, the longest hour of the night, ideas start jumping into his head, his imagination leapfrogging his emotions. Hal's threats on the football field keep coming back until at last he thinks he knows why. He must speak to Alice. The sky begins to whiten. He goes to the telephone. He has forgotten that the exchange doesn't open until eight. He walks around the farmyard, looking into tool shed, hay shed and shearing shed and talking to the pigs. He could almost be happy doing this if his stomach would stop turning over and his thoughts hold still. He goes looking for MacGillacuddy's. She is not there. He hopes she has been put out to pasture, but he fears otherwise. He has heard no car go past, so Hal has not driven off with Eddy and the child. Back at the house he contacts Maisy at the telephone exchange and asks her to connect him to the George Hotel.

When Giuseppe arrives at the Fischer farm all is quiet. He walks into the kitchen without knocking, under the circumstances a superfluous nicety, and through into the living room. Hal is asleep in an armchair in the gloom, an empty whisky bottle at his feet. Eddy is asleep in a bed with Claudia. Their room is crammed with sun. His racing heart settles a little. He places his hand on her arm.

'Breakfast?' he says.

'What time is it?'

'Eight-thirty.'

'Where's Hal?'

'Asleep. It is enough. We will go now.'

'We can't just go without telling him.'

'Then we will tell him. You can't stay here. What did you agree with him?'

Giuseppe lunges with this rest-of-his-life question and starts his heart racing again.

'We didn't agree.'

'Come. We will get breakfast at the farm for Claudia.'

'No you won't.'

Hal is standing in the doorway. Honeyed sun pours through the east-facing window of the room and hangs in globs on his dishevelled body, but his face is shaded, the line of the shadow slashing across his throat. Eddy hands Giuseppe the child's jacket and he bends and picks up her tiny shoes, holding them in the palm of his hand. Eddy gathers the child onto her hip.

'Claudia stays here or everything comes out in court. Adultery.'

'You will have things to answer in court too,' says Giuseppe. 'I would not be too eager to go there.'

'We're going now, Hal,' says Eddy.

They walk at a steady pace down the hall out onto the verandah and across the garden and get into the car. He doesn't prevent them. They don't look back at him. Giuseppe half expects to hear him yelling abuse. If he does, it is lost in a shriek of green and yellow twenty-eights flying over. Giuseppe turns the car up the drive. Before they reach the road they hear it. It is a flat sound, like a crack, not a bang. Gunfire. Giuseppe reverses to the back gate. He leaps out and races into the house looking into one room and then running to the next. Then he hears Eddy calling. She is standing on the front verandah calling to him as he walks on through the trees.

'He's carrying a dead twenty-eight. He's shooting birds.'

Giuseppe can see the slanting rays flashing on Hal's khaki jacket between the gaps in the trees as he moves. Eddy starts towards him. Giuseppe holds her by the elbow.

'He is dangerous.'

'He has lost his best friend.'

'That makes him more dangerous.'

Giuseppe puts his arm around Eddy's shoulders and draws her back towards the car. She lets him persuade her to leave. He is not used to this. Before, she had always insisted on making up her own mind. If decisions were difficult she would take them as a challenge. Who was this Eddy? Would he love her as much as the old one, always fighting to make sure things were done properly or to her liking? They get back into the car where Claudia is becoming drowsy in the sun. They drive slowly back out to the road and head towards the Nash farm.

'You didn't tell me that Hal broke your arm,' he says.

'He didn't mean to.'

'I telephoned the hotel. Alice told me. It all started to add up, why Max was so friendly. Why Alice wanted to meet me. I asked her if he was violent when we met two months ago, she said nothing.'

'There was nothing to tell. It was an accident.'

They drive along in silence.

'Hal was afraid you would come back for me one day. He needn't have been. If he'd been kind to us, I'd have stayed with him,' she says.

'So I am just an escape route.'

'In a way I suppose that's true, but they are different

things, leaving Hal and coming to you. In truth though, they seem to have got entangled because I don't know if I'd have had the strength to leave. I might have crumpled without you.'

'You have your family.'

'Yes. You and Claudia.'

This should fill him with joy, but he has things to think about. She has made it clear that Claudia comes first in her affections. He had expected her to fall into his arms. He had expected her to be the same feisty woman he left behind three years ago. If Hal had been kind, she'd not have come to him at all. Her feelings are more complicated than he has bargained for. He senses risks.

They arrive at Grey Tamma Farm to find Max unloading his case from Ernie Spry's delivery truck. Eddy takes the child into the house. The two men stand outside on the path.

'Hal is not in a good frame of mind. He has a gun,' says Giuseppe, relieved to give the problem to Max.

'Poor bugger. Where is he?'

'In the bush to the south of the house.'

Max gets into his car and skids off down the gravel drive under a mantle of red dust.

Eddy stands at the kitchen window and watches him go. Max is the only person who could possibly have any influence on Hal. He has a talent for that sort of thing. He is not unlucky. He will not get shot. He is reliable and brave. She fears that Giuseppe is none of the things she has so admired in her brother. In spite of this, she wants him. Love is quirky that way. He steps into the kitchen and stands inside the screen door looking at her. She remembers that look from when he was a prisoner here. He is fascinated by her. She smiles half a smile and shakes her head.

'Why has it taken all this?'

'We thought we could make our lives, but it is not so easy. Lives seem to like to make themselves.'

'However we mess it up, I think we must do it together.'

'Yes.'

He bends down and lifts his daughter into Jenny's high chair.

'To leave Hal on his own, full of whisky with a rifle full of bullets is a dreadful thing,' he says. But he has decided that the only heroics he is interested in now are those that benefit his child and Eddy. He can solve problems for her. She needs him, maybe more than he needs her.

He smooths her hair and rests his hand on the nape of her neck. Claudia, unlike either of her parents, will grow up in the certainty that her father loves her mother. Since his childhood, he has never had much use for faith. Coming here like this and claiming Eddy and his child is a true act of faith.

And Hal was like the war-dead and maimed of any nation. He was their living martyr and they would have to bear the weight of it. There would be few days in the years to come when they would not think of him, walking through the trees with a rifle over his shoulder, holding a dead parrot by its spread-feathered wing, reddening the red earth with its blood.